redux

ALSO BY A.L. DAVROE

nexis

redux

A TRICKSTERS NOVEL

A.L. DAVROE

This book is a work of fiction. Names, characters, places, and incidents are the product of the author's imagination or are used fictitiously. Any resemblance to actual events, locales, or persons, living or dead, is coincidental.

Entangled Publishing, LLC
2614 South Timberline Road
Suite 109
Fort Collins, CO 80525

Entangled Teen is an imprint of Entangled Publishing, LLC.

Visit our website at www.entangledpublishing.com.

Edited by Robin Haseltine
Cover design by L.J. Anderson, Mayhem Cover Creations
Interior design by Toni Kerr

ISBN: 978-1-63375-507-9
Ebook ISBN: 978-1-63375-506-2

Manufactured in the United States of America

First Edition March 2017

10 9 8 7 6 5 4 3 2 1

They find themselves in the mind of a man who does not exist;
come home on the shores of an imaginary land;
who are most themselves between the pages of a book.

part one:

ELLA GOES UNDERGROUND

chapter one

POST-AMERICAN DATE: 7/4/232

LONGITUDINAL TIMESTAMP: 7:23 A.M.

LOCATION: DOME 5: EVANESCENCE

Droids circle behind us as we draw deeper into the shadows of the doorway we're standing in. We're on Citizen's Way, the main artery of my home, Evanescence. But where there were once bustling crowds along streets lined with shops and vibrant screens airing The Broadcast, the vast expanse of the city's corridor is now littered with broken holo-glass, abandoned pods, and far too many bodies.

I try not to look at the distorted faces of the dead amid the piles of colorful fabrics, but it's hard. The Aristocrats around me were once so perfect—dressed in the latest Designer clothes, their hair Primped to unfathomable heights, their genetically Customized bodies made into masterpieces with cosmetic augmentations—Modifications (Mods) and Alterations (Alts). Their life goals were to be noticed and it's hard not to do just that, to stare at them. But their unblinking eyes and wide-open mouths blame me. It's my fault these Aristocrats are dead, after all. I'm the one who planted the computer virus that caused this mess—made the city's artificial intelligence rebel against its occupants.

Gus presses his arm across my chest, tucking me closer to the wall as two more droids march past, their red eyes scanning the road on either side. Unlike the domestic androids, these security units are without aesthetically pleasing chasises and without the humanoid illusion of skin. Their bare parts are just as cold and unforgiving as their intentions. I hold my breath until they are out of sight. Thank goodness they aren't equipped with thermal tracking units; they'd find us in an instant.

"We're almost there," Quentin whispers. He glances both ways down the road, his starry hair falling across his twinkling eyes, then he motions for the two of us to follow.

I lift my gun, hold it at ready as I limp after him. I hope no one attacks us. I don't want to use this gun. I, Ellani Drexel, have already caused the deaths of so many and I don't want to kill anyone else. Gus steps in beside me, his dark eyes scanning up, down, around, searching for any sign of ambush. How he can identify anything in the chaos happening in the glistening, high-rise buildings above us is beyond me.

My heart aches with every adrenaline-filled beat. This domed city was once a safe haven, a place where people closed themselves in against the chaos and death of the world outside. They built a utopia, a shining city of white light where everything was ordered and peace was maintained—the chips implanted in our brains made sure of that. But the chips don't work anymore. The virus I planted in the city's Main Frame did something to the chips—made it so that they can't communicate with the city anymore, or perhaps made it so that we are no longer accepted by the city. The virus didn't do what I thought it was going to do, I was tricked. Now, the spun-sugar world is dissolving in a torrent of blood and tears.

The city is turning on us.

We continue down an alley lit only by a flickering LED bulb hanging over the service door of one of the stores. This used to be one of my favorite shops, one where my best friend, Delia, and I would go shopping for shoes. Thinking of Delia makes me remember how she laughed at me earlier this evening. Granted, she didn't know it was me she was mocking, because my face is hidden behind a false one provided by my holo-mask, but that doesn't matter. It means something important. It means that Delia has become one of the very people she and I used to fear: the Elite Aristocrats—those who would step on others to gain what they want.

But am I any different? I wanted legs to replace the ones I'd lost in the accident that also took my father from me. I wanted Gus, the boy I fell in love with while playing Nexis—the virtual reality game my father created. I wanted freedom from the prison I'd been forcefully kept in for a year. I'd been given the opportunity to have all of that; all I had to do was plant the Anansi Virus for my uncle, Simon. Granted, Uncle Simon lied to me about the virus and if I'd known the true extent of what the virus was going to do, I never would have planted it. But do people who are blinded by desire ever see what they're doing?

"Ella? You all right?" Gus asks.

I glance over my shoulder, smile despite the coldness I feel inside. Just seeing him, just hearing his deep gravelly voice and knowing I finally have him for real, and not just when I played the game, warms the cold.

"I was thinking about how different things are. How they will be." I try to sound hopeful. I have him, I have Delia—despite her having changed in the year I've been separated from her. My cousin, Bastian, is also safe. And I have my new path in life—to eventually undo the momentous wrong that's unfolding around me. I'm not sure how to do this, because it's only been a few hours since the virus hit, and getting out alive is more important. But, even now, it's clear what I have to do and I hold on to that promising light.

Despite the light, the darkness pummels in on all sides of my mind. I've lost so much. Friends. Family. My home and the city that houses it. All gone because I played a game and planted a virus. It was only supposed to cause a temporary blackout. Gus and Quentin thought it was going to open the doors to the city and let in the Disfavored—genetically inferior people who live outside our domed city. The unwanted.

It did both those things. And more. No one knew my uncle Simon rewrote the virus. We're not even sure what, exactly, he did. All we know is we're being hunted by the very machines meant to make our lives easier.

The only option is to run, escape to Cadence, the domed city next to ours. But who knows what will be waiting for us there. The post-Bio-Nuclear war cities haven't communicated in over a hundred years and there's no way to start now. No way to let them know what's happening here, no way to ask for sanctuary, no way of knowing if life there isn't just as bad, or worse, than it would be if we simply wandered into the wasteland outside the city and handed ourselves over to the Disfavored who hated us for locking them out of Evanescence for centuries.

"There are a lot of uncertainties in front of us," I answer Gus. I reach out, brush his hand. His skin is cold and the Modifications beneath feel strange, but he's still the Gus I fell in love with in Nexis. Nexis. My father's game had been my salvation after my falsified death and imprisonment. It gave me legs, freedom, friends, love, adventure, hope. And it taught me so much: about my father, myself, the world as it once was before humanity destroyed it, and it opened my eyes to the injustice around me. But even that is gone. Not just for me, but for everyone. The promised escape into a virtual dream has been cut short by a true escape here in Real World. I managed to find a little piece of the game to take away with me… "At least we found each other."

His lips thin, and he looks down at the ground. There's blood on his black boots. Blood on my shoes and the hem of my dress, too, though you almost can't tell on my stain-wicking red fabric.

"What are you two doing?" Quentin hisses from farther down the alley. "Now's not the time for a chat. Come on!"

Gus and I step it up, trotting after Quentin and into a deserted street. Above us, someone is screaming. There's a baby crying. Something smashes, and glass rains down on us.

A moment later, a body tumbles from the sky, making me yelp and jump back. It's a domestic android, torn open from the fall so that its synthetic innards and fluids spill out in a splash, like a broken water balloon. It reminds me too much of the broken android I just left behind, my nanny and the only Real World friend I've had for the past year. "Meems," I whisper. I touch the small pocket sewn into my dress, making sure the chips I slipped in there are still safe. One chip I pulled from her broken body. The other is my father's G-Chip, given to me after the accident.

Gus steps close, grasps my hand, and tugs me around the android's twitching limbs. "Don't look at it."

A line of five Disfavored suddenly materialize out of an alley farther ahead. They must have heard the crash of the android hitting the ground or my cry. Our guns come up. Their guns come up. For a long moment, we just stare at each other. They're not like the Aristocrats fallen all around me. They're more like me, without genetic modification, so they have dark eyes, hair, and skin. And their Natural imperfections are made even more obvious by their threadbare, ugly clothes, their haggard expressions that speak of harsh lives, and the murderous hate that speaks of depths of emotion that most Aristocrats only imagine. Laser fire from another street adjacent to them flashes between us and their bodies fall.

One of the boys shoves me. "Go!"

I go. They follow. We take cover around a corner, watch the skirmish unfold. Five Disfavored, two droids. Bodies fall and one droid walks away, its arm hissing and spitting sparks, disappearing into a shop.

I breathe a sigh of relief and lean back into Gus. "Circuits, that was close."

"We need to get out of here," Quentin growls. "Now."

Gus says, "No one is fighting you on that."

Quentin turns, steps out into the alley. "It should be— "

"Halt! You there!"

My body freezes, but then instinct kicks in and I'm running. Gus and Quentin flee, too, both taking one of my arms and half carrying me along, since one of my prosthetic legs was damaged from the gunshot I got trying to rescue Meems.

Feet pursue, the pounding of them echoing up between the buildings, drowning out the sounds of androids killing Aristocrats above.

Bam. Someone shoots at us. The bullet strikes the holo-glass display at a corner store as we circle it, making the glass explode out and around us. I run harder, past intact and broken shop windows, the glass reflecting one word back at me.

Persevere.

Persevere.

Persevere.

The one word offering a whole gauntlet of silent encouragement and behind all the chaos, behind the screams and the shattering and the gun shots and laser strikes—like some phantom background score—I can hear my mother singing "Itsy Bitsy Spider" over the city's speaker system. The word had appeared and the song had started playing just after the virus went into effect. They're a message my parents left for me. And it still hasn't stopped. It's a mockery. Persevere, although you're dying. Keep climbing, although you're being chased down, shot at, killed. I just want to stomp my foot and scream for it to shut up, but it's part of the virus.

The gunfire comes again, striking at our heels, clipping walls and windows.

"Faster!" Quentin says.

I oblige as best as I can, gritting my teeth through the pain and trying to stay upright even though the piston in my leg keeps giving out like a bum knee. We turn down one last narrow alley and finally, the door comes into sight. Inconspicuous, unmarked. Once inside, Quentin slams the door shut behind us, throwing the dead bolt—the only thing standing between us and them now that the electronic locks throughout the city are disabled. It thumps and bucks as our pursuers attempt to follow us.

I back up a few feet, until I'm practically pasted against Quentin. Normally I wouldn't touch him. He's Gus's best friend and I even had a crush on him once, but he represents something that I've come to hate in the past year. But right now? I hate those Disfavored rebels out there more than I hate him, so I stick close. For a long moment, we stand there, staring at the door handle as it jiggles.

"Please hold," I pant. "Please hold, please hold, please hold."

Quentin's fingers touch the small of my back, as if somehow trying to lend strength toward my chant. Minutes pass and the door holds. Eventually, they must give up, because the handle stops jerking and the shouting on the other side lessens, disappears. Quentin is breathing hard behind me, his breath hot and humid against the back of my neck.

Gus tugs at the fabric of my dress. "Come on. Let's get out of here before they figure out a way to bust down the door."

With a nod, I pull away from Quentin and follow Gus back down the many stairwells leading deep under the city, past the service levels, to the Undertunnel where we will be meeting the refugees who will join us in fleeing our home.

We find Sid, one of Quentin's Dolls, and the rest of the survivors on the opposite side of a pair of steel doors that sit wide open. As we step past the doors, which I assume Sid hot-wired open, I see a great round room on the other side. To either side of the space there are more doors being opened by more of Quentin's Dolls—Disfavored boys who agreed to have experimental Mods and Alts before they were used on Quentin. In return they were brought in from the Outer Block where the Disfavored lived in famine and squalor.

Inside the rooms they open, there are storage containers. Beyond all the rooms, on the other side of the hall, is a yawning maw of blackness.

"Is that the Undertunnel?" I whisper.

"Yeah," Gus says.

I swallow hard, terrified of the impenetrable darkness of it and what lies just beyond—the *unknown*, the outside of the dome—and quickly turn away, trying to find something else to focus on. I stare at the thirty or so people standing or sitting in small clusters around the hall. The people are various ages, from my contemporaries from school to older

Aristocrats who must have been friends of Quentin's parents. But no matter what age, they all look tired, shell-shocked. Some are shaking, some are crying. Some are just sitting there, staring into nothingness.

I don't blame them. These people grew up in the sheltered utopia of Evanescence. They've never known true pain or need. Never seen murder or felt terror. This world must be just as foreign to them as waking up in the Utopia Zone was for me the first time I entered Nexis. Only this new world is not safe, not clean, and not escapable. This is Real World and I have a gnawing suspicion that life for these cloistered and clean Aristocrats is about to get as ugly and messy as it has been for the Disfavored they gawked at from the safety of their cushioned parlors. It's so much easier to judge and call someone an animal when you're watching them on a screen.

I search for Delia, who's still unaware I'm alive, to find her glaring at me with this awful scrutiny. She's so different from the last time I've seen her. Underneath it all, she's a Natural like me. But it's not okay to be a Natural when you live among the Custom-perfect Aristocrats, especially the Elite we went to school with. She's become like them, used Mods and Alts to the extreme to hide that she's not one of them. And the expression she's giving me is like the expressions we both used to shy away from. Judgment and disgust, the sort of condemnation one gives to those who don't belong. I try not to take her personally. It's not my face she's seeing, it's not me she's judging. It's just the face I've programmed into my holo-mask. But still, if she looks at a face that's meant to fit in like this, then how would she look at someone who is a Natural like me? How can she hate her own flesh that much?

Unnerved, I step closer to Gus as we walk, only to find that he's staring back at Delia with a different sort of expression I can't read—especially because his face is so difficult to interpret under all those Alts and Mods. He, too, looks nothing like how I remember him. In the game he looked like a Natural. But here, he's like Delia.

Sparks, the things Aristocrats willingly do to themselves to look unique among their too-similar genetically perfect peers—that's what genetic Customization did. Made everyone perfect. But when perfect is normal it's not special anymore. So they sought something more. More surgeries to modify structure. More nanotechnology to alter skin and hair and eyes.

More, more, more.

Until they are less and less like anything resembling human.

Until they look like Gus and Delia.

Quentin leads us to Sid, who is standing at a small command module fussing with wires. He seems annoyed.

"Is this it?" Quentin asks, voice tired and hollow as he tips his chin toward the people behind us.

Not looking up, Sid nods. "Yeah. Just a few more of us Dolls and whoever they could grab on the way out. We're lucky we got this many people, considering."

Quentin rubs his face. Carsai comes running up to us. I've never liked Carsai and I try not to let it show. She was my bully when I went to school. And she's the epitome of an Elite. Spoiled and self-centered beyond reason because she was born at the top of an already privileged Aristocratic pecking order. Dad used to say all Aristocrats were born with silver spoons in their mouths, but the Elite were born with diamond-encrusted ones. I didn't understand the significance of what that meant until I played Nexis, learned the value of silver and diamonds—they don't exist in Real World anymore.

Plus, she's Delia's best friend now that Delia thinks I'm dead, so I'm a little jealous of her, too.

She steps up to Quentin, grasps at his arm, pets him. "Quent, darling, what's going on? Are we safe?"

I roll my eyes at her false endearment. It reminds me of how Delia and I once talked to each other, so maybe my eye rolling is a little out of jealousy, too.

Emboldened by her move, other Aristocrat girls from school follow until there are six of them crowded around us and chattering over each other like tropical parrots.

"Where's my mom? Has someone alerted her to my whereabouts? I demand to vis-call her immediately." Farouza doesn't understand that she's not the only important person here. The Aristocrats are raised to think they and they alone are the center of the universe.

"Are we shutting the androids down? Will they be down long? Who is going to prepare my clothes for tomorrow?" Veronica doesn't know how to live without the technology that has handicapped the Aristocrats.

"I have a report due in the morning and my flex-bracelet isn't connecting to my G-Chip. What's being done?" Angelique has clearly been given her job placement and it is now the biggest source of stress in her life. I wonder if she's like me and got forced to follow a career path she never wanted. I didn't want to be a Programmer. I wanted to be a Designer, making beautiful clothing.

"When can we go home? I'm missing tonight's Broadcast. What am I going to talk to my intended about if I don't see it?" How sad that Kleary is being forced to marry a man she can't even talk to. Thank fate that I know real love and all my guardians are dead, so now I can choose who I want to marry.

"Ugh, look how filthy I am. I need a bath and a change of clothes." Like all Custom Aristocrats, Jewel probably doesn't even sweat, so the idea of blood and dirt are anathema to someone who grew up in a bacteria-free environment where clothes were incinerated after a single wearing and one could get Alts that made them smell like perfume and soap.

Quentin's shoulders droop like he can't handle any of them, and I don't blame him. I wouldn't want to be in his shoes, having to step into the new role as Leader now that his parents are dead. Having to convince these sheltered, self-absorbed people to traverse the Undertunnel while hungry, isolated, grieving, dirty, and harried by who knows what for who knows how long.

All in the hopes that once we get to Cadence, they don't do to us what our own city did to the refugees of Adagio—lock them out, leave them below in the darkness of the Undertunnel for months.

No one would have gotten in, either, except the old President Cyr died and the new one decided he'd be more merciful. We may not be that lucky.

"Not now, Carsai." Quentin pulls his arm out of her grasp and straightens his jacket with his uninjured hand. "I'll answer everyone's questions once I know we're 100 percent safe and we have time to discuss this, but right now I need all of you to just cooperate."

Carsai blinks at him. "But—"

"Later," he growls, turning on his heel. "Sid, let's get this gate closed."

Sid rolls his eyes. "Oh yes, because my G-Chip is fully functional, just like yours, and I can just wish it closed, can't I?"

"Sassiness is not warranted," Quentin mutters. "Just close the door."

"That's what I'm trying to do, but getting a door to open by crossing wires is a lot easier than closing it." He holds out some wires. "You're welcome to try. My fingers are quite burned at this point, and I'd like to remind you that, now that our G-Chips are currently useless and our currency system locked away on a Main Frame we can't access, I'm no longer getting paid to be your Doll. So, do be nice."

Quentin chews his lip for a second. "You're right, I'm sorry."

"We could manually shove it shut," Gus suggests.

Looking back, I stare at the two-story-high doors. They must each weigh a ton. I sense a few of the other Dolls materializing at the side of my vision. One of them with golden hair and delicate features pushes up his sleeves and says, "I hope you all ate your nutra-packs for breakfast today."

chapter two

POST-AMERICAN DATE: 7/4/232

LONGITUDINAL TIMESTAMP: 9:07 A.M.

LOCATION: SUB-TUNNEL 6

Click, click, click.

I reach into my pocket and squeeze the two plastic chips against the palm of my hand. One is my father's G-Chip. This little chip, like mine and everyone else's, was once implanted in my father's frontal lobe as both his key to the city and his psychological lock. It was the thing that made him part of Evanescence and also the thing that made him want to be something apart from it. The other is Meems's personality chip. Even though it's burned and I could never restore her, even though she'd hate me if I did, I couldn't bear to leave her behind. She might have only been an android, but she was so much more to me.

Persevere.

Meems had wanted me to do that—to overcome my trials, no matter how insurmountable. And now, most certainly, the stakes are at their highest. The game has become real, and I find myself grossly ill-equipped to play.

Click, click, click.

Someone wails. The Aristocrats are mourning the loss of their city, their kin, their lifestyles.

I close my eyes, trying not to listen or think. The door between the world I know and the unknown is closing. In front of me, there are six boys, shadows of each other, shoving the heavy steel door closed.

Click, click, click.

Quentin groans. He's putting too much stress on his already injured shoulder and hand. Stupid, shouldn't have gotten himself shot. Or punched an aerovator door. I turn away, dismissing the thoughts. I don't care. He's evil. He's from Cyr stock. The Cyrs killed my parents. Quentin killed my uncle Simon. Shot him in the head. Point-blank. Right in front of me.

In my mind, the memory of the sound of Quentin's gun going off ricochets about, making me suddenly jump. And behind my eyes, the image of blood and brain spattering and oozing against Lady's Cyr's white dress forces me to open my eyes and blink it away.

I try not to feel the loss of my uncle. He was a bad man. He caused the death of so many people. Made us lose our home. Used me as a pawn. Whatever his motives were, the stakes were too high and he deserved the death that Quentin dealt him.

I've seen lots of death. I've even killed. But that was death and killing in a virtual world, in Nexis. When you die in Nexis, you simply wake back up in Real World. Your game is over, your character dead forever, so it feels like a loss. But it's not like real dying. When I killed in the game, I wasn't killing for real, wasn't taking people away from friends and family for real. Not like what my actions have done to these people standing around me. My actions inside Nexis have killed. Real World killed. And that's not a game.

I close my eyes again as hot tears gather on my lashes. *What have you done, Ellani Drexel?*

Desperately trying to grasp at some shred of hope, I try and find the good in me and this situation. Something to appreciate.

I come up with only one thing—the knowledge that what I've accidentally done is wrong and all I can do is try to undo at least some of it. Get these people someplace safe, for starters. And then maybe see what I can do to regain the city.

The city is alive.

If I can just somehow access the Main Frame without my G-Chip, perhaps I can figure out what's wrong—figure out a way to get it to read the G-Chips again.

I open my eyes, look around, and nod to myself as I wipe away my tears.

Faced with this chaos, everything I have learned about myself and the world via Nexis is even more important. It's imperative to persevere, to believe in myself, my abilities, and the people I choose as my allies. I hope I still can.

But the idea of it is daunting, makes my breath come heavy and my heart beat faster. I'm scared. I'm no longer in a game. This is real life, a real-life adventure. One that I may not come back from. One that so many others have already lost. But I can't afford to lose. The weight of knowing that this adventure can't just be logged off or restarted makes me fear my ability. In Nexis, I was a good player. I had a team, the Tricksters, that trusted me. I usually made the right decisions. I was a great fighter. Can I be all those things here?

I have to be.

Echoes of gunshots and screams from above intermingle with the steady *click, click, click.*

I focus on the real noise, not the remembered ones, or

the ones I hear over my head.

The door is almost closed.

My hands reach out, possessed, and grasp at my legs. They do that. Ever since the accident that took both my father and my legs, my hands have secretly been checking when I'm not looking. Searching for something that is no longer there.

But today, they are pleasantly surprised and satisfied. There are knees to hold. There are legs where there haven't been for the last year. Prosthetics, a gift from my uncle for planting his sinister virus—a promise for a more permanent fix. One he never intended to keep.

I glance across the room at my cousin Bastian. He's one of the ones staring blank-faced into nothingness. *Does he hear the screams, too?* I cock my head. It's bad enough knowing what Uncle Simon did to me and all of the citizens of Evanescence, it's another thing entirely to think about what he did to his own son.

But then again, my parents did the same thing to me. Made me a tool. Sacrificed me to something greater. My mother and father programmed Nexis, made it so that my game and the people I played with would lead me to exactly where I was supposed to be. Gus, Morden, Nadine, Opus—each one, including myself, represented one of the Trickster archetypes. Fox, coyote, rabbit, crow, spider. And each one of them carried a code I'd pre-cracked which, upon the death of their avatars, broke through another layer of Main Frame security.

When my avatar finally arrived in the very heart of the Main Frame, I delivered the Anansi Virus that created all this chaos. But between my father's untimely death and my inability to trust my uncle, I can't possibly know what my parents truly intended.

My mother, father, Uncle Simon, Lady Cyr, and Quentin

and his Dolls were all part of that plot. My parents considered themselves spiders. The wise web weavers. I'm clearly expected to carry the mantle. From what I can tell, Gus is the fox here in Real World, too. I don't know if the other three archetypes are out here in Real World, nor do I understand what the real goal of this group actually is or was.

I look away, unable to keep looking at Bastian lest I start crying. For him and for me.

I refuse to shed a tear. Too many people around me are weeping and I have no right to join them. Not when it's my fault. So I stare at my new legs—the price paid for all of these people's tears.

I close my eyes, knowing I have to be more honest with myself. I planted that virus for one reason and one reason only. Because I wanted to be with Gus in the Real World and I didn't think I could do that without legs. I wanted to be whole again so I could escape from the prison of social ostracism and the isolation my guardian and my uncle forced upon me. So I could be who Gus expected me to be.

I turn and squint at him, pushing with his might against the door, and warmth blossoms in my stomach and chest. He's worth it.

And yet, one person's life is never worth anyone else's. Dad would have told me that.

Evanescence once had hundreds of thousands of citizens, and now the only people alive are these few dozen. Already, their Alterations are fading. Without the G-Chip to control the nanites and convert their kinetic energy, the argent skin and fiber-optic inlays of the Aristocrats behind me are winking out, taking their rainbow light and leaving only the faint emergency LED light over the door. In the growing shadows, these people sound like moaning ghosts. Reminders of a world that is quickly dying and will soon be a thing of the past. Haunters… Like the screams of the dying in my head, like the spilled Aristocratic blood I see behind my eyelids when I close them.

They're so broken, these Aristocrats. So tragically human. And that's beautiful.

I know we're not perfect, but what made those androids above want to kill us so very much? Perhaps they didn't have a choice. Perhaps the lack of G-Chips made them believe we were all intruders and enemies. Perhaps their uprising was part of the virus itself. Was it a fluke, or something programmed? And, if that's the case, what made Uncle Simon want to kill us so much?

Click, click, click.

Chilled, I turn away from the mournful howls of the people around me and look in front of me, hoping I can escape reminders of the last day for a moment. But looking at the door makes me realize just how intense a moment this is. The domed city of Evanescence—one of the cities that was the salvation for mankind after the Bio-Nuclear War, a city my mother almost died to get into—is being closed off. Soon it will be empty and abandoned, like my mother's city, Adagio.

Part of me wants to jump up and tell the boys to stop, to leave the door open. But beyond that door, there is no salvation. There is only death and destruction. Thousands dead at the hands of crazed robots and angry Disfavored rebels roaming the streets.

Click, click.

Trapped by both my thoughts and my setting, I glance over my shoulder again, beyond the Aristocratic refugees. The Undertunnel awaits. Dark, empty, long forgotten. I do not know what lies within it. I only hope that it brings us to Cadence, our sister city. Once there, I hope that I can do something to right the wrong that I've done. I hope I can one day return, regain, and rebuild Evanescence. Make it better.

Offer these people a future.

Click.

Door closing between death and uncertainty.

Click.

Door closing off the only home that I have ever known.

Click.

Door closing on me, Ellani Drexel, leaving another one—a stranger to herself—living in my body.

Click.

My heart is hammering faster. Faster. Faster. There's a lump in my throat. I want to scream. I cover my eyes as the massive steel door slides the last few inches, sealing my fate.

Boom. It slams shut. I take a breath, force myself to watch between my fingers as Sid begins to cross wires, creating sparks and acrid-smelling smoke, locking the door as best as he can against the killer androids and the Disfavored beyond. When he's done, he steps back and nods.

"It's okay everybody," Quentin says. "We're safe now."

A collective sigh tickles the back of my neck. Someone even chances a nervous laugh, but the bubbly, tinkling of it sounds off. The vocal Modification is an unwelcome reminder of better moments and things lost, like glitter on a battlefield. Just like that the tension returns.

I force my hands down. Gus and Quentin are both leaning against the door, panting and looking proud. Their smiles show that they didn't catch the laugh and what it means.

I let myself forget the sad reminder of the laugh and instead smile with the boys, because Gus's pleasure is my pleasure. His smile warms my heart, even if he doesn't look like the boy I fell in love with in Nexis. He's been too badly Modified and Altered because he's Quentin's Doll and even with fading Alts, his Mods will never go away.

Gone is his tussled, dark brown hair; gone are his

laughing, nearly black eyes; gone are his impish smile and bold, handsome face. I can't hold that against him. My body in Nexis was also a lie. I had legs in Nexis. And I almost let that truth, that shame in who I'd become, destroy our love.

I reach up and finally take off my holo-mask, dismissing the false face I've been wearing for the past few hours. No need to continue that lie anymore, either. Gus already knows and accepts who I am and what I look like because I wore my real face in Nexis, and now that the G-Chips are fried, my mask will soon lose power. When that happens, the others will learn what I look like—that I'm nothing but a Natural parading as a Custom, a dead girl come back to life.

Let them see my dark skin and unsymmetrical face. Let them see the scar on my forehead from the accident that killed my father. Let them see the gray eyes and arched brows my mother gave me. Let them see the thick, unruly brown curls and my oddly judgmental mouth.

As I lower my mask, Quentin is watching me, smiling.

Bristling, I glare at him in challenge. As the late President's son and the very top of the Elite, he represents the Aristocracy of Evanescence that I want to move beyond—secrets, lies, and confusion. Because he's a Cyr, because he knows things I don't, because he's half behind the chaos unfolding in the city above, because Quentin knew who I was, even with my holo-mask on, because he kissed me and I liked it and that confuses me.

Turning away, I meet Gus's eyes and smile again. Gus is certainty and truth. That's how I know he's right for me. That's how I know, even though Quentin's kiss confuses and tempts me, Gus is the right decision. Where Quentin is the wolf in sheep's clothing, Gus is the beauty in the beast.

Still holding his gaze, I take a step toward Gus. I want to be by his side, hold his hand. Kiss him so that I can prove that his kisses undo all the confusion Quentin's caused me. He'll prove that he kisses like game Gus, too—because he *is* game Gus.

Someone crosses my path, red hair cutting between Gus and me, forcing me to stop.

"Hi, Sadie," I say. Some part of me wonders why I'm not being vehement and salty toward her. She, with her foster mother, who was caring for me, was part of the plot to hide my imprisonment from the rest of Evanescence. Sadie could have gotten help for me, uncovered my uncle's diabolical plans, but she didn't.

I should dislike this girl. Her bloodshot eyes and shaking hands should make me gleeful, but they don't. I should hate her, but all I can wonder is if she hates me. Really, neither of us should care. Our world just ended. We're both suffering. There is no place here for blame and grudges and rights to sensitivity.

I'm so tired. All I want to do is lie down and sleep for a thousand years, dreamless and thoughtless.

"You're standing. Walking."

"Yeah," I say, closing my eyes. I have an awful headache. It's pounding behind my eyes, making my ears feel like they're going to explode. "Uncle Simon gave them to me."

"Oh," she breathes. There's an awkward moment of silence. I open my eyes and look back at her. She's picking at her dress, which is cornflower blue with iridescent shots of silver, periwinkle, and orange. It's a nice cut on her, accentuates her décolletage. "Suppose that makes sense."

I nod.

For a moment, she flounders, her eyes shooting around the room. Then they fix sideways at Quentin and his Dolls, a group markedly separate from the rest. There are seven Dolls. I know only Sid and Gus. Sadie looks back at the other

Aristocrats. I'm standing in the middle of the hall, by myself. I suddenly realize that I'm still an outcast. Still a Natural with no Modifications or Alterations. And, while most Alts are fading, leaving many Aristocrats in their original skin, they're still Custom, still perfect.

"What exactly is going on?" she asks.

For a moment, I don't understand what she means. It seems like the answer is obvious. But then I realize she wants to know what the situation between the boys and me is. They've all seen how Quentin and Gus treat me. The two most sought after and aloof young men in Evanescence and they both acknowledge me, despite being a Natural, and worse, someone everyone thought dead for the last year.

I shrug. "We're friends."

She narrows an eye at me, the glistening Alteration under it catching the LED light over our heads. "You don't have friends, Ella."

I know she means I shouldn't have friends because a year ago, all my friends watched my dead body paraded down Citizen's Way in a grand memorial procession. But all of that was an act, something my uncle cooked up to make everyone think I was dead. He claimed it was for my safety.

I glance over my shoulder at Delia, once my best friend. She notices me watching her. Now that the holo-mask is gone, recognition dawns in her expression, and suddenly she seems to be unable to stop staring. There's a bubble of hope inside of me, a desperate desire for her to come running at me in laughing relief. But her face, alien and strange as it is under those Mods, turns sour, the meaning clear. Hate, resentment, betrayal. All those emotions are there, aimed at me.

She must wonder why, if I was alive, I didn't come to her. Why I didn't heed all those messages she sent me in her darkest moments. Instead, I let her suffer without me, let her turn herself into one of *them* just so she wouldn't be alone anymore. There's no way she would know that I *couldn't* go to her no matter how much I wanted to. I had been cut off from the outside world, imprisoned in one small room with only Meems to keep me sane. Even in the moments when my ability to hack my habitation unit proved useful, I still couldn't go to her. I couldn't run away for the simple fact that I didn't have legs to run on. One can be a prisoner, even in their own body. Perhaps it's too late for her to understand that, perhaps the damage is already too deep, the hate too strong.

Heart falling, I turn away and stare at the floor.

Perhaps I've lost Delia for good.

But Delia isn't my only friend. "You're wrong," I say. "I've always had friends. Meems…" Thinking of Meems, I smile. And I feel it falter almost as quickly as I realize that she, like so many others, is gone.

"She was an android, Ella," Sadie says. As if that make some sort of difference. At my confused expression, she adds, "She was programmed to like you."

Perhaps that was true initially, but I honestly believe that Meems came to love me on her own—with her own free will—but I doubt Sadie would understand that. Most citizens of Evanescence wouldn't, so I don't argue.

"I made many friends in the game," I reason. "In Nexis. I played it often, didn't have anything else to do."

"AI isn't any different than an android."

I glance at Gus. "Not everyone in Nexis is AI, Sadie."

She bites her suddenly trembling lip and when she speaks, her voice wavers like the tears threatening on her eyelids. "They're gone, too."

I let out a long breath. She's right, of course. If there are only these few people from Evanescence alive, then most of the Real World avatars we all played with are also dead.

Nadine is most likely dead, like Meems.

But I *still* have Gus. "Not all of them."

"Shadow and Quentin, you mean?"

I nod. "Guster," I say, refusing to call him by the detached nickname I used to know him by. He's no longer anyone's shadow. "And with him comes Quentin."

She nods. "Because they're inseparable. I suppose that explains why he'd be friends with someone like you. He doesn't have a choice, really."

I ignore the simple, matter-of-factness in her voice. She's right. Quentin doesn't have any more of a choice than I do. Gus loves us both. And we both love Gus. And because of that, I need to play nice with Quentin.

But he can't be that awful, can he? Gus wouldn't be friends with him otherwise. Perhaps Quentin is a victim of circumstance. Like me. After all, I'm sure some would consider me an enemy now that I've played a hand in the destruction of their homes and the massacre of their loved ones. But I'm just an unwitting pawn in a much larger scheme.

Maybe I should try and look beyond my assumptions, give him the benefit of the doubt I'd want others to give to me.

And if I'm going to try and make unlikely friends with Quentin, perhaps I should think about making friends with a few more. Maybe re-approach Delia. Maybe Carsai. Maybe Sadie. After all, the world that drove us apart is falling to pieces above our heads. Maybe it's time to erase and rewrite our own programming. Perhaps it's time for me to let go of my newfound dislike of the Aristocracy and their sheep-like mentality.

I look Sadie straight in the eyes. "I think you're the one without friends."

Her lips part and close, part and close, like she's a fish I've grabbed out of the water and thrown on the hot sand.

Confused by her reaction, I mentally reassess and try over again. "Sorry, that didn't come out right. I meant that you've experienced a lot of loss. Lost friends. We all have. And...we could be friends, you and me"—I gesture to the others—"and them. Things are different and we've become all the other has got. We should act like it."

Her mouth closes and stays that way, then she draws a deep breath. "That's not how things work."

"It's not how they did work, you're right. But it could work. What's going to stop it?"

She stares hard at me for a long moment, level and intense. Then, she turns on her toe and clacks off, her plastic shoes ringing on the cement floor.

I smirk at her retreating form. She's rejecting me for the moment, but I know I've gotten to her. There was a spark there, in those grassy-green eyes of hers. Hope.

That hope warms my chest, despite the pounding in my head, despite the ache and exhaustion that have been creeping in since adrenaline from fighting to get to the Undertunnel has started to fade. I back up against one of the stationary control panels and lean my weight against it.

It feels good to be off my feet. I've been awake for at least twenty-four hours and on my feet for most of it. I've only recently gotten my prosthetics and even though I trained for them, I still feel how my body has been working to adjust to them. It's not just the legs making me tired. It's mental and spiritual exhaustion, too. Closing my eyes against the brightly colored Neo-Baroque clothing of the Aristocrats, I reach up and knead my shoulders.

A moment later, a hand slides under mine, rubbing deeper. A male body sits close, inhabiting my space like he owns it. Afraid that it may not be who I think it is—I have mistaken Quentin for Gus before—I glance out of the corner of my eye. The black outfit indicates a Doll, the blue and green on the forearm means Gus. Sighing in relief, I close my eyes again and let my hand rest over his. "Knew you couldn't stay away."

Chuckling, he presses his lips to my temple.

It's strange. So much has happened to me in the past few days. Reuniting with Uncle Simon, planting the virus in Nexis, getting my legs, finding Gus again after thinking I'd never see him when he'd died in the game, the destruction of the G-Chips, the android uprising, the rebellion of the Disfavored, the deaths of thousands of Aristocrats, including Uncle Simon…the death of Meems.

"You're tense," he breathes into my hair.

I lean into his massaging fingers. It hurts, but in a good way. "Mmm," I breathe and add a sarcastic, "I wonder why."

"We're okay now," he reasons. "We're safe. And we're together."

I open my eyes and tip my chin so I can meet his gaze. We're so close, almost nose to nose. "Are we?"

His hand goes still and he stares at me, troubled. His eyes are so deep, so predatory, and his voice is a low growl. "Of course we are."

I grin at him. "I meant are we safe."

He sits back a bit, relaxing. "They can't get through the door."

I interlock my fingers with his, entwining us. "That's not what I'm talking about, Gus." I glance at the dark maw of the entrance to the Undertunnel.

"Oh," he says. Then after a moment of thought, he continues, "We have plenty of food and water stored. The Cyrs have always kept a secret emergency stock here. We'll be okay until we reach Cadence."

I resist rolling my eyes. My fears are beyond a dry mouth

and rumbling stomach. I've lived through both of those things while playing captive to my uncle's schemes. "And what happens when we get to Cadence? Do you know what happened to the refugees from Adagio when they came here?"

Gus purses his lips. He must know. He's Quentin's best friend. Quentin's mother, Lady Cyr, had been one of those refugees. So had my mother. They'd apparently been friends. Chances are, Lady Cyr is the reason there's a stock of food and supplies kept here. "They got in. Eventually."

"But we very well may not get into Cadence," I say. "Or, worse yet, what if we get in and find it destroyed like Adagio or overrun by robots like Evanescence? What if it's like what Evanescence was to my mother? A city overrun by unnatural abominations who forced their ideologies on her—implanted a chip inside of her and killed her for not conforming."

Gus tips his head, and his eyes, so much darker and more animalistic than the ones I knew and loved in Nexis, take on what little air of softness they can. He reaches up with his free hand and cups my jaw. "We can only hope for the best, Elle."

I frown at his consolation.

His touch slides down my jaw, cupping the side of my neck and getting caught in my curls. "It's the only option we have."

Closing my eyes, I nod. "I know." It's stay and die, or run and maybe live. But when I was legless, imprisoned, and being starved by my uncle, I lived in hell and I clearly remember wondering if it hadn't been better to just die.

Persevere.

No. I can't die. I have to carry on. I can't be like Uncle Simon, blissfully relieved of all the responsibility for what he did by a bullet to the head. I have to see this through, hold myself accountable for what I've done. I have to try and maybe make it better. I can't let myself down.

I nod harder. "Okay. Okay, let's do this." I move to stand, but Gus's grasp tightens on my shoulder, holding me down. I turn questioning eyes on him, concerned.

In response, he drops his hand and grasps my thigh, his grip finding and circling the seam where the prosthetic attaches to my stump. "What happened?"

I blink at his hand. I knew this would come up. This is why I feared meeting him in Real World. "The accident that killed my father—"

"The one you were supposed to have died in?" he clarifies.

I nod, drawing my tattered dress up so he can see. I run my fingers along the silken red fabric as I say the words out loud for the first time in my life. "Double amputee."

He draws his hand away and stares for a long time. I stare, too. Really, one can't tell the difference between what a real leg would look like and my prosthetics. Uncle Simon got me the good ones. These are expertly wired and hooked into my own nervous system so that I can feel any sensation and make any movement with a thought. They are warm to the touch and pliable. The only giveaway is the seam. And, of course, the ugly burn hole from the laser strike I got when we attempted to rescue Meems.

Quentin managed to repair it as best as he could before we made the trip back to the tunnel from my house. I limp a little now, as one of the pistons was bent by the heat and he couldn't do anything about that. Normally damage like the limp and the burned silicone coating are fixable, but with Evanescence on lockdown, fixing aesthetic problems like this are out of the question. It's sad to damage my perfect new legs so soon after getting them, but at least I can still walk. It could be a lot worse.

I look up at Guster. He's still staring, his expression withdrawn and unreadable.

"Gus!" someone calls. The voice is familiar, but I can't place it at first.

He turns to look at her and something within him goes very still. I turn to see who it is. Delia. Why is Delia calling for Gus? Well, she's friends with Carsai now, part of the inner circle of Aristocrats who orbit around Quentin and his Dolls. Why wouldn't she call out to him? She probably wants to know what's going on. I turn back to Gus. He's still staring at her, as if lost somehow.

I reach out and grasp his arm. "Gus?"

He flinches.

I jump, startled by the response.

He blinks at me, eyes wide. "I'm sorry, I uh…"

I swallow, hurt that he'd shy away from me. "Delia's calling you." I gesture with my chin.

He gets up. "I uh, yeah. I've gotta go."

"Go?"

"Yeah. Just for a few minutes. I'll be right back."

"But we just got back together."

He leans in, touches my shoulder. "I'm not going anywhere, Elle."

Indignation wars inside of me. I want him all to myself, but I can't. He's not all mine in Real World like he was in Nexis. I have to share him. "Go on, then." I shoo him away.

Grinning, he turns away.

I watch him trot up to Delia; his anxiety and tension seem to melt away and he smiles at her. He's good at putting on airs, just like Quentin, but she doesn't seem swayed. Delia is angry, annoyed. They start to argue, which is pretty much what I would expect, considering the last time I saw the two of them together was on The Broadcast of my falsified memorial service and Delia was attacking him on Citizen's Way.

Smirking at the memory, I stand and gravitate toward the

throng of Aristocrats. It's so quiet. No words. No cries. Nothing. They're all in shock. All numb. At some point, it will all sink in.

No more laughing with friends as they walk in and out of shops on Citizen's Way. The only way is forward, into the dark Undertunnel, and no one is laughing.

No more fructose bubbly. Only water—if we can find it.

No more Designer outfits. We'll have to put our own clothes together, scrap to scrap.

No more constant din from The Broadcast. We will remain uninformed and have to make our own decisions.

No more perpetual light from all the Alts and Mods and holo-glass screens. Only true darkness.

No more androids to keep us company, entertain, or work for us. No more habitation units to monitor us, feed us, clean for us. We have to reassume many of the tasks we evolved to do.

No more doors opening at our approach, no more Central Staffing job placements according to our genetic predispositions, no more arranged marriages to advance up the social chain, no more crime-free city, no more fancy nano-fabrics, no more cyber-stars, no more pods to drive us, no more holographic gardens, no more credits to run the economy, no more high-tech solutions for all our ailments and injuries.

I glance over at where Quentin is standing, staring and brooding in that way he does as his Dolls drag the storage bins out into the main room. Meeting my eyes, he peels himself away from the wall and comes to stand beside me. He watches the people, too, quiet for a long time before saying, "Hard to think about everything we've just lost, what it's going to be like now."

It's as if he can read my mind.

"You're still blaming yourself," he reflects in an almost teasing voice.

I don't look at him. "For the part that I had to play in it?

Yes." I give him a pointed glare. "I also blame others." My uncle. My parents. Lady Cyr. Quentin. Even Gus had a part.

He looks away. "Regret and blame will do nothing for you."

I straighten and this time I do turn and look at him. "Do I look regretful?" I demand. "Have I pointed a finger at anyone?"

He stares at me. Without the nanos making his eyes twinkle like diamonds, they're turning a deep, warm amber. I wonder if that's the color his mother chose for him when he was Customized or if the amber is a Modification. "You look tired, Elle."

A part of me cringes internally. Elle is Gus's pet name for me, and I hate that Quentin has taken to calling me that, too. I turn away. Despite that, another part of me likes how he says it. Stupid Aristocrats with their smoky, sexy Modified voices. "I *am* tired."

He sidesteps a few inches closer as if gaining ground lost by my withdrawal of eye contact. "How's your leg?"

My fingers slide over the burn hole in my dress, hiding it like a weakness, which is stupid, considering he knows it's there already. I yank it away. There's no point trying to be perfect anymore, even if I'm standing next to the boy that years of socialization inside of Evanescence has taught me is perfection incarnate. "It's fine."

"It's only a temporary fix for now. I'll have to work on it more. I'll have you up to specifications in no time."

"I know," I say, irritated at his choice of words—as if I need improving. "You already told me."

Out of the corner of my eye I see him cock his head and examine me from down his nose as if I'm some kind of strange code that needs cracking. "Are you angry at me?"

"No."

"Yes, you are. Your brow is twitching."

Lifting my hand, I rub at my brow. "Who said a twitching brow had anything to do with me being angry?" I'm going to kill Gus when I see him. I can't believe he told Quentin about my twitchy eyebrow! Is nothing sacred?

He smirks at me. "He's right. It is cute."

Blushing, I turn away.

He lets the awkward set in for a few moments before blissfully changing the subject. "So, what are you going to do?"

I can't help but turn back toward him, but I find it hard to meet his eyes. "What do you mean?"

He switches his cocked head to the other side, reminding me of a bird of prey I once saw in the game. "That message we saw—Persevere—and the video of your mother singing to you, those were obviously meant for you. Your parents trying to tell you something."

I lower my chin. "Uncle Simon told me they wanted to continue on with what they were working toward with Nexis."

"What's that?"

"Honestly, I'm not sure anymore. I'd thought Nexis was originally meant to teach people, Aristocrats and Disfavored alike, about the greatness we could achieve as humans, inspire them to be greater and to maybe remember our ancestors' follies so we don't make the same mistakes. But the Anansi Virus confuses me. I'd thought, when Uncle Simon told me it was just for a power outage, that it aligned with their goals—to open the Aristocrats' eyes to their overreliance on technology. But that's not all the virus did, and now I'm wondering if there wasn't something else they were aiming at." I gnaw the inside of my cheek. I don't know why I'm telling him this.

"What are you going to do?"

I tense the muscles in my back, drawing my shoulders wider. "My best."

And then Quentin grins at me in an almost mischievous way that reminds me too much of Gus's expression in the game and I have to look away again. I focus on what the Dolls are doing instead and Quentin is, blissfully, content to stay quiet and watch with me.

chapter three

POST-AMERICAN DATE: 7/4/232

LONGITUDINAL TIMESTAMP: 10:02 A.M.

LOCATION: SUB-TUNNEL 6

The first storage box lid hits the floor with a clang and, grinning in satisfaction, one of the Dolls tosses his prybar to the side and glances in. His eyes—one a green cat eye, the other human, but red as blood—turn troubled. His skin looks like the skin of a golden snake and when he licks his lips in agitation, his tongue looks forked. "Uh, Quent?"

"Excuse me," Quentin says as he steps away from me and heads toward the Doll. They exchange a few words, Quentin checks the bin, his lips thin, and he quickly glances around. I glance, too, uneasy, but no one is paying attention. They're all mostly sitting, huddled in little groups at the far end of the hall.

He says something to the Doll and turns away. As Quentin walks back toward me, the Doll picks up the lid and quickly replaces it. Confused, I turn my attention back to Quentin who, somehow I can tell, is rattled even though his face seems perfectly calm and serene.

Crossing his arms, he stops beside me and turns to watch

as the Doll he just left goes to another bin where the Doll who made the nutra-pack comment earlier is working the lid. The Doll with the snakeskin doesn't seem to have any urgency in his movements or the words he exchanges with this new Doll, but I can tell by the slight pause in the new Doll's movements that what Snakeskin just said is significant. Snakeskin waits as this Doll opens the bin. They both look inside, exchange a few words, and then the new Doll replaces the lid. Snakeskin moves away and calmly speaks with another Doll.

I keep my voice low and my eyes on the floor as I say, "What's wrong?"

Quentin is quiet for a moment. "What makes you think something is wrong?"

"I can see it in your eyes."

Despite himself, he scoffs. "Really? I didn't know you looked at my eyes."

Choosing to ignore the lure, I say, "In your eyes. In their eyes." I resist the urge to point at the Dolls. It's clear that whatever is going on is secret and my instinct tells me to keep it that way, so I don't want to draw attention. "Tell me I'm imagining it."

Another moment of silence. "No, you're not imagining it." I wait for an explanation. "The storage bin Cam just opened is empty."

Lifting my chin, I angle my head so that I can see him. He's still looking on, calm and serene as a Cyr. "You're certain?"

A dimple appears on his cheek. "I saw it with my own eyes and I'm genetically enhanced to have superhuman vision, so yeah, I'm pretty sure."

I purse my lips.

He continues. "The one Jayn just opened, too. And Beau. They're all going to be empty, I'm certain."

I swallow. "They're not supposed to be empty."

"I'm well aware of this."

His sarcasm makes me frown. "This is no laughing matter."

"I'm aware of that, too."

Sighing, I drop my shoulders. "I suppose it would be useless to ask what happened to the supplies that were supposed to be stored here."

"I have a few theories. But does it really matter?"

"No. Either way, we're screwed, aren't we? We just sealed ourselves into this tunnel with no provisions and at least a week's worth of travel ahead of us."

"Look on the bright side," he says, glancing down at me, "at least we have each other."

Turning, I take in the battered group of Aristocrats. Bastian sitting quietly next to Sadie, who has her head on his shoulder. Delia and Gus, still arguing. And all the others… Some are contemporaries from school, many are older, but because Aristocrats are so capable of counteracting the aging process, I can't tell just how much older they could be. Selfish, shell-shocked, and naïve as they are, none seem to have noticed that nothing is coming out of the storage bins. In fact, they don't seem to have noticed the bins or the Dolls at all. I'm not sure if they'd notice a dragon in their midst at this point.

Rolling my eyes, I say, "I'm not terribly relieved at the prospect."

His glance becomes a full-on gaze. "Come on, I'm not *that* bad."

I open my mouth, uncertain what to say to him. I had thought he meant all of us. Not just him and me. I close my mouth and look away, cheeks heating. "I wasn't talking about you."

"What? You mean them?" He juts his chin toward the Aristocrats. "They'll be just about as useful as a stick of gum in a tornado."

I scoff despite myself. A normal Aristocrat would know

nothing about gum or tornados. "You've been playing Nexis, haven't you?" I saw both he and Carsai in Central Dominion, and surely they wouldn't have encountered terms or experiences like that on that level. Unless he's got an adventuring streak like Gus does, which wouldn't surprise me.

He closes one eye and turns the remaining one on me. Everything about his expression seems to be laughing at me. "I've been known to play a round or two."

"This isn't a game."

"You already said that."

"No, I said it's no laughing matter. Totally different."

He sighs. "Semantics."

"What do you plan to do about the lack of supplies?"

His good shoulder lifts in a shrug and he picks at the makeshift sling on his bad arm. Miraculously, his fingers seem to be working just fine. "Seems like there's only one answer to that. We're going to have to get supplies. Can't get to Cadence without them." Brow wrinkling, he turns toward the door that was just sealed shut. "Though, I don't really know how to get out of here now unless you're packing explosives in some hollowed-out crevice in your leg?"

I scowl at him. Brazen ass. I'll show him. "We don't have to open that door up." I can't believe he hasn't put this together yet!

He lifts a brow.

"Is there anyone in Evanescence who would have any reason to steal these supplies?"

"No, I don't think so. They were rudimentary, the very basic. Any citizen would have access to far superior."

"Right. So, either someone who had access to this stash sabotaged this equipment or someone who actually needed it found it and stole it. Sound about right?"

He nods, his eyes darting back and forth in calculation.

"I'm certain that everyone who knew about this stash is trustworthy."

"I thought Simon was trustworthy," I counter.

He shakes his head. "No. There were only three people besides myself and the Dolls, and I trust those people with my life."

Sighing at his stubbornness, I say, "Okay. When all other possibilities have been explored, then it's the impossible thing that must be the answer." Or something like that. Dad always said it better.

Quentin bites his lip. "So, you're telling me someone happened upon this stuff and stole it?" He glances around, bewildered. "How? These tunnels have been sealed for hundreds of years."

"Well," I venture, fisting my hips, "Obviously they're not sealed anymore. Someone got in and if they got in?"

"We can get out," he finishes.

"And you better hope it leads to food and water for these people, otherwise you just killed us all by closing that door."

"To be fair, we would have been dead either way."

I smirk. And then, realizing that I'm actually enjoying myself a little bit, I shake myself out of it and glance around, ready to escape. But I find there is nowhere to go. "Ugh, why are Gus and Delia *still* arguing?" I can't imagine they'd have that much to talk about.

"Uh, you might want to ask him that."

Turning, I move to storm away, but Quentin catches my arm. "Don't."

I spin on him. "You just told me to ask."

He lets my arm go. "Not right now. Don't insert yourself. Wait until he's alone."

I frown at him. "He's my boyfriend. I can talk to him whenever the hell I want to."

A strange flicker dances over Quentin's features and he looks away from me. "*Is* he your boyfriend? Because you had a relationship in a virtual reality game? Does that make it true in Real World?"

I purse my lips. "I—" I don't really know. I had just sort of assumed that we'd pick up where we left off. "He's been acting like it."

"Of course he has. He's happy to see you," Quentin says, gently. "But he has responsibilities here in Real World and those take priority."

I squint at him. "Are you telling me Delia is a priority?"

He takes a deep breath, grasps the back of his neck. "I'm telling you that all of those girls think they're a priority. If you go over there and insert yourself, monopolize him, you're just going to make it worse for yourself."

"Worse for myself?" I scoff. "Circuits, Quentin, why don't you just come out and call me an outcast."

"I'm only pointing out the fire that *you* started." At my confused frown, he clarifies. "Earlier, in the aerovator, when you admitted to helping to plant the virus." When he sees my dawning recognition, he continues, verbalizing what my brain is already realizing. "It was stupid of you to have admitted anything about your involvement to these people. As soon as the shock wears off, they're going to want someone to blame, someone to string up and make accountable. You put a giant bull's-eye on yourself, and it doesn't help that you've been isolated for the past year and are already considered an outsider because you're a Natural."

I glance back at Gus. He and Delia have finally moved and are sitting among the other Aristocratic girls. They're all chattering excitedly, but a few of them look up and stare back at me, their attention on the Natural talking to their prince. "It's certainly not winning me any points standing here and talking to you now, is it?" I turn away, intent on leaving, but he steps in front of me.

"Let's be clear on something, Elle. The only thing that will prevent arrows from hitting that bull's-eye is my protection, Gus's protection."

I take a step back, putting distance between us. "I want to help them—fix what I've done. I can't help them if they don't trust me, and how can I get them to do that if they don't consider me one of them?"

"We all want that," he reasons. "But believe me when I tell you the easiest and safest way to do that is to remain as close to me and my people as you can. You're one of us now, whether you like it or not. As one of my people, they'll automatically have faith in you because they do me."

I sigh. He's making sense. I just don't want him to be.

Seeing he's getting to me, he continues. "Look, if you stick with us, help us make an effort to supply and get these people to safety, then I'm sure they'll see you mean them no harm."

"I was going to do that anyway."

"Good, then we're in agreement. You're one of us."

"I'm not. I don't even know what being with you means. I don't understand what happened up there." I point at the ceiling above us, indicating the city that just went insane.

Quentin lets out a long, deflating breath. "I don't, either."

"What?"

"Not all of it, anyway. But I want to find out. And I can't do that until I'm certain all these people are safe. After that, I'm getting answers. Because that"—he glances at the ceiling and his voice quavers a little—"that's not what I signed on for."

Not for the first time, I feel my insides melt a little bit for Quentin, but I steel myself against him. I'm still not ready to forgive him for blowing out my uncle's brains, even if he was a murdering liar. "What, exactly, did you *think* you were signing on for?"

"To help create a rebellion, a coup. I wanted to be a revolutionary—a Trickster seeking to right the wrongs by making fools of the complacent sheep who allowed themselves to be corralled and controlled by a corrupt regime. I wanted them to see. To feel something for someone other than themselves. I think that's what you wanted, too."

I stare at him, still and unmoving, his words hitting too close to home. Trickster. That's what I was in Nexis. Me and Gus and my other friends. That's what we wanted there. But what does it really mean here?

Seeing my reaction, he says, "It's in your blood and bones, just like it's in mine." There's a passion to his voice, a light in his eyes, a madness to his sudden grin that stirs something deep inside of me. "Whether you want us to be or not, we're the same, Ella."

Before I can say anything else, someone comes trotting up to us. "Quent."

He turns to meet Sid as he comes to a halt. "They're all empty. Every container."

"Shit."

"There's one thing they didn't get."

Quentin's relief is palpable. "Sparks, tell me it's something useful."

"Looks like it." Sid's cat eyes narrow in mirth, making him look even more like a predator. "That little stash? The one Zane built into the floor? That's still there."

"Well," Quentin reflects, "I guess that proves that it was someone from the outside, then."

I cock my head. "Is that enough?"

He shakes his head. "No, they're packs, already made up—food, water, bedrolls, light-sticks—but not enough of them."

"So, we're screwed."

I jump at the new voice behind me, familiar as it is.

"Gus!" I breathe, "You scared me!"

He smirks at me. "I'm used to that."

I open my mouth to retort, but he continues speaking to Quentin. "What do you think?"

"As you put it so succinctly, we're screwed."

"How much food and water are in the packs? If we were to split it evenly between everyone here?" I ask.

Sid straightens, obviously put off by my sudden interjection. He glances at Quentin, who nods for him to divulge. "Not much, maybe three, four days? If we're sparing. A day or two if we're not."

Frowning, Gus says, "That's barely enough to get us past the limits of Kairos."

"Kairos?" I ask.

"It's the name the Disfavored call the Outer Block," Gus explains. "This tunnel runs under the Outer Block on its way to Cadence. But without enough food and water, we'll exhaust our resources right about there."

"Maybe that's all we need?" I suggest.

Quentin squints at me. "What makes you say that?"

I shrug. "No one lives outside the boundaries of the Outer Block, right? At least, it didn't look like anyone did when I watched them from my room. So, chances are, whoever took the supplies found the breech in the tunnel *inside* the Outer Block."

Their eyes light at this sudden realization. Sid takes a step forward, eager. "So, we just need to get everyone to that breech."

I can't help my bitter scoff. "We just escaped a city filled with Disfavored who were killing Aristocrats alongside the androids. Have you forgotten that? You wanna take the last few survivors up to the Outer Block like lambs to the slaughter?"

Sid's open mouth closes and he looks away.

"Point taken," Quentin says. "Pass the packs out among the survivors. Remove the food and water first."

"Are you sure that's wise?" I say, "Monopolizing the food and water?"

"It is," Gus says. "These people don't know self-control. It will be gone in one sitting."

Grimacing, I nod. He has a point. To be fair, they don't control their own food normally anyway, their habitat control systems do. So, I doubt they'll miss it. "What do you want to do about the fact that these packs aren't gonna last?"

Gus says, "Obviously, you've got a plan already."

I smirk. He knows me way too well. "A bit of one. But I'm not sure."

"No one has a better idea." Gus holds out his hands. "Go ahead."

"Maybe," I venture. "We could leave the bulk of everyone here and send some scouts forward. We could see what's ahead of us and perhaps, if what I'm thinking is correct, the people who took most of the supplies came through some sort of break in the tunnel in the Outer Block, er, Kairos. If they came in then maybe we can get out—find some supplies, come back, and get everyone to Cadence as planned."

The boys glance back and forth at each other. I wait for one of them to pose the obvious argument—that the people of Kairos don't like us and *any* Aristocrat going out there would most likely be killed. But what other choice do we have? I steel myself, glance between the three of them, hoping for a better plan. But when their eyes meet mine—amber, green, black—none seem to argue.

Gus says, "Okay," and immediately looks to Quentin.

Quentin nods. "We'll send a small scouting group out tomorrow. For now, do like I said with the food and water, distribute the supplies. We'll rest here for a bit, regain some energy, then start out in a few hours."

"You're not afraid of them coming through the door?" Sid asks. "Wouldn't you feel better moving us all a little farther along?"

"No, at the rate these people would move? If the rebels or the androids were going to come through the door, they'd get us whether we're right here or a day's walk away. Besides, I don't want to push them. I want to give them some down time to rest and wrap their heads around everything." Quentin turns and examines the room. "Why don't you take these storage crates and push them against the doors. They're pretty heavy and it's more between us and what's on the other side. I want everyone to feel as safe as they can. We'll use the empty storage rooms for some privacy. Once they're settled, I'd like to speak with you and the other Dolls."

chapter four

POST-AMERICAN DATE: 7/4/232

LONGITUDINAL TIMESTAMP: 12:12 P.M.

LOCATION: SUB-TUNNEL 6

Sid and the other Dolls have done as Quentin has requested and now people are drifting into the empty storage rooms. I stand with my new bag slung over my shoulder, apprehensive.

"Aren't you going to set your bedroll up?" Gus asks.

I lift a shoulder, sheepish. "I don't really know where to set it up."

He smiles warmly. "Next to mine, obviously."

I open my mouth to ask where, but one of the Dolls calls to him. "Gus, Quent wants to see us now."

Giving me an apologetic smile, he touches my arm. "Set up wherever. I'll come find you as soon as I get everything all squared with Quent. Then we can have some time alone, I promise." He steps forward, kisses my forehead, and draws away, his fingers leaving a tingling trail of want along my arm.

I stare after him, longingly, even after he's disappeared into the room Quent and the other Dolls are crowded into.

"Are you all right, dear?"

Startled, I glance around. I hadn't realized anyone was close to me. At my shoulder is an elderly lady. By elderly, I mean she looks like she's maybe fifty, which probably means she's at least a hundred. She's a Custom I think, but from what I can see she has had no Alterations or Modifications. Her dark hair is peppered with gray and there are fine lines at the corners of her mouth and purple eyes.

"Uhm," I say, not entirely sure what she means by the question.

"It's just that"—she smiles at me and gestures to one of the occupied rooms—"I notice you're not bedding down with the other girls your age."

"They don't like me much."

"Really? And why is that?"

I blush, suddenly self-conscious, but she doesn't wait for me to answer.

"Could it be that Natural face of yours? Girls your age can be so catty." She touches her chin in thought. "Or perhaps it's your earlier admission to planting some sort of virus and causing this hullaballoo? I'm sure most of them heard you admit to that. I'm sure many of them believe you." Her eyes seem to be laughing. "Not that it's true, of course."

I swallow. "It *is* true, actually."

"About the virus? Sure. But you didn't cause this. Takes two to tango, my daddy always said."

I smirk at her. She has a strange accent. I like it. And I like that she doesn't take things at face value—she questions them.

"Or maybe," she continues, "it's because you're the walking dead? Kids don't learn anything about zombies and vampires these days, they're ill-equipped to deal with the undead, emotionally or otherwise. I'm sure they're terrified of you." She chuckles, coughs behind her hand, then shakes her head as if annoyed. "Damn lungs. This is my third pair."

I want to ask how old she is. It's possible she's older than a hundred. She could be two hundred. Talking about zombies and vampires and hullabaloos, whatever those are, I'm sure she just might be that old. You can live forever now, swapping out your dead or dying parts as fast as a new one can be grown for you or receiving gene therapy to reverse the aging process altogether.

"I'm Violet Von Baren," she says, stretching out a hand.

I take it and shake it, like I learned through my father's historic files. "Ellani Drexel."

"Oh, I know." She shakes my hand very enthusiastically. "That's how I know you're a dead girl, after all. I saw the memorial service—for you and Warren. Don't suppose he's still alive, too?"

The name pushes a pin through my heart and I look away. "No."

"Darn." Violet sighs. "That man was a genius. Fun to talk to."

I nod in agreement as I finger the chips again. At this point it doesn't surprise me that Violet knew my father. Feels like he knew just about everyone and I never even noticed. "He made me everything that I am." The girl who cracks codes and plants viruses that destroy cities. Wanting to change the uncomfortable subject, I glance behind me. "Well, Violet, it looks like it's just us." I indicate the now vacant hall. Everyone has found a room. "I don't suppose..." I lift a shoulder, feeling a little shy.

"You wanna be my roomie?" she asks, grinning huge pearly white teeth at me. Stepping close, she grabs my arm and drags me in a circuit, glancing into rooms as she continues talking. "Now, I have this whopper of a story to tell you. It's about my son, Leopold. That's a fine name, isn't it? I always wanted a cat named Leopold. And I wanted to call him Leo for short. That means lion, did you know that?"

"No, I didn't."

"Obviously I couldn't have a cat. We haven't had domesticated animals in Evanescence since that awful parasitic infection killed them all off, so I just named my son Leopold instead. It was almost the same. He was sort of cat-like, especially after he got himself a whisker Mod. Didn't land on his feet, though, poor fool. Didn't have nine lives, either." She starts cackling hysterically and even though I don't get the joke, I smile because I think I've just found a new friend, even if she's a little bit strange.

As we pass one of the rooms, Bastian and Sadie both look up at the intrusion of Violet's pneumatic voice. I pause, drawing Violet up short, and step into the room, which is empty save the two of them. I glance between them and attempt an awkward smile as I meet Bastian's dark eyes. "Hi."

Bastian gets to his feet and launches himself at me, tugging me out of Violet's grasp and suffocating me in a bear hug. "I thought you were dead," he whispers thickly into my hair. "Don't you dare leave. Not ever again."

I hug him back just as hard. I don't really know what to say to make it okay for him. It just feels good to have him back again. I wish it had been like this with Delia. I wish she'd thrown her arms around me and started to cry when she saw my face. Maybe she still will, maybe, like Bastian, the shock just needs to wear off.

Violet and I have just started setting up our bedrolls with Bastian and Sadie when the Dolls come door to door to summon us all back out. As we exit, I take the opportunity to hobble between the massing Aristocrats and slide in beside

Gus to grab his hand. He squeezes back and we shuffle forward so we're all crammed shoulder-to-shoulder facing Quentin, but Gus's arms snake around my waist, keeping me close and protected.

Quentin's gaze slides over all of us. His eyes look black in the low light. The Aristocrats have found the light-sticks in their packs and many have carried them out. The different colored light-sticks make the inlays on Quentin's skin twinkle in an eerie reminder of his dead Alts. I glance at the people around me. Some of those who'd only gotten Alts look almost like regular Customs, perfect but dull. Those who relied more heavily on the permanent Mods will never look like normal people without surgery to restore their original forms. Like Delia. Like the Dolls. Without Alts to make them colorful and pretty, they just look like aliens and mutants to me.

"I know you're all tired," Quentin says, and his voice reflects his weariness. "So I'll make this short."

I'm relieved by that, as I'm eager to finally get Gus to myself for a while. I wish there were enough empty rooms. I'd have him alone if I could.

"Some of you have questions. Others are aware of what's going on. I'm even hearing that this is some kind of elaborate plan to kidnap you all and sell you to Doll Houses." His lip quirks, like it's hilarious. And I suppose it is. "I can't give you all the answers. I, myself, am not entirely sure what went wrong or who was responsible." *Liar.* But I'm thankful he's not pointing fingers and throwing me under the pod. "What I do know is this: my mother is dead. My father is dead. Most of the people in Evanescence are dead or will be soon, and there is nothing we can do to aid them. The G-Chips no longer work. We can no longer control our own homes or androids. Evanescence has been overrun by robots and Disfavored rebels, and we don't have the power to dispel them and reclaim our home. Not *yet*, at least."

He lets that sink in for a moment, giving us hope, before continuing. I absently start stroking the ridges along the outside of Gus's arm. Sparks, it's so good to be back in his arms. I can't wait to sleep in them again. "I am sorry for all of your losses and for the loss of our home. I, like many of you, would like to be able to take time to myself to be alone and grieve for lost family and friends. However, I have a greater responsibility than my own life. I'm responsible for all of you."

I still my fingers and swallow. Part of me waits for someone, anyone, to stand up and challenge him. No one does. I glance around at the shadowed faces. Everyone is staring at Quentin, enthralled as if he's on The Broadcast. How lost these people are. They crave leadership. They crave a hive mind telling them what to do. Even if their new leader is just a beautiful nineteen-year-old boy, these human nanites will respond to whatever program he feeds them. The mere fact that he's a Cyr is what designates him the one in charge.

Quentin's continuing words draw my gaze back to him. "It is my goal to get you all safely to Cadence as quickly as I can. Once we arrive, I expect you to obey whatever law comes upon us and attempt integration. It seems a daunting task, I know, but it is the only way we'll survive our current situation."

I roll my eyes at the floor. Well, when you put it that way.

"It is my hope that, for the short time we traverse the Undertunnel, you're all civil and accepting of each other. We've all got our differences and we have hundreds of years of programmed thought backing our prejudices. However, Evanescence and her morals are now dead. Once we reach Cadence, there is no telling what she will have in store for us and what passed as normal and proper in Evanescence may not in Cadence. I suggest you keep that in mind and work on making yourselves more malleable."

A low murmur of frightened voices kicks up and Gus's arms tense around me. Bile pools in my throat. Those lines were meant for me. I'm the only outcast among them and it rankles me that Quentin feels he needs to discipline them against their prejudice.

"Get some sleep, everyone." With that, he steps back and the group breaks.

Some of the girls shuffle after Quentin, their voices calling out, "Can we sleep with you and the Dolls tonight? We'd feel so much safer."

"I suppose I should go help him dispel his groupies," Gus mutters, drawing away from me. "Where are you sleeping?"

I point to the room I'm sharing with Violet, Sadie, and Bastian. "We've got roommates," I say, regretful.

He smirks his devilish smirk. "Never stopped us in the past, isn't going to now."

He helps himself to a long, lingering draft of my blush as he takes a few steps backward. "Ten minutes."

"Five."

"Seven, at the most."

"I'll hold you to it. I'll start exacting bodily compensation for every second over."

"I'll just take my sweet ass time." Chuckling at himself, he finally turns away.

Face hot and heart warmed, I start limping back toward our room, but something catches my ear. "Oh, come on, please?" It's Delia's raised voice, nearly yelling.

I glance around, trying to find her through the few remaining people in the hall. She's talking to Gus, who hasn't gotten very far from where we were standing and is looking darker and more ominous than ever. His expression makes my floating heart sink just as quickly as it had risen. I move closer, drawn to his need of my comfort.

Gus shakes his head.

Delia pouts, her odd bird-like Modifications making the expression look more ugly than childish. "Why?" she demands.

"Things are different now, Lia. I'm…I'm really confused."

I lift a brow. *Lia?*

She stomps her foot. "What does she have that I don't?"

Gus sighs and closes his eyes. "You just don't get it." With that, he slips away from where she's cornered him and steps toward me.

I hadn't realized he'd even noticed I was coming back toward him.

"Of course I don't get it," Delia calls. "You can't have two lives, Gus. You can't love two women. You need to make a decision, her or me?"

"I can't. I'm sorry." He slides an arm around my shoulder and moves to lead me away. "Come on, let's get out of here."

"What was that all about?" I ask.

Delia yells after us. "You said he was disgusting, Ella. I thought you wanted nothing to do with him."

Gus goes still.

My blood freezes.

Gus's voice is a low growl, too low for her to hear. "Is that true?"

Heart pounding, I look up at him. Lie or tell the truth? I lick my lips. I could say that she's just making it up, that she's jealous. But it wouldn't be the truth. Once upon a time, Gus did scare me and disgust me. But that was a year ago, and I'm a different person now. Circuits, why would she say something like that when it's obvious he and I are together? What's she trying to do?

Delia continues speaking, her voice choking up. "You didn't want him. You said I could have him. So why are you taking him from me?"

I cover my mouth, suddenly sick feeling. Oh my sparks. I'd forgotten Delia had always had a crush on Gus. What sort of friend does that make me? She must think me horrible for stealing him. But it's not like I did it knowingly. I fell in love with a boy in a game. How was I supposed to know it was this Doll now staring at me with Modified eyes? Eyes demanding answers.

I push the issue of Delia away for a moment. I'll explain everything to her after I save my relationship with Gus. She'll understand, she'll give up this silly idea that she has some right to him. I take a deep breath. "There was a time that I felt that way, yes." His arm moves to escape me, but I grasp his wrist. "But I don't feel that way anymore. I've grown, Gus. You know that I have."

He tugs his arm, still wanting escape, so I release him. He takes a step backward from me, his eyes wild and hurt. "I thought you were different," he hisses.

I take a step toward him, desperate and confused. "I am different."

He continues backing away, shaking his head. He looks like he's about to punch a wall. "I-I can't deal with you right now." And as Delia makes a step toward him, he snaps at her, too. "Either of you." And just like that, he turns and disappears into the darkness of the Undertunnel.

"Gus, wait!" I call. "It's dangerous!" I move to follow after him.

"Don't," Delia growls, grabbing my arm. "You've done enough."

Tears and sorrow sting my heart. I whip around and face Delia, who just watched her poison cripple my relationship with the only boy who will probably ever love me.

I glare at her, hateful. "How could you say that to him? What are you trying to do? I thought you were my friend."

My words are tight and clipped.

For an instant there is a strange wave of uncertainty in her expression and she drops my hand. But then she shakes herself. "So did I. But obviously that was a lie, just like everything about you. You're supposed to be dead. You should have just stayed that way."

I open my mouth to say something—anything—but someone places their fingers against my spine. I spin around to find Bastian standing there, his expression dark and troubled.

"Let it go." He glances at Delia. "Both of you." He draws himself closer to me, protective as I remember him being. I haven't been close to him in over a year and it feels so good. I just want to melt into his brotherly shelter. "Come on," he whispers.

I turn back to Delia, fists balled and spoiling for a fight, but she's already stalking away. The other Aristocratic girls rally around her, throwing me dirty glances as they shuffle into their room.

"What-what just happened?" I whisper, tears stinging my eyes.

Bastian tugs on my arm. "Let's go."

Feeling like a puppet, I follow him back to our shared room. Sadie is sitting on the sleeping bag beside mine, and Bastian's is on her other side. Sid and Cam—Snakeskin—are there, too. That doesn't surprise me; there are a couple of Dolls setting up in each of the rooms.

I sit beside my pack and promptly fall into a fit of burning tears. "How?" I cry. "How did it come to this?"

Bastian's voice is grave. "Things change, Ella."

"No!" I whip my head up, pegging him with my glare. "Not my best friend. Not Delia. Delia is Delia. Not that— Not that *thing*," I nearly scream, emphasizing my words with my finger.

Bastian sits back and lets out a long sigh, his eyes

wandering the floor. "I don't know what to say, Ella. Things were really hard for her after you. After you…"

"Died?" I offer, bitter. His lost expression sucks all the fight and anger out of me, and I sag against the wall, hugging myself. "She sent me messages every day for months. All that pain. All that pining and crying over my death. And I have hundreds of letters where I wrote my deepest, most heartfelt feelings to her almost every day for more than a year on my flex bracelet." I touch the bracelet around my wrist, useless without my G-Chip to control it. "She was my best friend. And now this? Why would she say something like that? Why would she wish me dead?"

"Perhaps you should ask her that yourself? She's your friend, after all."

Feeling hollow inside, I shake my head. "Have you looked at her? Delia isn't in there anymore." This hollow feeling—it's like she's dead. Like how I felt when Nadine and Gus died in Nexis. "I've lost her. And now I've lost Gus again, too!" I wail, tears coming hard again.

"I'm sure you'll make up."

"No. You didn't see the look on his face."

"I can't make out any sort of look on that face of his," he admits.

"Well I can. I *know* him, Bastian, front to back. He'll never forgive me."

A low growl sounds in his throat. "I suppose now isn't the time to ask how exactly you know Shadow." I shake my head and then he says to Sadie, "A little help?"

Her answering voice is confused. "What do you want me to do about it?"

"I dunno, give her girl advice or something." His words only make me cry harder because Delia used to be my girl-advice giver.

"I don't know anything about this kind of thing," Sadie explains. "I've never dated anyone but you."

"But you've lived with her this past year? That's what you told me."

"Well," Sadie says haltingly. "I never actually talked to her." Then, "Don't look at me like that, you're her cousin. You mourned over her for months. You grew up with her, you think of something to make her stop crying."

But Bastian doesn't know what to say. He never really did when it came to my being upset. It always just made him stare at me with this helpless expression on his face. Something I'm sure I'd find him doing right now if I looked up.

Gus would know what to do. He always does. He'd hold me and kiss me and tell me it was all right. But he's not here. Because my ex-best friend has some foolish notion that she has dibs on him.

"Love is a tricky thing," Violet finally offers. "Sometimes you think you've got it right, but you don't."

I don't want to hear that Gus isn't for me. He's perfect for me. He's mine. We've been together for a year! But Delia—she's my best friend. I could never hurt her, not knowingly. And now I do know. "What do I do?" I whimper.

"That's for you to decide. And her. And him," Violet says. "I've read a lot of journals. That's my favorite thing to read. From all different times. I have a standing order with the relic retrieval unit in the Outer Block. Everything I've learned from reading about people's lives from prior to the war is this: the pieces will fall as they will. You'll live. May not feel like it at first, but that's how life is. Sometimes we steal someone's lover. Sometimes lovers find out we used to hate them. Sometimes people can't accept it when friends and family who died in a war suddenly come back to life. They were prisoners of war or lost at sea and have finally come home after five, ten years—but the people they come home to have come to terms and moved on. They have new lovers, new family, and they don't like those wounds opening again so they push the returned soldier away."

Everyone is silent as those words sink in. What will I do if Gus pushes me away? The thought hadn't really occurred to me. What if I made all that sacrifice for a boy who doesn't even want me in Real World?

I sob myself raw and dry. My eyes feel like acid. Sadie, who hasn't moved from my side, lays her head on my shoulder and sighs. "I'm sorry, Ella," she whispers. And it's an apology for everything, not just what happened with Gus.

Something breaks then, and I suddenly find myself unfolding and pulling her into my arms. "I'm sorry, too," I sniff. "I'm so, so sorry." She's stiff for a moment, but then squeezes me back and a single sob escapes her.

As we cling to each other, I realize she needs this hug as much as I do. She needs a friend as much as I do. We're both lost. She's here in a room with me, Violet, and Bastian. Apparently she didn't find anyone who wanted to befriend her among the other Aristocratic girls. It doesn't surprise me. Most of those girls are Elites. Sadie was a ward of the city. Cared for by a nobody. They wouldn't accept her. Even now, with Quentin's words of change fresh in everyone's head.

But I will accept her. Despite our past—her turning a blind eye while Katrina and my uncle kept me imprisoned and practically starved me to death. Because if I can't forgive, then how can I expect anyone to forgive me?

chapter five

POST-AMERICAN DATE: 7/4/232

LONGITUDINAL TIMESTAMP: 5:42 P.M.

LOCATION: SUB-TUNNEL 6

Dragon fire. A body falling from the sky. Nadine's blood trail leading under my feet and back behind me into the streets of Evanescence. My own screaming as the interior of a pod tumbles over and over, blasting into heat. Gus's bloody-mouthed grin as Damascus Knights thunder down upon us. I'm running, faster, harder, heart hammering. The tunnel just goes on and on and on, escape never coming to me. A hand grasps my throat in the darkness. President Cyr's intestines spill from the dais. The door slams and guns start firing, people start screaming. Meems's face twists, contorts.

You led us here to die!

I flinch awake, gasping, then lie there, still and sweating, gulping in mouthfuls of cold, stale air. And then I hear Gus's voice. Blinking hard and fast, I try to get my eyes to adjust. The light-sticks have burned so low I can only see shadows in the darkness.

As my eyes adjust, I find it's not Gus at all, but Quentin

speaking. Circuits, I hate that I keep mistaking them for each other! It's unfortunate they both have the same voice Mod. Quentin is hunched beside Sid.

I hear Sid say, "—do this in the morning."

"No, I need it done now. Get up."

Sid sits upright and glances around, then turns sapphire cat eyes on Quentin, who tips his head toward the open door. Quentin moves on to Cam.

Cam doesn't respond as quietly. He murmurs and mutters, "Not now, Beau, I'm sleeping."

As Quentin grins at this, Sid softly mutters, "Jesus H, what an idiot."

When Quentin shakes Cam harder, he flails and starts speaking. "Wha—" Quentin slaps a hand over his mouth and shushes him.

Cam's face turns toward the rest of us and then back to Quentin, who lowers his hand. "What's going on?"

"Get up and come with me," Quentin whispers back, grabbing Cam's boots and shoving them at him. "I need you to help me."

As Sid gets to his feet, Cam pushes the sleeping bag away and groggily struggles to insert one foot in the wrong boot. "Why do you need us? Can't Gus help?"

Quentin's lips narrow. "He's offline right now, all bent out of shape about Ella and Delia. I can't deal with him, so I sent him to bed."

Cam grunts in response and, yawning, stands. "Okay, okay."

The three of them skulk out of the room. Suspicious, I slide out of my bedroll and follow after them. The concrete is cold and rough on my synthetic feet and my knee feels creaky and wrong as I limp after them. It's not hard to follow their whispering voices or keep my distance in the darkness, and Cam keeps up a steady stream of conversation that covers any noise I make as Quentin leads us into the dark unknown of the Undertunnel.

"What's so important that you need to do this now, Quent? You should be sleeping."

"I can't sleep," Quentin replies. There's a moment of silence. "How's everyone doing in your group?"

"Eh," Cam says. "Sid and that redhead seem to be hitting it off real well."

Sid speaks for the first time. "Her name is Sadie Turline."

"Oh," Cam says, "excuse me." He chuckles darkly. "Sid's got it bad for the prissy Aristocrat."

"She's with Bastian, if you haven't noticed them fawning over each other. At least I'm not swapping bio-matter with Beau."

"Oi," Cam grunts. "There's nothing wrong with Beau."

Sid scoffs. "Except that Beau's a guy."

"So what? It's been legal for hundreds of years."

"Would you two stop, please? You're giving me a headache," Quentin growls. "Honestly, how long have you two been Dolls? How many times do I have to tell you to drop the Disfavored prejudices. If Sid wants to fall in love with an Aristocrat, that's fine. If Cam wants to be gay, that's fine, too. Seriously, I'm getting sick of it."

The ribbing comes to an end with that, and they walk in silence for another few minutes. Finally, Quentin speaks again. "Besides Sid having a crush on this Sadie girl, everyone else is okay?"

Sid says, "I don't have a crush on Sadie," at the same time Cam says, "You mean, is Ella okay."

Quentin doesn't answer.

"Gus gave her the total brush-off today," Sid says. "In front of everyone. She cried."

I almost stop walking. It feels too weird to be hearing

them talk about me, but curiosity has me continuing to put one foot in front of the other.

Cam says, “Delia got between the two of them and caused it. I told you saving her would be trouble.”

“Hey,” Sid barks defensively. “I’m not the one who grabbed her and Carsai and threw them into the aerovator. Personally, I feel that they both should have been left to the killer robots, but I wasn’t about to fight with Gus when he did. I like my windpipe open and functioning.”

Cam mutters, “I still have no idea what he sees in that girl.”

I blink, confused. Gus saved Delia and Carsai?

Quentin sighs. “I do. Delia has some pretty compelling qualities when you get to know her. Trust me, between her relationships with Carsai and Gus, I’ve had to deal with Delia quite a bit over the past few months.”

Whoa, wait a second. Is Quentin Cyr actually complimenting Delia? The girl he never looked at twice?

Quentin makes a disgusted noise in the back of his throat. “Ugh, but Gus is such an ass. Getting mixed up with her in the first place when he had it so good in the game. One in each world? That’s just selfish.”

“Dreams are dreams, and reality is reality,” Sid says quietly. “One would think you’d know that better than anyone.”

“Oh,” Quentin’s voice is a dark chuckle, “trust me, I do. Doesn’t mean I can’t be upset about it.”

“What are you going to do?” Sid asks.

Quentin is quiet for a long time. “Nothing.”

Cam says, “Uh, what does that mean?”

“It means what it means,” Quentin replies. “If Gus wants to act like an ass, then let him. She doesn’t deserve it, but I don’t think she deserves me keeping him in line, either. She deserves to know the truth about him. Don’t you think?”

No one objects, but I don’t expect them to; they, after

all, know what the hell is going on and I can't, being the eavesdropper that I am, exactly demand clarification.

Quentin changes the subject. "Keep her occupied. I don't think she's handling what happened very well."

"Not sure if you noticed, but no one is," Sid mutters. "They're in shock now, but wait a day or two and you're going to end up with quite a few problems, and Ella is going to be the least of them."

A bitter scoff escapes Quentin and he says, "If anyone thinks they have more of a right to act out than anyone else does, they've got another thing coming. I don't have the time or the energy to deal with everyone else's grief. Ella is my top priority."

Wait, what? Me? Why me?

"Poor girl," Cam says. "She shouldn't have seen all that. With her uncle and everything."

"Yeah, well" —Quentin breathes— "it had to be done. Who knows what he would have done if he got loose. Anyway, I'm glad she was there, she may not have escaped otherwise. I don't think I could have dealt with that."

His words make my chest flutter. Never in all my life would I ever have expected Quentin Cyr to care about my well-being for an instant. And this? Being a priority? But why? I can't help but wonder if his concern for me factors into some greater plan, some other thing the Cyrs had planned for me.

I turn those possibilities over and over in my head as the boys walk on in silence and I follow like a shadow. I wince against the pain in my leg and that makes me start to wonder just how long Quentin's quick fix is going to last.

"Here should be good," Quentin says. And I hear his pack fall to the floor. "Try a light-stick. I don't think anyone will see it from this far away, there's a curve to the tunnel."

I take a few hasty steps backward, biting my lip against

the pain as I go, so that I don't show up in the circle of light.

Crack. Orange light floods around them, making me squint. Cam puts the light-stick down between them. "Okay, what's this all about?"

Quentin's fingers fly to his sling. "This. Something's wrong."

Sid purses his lips. "Have you even bothered changing the bandages since the attack?"

Quentin's lack of eye contact is answer enough. Sid throws his head back and sighs, but he steps forward and helps slide the sling over Quentin's head. I watch, uncertain if I should or shouldn't divert my eyes as Cam and Sid help each other strip a wincing and sweating Quentin's doublet, shirt, and bandages away.

Quentin is no disappointment to what I had always imagined he'd look like under those clothes. Perfect. Too perfect. Hairless and pale with just the right proportions. Muscled like those Grecian statues in Dad's archival files. I can see the tiny swirls of fiber-optic cable under his skin, but without the energy to light them, they look like fine scars. But even if they were scars, they'd still be beautiful. He's just too pretty. It's so fake. So… Customized. Not like Gus, who is so very real in his imperfections and flaws.

Sid moves to one side and I see the wound. Redness and swelling, dried blood, bruising. Ugliness. I wrinkle my nose, hating how wrong it looks on him.

"Circuits, Quent," Cam says. "Why didn't you say something?"

Quentin stares at the floor. He looks like he wants to punch someone. I realize that he doesn't like that he's wounded. Well, no one ever does, but his hatred is beyond the pain and the marring of his perfection. Quentin doesn't like that his injury makes him weak. Even from this distance, I can see the stubborn resolve in his eyes. That's why he refused to have the bandages changed until now. He's a fighter, I'll give him that.

Sid must also see or know that, because he says, "Being stubborn about it isn't going to help anyone. You're useless if you lose that arm."

For whatever reason, his words make my fingers go to my stumps. *Useless.*

"I won't," Quentin says. He lifts his hand, the one he punched the aerovator door with, and flexes it. The swelling is down, as is the bruising. "It should be healed already."

"Those experimental regeneration nanos only work unhindered. Something's probably preventing them." Sid kneels down and begins shuffling through the pack. "Sit over there." He gestures to the wall.

Quentin, straight backed and too pretty, marches over and slumps down like a rag doll, good arm slung across upraised knees. As he stares off into the nothingness before him, his lids droop. He's got to be exhausted. "Do you think it's possible anyone survived?"

Sid goes still and his gaze shoots to Cam, who hoods his eyes and looks away. Cam says, "I don't know. And there is no way of knowing. It's best to make peace with it and not get your hopes up."

Quentin closes his eyes and nods, leaning his head back against the wall.

My mind wanders, wondering who else Quentin must care about back home. His mother, obviously. A good number of friends, some other Dolls who hadn't made it out. A whole year has passed since last I saw him. Had his parents arranged a marriage for him yet? Had he liked her? Is he thinking about her right now?

Sid puts together some medical supplies while Cam squats beside Quentin and tries cleaning the wound.

Quentin hisses air between his teeth and looks away. "Fuck."

Cam grins at him. "You deserve it, big baby."

Quentin's amber eyes open and light up as he glances back at Cam. "I'm going to smother you in your sleep," he rasps.

"Oh really?" Cam visibly pinches the skin around the wound, making Quentin yelp to such a pitch that he makes no sound at all, then he groans, "Mother fucker."

"Hey," Sid snaps. "Take it easy."

Cam lets go. "You kiss your momma with that mouth?"

Quentin jerks his arm away and glares at Cam.

"Uh," Cam grunts, probably noticing his faux pas. "Sorry, I wasn't thinking."

Looking wounded and dejected, Quentin glances away again. That pity feeling I get for him creeps up. I know what that feels like. To not have parents anymore. To feel alone in the world. Part of me wants to rush forward and hug him.

Sid slips over and examines the wound, his face turning grave. "This… This is bad, Quent. They may not be able to fix this."

Quentin's eyes die and he nods. "Do what you can."

"It's infected," Sid says. "I'll need to strip away some of this tissue. It's going to hurt. A lot."

"Great," Quentin adds, balling his fists and going rigid. "It'll give me something else to think about."

"You might want to hold him down," Sid says to Cam.

Cam reaches out and takes Quentin's hand, prying his fingers open and cupping them around his. He plants his knees on either side of Quentin's legs, sitting on him, and shoves his palm against Quentin's chest. He leans in close. "Hold your breath—that always works for me."

Quentin draws a deep breath. I do, too. I suddenly feel cold and wooden. I shouldn't be watching this. This is

Quentin's pain and weakness, it's not my place to see it. Yet, I can't look away.

Sid's first cuts drive a winced wail to Quentin's throat, but he holds it back, making the blood rise to the surface of his skin so that pale becomes red and the veins stand out on his neck and forehead. Tears streak down his cheeks.

Teeth clenched, I dig my nails into my palms. I'm shivering and cold sweat is dripping down my spine, soaking the back of my neck. *Look away. Look away*. But I can't. I watch the blood dribble down Quentin's bare arm, over the tattoo under the wound.

A fox. Like Gus's. Do all of Gus's friends have it?

Flakes of discolored and crusted skin fall to the cement floor. I hear Cam make a shushing sort of cooing noise, which feels out of place and strange coming from a big guy like him. It reminds me of the noises Meems made for me when I was lying in bed, delirious and weak from the accident and subsequent discovery of my father's death.

Quentin is panting now, sweat pouring down his forehead, neck, chest.

A whimper wells inside of me, escapes in a long, low squeak. *Hold on. Hold on just a little longer. He's almost done.*

Sid's hands move quickly, cleaning away the dead skin, wiping away the blood, plucking out scraps of fabric that got stuck in the wound. He frowns and mutters something now and then, but neither Cam nor Quentin respond to him.

I count the seconds, keeping time. Minutes pass. Quentin's eyes have drifted closed and his body has gone limp. Part of me fears he's dead, but Sid and Cam don't seem concerned so he must still be breathing. He's probably passed out from the pain. I would be. Sid sprays the wound with nano-knit to help rebuild Quentin's muscle and skin, and over that, he applies antiseptic sealant to keep it clean and seal the nanos in. He should be healed within a couple of days. That's if Sid got all the infection. If not? Quentin might die. And as for the use of his arm? Who knows? Maybe it will have to be removed. Maybe he'll only be part of a person, like me.

Absolute dread at the idea pools in my stomach and panic makes my breathing speed up once more. I stand there, dumbfounded by the concept of actually caring at all for Quentin Cyr. The thought of something that awful befalling him makes acid churn up in my throat.

Suddenly, Sid and Cam both stand.

Realizing that they will want to start heading back toward the group soon, urgency makes me swallow my nausea. I totter around on my busted leg and hobble back to my sleeping bag.

I nearly trip over Sadie, because the light-sticks have all died to nothing and the room is in total darkness. I feel around for my sleeping bag and crawl into it, relishing the dry warmth of it over the dampness of my sweaty skin and the biting cold air. I curl into a ball and squeeze my eyes shut, willing what I've just seen to leave my mind's eye, but I can't sleep. There's a lump of anxiety inside of me that keeps my muscles tight no matter how hard I try to relax. So I lift myself into a sitting position and lean against the wall like a caterpillar in a cocoon.

When Cam and Sid do return, Cam's carrying Quentin on his back. Sid grabs his own sleeping bag and drags it a little away from the others. Cam squats down, and they both lower Quentin onto the ground.

Cam notices me sitting up and watching. "What are you doing up?" he whispers.

"I-I"—best stick to the truth—"I had a nightmare and then I couldn't fall back to sleep," I say. Desperate to know the prognosis, I tip my chin toward Quentin. "Is he okay?"

Sid slides the top flap of the sleeping bag out from under

Quentin's deadweight. "I think so."

"What happened?" I ask, trying to sound like someone who doesn't know.

Cam says, "He's just tired, that's all."

I grumble, annoyed that he's saving face for Quentin, covering his weakness. It must be nice to have people who are so loyal to you. Though, why they choose loyalty to Quentin, I don't understand. I slump my shoulders. Maybe I do. Just a little bit. He's genuinely worried about everyone here—including me—and he wouldn't express that kind of concern to his Dolls, who know the real him, unless he meant it. So maybe he's not as bad as I thought he was. I close my eyes, but suddenly remember that harsh, vacant expression Quentin had on his face when he squeezed the trigger and blew my uncle's brains out. I shiver. Maybe he is as bad. He's still a Cyr. He's still an Elite. He still willingly helped to destroy our home, played a part in his father's murder.

"Try to get some sleep," Sid says, dimming the light-stick.

I lay back down and close my eyes, but sleep doesn't come for a long, long time and when it does, there's only darkness.

part two:

THE THREADS CALL TO ELLA

chapter six

POST-AMERICAN DATE: 7/4/232

LONGITUDINAL TIMESTAMP: 10:58 P.M.

LOCATION: SUB-TUNNEL 6

I flinch awake and sit up. Someone pushes a cup into my hands. “Here, drink this.” The voice is an instant balm that soothes aching muscles and tired bones.

I take a few sips and stare into the lolling fluid, letting the vita-pep solution take effect, dragging my brain out of its catatonic state before I glance at the white-clad boy behind me.

Quentin’s watching me, his expression closed off and troubled. “You sleep okay?”

Swallowing, I look away and shake my head.

“Me, neither.” He looks down at his own hands clasped around his mug. “I don’t think many people did. I woke up to someone screaming.”

Shuddering at my own bad dreams, I pull my legs close to my body and hug them, balancing the cup between my knees. The silence stretches and I need to fill it. “I miss coffee.”

A soft breath escapes him. “Me, too.”

“Me three. Even the instant stuff. Anything is better than

this drivel." Blinking, I glance up, finally realizing everyone else is awake and sitting in a circle, huddled around the sterile glow of pooled light-sticks. Purple, blue, green. Together, they make our group look morbid and ghostly. We're disheveled, stained with blood, dirt, and tears, the dark hollows under our eyes noticeable. Our souls must look even worse. Violet lifts her cup and, grimacing into it, continues speaking. "Energy drinks. Who would have thought that would be a staple of the future? Here"—she tosses me a nutra-pack—"I saved you your share of breakfast."

I open the nutra-pack and squeeze some into my mouth. It tastes like salty apricot jelly, but I continue to swallow knowing I need my strength for the days ahead.

After a long silence, Sadie says. "I can't stop thinking about it."

"Stop it," Bastian growls.

She peeks up at him, her expression sad. "Stop what? The thoughts? The images? The screams?" She shakes her head, tears brimming on her lids, and whimpers, "I can't." She breaks down into sobs and Bastian, looking apologetic, pulls her close, smoothes her hair, and says he's sorry.

I can't help weakly smiling at him as he gives me the helpless look. Bastian obviously loves this girl. I want them to stay together, to love each other this much always, to have a big wedding with a Harley Dean gown for Sadie and a— No, that can't happen. Harley Dean is dead. Katrina who, smiling, would have given Sadie away is dead. And likewise Uncle Simon, who would have stood beside Bastian, is also dead. It would be a wedding of ghosts.

Feeling my smile fade, I look away.

"Now that we're all here and have had a chance to wake up a bit," Quentin says. "Ella, Bastian, Violet, I want to speak with you. Would the rest of you excuse us?"

Cam and Sid both stand. Sid holds out his hand to Sadie, who, sniffling, allows herself to be led away. Cam shuts the door.

A few seconds pass in silence before Violet becomes impatient and says, "Out with it, boy."

Quentin shakes himself. "As Ella already knows"—he glances at me furtively—"we are in a bit of a bind."

Bastian frowns and Violet urges Quentin on. "Explain."

"Our stores have been compromised, and we don't have enough supplies to last the group the distance between here and Cadence."

Violet whistles low under her breath as she leans back against the wall and crosses her arms. "That is a pickle."

"We do have a plan," Quentin says, "but I think we're going to need your help." His chin lifts and he looks back and forth between Violet, Bastian, and me. "All three of you."

Unable to help my sarcasm, I lower my brow. "You? Need us?"

"Strange, I know," he says, matching sarcasm oozing out of his voice and expression. "I know it seems like I'm entirely capable of everything, but it's a clever ruse, I assure you. In fact, I need help dressing and bathing and wiping my— "

"Okay," Bastian says, "cut to it."

Quentin clears his throat. "We plan on a small group going up ahead, trying to see if there is a way out and up. Hopefully, get some supplies topside."

"In The Waste?" Bastian asks, dubious.

"The Outer Block, actually," I say.

"As if that's better." Bastian rolls his eyes. "People can hardly feed themselves in Kairos, and you want to see if they'll give you supplies? You? An Aristocrat? A *Cyr*, nonetheless."

Quentin has the good grace to look a little bit embarrassed. "My Dolls have assured me that supplies can be had. They do exist. Just—for a price."

Bastian stares at him for a long moment, his eyes pinched.

I look back and forth between the two of them.

Finally, Quentin lets out a long breath and looks away. "I'm not thinking of the skin trade, if that's what you're referring to. I want to stay as far away from Doll Houses as I possibly can."

Bastian's words are low and clipped. "That's a relief. I've been there and I can't say I'm fond."

Quentin's scoff is bitter. "I've heard. Look, my Dolls... They're not just my Dolls. They're my friends, Bastian. I know about the skin trade. I know about the Doll Houses and what happens when you end up in one. I wouldn't do that to anyone. Not even to sacrifice one to save many. There's got to be another way."

"What way?" Violet asks. "I've been out there on relief missions. You don't approach a trader unless you've got a deal in mind. And you need to be good at deal making. Trust me when I say that."

He nods. "I do trust you. That's why I'm asking for your help."

When neither Violet nor Bastian speak, I sit forward and slowly say, "What do you need us to do?"

Quentin meets my eyes, stares into them for a long moment. It's like he's trying to tell me something, but I just don't know him well enough to know what it is. "I'm going to go up there."

"What?" Bastian barks. "You can't go up, you're the new President. What if something happens to you? These people will fall apart."

Quentin still doesn't look away from me. "I have to. I'm the only one of us with skills in negotiation. I'm the only one with anything to bargain."

"What could you bargain?" I ask. "We don't have anything."

"Leave that up to me. I'll take care of it."

Violet says, "That still doesn't answer the question of why you need us."

Quentin says, "I need you. I can't do this without you." He's saying it to me and me only. I know that. Deep in my bones, I know it.

"I don't understand," I say.

"That makes three of us," Bastian mutters.

Finally, Quentin breaks away and blinks. "I can't go up there alone. Bastian, you've lived out there—you're one of them."

"So have every one of your Dolls," Bastian reminds.

"Yes, but they've all been too badly Modified at this point. You're the only one who could remotely pass for a Natural. Even then, maybe only an Unmentionable. But one of them, nonetheless."

Bastian looks away, his mouth tight.

"Violet, you've worked among the Disfavored. Some of them may know and trust you. If not, you at least know your way around Kairos."

She nods once, the gesture clipped and tight.

"Ella..." He looks at the floor and rubs his neck. "I need someone to have my back."

Bastian uncoils from his brooding manner. "What? You want someone to have your back? Then take Gus, not Ella. She wouldn't know the first thing about being a bodyguard."

Quentin's eyes narrow in dark humor at the comment then slide sidelong at me. "I wouldn't say that. Would you, Ella? Last time I checked, you could hold your own pretty well. You're smart. You keep your head under fire. You're good with a gun. And you care about your companions, you look out for them. I don't think I could ask for more."

Swallowing hard, I look away.

Quentin turns his attention back to Bastian. "She's good for it. I trust Ella with my life."

Silence falls then, like a door slamming against an unauthorized G-Chip, and I refuse to look at Quentin or the others. Why would he say that about me? I barely even know him. He trusts me that much? Just because his best friend dated me in a game? Gus must have really blown me out of proportion. Still, I feel my cheeks heat. It's kind of flattering to be thought so highly of.

"What if I refuse?" Bastian says. "Sadie's pregnant. I can't be taking these sorts of risks."

I bolt upright. "What?"

"Oh, yeah." Bastian blinks and his mouth quirks in an awkward grin. "It just sort of…happened."

"Why wasn't that the first thing you told me?" I demand, suddenly torn between the urge to shake him and hug him.

Quentin snaps his fingers. "Focus you two. If we don't find food and water, you're not gonna live to see this baby born. I'd think that's the only motivation you need—to protect that girl and your unborn child."

That changes Bastian's mood immediately. His dark eyes go stormy and he shovels his fingers through his thick hair, salt and pepper now that the fiber-optic shots of silver are dead and have turned white. "Fine, I'll go."

"Violet?"

She shrugs. "I'm living on borrowed time anyway. Might be nice to see some old acquaintances, breathe that awful air once more. Always tastes like biting tin foil. You wouldn't know what that's like, but it's awful, lemme tell ya." Then she giggles.

Quentin turns questioning eyes on me.

I can't help the desperate expression that passes over my face. "I'd really feel better if Gus came, too."

Chest rising and falling in a deep breath, Quentin's lips

purse and he looks away. "Knowing his past, do you really want to ask him to go back into the Outer Block? Because I don't."

The nail hits home. And it hurts. He's right, of course. Gus is from that place—Kairos. They nearly killed him the last time he went there. For being a Doll. To bring him back there would be tempting fate. I couldn't ask that of him, not for my own selfish need to have him by my side—to feel the safety of having him at my back.

Quentin's voice is soft as he says, "You'll have to make do with me. But I promise I'd never let anything happen to you."

I can't help but flash a morbid smirk. *He's* going to protect *me*? Even though he's asking me to protect him? I want to say no. I'm scared. I've only just escaped danger and I want to remain here where it's safe. But Quentin is important to the Aristocrats. They need him to come back alive. Gus needs him to come back alive. And because I care about making both the Aristocrats and Gus happy, I should make sure he does.

But what if I fail at covering Quentin or the others, and one of them gets killed? That failure is on my hands.

And what if I succeed in protecting them? I probably could. Yesterday proved that my training in Nexis translated over to Real World survival skills. Threads or no, I've just spent a year in a crucible, fine tuning my mind and body in an effort to protect myself and the people I love.

What if that means killing? This isn't a game anymore. Killing here means real death.

But I've already killed a lot of people, haven't I? Innocents. It's not okay and I don't forgive myself, but I've somehow managed to live through the shame of it. Killing someone who is attacking us would be far more justified.

Still…an accidental virus and a gun to the head are far from the same thing. "Okay," I say quietly.

chapter seven

POST-AMERICAN DATE: 7/5/232

LONGITUDINAL TIMESTAMP: 1:32 A.M.

LOCATION: SUB-TUNNEL 6

"Make sure to keep the provisions under tight guard," Quentin is saying to one of the Dolls. This one, with bright florescent-orange eyes and curly cocoa-brown hair, is called Karl.

Karl nods and touches the gun at his belt.

"But don't come off like you're bullying or throwing your weight around. There are more of them than those of you I'm leaving behind."

Cam pauses from helping me repack my bag. "You shouldn't be leaving any of us behind."

Quentin shrugs. "We've gone over this. You know my logic."

"Yeah, well, I think you've got some wires crossed up there."

Bastian and I share a furtive glance. I'm sure we both think the same thing. This plan is insane, but I haven't been able to come up with any alternative.

Ignoring Cam's comment, Quentin looks back to Karl, who is standing in the doorway of our room. "Have all the Dolls filled everyone in?"

"They're working on it. I can't say they're happy about it."

As if in answer, I hear a "Move out of the way, Karl, I need to speak to my intended." The voice is Carsai's, she's unmistakable.

I lift a brow at Quentin and he rolls his eyes in response. "Let her in."

Carsai comes storming in, her dove-gray gown, torn and stained along the edges, sweeping and billowing in a way that comes with the countless hours of practice that only Elite Aristocratic girls have time for. She comes to a halt in front of Quentin and plants her fists on her hips, her perfect chest heaving against the laced bodice. "What is the meaning of this, Quentin Balthazar Cyr? I'm told you're abandoning me."

Calmly, Quentin finishes zipping his own pack and stands, smooth as silk. He towers over her as he stares down into her upturned face. Neither looks anything like they did just a day ago. Alterations dead, both have a network of fine scars across their Custom too-pale skin. Where Quentin's eyes have faded to their genetic warm amber, Carsai's have gone a washed-out blue. His hair is white, dead from the fiber-optic nano-plugs. Carsai's is a strange salt-and-pepper gray, like Bastian's. While he has some light and tasteful Modifications throughout his body, hers are more extreme—typical of a female Aristocrat—so her body still sports unnatural lumps, inclines, and spikes.

"Good morning to you, too, Carsai."

She lifts her chin, petulant.

He closes his eyes. "Look, let's be clear on something right here and now. My parents are dead. Your parents are most likely dead. Our city is in shambles and our social system is shot. I want you to understand that I'm no longer operating under the terms of the marriage our parents arranged for us. I can no longer show you special favor."

"What?" she squawks. "But Quent—"

He holds up a hand. "I'm sorry, Carsai. It's not what I wanted in the first place and I'm not sure it's what's best for you, either. You should know that I'm in love with someone else and it never would have been fair to you. So now that we're no longer duty bound, I think it's only right to dissolve the contract."

Carsai's mouth is hanging open in shock. So is mine. I try not to stare, but it's hard. She was always so high and untouchable. Inhuman in her effort to be better than anyone else. And now? She just seems so very human. Her world just dissolved to a tiny puddle, and here Quentin is taking the last vestiges of normalcy away from her. I feel bad for her. But then, I don't blame him, either. It's hard to be married to someone you don't love. Nadine taught me that while we were in Nexis. I can only imagine it would be doubly awful if the person you were forced to marry were a heartless social climber like Carsai.

She manages to sniff, drawing her jaw up as she does so. I can see tears gathering on her eyelids. A shaky, "Well, I never… This is highly irregular."

Quentin says, "You'll get over it, I'm sure."

Her nostrils flare as her eyes wander around the room, taking in Cam, Bastian, Sadie, Violet, and me. Then she turns on her heel and exacts a hasty retreat, bumping into Karl as she does so.

Quentin's shoulders fall and he lets out an audible breath. "That went well," he mutters.

"I was pretty sure she was going to scratch out your eyes," Cam says.

"Me, too," Quentin admits. "I feel bad for her. She doesn't

do well without plans, and I'm sure I factored into a good number of them."

"Don't," Bastian says. "She's a scheming, spoiled brat. She needs to be cut down a few pegs. Especially if she wants to live."

"Bastian," Sadie says, "that's harsh."

"He's only saying the truth," Violet adds. "Saying what we're all thinking." She turns to Quentin. "'Good riddance to bad rubbish,' my daddy always said. If I had a bottle, I'd crack open some champagne and toast to your near miss. Though, I doubt she'll take the rejection lying down. Girls like that rarely do." She makes a strange hand gesture to her forehead. "I salute your bravery, sir."

"It needed to be done. I don't believe in arranged marriages. People should marry for love."

I blink at him, a little proud, despite myself. "That's a very arcane, un-Presidential sentiment."

He shrugs. "There are a lot of people who put aside what they truly believe out of duty and obligation. Doesn't change who they actually are. Is it so wrong to want to be who I actually am?"

"Making waves, I see." Gus's voice draws Quentin's intense gaze away from mine.

I turn, too, finding Gus standing where Karl was just moments before. He's leaning against the jamb, arms crossed.

"Only little ones," Quentin admits.

"Carsai isn't a little wave. She's a tempest. She's already in a tizzy, proclaiming you're going to shake the very foundations of Evanescence."

Quentin rolls his eyes. "She must not have been paying attention when Robopocalypse hit back there. Evanescence is already experiencing aftershocks."

"It's doesn't have to be. We could try to get it back," I reason.

He glances at me. "That would take a miracle."

Shy and uneasy, I shrug and glance at Gus then back at Quentin. "Wouldn't be the first one I've encountered."

Quentin clears his throat. "We'll keep an eye out for any convenient miracles while we're out there. Okay?"

"Speaking of..." Gus says. "How come I wasn't consulted on this suicide-run plan of yours?"

"You were too busy moping," Cam mutters. "Some of us were planning bigger things."

"Cam," Quentin growls, voice low, his eyes roving over us. "Will you excuse us for a moment?"

Nodding, I stand and move to file past Gus with the others, but Gus catches my arm. "Not you." He eases me back into the room where I stand trapped in with the boys and their palpable tension.

As soon as the others are far enough away, Gus turns his attention to us and hisses, "What the hell kind of plan is this?"

Quentin doesn't speak, and I'm not sure if I'm supposed to. I don't know who Gus is talking to. Quentin, I guess, as he rounds on him, stepping into the room as his words take on heat. "Never in the entire time I have known you have I seen you make such a foolish and deadly decision. What do you think you're going to do? March right up to the nearest Disfavored door and ask for alms for a score and a half of displaced Aristocrats? 'Oh, pardon me ma'am, but I was just hoping you could spare some pity for the pompous, ignorant assholes who have been shitting on you and your kin since the day you were shunned and locked out of salvation?' Yeah, that's gonna go over really well, Quent," he huffs.

Quent waits a moment more then says, "Are you finished?"

"No."

"Well, hurry up and fucking finish. I have work to do."

Gus scowls at him. I can see hurt in his eyes. Hurt, betrayal, anger, and fear. I reach out and touch his wrist, but he doesn't respond, just glares at Quentin, who glares at him right back. Gus says, "I'm coming with you."

"No you aren't."

"Fuck you. I'm not letting you go and get yourself killed."

"This isn't up for discussion. It's an order."

Gus gets right in Quent's face, making me step back, because I'm certain one of them is gonna throw a punch. "Screw you and your orders. The laws, the rules, don't exist without a city to uphold them. You can't and don't own me anymore and I'm not following your orders—especially if they mean you walking into danger where I can't protect you."

"Guster," Quentin warns, voice icy, "if I have to get every Doll to hold you at gunpoint to keep you here, I will. If I have to get them to hold guns on Delia, I will. You're staying."

Breathing hard, Gus takes a step back like he's been shoved or slapped. Finally, he says, "Why?"

Quentin softens his voice. "You're the only person I trust to act in my stead. I need you here. Be my eyes. Be my ears. Be my mind, my voice, my authority. I know you'll take care of these people when I can't."

Gus pouts at the floor. "The roles should be reversed."

"You can't go up there. You're too obvious, too much of a target. I've made you that way and I'm sorry for it. I know you want to be there, but you'll just have to trust that we can do it on our own."

Blinking, Gus turns back to us. He must just now realize I've got my bag over my shoulder because he shakes his head. "Oh no. No. No. No. You're not going with him."

Shrugging, I say, "It's not your decision to make."

Gus is still shaking his head, his shaggy hair dancing around his ravaged face. "I can't let you. It's suicide. What if something happens to you? I-I couldn't— "

I reach out, grab his arm at the elbow, and jerk. "Gus, look at me."

He goes still, stares down at me.

"You need to trust me. You need to have faith in me."

His brows pinch in desperation. "What if something happens to you? To either of you?" He glances at Quentin. "You. Out there. In danger. And me... Here—"

"Protecting the woman you love," I finish for him, shoving the blade where it needs to be inserted, because nothing else I say will sway him to my side and he's ready to stop me if he has to. My words have an instantaneous effect on him and I know them to be true. Gus loves Delia. I wince at this truth, this reality I didn't want to recognize. It has a weird, unhinging effect on my head and things no longer feel real, like I'm floating somewhere on the inside. I force myself to speak, even though there's this sudden ache in my chest and my words come out wobbly. "Are you going to leave Delia here?" I think I'm going to cry. "Un-Unprotected?"

His mouth opens, closes. "How—"

I force a smile and somehow it makes my chest hurt even more. "It doesn't take a Master Chemist, Gus."

He steps back, leans against the wall. "I was gonna tell you. I just didn't know how."

"How," I whisper, echoing the words.

There's this weak little smile he throws at me, a little breath of a laugh. "We bonded over you. Actually."

"Me?" I say, as if on some sort of autopilot. I'd been asking how he'd managed to love two girls—because I don't doubt he loves me, too. And here he's giving me the explanation of how that happened. And there's some morbid sense of curiosity I have about it. A need to know, so I prompt him and keep listening.

"Yeah," he laughs, shaking his head, and it's so adorable,

that candid weakness he has for her. I suddenly want to vomit, but he shoves the urge down with words. "She attacked me at your memorial service. Screamed something about making you unhappy before you died. I—" He pauses, meets my eyes. Something in my expression must tell how unhinged I suddenly feel because he reaches out and grasps my wrist. "I went to see her after that. I guess I needed her forgiveness for hurting you. Because"—his fingers squeeze affectionately at this—"I'd always had a thing for you."

When I don't respond, he drops his hand and adds, "Things just sort of developed from there. I guess we found comfort in our shared grief."

For a long moment, I don't know what to say or do.

"I didn't mean for things to happen like this. You have to know that. It's just that…this is real and that was a game, and now you're both real."

"I know," I finally manage. "But I can take care of myself and she can't, so…" I shrug, pretending it doesn't hurt like hell to tell Gus to leave me and stay with her. But I want Delia safe. I want the other Aristocrats safe. Most of all, I want Gus safe. I know he's capable of doing that when I can't. Just like he knows, deep down, that Quentin is safe with me. "Promise me you'll take care of her." Then I add, very quietly, because I have to remind myself now that all I wanna do is fight her, "She's my favorite…"

He nods. "She's pretty special."

It aches to hear the man you love say that about another woman, but I nod because I have to. Because I need him to move and let me out of the room, sooner than later, before the tears I feel burning start to fall.

"I'll never forgive myself if something happens to you, Elle. I love you."

"I know," I say again. *You just love her more.*

Quentin steps into me, puts his hand on my trembling shoulder. "I'll take care of her, Gus. I promise."

Gus draws close, pulls Quentin into a hug, then stoops down and gives me a long, desperate kiss that I dread, in my very bones, is the last one. If I go and he stays here with Delia, that's the decision made. Her over me. He turns. "Take care of each other." He meets my eyes one last time. Then he turns and he walks away.

I stand, staring into the blackness of the empty hall beyond the doorway, listening to myself breathe hard for longer than I know. Eventually, Quentin's fingers close over my elbow, reminding me I'm clutching myself like I've been shot in the stomach. Feels like I've been shot all over. I sway in his grasp, but he holds me up.

"That was very brave of you," he says, voice quiet.

Blinking hard, I pull away and take a few steps. "I don't want to talk about it. I did what had to be done."

"But it couldn't have been easy," he whispers, more to himself than me, I think. His hand appears on the small of my back, warm and comforting. "Come on. Let's get out of here before someone changes their mind."

As Quentin and I emerge from the room, we're confronted with most of the Aristocrats standing outside the rooms, silent and frightful looking.

"I suppose I should say something to them," Quentin notes as he draws away from me. "Gather around, everyone, I have some things to tell you."

I remain behind, feeling awkward and strange. Still unhinged about everything. I realize Delia is standing on her own, away from everyone, her arms crossed like she, too, just got shot, and I hope that Gus didn't just say something stupid to her. Biting my lip, I step toward her.

"Are you all right?" I ask.

Her face changes suddenly, like she smells something sour. "Leave me alone."

I take a deep breath. I don't want things to be like this. "Delia, I…I'm sorry." That's all I can say to her.

She turns and glares at me. "Are you? Are you really, though?"

"Of course I am."

Her eyes narrow. "And sorry is just going to fix everything? Make me forgive you for abandoning me, killing off my family, and stealing the man I love?"

I stare at my fists, balled before me. There's no way to put into words the utter despair and loss I felt after my father's death. After the loss of my legs and discovery that I could no longer see Delia. Yes, I managed to put her out of my mind often, but I never forgot about her. How could I? Even during my happiest moments, I always thought about her and her happiness as well, wished the same for her. How will she ever understand that while she was falling for Real World Gus, I was falling for the same boy wearing a different face in another world? I reach into my pack and pull out my flex bracelet. I take a second to remove the chip containing the sonnets of William Shakespeare, slip it into the pocket with the other two chips for safe keeping, and toss the bracelet to her.

She catches it, turns it over in her delicate fingers. "What's this?"

"What's it look like?" I say, turning away from her because there's this awful lump in my throat and I think I might lose it. "There's a file, Letters to Delia, maybe you can read sometime. Maybe you'll understand then."

She remains quiet, her fingers playing over the flex bracelet like it's some kind of relic.

"I didn't steal him from you, Delia. He's not gone, he's right here with you. And that's where he's going to stay." I say these words even while some part of me hopes they're not the truth, some part of me doesn't want to let him go and wants to fight still, but right now I can't do that. Right now, I need to feed these people and make my best friend believe I'm not out to destroy her.

Her eyes slide up, she stares at me for a long moment, then she lowers them again.

"Anyway," I say, "I'm leaving. I hope maybe we can talk when I come back. If I come back." I walk away.

"Good luck," she says, voice so quiet I can barely hear her, and I'm not sure if I'm imaging it. Part of me wants to turn to make sure, but another part of me is afraid I did just imagine it, so I don't. I just keep walking away.

chapter eight

POST-AMERICAN DATE: 7/5/232

LONGITUDINAL TIMESTAMP: 3:45 A.M.

LOCATION: SUB-TUNNEL 6

The Undertunnel is a cloying cement corridor, perhaps no wider than ten feet. I have no idea how thick the walls are—not enough to keep out the moisture if the puddles are any indication—or how far underground we are. It feels like we're in the very center of the earth. I have the same prickly, nauseating feeling here as I did in the Minotaur's labyrinth back in Nexis, and what happened earlier with Gus only makes the suffocating feeling worse.

Ahead of me, strips of bright-colored light attached to backpacks indicate where Quentin and Violet are, lighting their grim outlines. I place one foot in front of the other, using the purplish light of the light-stick attached to my backpack to guide myself over cracks and tepid puddles.

Bastian stays close. "Are you sure you don't want me to take that?"

"For the millionth time, no. I need to get used to it."

"I know," he grumbles. "It's just… Your leg—"

"I'm fine," I snap. Then, realizing I'm misplacing my emotions, I try to honey it by reaching out and touching his arm. "Really. I'm all right."

His eyes bore into me. He knows I'm lying. "You're not."

I deflect what he's really getting at because I don't want to talk about it. I've managed not to cry about Gus, and I'm going to keep it that way because crying would mean accepting it's true and I don't want to. "You'd be limping, too, if someone shot you in the leg. It's okay. I'm not bleeding, and I can't get nerve damage or anything. It's just some damage to the prosthesis."

Humoring me, he says, "They're delicate instruments. You should take better care of them."

"I will," I promise. "I'll have Quentin take another look at it when we stop. Okay?" I should have had him do it before we left. But I just needed to *go*. I regret it now.

He grumbles under his breath about something not being the point, but this seems to satiate him for the time being and he lets it go.

Violet drops back to join us, and seeing that we're all lagging, Quentin slows his pace as well.

"This reminds me of a book I once read," Violet says, voice breathy and crackly. I wonder if her lungs are all right with all this walking. "Back before we completely butchered the English language—all this misspelling and changing definitions of words and capitalizing things unnecessarily. Honestly, my mother would have rolled over in her grave—she was an English teacher. Anyway, this book was called *Journey to the Center of the Earth.* Marvelous little tale about a group of subterranean travelers, much like ourselves. Would you like to hear about it?"

I grin, thankful for the distraction. She reminds me so much of Dad with his crazy Pre-War stories. "Sure."

As Violet regales us with the story of this group coming across all manner of strange adventures and people, we press on.

After a few hours and a few more stories from a seemingly tireless Violet, my pack begins to feel like I'm carrying a progressively larger load of bricks, and it starts to knock me off balance so that I have to keep my hand against the cement wall as I walk. I grit my teeth against the pain and try to tamp down my frustration. This walk and the weight of a pack wouldn't have fazed me in the game. But my Real World body is weak and tired. I'm sweaty and my dress clings around my legs, heavy and foolish in its opulent Neo-Baroque cut and cutting-edge synthetic fabric. I try to remind myself that I've endured far worse. Worse pain. Worse frustration. Worse loss and fear and emotional turmoil. At least now I know I'm doing something about it. Most of it. Who knows what to do about Gus and Delia.

Eventually, the stories stop and we walk in dark silence for a long time. Quentin keeps a steady pace in the front. Bastian gains ground, coming even with Quentin. I can hear them talking, but not what they're saying. I focus on the scuffing of my shoes, the feel of the cool stone under my fingers. Violet keeps pace with me, her wheezing a strange comfort.

"I used to be able to do this without a problem," she huffs. "Climbed Everest once."

"I don't know what that is."

"A mountain." She chuckles. "A big one. And now here I am, below sea level with a five-pound pack and I can't even catch my breath. Don't ever get old."

"I suppose I don't have a choice in the matter."

"Sure you do. We all have choices. And let me tell you, when we stop I choose to sleep like the dead!"

At my frown, she realizes her slip. "Sorry. I shouldn't have said that."

I touch the tiny rectangular outlines of the chips in my pocket. "Did you lose anyone back in Evanescence?"

Violet looks up at me, her purple eyes—maybe her namesake—lost and sad. "I've lost many people over the years. But I lost the important ones a long time ago. So," she says, voice quiet, "I guess I can't understand what you're all going through."

"I don't think that's true."

"No?"

I shake my head. "You've probably had more loss than most of us. You've had entire lifetimes of it." I think about how old she must be. More than three hundred years old. How many husbands has she had? How many children and grandchildren? How many friends and coworkers? To have climbed a mountain, she must have lived through the war. Seen the opening and closing of the domes. To see that much death… Even when someone chooses to die, it's still hard. I've been there. Gus sacrificed himself in order to help me advance in Nexis. It was awful knowing he chose to leave me alone. "What kept you going? Why'd you choose to stay alive?"

Her pink lips fold up in a small smile. "Knowledge."

I knit my brows. "You've been alive this long just because you like reading the archival files?"

She laughs. "No! Well, yes, I like to do that and there is so much literature and history, I could live for a thousand years and never cover it all. But it's about what's coming, not what has happened."

I stare at her, waiting.

She glances wistfully into the darkness. "I wanted change. I wanted to be free from all that." She waves her hand dismissively back the way we came. "After we fell, well, I saw what we became and it made me so sad. I told myself I'd stay alive and I'd remember. I'd help others to remember. I've been tutoring every President this city has had." She gestures at Quentin's back. "Some are better than others. I figured I'd hold vigil until we made something of ourselves again. I want humanity to realize it could be great again. To step outside the bubble and go back into the world."

"Like the old explorers," I say. "Columbus and Louis and Clark?"

She nods. "But not just here on land." She looks up. "We once walked on the moon and sent probes into the stars. We've wasted so much time and effort on piddly things like immortality and odor-resistant fabric," she notes, lifting her dusty-rose-colored skirts, "and we could have inhabited space colonies by now! That's what I've always wanted. To go up into the stars."

I smile at her. A who-knows-how-old genetically enhanced woman with none of her original parts, and she's holding out for a space adventure. Dad would have loved this woman. "My father would have called you an American Dreamer."

She giggles. "I'll take that as a compliment. They built this world. The dreamers. Like your father. Now, he knew how to dream up a thing or two. I would have been proud to call him my son."

Part of me wishes she were my grandmother, that I could have some of her spirit as a natural gift, like I do my Programming skills.

But I do have it, don't I? I went into the game, explored entire worlds. Who cares that they weren't real? They felt real. Dad made the places and people as real as he could. And now I'm on a real adventure. Off through the Undertunnel, off to see the Outer Block and another domed city.

I smile at her. "You're enjoying this, aren't you?"

She grins back, her eyes bright. "Immensely, dear."

I hitch my pack. "I'd enjoy this more if I were a little

more fit for the task."

"At least you're not an Aristocrat," she comforts. "Naturals like you, me, and Bastian, we're built for this sort of thing."

"If you're a Natural, how come your eyes are purple?"

"These?" She points to her face. "Liz Taylor. Always liked her; some say I look like her. When it came time for a new pair to be grown for me I couldn't help indulging myself a little bit. I did that with quite a few parts as I've aged. Have to keep up with the times."

Though I don't know who Liz Taylor is, I get her meaning and I say, "Oh." Then squirming, I adjust my pack again and mutter, "Quentin doesn't look like he's having much trouble."

Violet beams. "Did you think he was just another soft Aristocrat with implants to make him look brawny?"

"I suppose I did."

"He's nothing like the other Aristocrats, Ellani. You'd do best to remember that. He's stronger than any one of them. He's much more like his Dolls, though I daresay he's a might bit better."

I wrinkle my nose in distaste.

"He's like you and me. A survivor." As an afterthought, she adds, "I like survivors, especially handsome ones with good manners and devious little grins. If I were a few hundred years younger? Let's just say there would be some debate on who would be breaking whose hip." She cackles to herself and it echoes throughout the tunnel.

chapter nine

POST-AMERICAN DATE: 7/5/232

LONGITUDINAL TIMESTAMP: 6:07 A.M.

LOCATION: SUB-TUNNEL 6

I don't have a working flex bracelet, so when Quentin comes to a stop ahead of us, I'm not sure whether we've been walking for ten minutes, ten hours, or ten days. It feels like ten days. After Violet and I catch up, she pulls off her pack and leans against the wall. "Finally."

"Why'd we stop?" I ask.

Quentin gestures to follow him. He leads me forward a few paces and holds his light-stick up so that I can see. I find myself staring out over a large chasm before us.

"That's a good reason," I breathe, taking in the massive hole that stretches from one end of the tunnel to another. "How are we going to get across?"

"We could try climbing down and up again," Bastian offers.

Quentin squints down into the abyss, offering nothing.

I ask, "What are you thinking?"

Instead of answering, Quentin spares me a glance then responds with a question, "What do you see down there?"

I stare with him, the angle of my shoulders matching his so that I can see what he sees. "Rocks, I think."

His head bobs. "What do you hear?"

I tip my head. "Water?"

"Water," Quentin agrees.

I glance back and forth, trying to make sense of things. To either side of us, the tunnel opens up into darkness, the cement walls now a cascade of broken stone and dirt. "Earthquake?"

"It's possible," Quentin concedes, his voice a low purr that skitters up my spine. Without thinking, I reach out and brace myself against the wall. "Or perhaps explosives. Someone purposely trying to destroy the tunnel."

"How would they even know it was here?" Bastian asks.

"Perhaps they were looking for water," Violet suggests. "It's at a premium, since anything that's out there would be poisonous."

"Wouldn't that be true of what's down here?"

She shakes her head. "Possible the biospores haven't gotten down this far. Possible an aquifer would be safe. Possible that people come down here to draw water or perhaps there's a well drilled down here."

I say, "If it's intentional, then we're certain to come across someone down here."

Quentin turns. "I think we need to scout."

Violet's hand shoots up. "I'll go."

"Are you sure you're up for that?" Bastian asks.

She scowls at him. "I'm more experienced at rappelling than you'll ever be, Pansy." Violet turns and stares down into the abyss. "We'll find caverns down there, no doubt. Maybe a network of caves inhabited by savages who've never had contact with other humans."

"Oh, here we go," Bastian mutters and moves away. "Come on, Quentin, let's get this ready and over with."

Humoring her, I cock my head. "You're so certain?"

I receive a glance over her shoulder and a smirk. "Not at all, but wouldn't that be fun? If they captured us and scalped us?"

I have no idea what scalping is, but by her mischievous grin, I don't think it's a good thing. "I wouldn't want to meet anyone or anything down here."

She turns and plants her fists on her hips. "Where is your sense of adventure? Remember *Journey to the Center of the Earth*? You should come with me. We'll go spelunking and find the diamonds and secret treasure before everyone."

I gesture at my leg. "I'm not sure what spelunking is, but I don't think I'm in the best shape to do any sort of extensive exploring. I think we should focus on finding food and water for the others." At her petulant face, I say, "Perhaps we'll come back and look around some more. *After* we get everyone to safety."

She stares at me for a long moment, her eyes even more purple from the plum-colored light-stick I've got in my hand. "You can't save them all. As soon as you accept it, the further you'll get in life. You can't make anyone happy but yourself."

I lick my lips. Violet is a conundrum of mischief and harsh reality, and her fluctuation from one to the other leaves me feeling like I'm losing my foothold on something very important. Looking away, I say, "I know."

"Being alive means leaving a trail of the dead behind you. That's what it means to go on living—to walk away from death whenever it comes knocking. And I'm not just talking about physical death, Ella. Everything dies eventually. Ideas, relationships, lifestyles. You walk away from them, they walk away from you."

Her words feel too much like a reminder that I left Gus, and now he's likely to leave me. I scrub my hands on my thighs and stare at the stone under my feet. "Walking isn't the same as running. Walking is deliberate, thought out. Running is just panic. And I've been doing a lot of that lately. I really shouldn't. I should be facing things head-on, fighting them or making a decision that they're not worth the fight." But by that logic, my walking away from Gus would mean that I don't think he's worth the fight, when that's the complete opposite.

I spent a year playing Nexis and Gus was with me nearly every moment of my daily six-hour limit. He taught me how to play, introduced me to the other Tricksters, brought me purpose, and helped me learn to love my Natural body when I'd been taught to hate it in Evanescence. My point in playing Nexis had been to experience the masterpiece my father had programmed, and Gus made that dream a reality. Scores of adventures, scores of battles and victories. Hardship, loss, love. Nights spent curled in each other's arms. I trusted him with everything, knew he had my back no matter what. We shared all of that—together. I thought I knew him better than I knew myself. You don't walk away from people like that. You fight for them.

As if reading my thoughts, Violet says, "Look back all you want, Ellani, but keep moving. Even if it means leaving someone or something you love behind. You have to do it. To live. That's what it means to overcome adversity."

I glance up at her. Violet is closer now, close enough that I can see the fine lines in her slowly aging face. She meets my shocked gaze, leans in. "I know that's what your real goal is. Don't lie to yourself by thinking anything else. You live. Even if it means leaving all of us in the dust. I can see what's in you, and you're worth more than any of us."

My chest crimps. "I can't leave some things."

She smiles. "Love, you mean? Look, I've been alive a long time and if there is one thing I know, it's that if something is meant to be, it will figure itself out. If you have to leave us in the dust, then do it. Maybe someone will follow you." She steps parallel to me, places her hand on my shoulder. "I wish I had been born to be you. It would have made life far more exciting." With a squeeze to my shoulder, she leans in, gives me a kiss on the cheek, and goes off to help Bastian and Quentin. "No, no, you're doing it all wrong. Move over, boys, let a woman show you how it's done."

Bastian takes a step back so that Violet can inspect the area for a good place to anchor a rope. She chooses a thick, jutting loop of steel that's sticking out of the concrete.

I glance down the drop. "What should we do once we're down there?"

Bastian says, "You're not going down."

"What?" I ask, looking back up. "Who's going to stop me? Besides, *he* can't go"—I point at Quentin—"he's injured, and you can't go. If you fall, Sadie will kill me."

Flexing his arm, Quentin says, "Nah, I'm fine. I heal fast."

I frown at him. Remarkably fast. What kind of experimental nanos are floating in his bloodstream? And what do they run on now that his G-Chip is down?

"There's no reason you should test that," Bastian says. "I'm able-bodied and willing." He fixes me with a glare. "I'm going."

"But you're inexperienced," Violet notes. "Both of you. This method is gonna be hard, and that's a long drop to make a rookie mistake."

"So is he," Bastian reasons.

"Nonsense," Violet says, tossing the coil of rope from her bag to Quentin. "Trained him myself. Kid's a pro. Quent and I will go."

"We're all going to go." Quentin loops the rope around his now perfectly mobile shoulder. "We will get more ground covered and we'll all have to go down eventually if this is the way out."

Violet frowns. "They can't handle this."

Quentin gives her a steely glare. "They're gonna have to. All of the Aristocrats are, so best brush off your tutoring skills by practicing on a couple people who are less likely to freak out about dust or complain about a broken nail."

And that seems to settle it.

Violet goes down first and Quentin points out the way she's standing, how the rope sits at her back, around her groin, and around her backside.

"It's gonna hurt," he says. "You'll be holding your own weight. You'll get rope burn, but you can't let go. As long as you keep the rope at this angle and let a little out at a time, you'll be fine."

Stomach in my throat, I hold my breath as Violet backs over the edge. Just leans and leans and leans until she bends her knees and takes a step backward and down. I gasp and run to the edge, but she's there grinning up at us as she slowly lets out slack from the double lengths of rope in her hand, takes a few steps backward, lets out some more. Down and down and down. The ropes creak against her weight. Quentin and Bastian nervously adjust their grasps on the third length of rope they've tied to her in case her grip fails, letting out more length as she descends. Her grin becomes gritted teeth the farther she goes. Her light-stick sheds a feeble glow into the nothingness around her.

Finally, she finds her feet some thirty yards down and my muscles relax a little bit. I realize I'm heaving like I've been running a marathon. She unties her security rope, looks up, gives a thumbs-up.

Quentin pulls the security rope back up and over the edge and holds it up. "Who's next?"

Terrified, I glance at Bastian. He wordlessly steps forward and takes the rope. As he ties it around himself, Quentin pushes a length of it into my shaking hands and steps forward.

Silent with horror, I watch as Quentin wraps the rope around my cousin's rib cage, instructs him to step over the ropes, lifts them, and wraps them around Bastian's wrist. "Ready?"

Bastian nods, though I can see the horror of what he's doing in his wide black eyes. He backs to the edge, shores up his grip as Quentin comes back to me, and draws the security rope taut against his back. "Remember. Go slow. Don't let go."

I keep my eyes closed as Bastian goes over, and I let the rope slowly slide through my fingers, giving him slack. Forever turns into eternity as inch by inch, he descends.

And then suddenly there's a yelp, a sharp yank, and the rope falls from my loosened hands. Quentin is pulled forward a few steps before regaining himself. With a grunt, he leans hard against the rope, the length of it biting into his skin. Scrambling, I regain my length of the rope and pull with him, levering all my weight against the dead-weight on the end.

Beyond my ringing ears, I hear Violet yelling from below. "Get your feet back under you! Don't lose track of that rope."

There's struggling on the other end of the creaking length that is the only thing holding my cousin from certain death. Quentin is breathing heavy against me, my body is soaking with perspiration, and it feels like the rope is going to slip out of my grasp at any moment.

"Hold on," he grunts. I don't know who he's talking to.

"That's it," Violet is saying. "Now pick 'em up and get 'em back 'round your wrist. Stay calm." A few more minutes. "Okay, give him some slack."

Quentin nods to me, and we ease off the rope, let it slide again. Time creeps. The rope inches through my twitching fingers. I stare at it, intent, ready to grab instead of drop it this time. And then finally he's down.

I sag to the floor, a shaking mess.

Slowly, Quentin gathers the rope up once more, coiling it around his arm. Then he's still for a long minute. I can tell he's staring at me, waiting. "Elle?"

I shake my head. "I-I can't."

He crouches down in front of me, meets my haunted eyes. I feel him take up my hands, hold them against his chest. "You're shaking."

Of course I am. I don't want to die.

"You can do this," he whispers.

Mute now, I shake my head again.

"Hey." Shifting both my hands to one of his, he reaches out with the other, stills my head with a palm to my cheek. "Look at me."

I do, only because I don't have a choice. He has me trapped.

His expression is calm. Serene, like the boy who shot my uncle in the head. I wish I could turn off like that, become cool and calculated and unfeeling. "I will not let you fall. You need to trust me. You need to trust yourself. Stand up."

Swallowing hard, I get to shaking legs. I don't know how I'm going to go down on such unstable things. One is injured as it is.

"Shoes," he prompts.

I slip out of my heels, let the cold stone touch my synthetic skin. It feels strange being on flat feet. I've grown up on heels. Without them he seems like a giant as he bends and comes around to my back, putting them into my pack as I stand like an idiot. Seeing that I'm being useless and silly, he bends at my hip and I feel him tugging my skirts. I wince as I hear the tearing noise of him splitting my beautiful dress from hem to seam.

Four times, like Violet did with hers.

And then he's winding the strips around my thighs, his

fingers passing in and out like butterfly wings. My legs go from shaking to jelly and I have to hold the wall to keep myself upright.

When he's done, he stands in front of me, stares at me, and frowns. After a thought, he unbuttons his jacket and slides it off his shoulders.

I blink at him, confused.

"Put it on."

I do as I'm told. It's big on me, stiff in the shoulder from all the dried blood. It smells like him and the weight of it makes me feel like I'm being held. My fingers fumble on the buttons and he steps into my space to help, his knuckles grazing my hitching chest. The warm certainty of his presence disappears for an instant as he bends to retrieve the rope and then he's back, tying it under my arms.

When he finishes with the knot, he just sort of goes still, his body close to mine and me wavering against the solid weight of him. His fingers slide from the knot, inch up, flutter along my clavicle, against my neck. One hand slips back behind my neck and into my hair, tugging just slightly, as the other tips up my jaw.

His breath is warm and minty as he breathes something that seems like relief, and if it's possible, something about him—his expression, his body—eases me. He stares down, his eyes clear and true, and that melts me into his body and his touch.

And then he's kissing me again. And I'm kissing him. It's just like it was in the aerovator during our escape. That heat, that familiarity. That instant awakening and settling inside of me—like a flock of birds and a lazy pool of molten heat exploding through my veins and muscles at the same time. That feeling like it's perfect and sound. It's everything I ever wanted of a kiss from Quentin Cyr before...before...Gus.

I shove at him, step away from him, gasping. "What are

you doing?" I demand. "You can't keep kissing me, you're-you're in love with someone. I heard you tell Carsai."

Unapologetic, he grins at me. "Hmm, that's something to think about, isn't it?"

"You're a cad."

He shrugs. "You're not scared anymore, though, are you?"

Heaving in confusion, glaring in heat, I growl as I have to admit that no, I'm not scared anymore.

"I'm not sorry," he says, voice quiet. "I like kissing you."

Gritting my teeth, I march over to the ropes and pass them around myself as I saw Violet and Bastian do before. I shore up my grip on both ends of the rope and I don't look down. To look down would be to see where I'm going and right now, I don't want to.

"Hey," Quentin calls to me from where he's standing, lifting the security rope around him as he backs his weight against it. I feel it tug a little against my chest, like he's drawing me back to him.

I pause, look at him even though I don't want to make eye contact.

"Go easy," he says, voice like honey. "Just breathe."

Something nags the back of my mind, like I've heard those words in that tone before, but I can't remember where. Holding with all my might, I lean backward.

Going over is hard, it's fighting every instinct I have to catch myself from falling. To remain upright when all I want to do is ball up. The rope bites at me, against the back of my ribs, against my legs, against my wrist and my arm. The dress wrapped around my legs and Quentin's jacket help to ease the burn as it slides and catches…slides and catches…as I give myself a little slack and squat back into it. What's left of my thighs burns, the knee of my injured leg creaks. "Please hold," I whisper-pant. "Please hold." My feet scuff against jagged rock, and I hope I'm not cutting the delicate coating on them. I feel dizzy, shaky. My arms and abs scream, and I find myself thankful to Meems for training me for this moment, for making me exercise even though it never seemed like it would matter.

I force myself to school my breathing, keep my head despite the shaking, despite my pulse pounding in my throat. Bit by bit. Foot by foot. I make my movements mechanical, methodical. Like an android's. I think of other things than the distance growing between me and the top. A design for a new ball gown. Blue with a sweetheart bodice and a portrait neckline, opaque sleeves with pearl buttons. Layers and layers and layers of gauzy skirts. Pearly slippers, a white feather hairpiece, glistening diamondesque and pearl jewelry to match. Maybe a fan. Yes, a carved one, with—

I feel hands touching my back and I ease down, and then there's a big grin spreading across my face as my legs finally give out and I pool to the floor. I did it. I made it. "That—" I whimper as Violet unties the security rope from my chest. "That wasn't so hard."

"That's the easy part." Violet grins. "Going up is the hard part."

Bastian and I both groan.

"Quit your bellyaching and help me," Violet scolds as she tosses us my end of the security rope so we can hold it for Quentin, who should be tying himself to his end.

Finally it's Quentin's turn, but his descent is much smoother. He doesn't seem bothered by his arm or the rope cutting into his bare forearm as his feet touch ground and he straightens, smooth breathed and stoic. "Haven't done that in a while."

"Fun, right?" Violet demands. "We should do it again."

"I'll pass," Bastian huffs.

"Unfortunately, I'll have to agree with Bastian. We've got work to do." Quentin turns and examines the vast cavern we've rappelled into. "Can't see much in here."

"Ceiling's high," Violet notes. "Can tell by the echo."

"It's damp, too," I say, touching the rock. Not that I need to, I can feel it in the air, can hear the droplets hitting the floor.

"Violet, you and Bastian will go this way. Ella and I will go that way."

"No," I say, stepping up close to Bastian. "I'll go with Bastian, you go with Violet."

Quentin narrows an eye at me, but he grins like he knows what I'm trying to do. "Okay, have it your way, Elle. We'll meet back in three hours." Without another word, they split away and disappear between two massive spires of rock.

For a long time, I just stare, watching the blue and white of their light-sticks become dimmer and dimmer in the distance.

"I'm sure it's going to do us all a great amount of good that none of us have anything to keep the time on us," Bastian mutters.

"We'll be all right," I say, pulling my shoes out of my bag and putting them back on. It feels good to have three inches and solid ground under my feet. "Come on."

chapter ten

POST-AMERICAN DATE: 7/5/232

LONGITUDINAL TIMESTAMP: 8:02 A.M.

LOCATION: DISFAVORED TUNNEL SYSTEM

Hobbling worse than ever, I take the lead in the direction opposite from where Quentin and Violet disappeared. We weave between strange columns and pools; the floor is mostly smooth here and there are strange stripcs along the rock. "Look at all this water."

"And it could be drinkablc."

I smirk at him. "Wanna test it?"

"Mmm, no." He reaches out and touches the tip of a pointed stone. "This place is weird."

"Natural cave," I say. "I read about them." I point. "Stalagmites. Stalactites."

"Fascinating," Bastian mutters. "Wherever we are, it's deep. And lonely."

"Yeah," I say quietly as I walk beside him.

A long few minutes pass as we circumnavigate a massive pool, so still it perfectly reflects our upheld light-sticks. "You think the ocean looks like that?" he wonders.

"No. I saw it once in Nexis. It's bigger. Smells less, I dunno, earthy. It's salt and there are these birds, gray and white. They make this weird noise." I pause trying to think about how to emulate the sound of a seagull.

"You sound like Uncle Warren."

My heart tugs and I impulsively check to make sure the chips are still there. "Is that bad?"

"No," he says. "Uncle Warren was good. Not like… Not like…"

I touch his arm, willing him not to say it.

Sighing, he lowers his light-stick between us, illuminating the path. "I didn't think I'd miss my dad…but…"

Trying to ignore the lump in my throat, I let my fingers slide down his arm and grasp his hand. "I understand."

He nods. "Uncle Warren. Aunt Cleo."

"Meems."

"Meems," he agrees. "You must miss her a lot."

"Yes. And Dad. I miss Delia, too," I admit.

He glances at me. "Yeah?"

I shrug. "Seeing her again after all that time brought all this hope back. She'd been dead, but then she was alive. Yet, I lost her almost as quickly. She didn't embrace our friendship, in fact, I made things worse. And now I feel like my hope has been snatched away again. I feel like I did when Uncle Simon first cut me off from her."

After a long time, he says, "I'm sorry for letting Simon do that to you."

I glance at him. "You didn't know."

Bastian kicks at the loose stones near his feet, making them skitter into the water with a *plop, plop*. "I didn't. But that's no excuse. I should have." He's quiet for another long minute. "Ever since I saw you and realized who you were, I've been obsessing over it, turning things over and over in my mind, trying to put everything together. Sparks," he whispers, "it's like he was dropping a trail of candy for me to follow, and I never made the connection." A harsh breath escapes him. "I think about how many times I went in and out of that house. It was like walking into some surreal nightmare because even though I wanted to be there for Sadie, I wanted to run away, too. I kept feeling like any moment you or Uncle Warren would walk around the corner. And you were right upstairs!" This last bit comes out as a breathy laugh, but there's no humor behind it, only bitterness. He cups his face in his hands. "I'm so stupid."

I look away from him. "I suppose that makes two of us." And I intend it to encompass all of the stupidity I feel. "How can people be so smart, yet so stupid?"

He squints at me. "What do you mean?"

"I'm a child prodigy. A brilliant Programmer. Yet, I can't figure out the simplest things sometimes. Not my feelings or how to react to them. Not what other people were doing to me. From day one, I was manipulated into playing a key role in a rebellion I knew nothing about. I should have seen it, should have been able to protect myself and the people I love better."

"There's nothing wrong with trusting the people who are supposed to love and protect you."

I shake my head. "I feel so used. Like a puppet."

Bastian gnaws his lip, his eyes hidden from me by his new hair. "I understand the feeling."

I give him a little nudge with my hip. "Do me a favor?"

He looks down at me questioningly.

"When Sadie has this baby, don't do what our parents did, okay? Put the baby and its happiness before your own. Teach it to be better than what our parents did for us."

Swallowing, Bastian looks away. "I'm terrified of her

having a baby, Ella. I had no idea she'd disabled the birth-control element on her chip. We aren't even married yet."

My jaded mind believes the most plausible reason for Sadie to do such a thing likely involves Katrina and wanting to ensure a marriage to Bastian. Katrina wouldn't want what happened to her and my father. Katrina wouldn't want Sadie's potential suitor to suddenly run off with another woman like my father did to her. She'd want her and Sadie's newfound places among the Elite set in stone. She'd want Sadie to ensure Bastian wouldn't leave her. I think of bringing that up, but decide it's best to leave it unsaid. It would cause trouble between Bastian and Sadie, and I want them to be happy. Instead, I say, "You love her, don't you?"

Bastian examines the darkness for a long time. "Yeah. More than I thought I would." He scoffs. "I always knew I'd end up in an arranged marriage. We all do, but for the longest time I operated under the idea that you and I would get married."

"What?" I ask, laughing despite myself.

He gives a helpless shrug and blushes. "My father was the first one to mention it to me. And a Drexel marrying a Drexel would have kept all the assets within the family. He thought a lot about that sort of thing."

"But we're cousins."

He gives me a sidelong glance. "Only by adoption."

"Still," I say, wrinkling my nose. "You're like my brother."

He looks away again. "I know. Doesn't stop the cruel logic of the social climb. Things like cousins marrying cousins happens all the time in Evanescence, you know that. I got over the awkwardness of the idea a long time ago, had come to accept it as a very real possibility. It wasn't until Nexis came out that you even had other prospects."

I hood my eyes, because he's right.

We come to a jumbled section where the columns become thick and we have to climb between them. On the other side is a break in the rock. "Go in?"

"That's the point, right?"

He helps me slide through the crack and then he follows. It's painfully close at first, making me feel like I'm slipping into a crack I won't get out of and panic is just about to set in when it loosens and widens into a sharp incline.

Bastian grunts as he squeezes through behind me. "In some ways, I'm glad you died. It made Simon give up on you, made him think of options where for a long time he simply hadn't. And it gave me hope. I'd been resigned for so long."

"Gee, thanks." I give him a playful punch on his side, but I understand what he means. Without my staged death, the arrangement between Bastian and Sadie would never have been made.

"It's not as though I don't love you, Ella."

I nod. I've always known Bastian loved me, but I always suspected it was slightly displaced. "But the love you have for me is different than what you have for Sadie. Isn't it?"

Bashful, he nods. "I didn't think there were different kinds. There's love and then there's *love*."

We're both quiet for a long time, each of us deep in thought. Eventually Bastian says, "I'm terrified of being a father. I have no good examples to work off of."

I bite my lip. He's right. Not his adopted father, Simon, who only adopted him to look good to my mother. Not his uncle, my father, who buried his head in a virtual world and got mixed up with rebellions that endangered his family. Not his biological father, an abusive slap-patch addict who sold Bastian to a Doll House and whored out Bastian's little sister, Ava, for credits. Sometimes I think Bastian took to being so big brotherly with me because he no longer had Ava to look out for. Or perhaps he wanted to protect me where he couldn't protect her. "Just be yourself, Bastian. Love that kid as much as you love Sadie and everything will be okay."

"Will it?" he wonders. "Is everything going to be okay? When everyone blames us for what happened and we don't even have a home anymore?"

How to answer that? The past year of my life I spent as a prisoner in my own home. But it no longer felt like home. Consciousness in Evanescence took a back seat to going into Nexis, being with Guster. I sacrificed everything to be with him, only to find he's had another girl in Real World all along. I don't understand; he'd wanted to meet in Real World. Uncle Simon had claimed that Gus had come to him trying to find me. Are his feelings for Delia not as strong as I think? Does he love me more? Can I let him walk away from her in favor of me, knowing her feelings for him are so strong? Can I survive letting her have him? I close my eyes, willing the tears not to fall. "What's that stupid thing Dad always said? Home is where the heart is?"

Bastian smiles. "Yeah, I think that's what he used to say."

"I envy you," I say. "Your heart is right here. Right with you. And it's only getting bigger. Even though all that awfulness happened back there in Evanescence, even though Uncle Simon is dead, I think you managed to save your true home from all of that."

He stops short, making me stop, too, and we stare at each other for a long time. Bastian has always had the sort of face that was too heavy and angular to really be called handsome. At least, not in the Aristocratic sense. But with my new eyes that appreciate the natural beauty in people, I can see his Natural features for the comeliness they represent, even with the Mods and Alts he's added to hide them over the years. He lifts his hand, smoothes it over my curls. "You really do have a beautiful mind."

A sudden stabbing of hurt in my heart and insecurity in my belly make me look away and hide my face in my arm. "I don't feel all that beautiful."

He sighs in a way that lets me know he's annoyed. "Shadow?"

"His name is Guster," I correct. "And I'm sad about Delia, too. About getting between the two of them."

"I don't really understand how you can come between the two of them. You've been dead to all of us. Trust me, I know they both thought you were dead. That's what they bonded on initially. I was there. So, how did the unflappable Shadow come to fall in love with a dead girl?"

"It's a long story."

He glances around, takes a few steps away from me. "We've got time."

I tell Bastian all about the accident where I lost my legs and subsequent captivity. He knows some of that part since Sadie has told him what she knows already. When I get to explaining Nexis and my experience in the game, he stares at me in fascination. He stares like a Programmer should, enrapt in my experience, sometimes interrupting to ask questions about the tiniest details. He's incredibly interested in how my extracurricular codes were integrated into other avatars, whose specifically timed deaths at key locations unlocked security levels that no known person had even gotten close to.

"Aunt Cleo was a genius, I'm telling you. What a way to plant a virus! Designing the game to mirror Evanescence's Main Frame OS then programming it to superimpose itself over the Frame once it was released. You didn't have to even try to circumvent the G-Chip's security measures because it's so convoluted, the G-Chip wouldn't have picked it up." He shakes his head. "Even when they had a freaking chip implanted in your mother's brain and monitored her day and night, she still managed to bring them to their knees."

I agree. My mother was a genius. As were my father and even Uncle Simon. The terrifying part is that I'm the next generation of Drexel. I have the cells that made them who they are. And they trained me. Made me into them whether I wanted to be a Trickster or not. And I lived up to what was expected of me, proved my genes work just as well—better. Dad gave me the codes, after all, codes neither he nor Mom nor Uncle Simon had managed to crack. And I cracked them.

"So, that explains why Shadow is all mixed up. He thought you were dead in Real World, and you were just a manifestation of his internal wants and needs in Nexis. He never thought you were actually real. Never thought he'd actually meet you, so why not have a relationship with Delia? Seems harmless."

"Until you factor in that he knew I was a Real World player. He'd asked to meet me in Real World, Bastian. He'd even gone to Uncle Simon trying to find out who I was."

He rubs his chin. "Hmmm. Maybe he knew he loved you more than her? Maybe he wanted to be with the Real World player of you more than Delia?"

"How could anyone not love Delia? She's wonderful."

Bastian's voice drops. "Seems to me like you don't know her anymore. Trust me when I say this, Ella: the girl who was the Delia Haverfeld you knew is not the same. I saw firsthand the kind of transformation she went through after you died, and it had nothing to do with the amount of Mods and Alts. She changed on the inside. Became dark, cut-throat, and cunning. She'd do anything to anyone to get what she wanted, because she didn't care about anyone anymore. I even helped her."

I turn back to him, squint in the dying luminescence of

the light-stick. "What?"

He shakes his head. "I helped her with some programming. Things meant to help her cheat and advance. I did it because I felt so bad for her, saw how far she fell after your death. But now I wish I hadn't. Not at the cost of your happiness."

"I don't understand."

"She's a brilliant Programmer. Almost as good as you. It doesn't surprise me that Carsai would ask her for cheat codes. Though, she didn't have enough access to the game to develop the codes without help."

"You helped her get Carsai into Quentin's game?"

"Something like that," Bastian hedges. "Quent's game was locked up tighter than the Main Frame. Neither of us could access it, our chips wouldn't allow for it. I doubt even you could have. But Delia developed something just as good, and I helped her plant it."

I lift a brow, waiting.

"She figured out how to manipulate the game. Get it to give players everything they wanted."

"The game was meant to do that anyway," I reason.

He shakes his head. "Not everything. She figured out how to manipulate other avatars, AI and Real World players alike. She gave Carsai an AI version of Quentin. And after that, she had people lined up for blocks looking for her services. For the right credits, you could infiltrate anyone's game, you could destroy someone's game, you could influence anything that happened inside their game. She could do anything, so long as it didn't involve Quentin Cyr's real avatar."

"Because he had special defenses," I mutter. "But no one else was safe." I shudder, thinking of how awful it would have been if, in a fit of mass inspiration, Uncle Simon had decided to hire Delia to throw my game, make me lose my companions—Guster in particular—in an effort to push me over the edge and make the deal to plant the virus with him. Worse yet, what if Delia had sensed Guster was cheating on her with someone in the game and decided to end it before he left her? "How bad was it?"

"She would do anything anyone wanted, as long as they had the credits to pay for it. She was credit driven. Needed Alts and Mods like a drug. I think she didn't want to live in her own skin anymore."

I chew my nail. "That doesn't sound like her at all. And why would Guster love someone like that?"

"Because he's the same?"

I frown, knowing he's right. Gus had even admitted to hating his own skin. He loved me for being an idealized version of what should be, and her for being a real-life version of what was.

"Everyone is weak," Bastian continues. "We all make mistakes. Even Delia."

His words remind me of my own role in everything. My desperate attempt to reunite with Gus made me accidentally kill so many people. The memory brings images of the attack, and the images bring acid sizzling to the back of my throat. I swallow hard and shake my head to dislodge them. "I know what you mean." Desperate, I turn back to Bastian. "I know I was manipulated into planting that virus, but I still feel guilty. Still feel responsible. Am I ever going to be free of these feelings?"

"I ask myself that every day."

I lower my brow. "What did you do? I could swear by the expression on your face you had no idea what was going to happen with that virus."

"With the virus, no. Simon never trusted me enough for that. But Zane did trust me."

I lift my head, interested despite myself. "Zane?"

"Zane was the liaison between Lady Cyr and the Disfavored rebels outside."

"Makes sense." His documentary on the Disfavored provided the perfect alibi. He was certainly the type to be part of a plot to overthrow the current regime. He was always outspoken, championed the Disfavored, and spoke of starting fires. He had even encouraged me to start fires.

"One of his main goals was to gather intelligence on how the Nexis gaming houses influenced the Disfavored. I made tweaks to the game based off of his recommendations. The goal was to get the Disfavored as discontent with the Aristocrats as we could."

"So, my Dad's game caused the Disfavored to rebel as well?"

He wrinkles his nose. "More like, opened the door for the opportunity to cause the Disfavored to rebel. The game the Disfavored got was very different than the one you played. Zane and I made sure of it. We worked together almost daily."

"I thought you hated each other."

Bastian grins, shakes his head. "Clever ruse. It was important Zane didn't appear to have any influence on the development of Nexis."

I scoff. "Right, because covering my father extensively and actively courting me wasn't attracting enough attention already."

He narrows his eyes. "Believe it or not, it wasn't. At least not to President Cyr. He knew about Zane's arrangement to marry you. Given the relationship between Lady Cyr and your mother, it would have only been natural."

I pull my hand away from the wall I've been running it along. "Lady Cyr? What does she have to do with Zane?"

"Oh," Bastian breathes. "Zane was Lady Cyr's son."

I blink, dumbfounded, and then automatically deny it.

"That makes no sense. As firstborn, he would have been heir to the Presidency of G-Corp. Quentin is the only known son of the Cyrs."

"Of the Cyrs, yes. But Zane Boyd isn't President Cyr's son. Lady Cyr had him before she and the President were married. Before she was Kit Cyr, she was Kit Boyd. Kit and Zane were refugees from Adagio. Like your mother. That would also mean they were Naturals. Like us."

Suddenly feeling a little sick, I cover my mouth. The last moments at the ball in Bella Adona play out in my head—Zane grabbing my hand and shoving Bastian and me into the aerovator then grabbing Sadie and shoving her in, too. Guster saying they couldn't fit any more. Zane saying, "Just one more! My mother! And my brother, where's my brother? Someone find them!" Quentin appearing at the sound of Zane's panicked voice asking, "Is Mom in there?" The grave expression in Zane's eyes when he says, "No." Then the chaos of more gunfire, a bloody body falling in on us. A struggle between Zane and Quentin, then Zane tossing Quentin into the aerovator like a rag doll—like a little brother—as he turns to go look for their mother.

The door slamming.

Quentin screaming to get back out, to get to Zane, I realize. Because he must sense Zane is sacrificing himself. The stark terror in Quentin's eyes, his screams that rattle my insides even now, the insane grief that forces him to attack a steel door with his bare fist. Then more gunshots. Quentin's collapse into a crying fit in front of everyone, dignity lost. The moment Quentin Cyr fell from godhood and became a human to me.

I find a thousand little tiny things that tie Zane and Quentin together. Little, furtive glances at parties. Favoring comments on The Broadcast. The obvious way the Cyrs avoided speaking to Zane at social events. Some of their physical features, hard to see under Customization, Mods, and Alts, tie Lady Cyr to her two sons. Even the fact that I was drawn, above anyone else in Evanescence, to both of them.

"I can't believe I didn't see it sooner," I gasp.

"You weren't meant to," Bastian quietly remarks. "The stipulation for Zane being able to live in Evanescence was to deny any link with Lady Cyr. He became a ward of the city and she became the First Lady. All of their meetings were top secret. Of course, it became easier once he was older and on The Broadcast shadowing the Cyrs, meeting with them for exclusive interviews, becoming close friends with the heir to the presidency."

"They were so close," I say, thinking of Quentin's expression when the guns went off on the other side of the door. Less than two feet separating him from his brother's body being riddled with holes. "How can you get that close without having grown up together?"

"Zane and Quentin hit it off from the moment Lady Cyr finally told Quentin about Zane. They became more so after they started working toward the rebellion. It was their family project, a way to reunite because without President Cyr, she'd be able to acknowledge Zane as her son and elevate him as Co-President alongside Quentin."

I shake my head. "No one suspected? What about the other refugees from Adagio?"

Bastian forces a smile. "What other refugees?"

My stomach drops. "There *were* other refugees from Adagio weren't there?"

"Sure," he says with a shrug. "But when that door finally opened after months of them camping out in the tunnel, the only bodies left standing were your mother, Lady Cyr, and Zane. I don't think the former President would have ever let them in, so let's be thankful he met with an untimely end. Some say at the hands of Quent's father himself. And who knows why he wanted them inside so very badly. Considering he married one and gave the other one of the most prestigious positions available through Central Staffing? I'm willing to guess he knew they could provide valuable new information and training that would revolutionize our city."

"I'm sure the end result was not what he had in mind," I mutter.

He takes a deep breath. "No, probably not. But you can't expect anything else from Lady Cyr. Not after everything G-Corp put her through. Her first husband died in that Undertunnel. She watched the other refugees eat him just to stay alive as they waited for the gate to open. Zane was on his deathbed, and she and your mother practically sold their souls to get him the medical treatment he needed. A three-year-old child's life in exchange for chip implants and servitude to G-Corp. It was all a power play to President Cyr. More came after for Lady Cyr. Mods and Alts, genetic therapy, forced marriage, repeated rapes and beatings. Having her first son cloistered away from her so that she barely saw him. Having to stand by as her second son was Customized and mutilated so that he didn't even look like himself anymore. That's just what I know, I'm sure it's worse. Your mother was lucky she ended up with someone like Uncle Warren who loved and cherished her to a fault. Even so, that still ended in both their deaths. I'm not at all surprised Lady Cyr and her sons plotted to destroy both the President and his empire. And I'm glad I helped them escape, even if it ended in this awful way."

"When you put it that way," I breathe, now feeling awful for ever thinking Quentin was just another Aristocrat. "I suppose I am, too. To some degree. But the rebellion came with a heavy toll."

"I'm sure Quentin feels it. Personal vendettas often come with collateral damage. And they backfire, but I'm sure he never imagined he'd be walking this path alone. I'm sure he feels very lost and abandoned."

"He's not, though. He's got Gus. And the other Dolls. And the Aristocrats."

Bastian smirks. "Somehow I doubt they give him half the comfort he needs. Responsibility is a heavy burden. I bet he's happiest when he feels he can just be himself, and I guarantee there are very few people he feels that way with."

I never really thought of it like that. How one could be surrounded by a room full of people, but still feel vastly alone. One can be trapped in a dark corner of one's own mind, unable to get out because everywhere one goes there's a wall of expectation and obligation. How strange that must feel.

part three:

ELLA FINDS TREASURE IN THE WASTE

chapter eleven

POST-AMERICAN DATE: 7/5/232

LONGITUDINAL TIMESTAMP: 11:36 A.M.

LOCATION: DISFAVORED TUNNEL SYSTEM

The tunnel narrows out and ends up ahead. "What's that?" I ask, pointing in front of me.

Bastian steps up close. "Some kind of blockade?"

I step up to it; examine it in the fading glow of the light-stick.

"Here." Bastian snaps a new light-stick to life, adding blue to my fading purple.

I hand him my light-stick and examine around the edge of the blockade with my fingers. It's a combination of dry, brittle plastic, broken chunks of cement, various twists of steel poles, and corrugated metal like the walls of the Disfavored shanties I used to see from my vantage point in Dad's workroom back in Evanescence.

"I think we might have found the entry point." I pull at a few rocks and they tumble to our feet in a cloud of dust.

"Careful," Bastian warns, coughing a bit. "You don't want to cause a cave-in."

Squinting against the dirt, I nod and prod a little more gingerly. "It's warm," I say, putting my hand against the largest piece of corrugated board. "Is it hot outside?"

"Yeah. It's a desert."

I pull an old brick free and am rewarded with a small black hole beyond. I lean against the blockage, trying to see in the darkness on the other side. "I can't— " I say as I step on one of the metal pieces at my knee level, but "see" is drowned out by an awful creaking noise and then my shriek as my high-heeled shoe slips, knocking me forward, and the whole of the blockage caves outward.

I tumble headlong, rolling and thumping with bricks and dust and clanging metal down a long, sharp decline. And continue to roll even after the incline stops until I slam against something tall and hard. I lay there half buried under rubble, dazed, ears ringing, and wincing, certain I've just broken every bone in my body.

Eventually, I chance a stinging breath. I'm rewarded with a mouthful of acrid, metallic air that smells like the breath of the dragon I fought in Nexis and tastes even worse, I'm sure. Sickened, I cough and retch, and it sends knifing pain on top of all the other aches that are settling into my bruising body.

Bastian yells above me. "Ella! Ella!" I hear him clambering down after me and a moment later, a few more rocks and bits of trash come tumbling down to add insult to my injury.

He lifts a piece of plastic off of me and I'm suddenly assaulted with dull light. I close my eyes against it. "Ella?"

"Tell me I'm not paralyzed," I whimper. All I can feel is pain and I don't know how far it extends.

I sense him crouch beside me. His hands rove my body.

"Ow," I yelp, eyes flying back open. "Ouch, ouch, stop." I sit upright, shove him away. "Stop it!"

He sits back, lets out a breath. "I think you're okay." He

reaches into his coat pocket and draws out a handkerchief. "Just some bumps and scrapes." He presses it against my head, apparently staunching blood.

Lifting my hands, I examine myself. Hands and elbows are scratched and bleeding, my clothes are filthy and torn. Reaching up, I take over holding the handkerchief and offer the bloody palm of my other hand. "Help me stand."

He hauls me to my feet and I totter there, lightheaded. "Something's wrong with my leg." Slowly, I move to take a step and immediately regret it. Cursing, I pull at the lengths of the dress wrapped around my legs until they come free and then I tug them up. "Don't look away. Tell me how bad it is." Between the glaring yellow-white light and my dizziness, I can't seem to focus.

Bastian squats down, and stares at my leg. "This is highly indecent. What if someone should come by and see me with my head up your dress?"

I roll my eyes. "I could care less about decency right now. Can I walk?"

"You've got a decent burn here, but I'm assuming you're aware of that already. Looks like..." His voice trails off as he leans closer and prods my prosthetic with his fingers. "I'm not an Engineer by any stretch, but this looks like a structural injury of some kind. Something's broken. I have no idea what it is nor the first thing to fix it."

"Damn it." Straightening in annoyance, I drop my dress so that it falls over his head. "Where are we?" I ask, squinting around, as he makes a hasty backpedal to escape the skirts.

He stands, gains his bearings.

We're in some sort of field filled with what looks like scrap and refuse. Far to either side are scattered shanties—the concrete, plastic, wood, brick, and metal homes of the Disfavored. They stretch in a long diagonal that starts at the very edge of the yellow, rocky Waste in front of us and builds all the way back and behind us until it rests against the dark, impenetrable belt of the dome.

For a long moment, I just stare at the massive wall that is Evanescence. I can't see the top, only the high black wall that must be twenty stories high, and the very edge of the blue nano-glass dome. The rest is shrouded in ominous yellow-gray smog, smoke that rises from the city around me, and a strange, ever-lasting lightning storm that seems to be brewing overhead.

Eventually, I am able to turn away and examine the Outer Block: Kairos. The shanties to either side of us are more spread out along the city limits—the part closest to The Waste. As Kairos nears the wall of Evanescence, the number of shanties gradually grows until they're stacked one on another and another, leaving just enough room for rickety swinging bridges; narrow throughways; distribution tracks from above; and black, trash-strewn alleys. Occasionally, there is a break where rutted main roads cut through, but even here, the shanties are starting to stretch over the roads, blocking out the dim, bilious light.

There's a deep hum in the air, something that seems to vibrate my bones. A *whump, whump, whump*ing.

"We're in a dump field," Bastian says.

I turn to him, take in his tense shoulders, stiff posture, and balled fists. "Dump field?"

He jerks his head toward Evanescence. "It's our trash heap. Things come down from inside, the Disfavored comb through it and take what they can."

I look at what I'm standing on. Plastic frames for 3D printouts, android parts, discarded Primpers, muddied shreds of last year's fashions, worn-through shoes, bags, broken bits of costume jewelry, large chunks of industrial materials, containers for food, supplements and fuel, the stripped bodies of pods. Anything that would have been sucked down the disposal units is here. We're standing on a mountain of it.

"It's a lot."

"Imagine if the Disfavored didn't pick through it at all. The dumps come pretty regularly. Now that the city is dead? Give it a week, they'll have picked this and every one like it to the sludge."

"There are more?"

"There are at least four that I know of."

"I thought all our waste went to the incinerators."

"Only bio-matter. It's the most hygienic way to dispose of it. But everything else comes here—keeps the air pollution down."

I look one way and then the other. Out in The Waste, there is nothing but brown and yellow rock, and dirt with the occasional hump of some long-lost relic of America-past, rusting and useless in the nothing between us and the top of tiny blue marble that I know to be Cadence in the distance. "How far does the Outer Block extend?"

Bastian toes some of the trash. "It's built entirely around Evanescence in a giant ring. Quaint little suburbs." His voice is acid.

"But why so close? Why not spread out more? There's so much empty land that way."

"Access to resources," he says simply. "There's no water out there. No food, no aid from the dome. The cannibals live out there. The closer to them, the more likely you'll get snatched in a night raid. Plus, the farther you get from the dome, the weaker the nano-net. Scratch lung is enough to make people put up with living on top of each other, filth or no." He gestures to the tumble of buildings closest to the dome.

"Nano-net?"

He points above our heads. "That cloud, it's made up of nanites. We have hundreds of thousands of nests stationed on the dome. They're constantly patrolling, constantly taking out the leftover airborne biohazards from the last war."

"But we've been vaccinated against that. Why keep the nets operational? Not that I'm complaining, seeing how it protects all these people."

"Vaccines are only as good as the virus they match. Add the radiation floating around out here to a bunch of biological agents and you have a melting pot of mutation. It's possible some strain we've never encountered could get through. That's why travel outside of the dome is—or was—strictly controlled. Only sanctioned personnel were allowed out here. And only Dolls and adoptees were allowed in. And only after strict quarantine in both cases."

I nod.

"While I don't mind playing twenty questions, we're exposed out here and I don't relish being chanced upon."

"Are we not in a good section of town?"

He rolls his eyes. "This is Kairos, Ella. There's no good part of town. It's dog eat dog, kill or be killed. I'm not chancing that while you're injured."

Swallowing, I glance around uneasily. There are bodies moving in the city to either side of us, but there are large swaths of trash between them and us, and we're reasonably well hidden by the refuse stacked all around us. "You're right. We should get back and find Violet and Quentin. Maybe he can help my leg."

"You can barely walk. How do you expect to get back?"

He has a point. "I could find a walking stick maybe." Though, walking on my leg at all would mean possibly damaging it more. That would be foolish. Desperate, I examine the rubble around us. "What if I just waited until you came back? I'm sure Quentin could fix my leg if he were here." I hope.

Bastian's face folds into a grimace. "I don't like that idea."

"You have a better one?"

"No," he admits. "But there's likely to be a waste retrieval unit combing through at any minute. It's scavenge early or get nothing at all here."

"Well then, you better—" But my words are cut off as a strange *phft*ing, sizzling noise fries the air around us. There's a massive flash of light from the sky, which instantly blinds us, and the ground rumbles hard enough to knock me onto my butt. Blinking hard, I try to focus.

"What was that?" I ask, staring up at the sky. Something about it has subtly changed, but I can't put my finger on it.

Bastian frowns, examines the world around us. "I don't know."

I hear metallic scratching and a few moments later something comes flying from above. It clips the side of the dome wall, tailspins, and hits the ground with a clang. Another joins it just after. Then another.

"Those are falling from the top of Evanescence."

"It's the repair units," Bastian breathes. "Without those, any damage to the nano-glass will mean instant ruin to the inside."

"That's how Adagio lost her blue color," I whisper. I realize now that the subtle difference in the sky is that there is no longer lightning. The cloud looks lower, less active. And it seems like ash is falling. "The nanites," I whisper and then in dread, "Bastian, the net is failing."

"What?" he gasps, following my gaze. "It can't be!"

But it is.

"That's impossible. For something like the net and the

repair units to go down…"

Stomach sinking, I lower my chin. "Something is very wrong in Evanescence."

He looks back at me.

Something like this? It could only mean a dome security failure. A big one. Like, way bigger than what the Tricksters originally intended with their small power outage to allow some Disfavored rebels into the city via one door that Guster manually opened. Is this some kind of piggyback program? Something else Uncle Simon planted? Something someone else planted?

"If the main gate opens," Bastian hedges.

"Go get the others," I demand. "Now."

Not needing to be told twice, Bastian turns and runs back up the hill of trash. Rubble and plastic bits tumble down in his wake. A moment later, he ducks back into the cranny we came from.

I look back up at the sky. If the main gate opens, the androids will come out. And if they come out, everyone in Kairos is dead. I lift my hand and hold it there. While I can't see individual nanites, I can see a thick blanket of them, and within a few minutes, my hand is covered in a thin gray film. I can hear the people in Kairos making exclamations, screaming. People begin running back and forth, back and forth. Frantic, blind panic.

The nano-net is failing. Without it, the people here are at the mercy of the biospores that nearly destroyed civilization just a few hundred years ago. I lower my hand, let the nanites fall to the ground. Already, there is an ashy layer of them over the field. I've been vaccinated against the diseases of the past. But these people? They haven't. Even if the main gates don't open and let the androids out, these people are dead.

I turn, examine the field around me. Not far off is a

stripped pod, topless in the fashion of just a few months ago. I grab a nearby piece of corrugated board and hobble toward it. As I cover the pod, which is basically what the archives foretold as a "hover-car," I try to puzzle through what's happening around me.

Is what's happening to dome security because of the Anansi Virus? Some third layer of protocol within the virus? Layer one: create the blackout to allow the rebels in. Layer two: disable the G-Chips so that the city would go haywire. Layer three: completely disable the dome.

But why? If these system failures are part of the virus, then what's the point? What was Uncle Simon trying to do? More disturbing, if they aren't part of the virus, then what is happening inside of my city? I climb into the pod, shut the door, and ponder as the last vestiges of my technological world literally fall down around me. Nanites pile up on the windows of the pod, covering it. This reminds me of the story of Pompeii I read about in Dad's files. I just hope that living people rise out of this ash.

chapter twelve

POST-AMERICAN DATE: 7/5/232

LONGITUDINAL TIMESTAMP: 8:05 P.M.

LOCATION: KAIROS

"Elle," Gus whispers. "Ella, wake up." He puts a hand on my hip, brushes my hair to the side with the other, and the gesture sends hot tingles across my skin.

Moaning, I curl into a tighter ball. "I'm tired."

"I know. Me, too."

Something in the vulnerability of his words strikes me wrong, disjoints my perceptions. "Quentin," I breathe. It's an accusation, a realization, and a gasp all at once.

His fingers twitch on my hip, draw away. "Yeah. It's me."

Rubbing sleep from my eyes, I sit up and lean against the pod's interior. A quick examination of the surrounding area tells me that we're alone and I'm still in the pod that I covered earlier. "What time is it?"

Quentin scoffs. "You're joking, right?"

Right. No sun, no G-Chips, no way to tell time. Besides, what does it matter anymore? "Is-is something wrong?"

He cocks his head. The circles under his eyes are darker

than on the boy I once had committed to memory. But then, this man and that boy aren't really the same. Just like I'm not the same Ella, Gus isn't the same Guster, and Delia isn't the same best friend. This man has no luminescent skin or fiber-optic inlays, he has no sentient starlight hair, and no diamond facet eyes. This is an abnormally pretty man, marred by lost sleep and grief, with white hair, amber eyes, and a strange patchwork of delicate trails under his skin. "I don't think so."

"Then"—I rub my eyes and stifle a yawn—"why'd you wake me up?"

"Oh, I don't know, 'cause you're passed out, alone, and defenseless on a trash heap in the middle of the Outer Block?" he offers, grinning in sarcasm.

I blush. "I didn't mean to fall asleep."

He settles into a sitting position in front of me. "It's fine, you've been out for quite a few hours now. It took me awhile to find you and even then, I didn't want to wake you."

"Why did you?"

"You were having a nightmare."

"Oh." I look away. "Was I screaming?"

"You weren't screaming. Not out loud, anyway."

I squint sideways at him. "Then you just assumed I was having one?"

He purses his lips. "No. I can just tell."

Mocking, I lift a brow. "Disgustingly pretty, a Leader, and a psychic? My, your mother sure went the extra mile when she Customized you," I chide. The expression he gives me makes me automatically regret my sarcasm. "Sorry, I shouldn't have mentioned her."

He rubs his temple. "It's okay. Can't always walk on eggshells, right?"

Feeling like an ass, I lean forward and say, "I'm still sorry."

He pulls his hand away, forces a tired smile. "I know, Elle."

Sitting back, I stare at the ash-fall of nanites outside the pod's open door and let time unwind between us before I manage to find words. "I was dreaming about Meems. It was a good dream. Kind of. Just a normal sort of day. Well, as normal as it got for me after this." I gesture at my legs.

He nods. "I'm sorry for waking you, then."

"No. I'm glad you did. I hadn't wanted to fall asleep anyway. This isn't the time for it. I was trying to brainstorm, but I guess the last few days are catching up with me."

His gaze takes on a vacant expression and wanders off, distracted.

"How long has it been since *you've* slept?" I prod, aware that he's dealing with a lot of stress and grief, and I have no right to feel sorry for myself.

More silence. Finally he pushes a small tool box between us. "I made up an insert for your prosthetic while you were asleep. I'd like to try attaching it if you'll let me."

Nodding, I lean back against the pod's interior. Face hot, I turn away from him and stare at the floor as he scoots closer and his fingers find my ankle. His touch is a soft, slow tease as it glides along the inside of my leg, slipping aside the cuts of my dress to expose my leg to his examination. I hold my breath, rejecting how it makes my body react. I shouldn't like his touch. I should only like Gus's touch. His hand lingers on the inside of my thigh for so long I need to turn back and see what's going on.

He's just staring at my leg. The prosthetic, the wound, the band where it connects to my stump. I can't tell what he's thinking.

"Ugly, isn't it," I mutter, not really knowing what else to say to someone who is perfect.

His eyes slide up to meet mine. "I wasn't thinking that."

I press my back hard against the pod's interior, wishing I

could just become one with the plastic, synthetic leather, and metal; blend in like that chameleon creature Dad once told me about. I feel so exposed with Quentin, so fearful of his judgment, and I don't understand why.

He looks back to the prosthetic, lifts his other hand to trace the burned silicone around the wound. Even with the damage, I can feel that touch all the way up my spine.

"I was thinking," he whispers, his breath tickling my skin, "that I'm glad you have prosthetics and not a new set of engineered legs. Because this wound? It probably would have killed you. Would have hit a main artery. You'd be dead. Gone. So, in a way, I love this supposedly ugly leg for saving your life."

I hold my breath, try to stop my heart from beating. "It wouldn't have killed me," I reason. "Laser strike. Would have cauterized the artery shut."

"You would have lost your new leg. So, be thankful you've got this instead."

"Damaged and ugly as it is."

He glances back up at me. "They aren't as bad as you seem to think they are. These are really good prosthetics. I mean"—he traces a shape on my leg—"you can feel that, can't you? Even with the damage?"

I lick my lips. "A little." I refuse to accept he just drew a heart on the inside of my thigh. There must be some nerve damage.

He lifts one leg, plants it between mine so that he's straddling my knee. "I'm going to need a little help. My wound is healed, but my nerves aren't healed enough for some of the finer motor movements I'll need for this."

I squirm a little, trying to sit up as straight as I can, so I can both lean over and escape how close his knee is to an area I'm not sure I want him anywhere near. Yet the idea fascinates me, and part of my need to escape is fear of that fascination. “Just tell me what I need to do.”

He shifts to the side, his muscular legs squeezing mine, and opens the tool box. “I can do that.” He pulls out a slap-patch and holds it up to me. “This is a local anesthetic,” he says as he unwraps it and slips it under the edge of my dress. His fingers slide along my skin—my real skin—attaching it at my hip. They linger too long, wrapped along my upper thigh, and he holds my eyes. “You’re going to want it. I don’t want to hurt you.”

Swallowing, I nod and look away. “Just get it over with.”

“As you wish,” he says, voice quiet.

It’s all business from there, Quentin endeavoring to fuse a small splint against the bent piston with the set of small hand tools he took from my home when we fled the city. I don’t feel any of it. Not the pain, not his fingers on my skin. And I’m glad of it. It’s hard enough to focus with him sitting so close to me that I can taste him on my tongue and feel his breath on my neck. He’s more human now—his nanos are dying so his constant cloud of pheromone is gone, yet his breath still smells faintly of mint, which I like. He keeps making low requests for me to hold something a certain way or pass him something. His voice vibrates in every hair of my body, and I can’t stop staring at his throat. Once, he grasps my hand with his, adjusts how I’m holding something, and his fingers linger on my wrist, my pulse pounding against his strong fingers.

When he’s done, I push my dress down and he backs out of the pod and helps me to stand. My leg is still a bit unstable—I still have a limp—but at least I can walk.

“I’d like to keep an eye on it until the slap-patch wears off. I want to make sure there’s not too much pain from the pressure. Let’s sit and wait. It shouldn’t be much longer.”

As much as I want to get out of the stink of the dump

field, I do as I'm told, because I don't want to make a rash decision that results in unnecessary pain or damage. So I let him help me sit down and settle back into the pod. "Thank you. You didn't need to do this for me."

He smiles to himself as he disassembles a small fusion torch. "It's the least I can do. Perhaps when we get to Cadence I'll be able to replace the whole part instead of just patching it. Ideally, a 3D printer would have that fixed in a matter of hours, but I have no idea what to expect there, so perhaps we'll have to get something made, if I can't do it myself."

"Still," I say, "you have no reason to help me."

"I have plenty of reason to help you, Elle. I'm glad I had the opportunity today." He doesn't look up as he packs his tools back into the box.

"Where are the others?"

"I sent Violet and Bastian back to the main camp. The Dolls need to be told the main power failed in the city."

"You think that's what it is? That the whole city is shutting down?"

"Most likely."

"Any idea why?"

He shakes his head. "The Main Frame must be shutting things down for a reason. Or the virus is telling it to. I can't be certain what's happening."

The frustration in his voice resonates with my own. I try to focus on the things we can control. "What about food and water?"

He sits back, his fingers fidgeting on the seat of the pod's interior. "The water in the cave is drinkable. I'm having them move everyone to the cave. There's a large underground lake down there. That should at least get them some water. Once they're settled in, Violet and Bastian will rejoin us and we'll find food."

"You think it's wise to move them all down there?"

He shrugs. "Violet and I found a lot of caves and tunnels. I wanted the Dolls to investigate, find the one connecting to the rest of the Undertunnel so we can get to Cadence as soon as we have proper supplies. They can't do that where we left them."

"No," I agree.

Smoggy daylight fades to black, and still the nanites fall. Quentin keeps sliding out of the pod, investigating the surrounding area, and every time he does the ground crunches under his feet.

"Do you see anything?" I ask, not for the first time.

As he slips back in and pulls the door mostly closed, he says, "No. Nothing at all."

I try not to let it worry me too much. "It took a while for just the four of us to climb down. I'm sure it will take far longer to get everyone else down. I doubt some will come willingly."

"True." He works things over in his mind for a few minutes, his eyes pinched, then he gives me a look. "There's not much light out there."

"That's good," I say, watching as my breath comes out in a cloud. It's getting cold. "Means no one will see us. We're hidden."

"Yes, but it also means we can't see anyone coming at us. Makes me nervous, but I don't want to use the light-stick. We'd be a beacon in the night."

I turn and squint through the smudged window. I can see enough of the outline of Kairos against the sky to tell there are no lights in any of the windows, no fires in the barrels down on street level. There never was a lot of light at night. The Disfavored don't have much in the way of resources to burn or to fuel artificial light sources. They live as the sun and the dome provides for them. But I remember seeing some on the nights I'd sit up and stare out my prison window. There should be some and there aren't.

"It's too quiet," I note. "There should be more activity. Someone should have come to comb this dump site by now."

It's getting hard to see Quentin now, the last vestiges of sundown have disappeared behind the trash, leaving us in inky gray. He takes a deep breath, lets it out. The mint scent of it is a comfort in the stink of the Outer Block. "If the net is indeed failing, I doubt they're thinking about trash right now."

"How much of the biospores do you think are still out there?"

"Enough," he says quietly. He squirms, making the synthetic fabric squeak under him. A moment later, I feel a sleeping bag spread over me. "You're shivering."

I curl under the sleeping bag, thankful for the warmth of it. "I read that deserts got cold at night."

"Like Garibal," he says.

I stare at him in the inky blackness. "It unnerves me how much you know about Guster's game, how much he must have told you."

Quentin doesn't respond, instead he changes the subject. "If Bastian and Violet aren't here by morning, we'll have to resort to Plan B. We can't afford to wait long. Not with all those people back in the Undertunnel waiting on us, not if it becomes even more dangerous to walk around out here."

"Do you have a Plan B?"

"The dome does intermittent relief drops of food and potable water on a weekly basis. If we're lucky, there has been a recent one and we'll be able to find a distribution center that still has a reasonable stock left. Perhaps the fall of the nano-net has created a hiccup in daily activities and we'll be able to grab some of it."

I nod, though I know he can't see it. "Seems wrong to steal from these people."

"I hate to say it, but they're dead anyway."

I swallow hard, hating how right he is.

He says, "We should get some sleep."

I nod again and silence falls for a long time. I don't sleep, though; my mind is turning over and over. I'm so tired. So scared and uncertain. And, while I'm trying my very hardest, I just feel so overwhelmed. Before I know what's happening, I'm suddenly curled into a ball and sobbing.

I feel Quentin's arms come around me, pull me up and into him in comfort. "I've got you, Elle. It's gonna be okay." I grasp at him, bury my face in his neck and cry harder. He's real. He's human. He's warmth and comfort. He smoothes my hair, holds me tight. He's crying, too. I can feel the wetness of his tears. He rocks me, shushes me. Even though he's in pain, too. Even though he's broken, too.

"I'm scared," I admit. Why to him, I don't know. Maybe because he's the only one here. Maybe for a different reason.

"Me, too," he admits into my curls.

Making a fist around the chips in my pocket, I say, "I-I miss Meems," and my voice breaks, squeaks.

He's quiet for a long moment. "I understand your grief. I wish there was something I could do to make it go away for you. For both of us. Sometimes I can turn it off, block it out, but sometimes it feels like I'm drowning, like I can't get back up for air."

I whimper, terrified of the truth of his words. Pressing my cheek against the cool certainty of the blood pulsing in his neck, I reach up and touch my forehead.

His fingers continue to stroke my back. "We'll continue to deal with it. Us, the other Aristocrats. I can't imagine a goodly number won't come out of this scarred for life. PTSD, depression. Have you read about those?"

I shake my head.

"We don't have those anymore. We live happy lives. And if we're unhappy, there are drugs and new Designer bags and virtual reality games to solve it. But we don't have those solutions without the city, and the longer those people stay in the tunnel the more likely they'll develop light deprivation and mass hysteria. We'll be walking back to a mob mentality, I'm sure. That's why I'm concerned about moving them to safety as quickly as possible."

I know I should care more than I currently do. I know he's currently being better than me—thinking of the others before himself—but he's been trained to do that. I haven't. Right now, all I wanna do is find a safe, comfortable place for me. "You're better than I am," I whimper.

"No," he says quietly. "I'm no good at all."

The fabric of his shirt crumples as I make a fist around it. How does he not see what I see?

"I wish I'd had a different life," he admits.

"Yeah." Then I smile at the thought. "Like maybe what I had in Nexis. I could be with Gus then. For real. Without all this confusion and uncertainty, no smoke and mirrors."

He lets out a long breath, almost like a sigh. "That's a good dream," he whispers, his words faint. His face presses into my hair and I feel his lips move as he adds, "The truth."

chapter thirteen

POST-AMERICAN DATE: 7/6/232

LONGITUDINAL TIMESTAMP: 6:03 A.M.

LOCATION: KAIROS

The sound of movement outside wakes me. I make to sit up, but realize I'm being held down. For an instant, blind panic takes over and I rip at the sleeping bag, pulling it away from my face so I can see and breathe more clearly, but then I go still as the body wrapped around me moves and a familiar male groan lets out at the base of my neck. I shiver in delight as it slips and skitters down my spine, the back of my legs, then bounces back to curl along my ribs and settle hot and heavy in my chest—content and at home.

Gus. I find instant comfort in the arm wrapped around me, in the body cupped around my back, in the leg resting between mine, in the face that's buried in my hair, and I let my body relax and take pleasure in the moment. This reminds me so much of Gus. Quentin reminds me so much of Gus. I love it as much as I hate it—knowing that the boy who was the other half of my soul has been torn away from me, yet feeling like he's not actually gone. It's awful and wonderful and confusing.

I hear another noise outside. Rustling, crunching movement among the debris. My hackles go up and cautiously, I grasp the wrist underneath my hand and pick my head up, careful to stay low.

I feel Quent's breath catch, his body move as he comes awake, and his voicc is low and gruff from sleep. "What is it?"

"Someone's outside," I whisper.

His arm tenses protectively around me as he raises himself on one elbow and squints against the light breaking in through the gap between the board and the pod.

He snaps his fingers and I know, from months of training alongside Gus in Nexis, what this means. I reach for the gun among the bags on the floor. I've just gotten my hand around it when the corrugated plastic across the missing roof slides away in a cascade of nanite bodies and light floods in. I level the weapon at the silhouette, blinking in the harsh light.

A half second later, I focus in on wide, vibrant blue eyes staring at me from the cherubic, too perfect face of a little girl half hidden behind the plastic masks the Disfavored wear to protect thcir lungs. I stare at her, awestruck, and she at me, terrified as a rabbit against a wolf.

Quentin's hand folds around the gun, lowers it. His body relaxes against mine.

I hear, "Ani, what is it?"

The little girl looks away from me, toward where the voice came. I jerk my hand up, ready to fire, but by then there are more bodies, more shadows and silhouettes appearing. We're surrounded.

They're young. Most younger than me, some about the same age or a little older. One of the older ones turns, says "Go wake Claire," and another scampers off to comply. Quentin's grasp on me tightens as his gaze swings around the circle, taking in the masked Disfavored.

"You think they came out with the dump?" one of the kids asks, gazing up at the wall.

The older one who spoke narrows his eyes at us; they're just as blue as the little girl's. He's tall, broad shouldered, and his black hair is cropped close to his skull. He's uncharacteristically symmetrical looking for a Disfavored. Then he smirks, "That would be providence, wouldn't it?" His gaze pointedly fixes on Quentin. "A Cyr going out with the trash."

Despite the derogatory words, Quentin relaxes once more. Perhaps knowing this Disfavored man recognizes the white outfit—something only the Cyrs are allowed to wear—he expects that he'll be treated accordingly. But because the Disfavored just killed so many Aristocrats, I think the sentiment insane. I cock the gun.

I'm met with five other bullets sliding into chambers from five other guns that have suddenly been drawn around the circle.

The blue-eyed man grins. "Is this one of your Dolls, Cyr?"

"Something like that," Quentin says, voice self-satisfied. "Now, Delaney, if you wouldn't mind taking me to your leader, I would be much obliged."

Delaney's blue eyes go wide, mirroring the shock I suddenly feel at Quentin's recognition of this Disfavored. "It's not every day I come across a Domite who knows me."

As Quentin moves to stand I grasp at him, frightened this Delaney will attack him. The guns raise, but Delaney calls them off, allowing Quentin to step out of the pod. Here, the light falls on him completely, making him look ominous and frightening. Tall, broad-shouldered Quentin with his angel features, white clothes, and a cocky grin that lets everyone know they don't scare him a bit. "Do you know who I am?"

Delaney scrutinizes him and then a light enters his eye,

but his expression seems confused and troubled. "You're Quentin. The heir."

Quentin lifts his hands. "In the flesh."

"And, who are you?"

Grinning wider, Quentin says, "This is Ellani Drexel."

"*The* Ellani Drexel?" Delaney looks down at me again.

Confused at how *I* would be recognized, I say, "The only one that I'm aware of. But how do you know me?"

"Everyone knows that name." He grins. "And now a pretty face to a name that warms my heart. Tell me you're single."

Abashed at his forward comment, I open my mouth, but Quentin says, "She's not."

"Damn," Delaney breathes. He crouches down, leans into the pod, and offers a hand. "Enchanted to meet you anyway."

Feeling a blush creeping up my cheeks, I shrink back, cautious.

"It's okay. I don't bite. Hard, anyway," Delaney says, holding his hand out farther.

Steeling myself, I reach out and shake his massive, callused hand.

"Well," Delaney says, standing once more. "I'm sure you guys are hungry and could use a rest. Mac and Claire will want to see you."

Quentin perks up at this. "Mac and Claire?"

Delaney smiles. "You're aware of who they are?"

He nods, I shake my head.

"Good." Looking up, Delaney addresses another one of the Disfavored, who looks similar to Delaney with his olive skin tone, average build, and dark hair. But his face is less symmetrical and instead of blue he's got vibrant, almost grass-green eyes. They stand out even more because he's got a large scar over one of them. "Aaron, continue making the rounds with the crew."

Aaron grimaces. "Aw, come on, do I have to? What's the point?"

"The point," Delaney says, standing, "is to not count our chickens."

Rolling his eyes, Aaron mutters, "Would be nice to have chickens at all."

The little girl named Ani looks up at Aaron. "What's a chicken?"

"It's food," another little boy, this one with fair skin and hair, says. "Stuff we don't get to eat 'cause it don't exist no more."

"Oh," Ani breathes, and I can tell this disappoints her.

"All right," Aaron says, "let's get it on, then." He makes a shooing motion with his hands and the other Disfavored climb down and start shuffling through the rubble once more.

Delaney bends and picks up a large bag that clanks. "Shall we?"

I glance at Quentin. "Is it okay to leave? What if Violet and Bastian come back looking for us?"

"They're past their return time. The agreement was that we'd go on without them," he reminds.

"Still." I worry my hands together. "I feel like we should go back and get them, not go wandering off with someone we don't know."

"Perhaps I'm being too civil," Delaney says, showing his teeth in a fake smile and patting the gun now holstered at his hip. "You don't have a choice. I'm just trying to be nice. Show some decorum. Wouldn't want you Domites to think badly of us Disfavored."

Quentin gives me a tight-lipped expression, which means I shouldn't press my luck, so I don't. Instead, I quickly repack my sleeping bag and we follow Delaney as he leads us across the dump zone. I hear two more people skitter over the rubble behind us and take up our flanks.

"We're not going to try anything," Quentin mutters.

Delaney shrugs. "They're just making sure. They can be a little overprotective."

"Who," I ask, "or what, exactly, are you people?"

Delaney swings his bag over his shoulder and grins. "Just your friendly neighborhood trash pickers is all."

A low grumble escapes Quentin and I smirk. Obviously he's about as pleased with that vague answer as I am. "Delaney is part of the rebel group we orchestrated the raid with," Quentin informs. "Mac is their leader, Clairen's second in command."

"But if you know each other and are on the same side, then why the hostility?"

"They don't know me. They know Zane. He's the face of the Aristocrats in Outer Block. They only trust him."

"Correct you are," Delaney says. "Even then with a grain of salt. Especially after getting into the dome proved to be quite perilous to our people."

"But," I hedge, "that was an accident. Uncle Simon—"

"Yeah, yeah." Delaney waves his hand. "I know, wasn't in the plan, all that, blah, blah, blah. Look, I lost a lot of people in there. Good kids that shouldn't have died because your crazy robots went nutso-defuncto. So, I'm sorry if I ain't feeling forgiving, accident or otherwise, you Domites are on the naughty list, princess."

I grind my teeth.

After a few minutes of walking, the distance between us and him growing due to my slow pace, Delaney stops and turns. He looks like he's going to say something, but after watching us close the distance, Quentin's hand on my elbow to steady me on the uneven ground, he stays silent until we're close to him once more. "Claire's good with medicine," he says, turning to lead the way again, "Maybe she can take a look at your leg. I'm sure she would."

I lick my lips. "It's not really the sort of thing that just anyone can fix."

"Claire's not just anyone."

"Did you ask her if she was single when you met her, too?"

Delaney's eyes slide sideways and he examines me hard. "You're not like a normal Domite. How'd you end up in the dome? Drexel adopt you or something?"

A scoff chuffs out of me before I can stop myself. "Uh, no. Actually, I'm his real daughter."

He's looking all the way at me now, his handsome face close to mine. "But you're a Natural. He was a full-blown gene-tweak."

Gene-tweak? He must mean Customized. "I'm half Custom," I say, suddenly feeling like I need to justify myself. "Dad was an Aristocrat, born and raised. Mom was a Natural."

"Oh," he breathes, his face suddenly relaxing. "That makes way more sense. Me, too." He turns away, like that ends the conversation.

I stop short. "Wait, what?"

"I'm half Custom, too," he says very slowly, like I'm stupid. "Though, my father didn't claim me like yours apparently did." He shrugs. "I'm jealous. I would have much preferred to grow up in there than out here. I hear Aristocrats are assholes to Naturals, but it can't be any worse than being a mixed blood out here."

I stare at him, mouth open.

Quentin leans in close to me. "They're called Unmentionables out here, Elle. It's not a blessing to be a mixed blood in Kairos. It's the second-class citizen to the second-class citizen."

Face suddenly hot, I shut my mouth and look away. "I-I didn't realize there were others like me."

"Oh yeah, plenty," Delaney adds, "Natural by-product of Doll Houses, right?"

Yes, I'd forgotten that Doll Houses dealt in all manner of flesh, not just in selling Disfavored to people like the Cyrs to experiment on.

"You'd think," Delaney goes on saying, "considering how natural a by-product and how numerous we are, that those in Kairos would be a little more accepting of we Unmentionables. But you know how people can be. Natural, Aristocrat, when you come down to it, humans are jerks to each other. Nobody likes different."

I giggle at that. I like this guy. Then I sober as I come to a realization. Everyone who had just surrounded us had something uniquely un-Disfavored about their features. "Those kids back there. Are they all like you?"

"Yeah," he says, voice somber. "There's a whole group of us. Mac started it with me and Claire. Took us in, got me off the street, got her out of the Doll House, gave us honest, fulfilling work to do. She and I, we pay it forward—do it for others now. Safety in numbers of those who are like you."

"I suppose I understand that."

"My unit was bigger, but I lost quite a few in the raid."

"I'm... I'm sorry."

Trash gives way to rubble gives way to packed, dried mud as Delaney leads us farther down the dump zone and closer to The Waste. Here, the air grows staler and the stench changes to something more organic.

Quentin coughs

"You get used to it," Delaney says.

"I don't think I want to."

Delaney kicks a tin can and it clatters down the trash heap. "This is nothing. Some of the other cities smell even worse."

I cock my head. "There are more cities like this one?"

"Well yeah. I mean, every dome's got one. Would be pretty stupid for people not to build under the nano-nets, right?"

"But you've been to them?"

"Nah," he corrects. "Mac has only ever let me go on runs to Norsha. That's the city around Adagio. No one lives there anymore. Dome is dead so most of those people either moved here or to Adagio's sister city. Annex is the city around Cadence, but Mac won't let me go there. He says my mouth would get me into trouble." He reaches up and taps the mask on his face. "You might wanna put your masks on. Not sure if you noticed, but the net is down."

"Oh, right." I move to pull out the mask that was provided in my pack and I hear Quentin doing the same beside me. How stupid. I watched the net fall last night and here I am walking around mask-less. I'll have to learn fast to think about these sorts of things.

Wrinkling my nose, I adjust my mask, uncomfortable with how it sits on my face.

"You'll get used to that, too," Delaney says, grinning.

"You shouldn't have to be used to it," Quentin says. "Isn't that why you live under the net?"

"Those of us who live in thin air wear masks all the time," Delaney explains.

I lower a brow. "Thin air?"

"Yeah, the farther from the wall, the thinner the net. Eventually you're living in an area of thin nano-coverage. Hence, thin air."

"Oh."

The trash diminishes more and more until we're finally walking on flat, cracked earth. "Welcome to The Waste!" Delaney yells, flinging up his arms in a grand gesture. "Ain't she beautiful?"

Now that we're closer, I can see that while Kairos is built

in a ring around the city, there's another sort of ring around Kairos. A ring of the dead.

Interspersed between the bits of hollowed and forgotten bits of America's past are thousands of makeshift markers for graves. Some are bits of plastic or rebar tied to each other to make up crosses as some of the Disfavored still follow religion. Others are just pieces of trash with little things written or carved into them. One of the crosses closest to me has a half-rotten little doll propped against it. "It's a graveyard?"

"Well yeah, where else are we gonna put the dead? Leave them in the streets to rot? Place smells like shit anyway, ain't gonna make it worse. This way."

He acts like death is no big deal. Quent and I glance at each other.

We remain quiet as he leads us along what looks to be a cracked and ground-down old road along the outskirts of Kairos.

"Is it safe to be out here?" I ask, blinking at the sun, which is an unforgiving orange ball on the horizon. It's still low, so it should only be early morning, but already I'm sweating. I glance longingly at Quentin, who is engineered not to sweat at all, though he looks far more uncomfortable because of it. "What about the cannibals?"

"Oh them? Nah, they only come at night. If they came in the day we'd know they were coming. Those big rigs they drive kick up a lot of dust. They're gonna be pissed when they do their next raid, lemme tell you that."

"What do you mean?" I ask.

"Haven't you noticed something?"

"There aren't any people in the city," Quentin says. "I've been keeping an eye out, and I've seen barely a handful today where there were hordes yesterday."

He's right. I've noticed it, too. I can tell, even at this

distance. I've made a study of the living movements of the city that lurked in the shadow of my home. The arteries of her streets, the workings of her human cells, the beat of her heart of Disfavored determination. Kairos is dead. There are no people in her streets, no arteries clogged with the cells, and no beat to drive them anymore. "Why? What's going on?" Is it the robots? "The biospores couldn't have killed them all that quickly."

"They're scrambling, moving to safer ground."

"Safer ground?"

He grins and sing-songs, "You'll see."

After a good half hour of hobbling along the uneven road, we turn up an abandoned alley. Delaney lets himself into one of the shacks, low and squat with a torn bit of canvas across the doorway. We go to the back, through two adjoining rooms stacked with crates, and down a set of steps into the ground.

He leads us to the back of a basement where another Disfavored, this one sporting the more typical dark features I expect, is standing guard, a shotgun slung at his shoulder. "Hi, Faulk."

Faulk yawns wide and steps off to the side as Delaney unzips a door out of a wall that's nothing but a cleverly painted bit of canvas. "This way."

One of Delaney's men switches places with Faulk and Faulk steps in with us, leaving the other two outside.

Delaney zips the door closed, pulls his mask off, then reaches out and tugs ours off as well. "Boop! That's better. You don't have to hold your breath," he says, grinning. "The biospores can't get in here. And the radiation…well, you can't escape that, but we keep a counter on at all times. Hasn't spiked in a while. I think we're far enough away from the nearest ground zero."

Without his mask, I stare at him. Delaney is attractive,

and I understand why, now that he's explained his Custom heritage, but even he hasn't escaped the horrors of living outside of the dome. His tawny skin is finely scarred from acid rain and radiation burns. "Seriously," he whispers. "It's all right. I promise."

We follow him down the hallway—a metal framework covered in canvas. We're below ground, and I assume the canvas is to keep the damp and the dirt out. Eventually, we turn into a smaller hall lined with zip-closed rooms. We bypass all of them and head toward a central area where a large number of people are attending all manner of vehicles, setting up equipment, staring at small screens on antique bits of technology, and talking to each other in hushed voices.

Delaney angles us off to the side, toward a number of people who stand huddled together over a map. One of them I recognize, even at this distance. And when he sees us coming, he turns entirely and smiles.

"Zane?" Quent gasps. It's a word that reveals more weakness than I want to admit in Quentin, yet at the same time, it only seems to make him stronger.

Zane flashes his winning Broadcast grin and I instantly see the resemblance between them. How did I never see it? "Hey."

Quent begins to sputter, "What-but-I-I thought you... You were dead."

Zane puts his hands in his pockets and gives a noncommittal shrug. "I have to keep it interesting, gotta keep ratings up."

"Ratings for what?" This is from a new voice, one belonging to an astoundingly beautiful girl who has just materialized beside him. Tall and willowy with black hair, pale skin, teal eyes, she smiles and addresses us. "He still thinks he's on The Broadcast." She smacks his shoulder. "Idiot."

"Ow," he says, voice changing to a tone I've never heard

come from his mouth as he reaches out and touches her hip. "That's enough out of you."

"Who is that?" I breathe into Quent's ear.

"That, I assume, is Clairen," Quent muses. "The only woman on this earth my brother actually cares about."

"What? But how?"

"He met her out here when he started covering the Disfavored for that documentary he was doing." Quentin glances at me, eyes bright. "Fell for her the moment he saw her."

"Man," Delaney mutters from beside us. "I'm so jealous, everybody's so in-fucking-love."

"Don't worry, Laney," Clairen says. "One day your prince will come."

Turning away, Delaney rolls his eyes. "I've done the favor of the century finding these two for you ungrateful assholes. If you need me, I'll be in my cell writing sappy love songs."

Clairen lifts her hand to her mouth and calls out to him. "Behave yourself, you know what they say about masturbation."

He flicks her some strange one-fingered hand signal I've never seen before and stalks off.

"Charming chap," Zane says.

She takes on an apologetic tone as she says, "He grows on you."

Zane turns around. "So do tumors, but you cut them out and dispose of them."

She shoots a glare at his back before turning to us. "You must be Quentin." She offers her hand to Quentin, who shakes it awkwardly.

"I've heard a lot about you," he says, blushing slightly.

She smirks, and it's quirky and crooked. "And I you."

He grasps my elbow, practically throws me at her like he's afraid she's going to reveal something he doesn't want her to. "This is Ella."

Clairen isn't so ready with a handshake for me. "Ellani Drexel," she muses, crossing her arms. "You're not what I expected."

Uncomfortable, I glance from Quentin to Zane, uncertain whether I should be taking offense or apologizing.

"I dunno," she says, looking at Zane. "I thought she'd be taller or something."

Zane steps forward, places an affectionate hand on my head. "Good things come in little packages. Easier to deliver. Right, Quent?"

"Deliver?" I ask, turning to Quentin.

"Oh, don't look at him," Zane says, his hand turning my head back. "He's as clueless as you are." He steps in front of me, grasps both sides of my face. "Let's have a look." He stares at me, eyes sparkling. "Hm… You've lost weight. And you look like you could use a good rest. But, of course, you're lovely as always."

"Zane, we don't have time for your flirtations," Quentin growls. "The dome is down."

"Yes, the dome," Zane exclaims, brown eyes igniting—they were once purple—and he looks back down at me. "How did you manage to shut the dome down?"

"I didn't do anything," I snap, pulling away. "It must be part of the virus. Some tertiary protocol."

Zane taps his chin, turns away. "Maybe. Maybe. Kill the power, kill the chips, blow open the gate."

I stiffen. "The gate's open?"

My question is ignored.

"What were you thinking," Zane mutters, but I don't know who he's talking to.

"Whatever they were planning, I'd have preferred it if the net didn't go down," Clairen mutters.

"Maybe not, if the plan was to get the Disfavored to move into the city as quickly as possible. The job is done."

"A trap, you think?"

Clearly, they're in their own little world and I'm not involved in this conversation anymore.

"Wait, wait." I hold up my hands. "Someone explain what's going on, please? From the beginning. Zane, how are you even alive?"

"Oh, right. Sorry." He smiles and it's almost sheepish. "We've been in crisis mode. Too much vita-pep, not really thinking." He waves his hand dismissively. "Uh, where to start."

"The aerovator," Quentin prompts. "You were on the other side, looking for Mom." His voice wavers, drops a few octaves as he looks at the floor. "I heard the gunshots."

"My unit was the one to go into Bella Adona," Clairen says. "I saw Zane and Kat, surrounded by attacking androids." She shrugs. "Something just snapped."

Zane grins. "She was a thing of beauty, like an avenging angel. Saved our asses."

"Our?" Quentin repeats. "You mean Mom?"

"Yeah."

As if his legs are suddenly unstable, Quentin takes a step backward, grasps at one of the support poles, and plops down on a crate.

Zane says, "She's out with Mac. She's mental about the main power going down in the dome, so she demanded to be taken in and shown. They had to take half the rebels to keep her safe."

I look up from a very stunned Quentin. "You mentioned something about the gates blowing open?"

"Oh yeah," Clairen says, "Wide open."

My stomach sinks. "So, the androids are in Kairos?"

"No."

"No?"

"From what we can tell, the androids and droids alike are all dead," Zane says. "Like the city."

"So, it's as I feared." Not only is dome security down, the whole thing has shut down. But how? And why? "And the Disfavored?" I urge.

Clairen says, "They're moving into Evanescence."

"A mass exodus to safety," Zane adds. "Now that the net is down, their only hope is the dome."

"But the dome won't save them. They have to know that. The habitat systems won't work if the main power is down. The repair bots have already fallen from the frame."

Zane crosses his arms and lets out a long, low breath. "Eventually they'll realize that *if* we can't get the power going. But for now, they're simply celebrating the gates of paradise being opened for them. They're parading around in expensive clothes, eating like kings, and sleeping in comfortable beds for the first time in their lives. They're choosing to see only hope for the future. It's a new feeling for most of them."

"Well," I breathe. "At least they're safe for now."

"Yeah," Quentin agrees. "But we've got bigger, more immediate fish to fry." He turns to Clairen. "We need your help."

She blinks, confused. "*My* help?"

Quentin runs his hand through his hair, grasps the back of his neck. "All of your help, really." He glances at me, as if looking for reassurance. He's been so sure of himself, so in charge until this moment. It's clear he feels he needs to step down and hand the power to someone else. I wonder if he even wants it at all or if half of his relief at finding out his mother is alive is the new knowledge that the Aristocrats who've been relying on him are now someone else's responsibility. "We need food."

Straightening, Clairen steps forward. "Of course, you

must be starving."

"No," I say. "Not for us. We need supplies. Enough food to get us and at least thirty other people to Cadence."

Clairen's brows scrunch.

"I see." Zane rubs his chin. "So, there are others who survived, then."

"Of course others survived. You're the one that helped load that aerovator." Quentin puts his fist on his hip. "Or did you forget that part?"

Zane shakes his head. "I didn't forget. I just didn't hold out much hope. So, everyone made it?"

Nodding, Quentin says, "Most of my Dolls, Gus, Violet, some other Aristocrats."

"Bastian? Sadie? Angelique?"

"Them, too."

"Good."

"Angelique?" I ask, wondering what she has to do with Zane. To my knowledge, she's just one of Carsai's cronies.

"She's my assistant," Zane explains. "Very gifted, sees things no one else does. She'll make a wonderful Anchor when I'm done training her."

"Oh."

Impatient, Quentin says, "So, will you help us?"

"What happened to the supplies we planted in the tunnel?" Zane asks.

"It's gone."

"What? How can that be? No one knew about that stash but us."

Quentin shrugs. "Someone must have found it. There are ways into that tunnel from out here. That's how we ended up here."

"We know all about the tunnels," Clairen says. "We use them as bolt-holes when the cannibals come."

"So, your people took the supplies?" I ask.

"Of course not." She seems offended I'd even suggest it. "None of us even knew it was there."

"Well someone did," I push.

"All of the Disfavored know about the tunnels," she explains. "They're how we live. Sand storms, cannibals, late shipments of water from the dome. All that forces us down. Anyone could have taken those supplies if they happened upon them."

There's an awkward moment when I'm trying to decide if I should apologize for being suspicious of Clairen and her people, then Zane breaks it. "Where are they now?"

"We left them back in the caves," I explain. "Where there's a big underground pool, so they could at least have water."

Clairen says, "It's not safe down there."

"What do you propose?" Quentin asks. "Bring them up here so they can get strung up by Disfavored?"

"The Disfavored go down there, too."

"No place is safe," Quentin mutters. "We're trying to get them to safety. We need supplies to do that and once we have it, we'll be out of your wiring for good. You can have Evanescence for all we care. Just help them get to safety."

I open my mouth, ready to argue that Evanescence is our home and I can't get it back for the people I've hurt if he willingly hands it over, but I close it again. I have two groups of people to worry about now. The Aristocrats who I have displaced *and* the Disfavored who I've handed a death sentence to by somehow powering down the city entirely. There are a lot more Disfavored, and they need Evanescence more than the Aristocrats do.

Clairen stares at Quentin for a long moment, then looks to Zane, then me. She seems to be looking for some way out of a situation there is no escaping. Finally, she says, "I'd like to say yes to you, Quentin, I really would. But our resources are incredibly tight, and I don't make those kinds of decisions."

Quentin throws up his hands. "You have the entire city of Evanescence at your disposal. Enough food and water to supply ten times the number of people moving in from Kairos."

"There's potential for that, yes," Clairen says, voice even. "But we're out here and the other Disfavored are already in there, if you haven't noticed. We'd have to go in and try to find something that hasn't already been claimed. It's not like we're in a position to just walk in and demand people start handing us things."

"Aren't you?" I ask. "I mean, you're their resistance, aren't you?"

"We're a small group and we pretty much operate on our own. We don't represent the whole of Kairos, nor would they want us to. Most of us are Unmentionables. We're outcasts among the Disfavored and they're loath to even look at us much less carve out a space for us in their new utopia."

"So why did you help them at all?"

"Besides the fact that the system between the dome and Kairos was just fundamentally wrong?" Clairen looks down. "Because if things had worked out the way we had planned, then we would have had a proper spot."

"So why not make that spot now?" I ask. "Why not step forward and pretend you are the ones who gave them the dome?"

"Because the rebels are nothing and nobody to them. If there's anyone the Disfavored would listen to, it's you." Zane points at me.

"Me? Why?"

"Because you're Ellani Drexel. Their savior."

Confused, I look back and forth between them, then the man named Faulk and the other guard standing there with him. They both nod, as if this will answer something.

Clairen says, "Your father is a hero to the Disfavored. For bringing the game. And you're a hero, too, for bringing the virus."

Mouth open, I stare at her for a long moment. "I-but… How?"

Zane says, "Let's just say it was very well known that you'd plant that virus. It was just a matter of when." He holds his hand out toward the direction of the dome. "And when the gates of Evanescence blew wide open? They had their obvious proof. To the Disfavored, you are an avenging angel come down to smite the Aristocrats."

My stomach suddenly feels sour, and I plop down beside Quentin on the crate. A fine pair we must make.

"Well," I say, because words aren't really working for me. How surreal that I had no idea what I was doing, even as I did it, and all the Disfavored knew and waited, with baited breath, for me to do it.

How cruel. How sick. But it's done, and I can't do anything to bring the dead back. Only keep those who lived alive. Disfavored and Aristocrat alike. "If I have that power, then I'll have to ask them to help us."

"Are you sure you're ready for that?" Zane wonders. "You'd have to give them an extremely good reason to provide aid to the Aristocrats."

Quentin says, "Couldn't we appeal to basic human decency?"

Clairen shakes her head. "There's a point when humans become inhuman. You should have seen it," she says, voice low. "All those bodies, bloodied and beaten from the droids. The Disfavored paraded over them, strung them up, did even worse things. If any Aristocrats lived after those bots went down, I doubt they still do. There's a lot of hate for Aristocrats among the Disfavored. It terrifies me."

Taking a deep breath, I hold it. To prevent myself from screaming, to prevent myself from crying, to prevent a lot of things. Is this what the Tricksters really wanted? All of the Aristocrats to die? To turn innocent androids like Meems into killing machines and then destroy them, too? Did they mean for the Disfavored to take over the city? Why? What's the point of so much senseless killing? I force myself to my feet. "I *have* to make them see. I'll think of something."

Clairen holds up a hand. "If you can wait just a little, perhaps there's another way. Something less dangerous. Mac and Kit should be back soon. We have some supplies," she ventures, glancing at her comrades. "Perhaps if you explained to them."

"Fine," I say. "Then we'll wait and ask them."

"If they say no?" Quentin asks.

I ball my fists around my shredded gown. "Let's hope they don't." Because otherwise I may have to appeal to the Disfavored—tell them that some Aristocrats are still alive and somehow convince them to feed instead of kill them.

chapter fourteen

POST-AMERICAN DATE: 7/7/232

LONGITUDINAL TIMESTAMP: 8:23 A.M.

LOCATION: REBEL BASE, KAIROS

In the morning, we all sit in a strange silence that's both comfortable and tense as we eat our gruel. Quentin makes a face the first time he tries it, but continues eating without complaint, though it's clear he's struggling with it. I don't even notice the taste anymore. I ate gruel very similar to this for months while I was imprisoned in my own home with only Nexis to give me comfort.

"Did you sleep well?" Zane asks.

I nod.

He sucks his spoon for a moment. "I thought it was a little strange you two didn't spend the night together."

"Zane!" Quentin barks, obviously embarrassed.

"What?" Zane turns to him with a look of confusion and I can't tell if it's genuine or feigned—he's so good at acting. Cheeks warming, I pretend to be interested in my food.

Clairen scoots a little bit closer to me. "How do the clothes fit?"

"Good," I chirp, happy to grasp onto a new direction in the conversation. "A little big, but it's so nice to be in something clean."

"They're nothing too fancy. I'm sure you're used to much better," she says, lowering her eyes like she's a little ashamed she doesn't have silk pajamas to offer.

Reaching out, I touch her wrist. "They're wonderful. Honestly."

"Yes," Quentin adds, touching his own new outfit, simple black coveralls—similar to what the service droids in the dome wore—which seems to be the general uniform of the Disfavored rebels. "We're both grateful for the clothes and a chance to clean up."

Zane riffles Quentin's hair. "You two looked like you had a good roll in the dirt."

Quentin slaps his arm away. "Enough. I'm serious."

"Aw, come on. I'm only teasing you."

Aaron appears and squats down beside Clairen. "Mac's back. Kit's with him."

Clairen nods. "We'll be right there."

Zane stands and rubs his hands on his uniform, which he's got unbuttoned and tied around his waist, revealing a black, sleeveless shirt underneath. When he turns, he's got a different tattoo on his upper arm than Quentin does. His is a coyote, like Mord was in Nexis. "You guys should stay here until they settle in and I can explain things."

Quentin's hand tightens on his spoon. "What explaining does she need?"

Rubbing his forehead, Zane looks up at the ceiling and I can tell he's searching for patience. "It's more that I'd rather tell Mac about the situation you and the other Aristocrats are in. He can be a little difficult. If you want a yes, it's best to send someone he knows."

A scoff escapes Clairen. "That's an understatement."

Quentin leans forward. "So, you've gotten in pretty tight here?"

Clairen begins to tie her pin-straight hair into a ponytail as she speaks. "You can assume there's a reason Zane's not dead yet."

Zane grins. "He's smitten with my charming good looks."

The deflated glare that Clairen gives Zane makes me chuckle.

He touches his chest in mock pain. "Oh ye, of little faith."

"We, uh," Aaron says, voice a little nervous. "We should probably go. I'm sure they've unloaded, and he doesn't like waiting."

"We're right behind you," Clairen says, grabbing Zane's arm and dragging him away.

Zane glances back and winks at us. "Don't worry. I'll get you your food."

"I hope it's better than this stuff," Quentin mutters, setting his bowl of half-eaten food aside.

The abandoned gruel bothers me, makes phantom memories of a time when I was starving on rations the size of what he's leaving in his bowl. I get mad at him then. For making me remember that time when Uncle Simon held me captive, starved me on this same gruel. For being an Aristocrat and having the choicest of *real*, not even synthetic, food while people like Clairen and Delaney struggled with hunger and learned to be grateful for the dome providing them with rations of gruel. I want to scream at him, yell that he's stupid and doesn't understand. Instead, I ball my fists and bite the inside of my lip until it bleeds.

•••

Zane's expression upon returning a half hour later says it all. Quentin looks up from his hand of cards. Delaney has been teaching us a new game, one we didn't get a chance to learn in Nexis.

"Let me guess," Quentin says. "You didn't get us our food."

Slumping down on a crate, Zane balances his elbows on his knees. "He's got a stick up his ass today."

Delaney doesn't look away from his hand as he selects a card and lays it down on the table between us. "Are you surprised? He did just come back from the dome. Can't imagine he saw much of anything he liked."

Zane runs his fine fingers through his hair. "No. Seems it's just as we feared. The whole city is down. Half the doors are closed—stuck shut on whatever setting they were on when the city powered down. Some we could pry open, but the ones that count? The ones where the bulk of food and water storage are? Those aren't gonna come easy."

"You mean they can't get to the food and the water stores in the city?" I ask.

He shakes his head. "Not all of them. Enough that Mac's being stingy about not sharing what we've got without some guarantee that we could resupply. I'm afraid they're going to resort to explosives," Zane says, voice quiet as he nibbles a nail. "But that's dangerous. The slightest concussion could fracture the nano-glass on the dome and without the repair bots? I've seen how quickly a cracked dome can empty a city."

I glance at Quentin. "There must be something we can do."

Zane says, "Unless you know some magical code to restart a whole city, I doubt you can."

"No, but I did create the code that allowed the virus into the Main Frame, so, maybe I can write something to restore Evanescence?"

Zane lowers his hand and blinks at me. "Do you think

you could do that?"

I shrug. It's an absolute long shot, something I have no idea how to even start. But it's a bargaining chip we didn't have three seconds ago. "It's worth a try."

Zane stands and grabs my hand, making me drop all my cards. "Come with me." He tugs me to my feet and practically drags me down the corridor.

Zane approaches a thick bald man with a low, wide face who stands, beefy arms crossed over a massive chest. He's short, but both Quent and Gus could probably fit inside of him. Beside him Clairen leans against a table, hand on one hip, her sharp features distinct, with her hair pulled back and her eyes intense with interest in the conversation they're having.

Aaron stands at the doorway, looking bored, and grins at me when we pass.

Zane clears his throat.

"We were just talking about you." The man motions for us to come closer.

Lifting his hands, Zane makes introductions. "This is Mac. He was my rebel contact during the planning phases and *this* is Ellani Drexel."

"Drexel, eh?" Mac gruffs. "Got a lot to owe you for, little lady."

"So I've heard," I say. "Even though you all apparently owe me, you're unable to meet my one request."

Mac frowns at me. "You've got *cajones*, little one."

I scrunch my nose. "I have no idea what that is."

"Means you got a heavy ball sac."

Still not quite getting what he's saying, I glance at Zane for help.

"He's being a vulgar Disfavored man. Ignore him and tell him what you told me."

I look back to Mac, still cross-armed, still looking like a bull ready to charge. I search for the best way to frame things for a man like Mac. He seems straightforward and to the point. Simple, but not stupid, someone who likes a clean deal. "Do you question what I'm capable of?" I ask him.

The stoic expression on Mac's face slackens and his eyes tighten in distrust. "If everything that I've been told is true, then I think you're capable of quite a bit, Miss Drexel."

"You'd agree that I'm the one who, above everyone else in the entirety of my city, was the one who hacked into the Main Frame."

"With help, yes."

"With help. They laid the path, I unlocked the doors. I made the final plant. In the end, it was my straw that"—I touch my lip in mock thought—"what did Dad call it? 'Broke the camel's back' I think."

"What are you getting at?"

"What I'm getting at, sir, is that I have a set of skills that you need. I'd be willing to sell them to you at a price."

Mac's face turns a little red and he turns to Zane. "What's she all about?"

"Ella thinks she might be able to reboot the city."

Mac's thick brows rise and he examines me over a bulbous nose that looks to have been broken once or twice in his life. "You're trying to make a deal with me, I see."

I nod. "If I can start the city again, then you'll have access to all the resources you need."

"That's a big *if*."

"Seems that everything that has happened up until this point was a lot of plans hinging on 'ifs.' What's one more?"

His arms slacken, and he puts them in his pockets. "What's

to keep me from compelling you?"

"What could possibly compel me? Everything I love is dead. The people I care about are down in that tunnel, and you'd have to feed them to keep them alive to blackmail me, so you might as well just make the deal and make it easier on your guards."

"There's other ways to compel people."

"You mean do what my uncle did? Take away my legs, imprison me, isolate me, starve me to the point of insanity? None of that got me to plant that virus for him. What did plant that virus was a simple deal. Just like this one. I got what I wanted, and he got what he wanted. You catch more flies with honey," I say, smiling sweetly. "That's another one of my father's."

Mac scowls at me.

I shrug. "I can't guarantee anything, but I'm your best hope for even getting into the Main Frame, let alone rebooting the entirety of Evanescence. And all I'm asking for is some supplies for a few measly Aristocrats."

Mac stares at me. His face is stoic again—poker face. Another thing Dad would have said, now that all his little sayings are on my mind. I resist the urge to touch his chip. This moment is too tense to even move.

We're still for such a long moment, him staring at me, me staring at him in some sort of silent contest, that I wonder if I've miscalculated his personality and I've overplayed my hand. But then, suddenly, he bursts out laughing and his hand comes flying up to smack me hard on the arm.

Unnerved, I glance at Clairen over his shoulder. Her smile touches her eyes and they don't seem unkind.

"You drive a hard bargain," Mac is saying. "I'm starting to really gain some respect for you Aristocrats."

I draw a breath. "You'll do it, then."

"Sure, sure." His arm comes out and his hand splays across my shoulders. He guides me as he begins to walk. "I'll even send them along with a little guard. As a mark of good faith. Wouldn't want anyone saying I threatened The Savior with physical violence or any such nonsense."

"No," Zane mutters as he walks at my shoulder. "Wouldn't want that."

"Blowhard," Clairen adds from his other side.

If Mac hears, he doesn't indicate. "As long as everyone understands that they go and you stay."

"Stay?" I ask.

"Sure," Mac says. "At least until we're up and ready. Maybe you'll leave then. Maybe you'll stay. Who knows if we're going to continue needing you to update and maintain the system."

I swallow. What have I gotten myself into? At least everyone is safe.

"Claire," Mac says. "Be a button. Run down to supply and make up a few care packages for Miss Drexel for"—he looks down at me—"how many was it?"

"Thirty, roughly."

"We'll call it an even forty."

"But," Clairen argues, "supply is Dolman's job."

"Not anymore it's not. It's yours now. Along with your other duties."

"But—"

"No buts, Claire. Argue some more and I'll start feeling super generous and have you make up sixty," he warns.

She closes her mouth.

"That's what I thought. Next time you get the urge to get saucy and call me names, have the decency to say them to my face. A cuff to the ear hurts less than being overworked and hungry. I thought you learned that when you were ten."

Clairen growls under her breath, but she just says "Yes,

Mac" and walks away.

When she's gone, Zane says, "Whew, you're a mean son of a bitch."

Mac's hand leaves my shoulder and the next thing I hear is a meaty fist hitting Zane's bony shoulder.

"Ow!"

"You're part of the family now, kid, rules apply to you, too."

Zane's voice suddenly becomes bright and he's grinning like an idiot. "Oh, I'm so very pleased." He turns to me, expression and tone becoming stone sober. "Aren't you excited to become a part of this, Ella? Can't you just feel the love?"

I dart an uneasy glance at Mac, who is grinning and shaking his head. "You're a goddamned idiot."

"I know," Zane says. "That's why I fit in so well."

He doesn't get smacked for that.

part four:

ELLA LEARNS WHAT IT MEANS TO BE CHASED

chapter fifteen

POST-AMERICAN DATE: 7/7/232

LONGITUDINAL TIMESTAMP: 2:46 P.M.

LOCATION: DISFAVORED TUNNEL SYSTEM

As we walk through the tunnels I see evidence of the Disfavored who have been here in the past. Lost items—a shoe, a cap. Bits of trash, smudges of ash. Even some dried out and vulgar bits of human excrement. I keep pace with Faulk and Aaron. They're in easy conversation, Aaron often grinning at something Faulk says, but I can't hear them at this distance. Quentin walks beside me, brooding.

I speak, because the silence between us is getting to be too much. "You're quiet."

He smiles. "I'm thinking that I don't like the idea of leaving you behind."

"You think they'll hurt me?"

He scoffs. "No, you're probably the safest you'll ever be with the Disfavored. They don't see you as one of the Aristocrats, Miss Savior," he teases, pressing against me.

Looking away, I draw a deep breath and let it out slowly. My chest feels so tight. So much anxiety. "I'm scared."

"Of what?"

"Being this Savior I've been painted to be. Having that responsibility. What if I can't undo this virus? What if I can't get the city back online, and all these people are let down because of me?"

"If anyone can, it's you."

I touch the chips in the breast pocket of the new clothes that Clairen provided to me before we left. They're scratchy and threadbare, but they're clean. Despite a bath and clean clothes, I still feel dirty. Like ten pounds of something inexplicable and disagreeable is weighing me down. "That's an awful lot of expectation."

"Seems to me that you were born under a cloud of expectation. From day one, your mother had plans for you to carry out this crazy scheme. And ever since then, more and more people have gotten involved, ushered you down this path."

"You and me both," I note, not ignoring the path he's been shepherded down.

"Yeah. But at least I sort of knew what was happening. Granted, nothing has gone according to plan thus far. The only thing that was supposed to happen when you planted the Anansi Virus was a short power outage. Just enough time for some Disfavored rebels to infiltrate the city and storm Bella Adona. The only Aristocrat who was supposed to die was my father—everyone knows that Aristocrats are cowards and wouldn't fight a group of armed Disfavored. The rebels figured they'd probably lose a few to the security droids, but they signed on aware of that. The benefits of putting a Disfavored sympathizer like my mother into the Presidential seat far outweighed the cost. It was going to be the dawn of a new age. An age where Disfavored and Aristocrat might walk hand in hand. That's what I was told was going to happen. That's what

Zane thought was going to happen. That's what Mom and the Disfavored rebels thought was going to happen. But..."

"But Uncle Simon altered the virus."

He nods.

"I have a lot of trouble believing anyone intended to kill all those Aristocrats. I can't believe he made the city turn on us. I can't believe he'd turn off the nano-net. It just doesn't make any sense."

"Zealots only ever make sense to themselves."

I don't answer. It's clear Quentin believes Uncle Simon is entirely responsible for what happened after the virus was planted. I don't blame him—if not Uncle Simon, then who? Still, I'm not convinced. I want to believe in a person I've loved my whole life.

Quentin swings the light-stick back and forth, back and forth, examining the tunnel. Aaron and Faulk turn left up ahead. Finally, I say, "At least now everything is out in the open and we're making our own decisions."

"I don't feel like that," he says.

I pause, mid-step. "You don't?"

"No, I don't." Turning away, he continues walking and I follow. "I don't want to bring these Aristocrats to Cadence, because if I leave with them, I'll get sucked into maintaining those people for the rest of my life. That's what I was born into, but it's not what I want."

"I don't want to stay here with the Disfavored, because then I can't be with the people I know and love. And if I stay and you all go, then I'll never see any of you again. I'll be stuck with strangers and I'll get sucked into what I was born into, and it's not what I want, either. But," I reason, "it's what I have to do. To resolve what I stepped into blindly, I have to walk into something else with my eyes wide open. It's the only way."

"I don't like it. There's got to be another way."

Suddenly, I realize where we are—back in the cave with the big pool. We weave in between columns and jutting rock, drawing closer to the far side of the pool, where a weak bit of light-stick glow is emanating. I notice an abandoned shoe and a lost scratch-pad. Something about it seems very wrong.

"Quent?" I whisper, suddenly feeling like whispering might be a necessity.

"I see it," he murmurs.

Faulk and Aaron must, too, because their guns are drawn and they're prowling forward, using the columns as cover, their lanterns splitting apart and throwing lurking shadows in their wake. As they disappear ahead of us, Quent crouches and picks up the scratch-pad, thumbs through it. I crouch beside him, looking over his shoulder and squinting at the fading backlight of the pad. Soon there will be no power to it at all.

Drawings. Dozens of them. Of Aristocrats, of Disfavored. Of Zane and Clairen and Mac. "This is Angelique's," Quent says, reaching forward to pick up the stylus. "She doesn't go anywhere without this." He slides the stylus home and powers it off.

My stomach sinks. This silver shoe… This is Veronica's shoe. At least, it's a shoe that my Designer brain tells me would perfectly match the powder-blue gown Carsai's crony had been wearing. Those perfect crisscross bands would have accentuated the fiber-optic pattern on the bodice.

"Something's happened. Something's wrong," I breathe, sudden panic climbing up my ribs. It's like my muscles are being drawn tight, like a slingshot about to be fired. I get to my feet. "I need to find them."

"I don't think we're going to like what we find, Elle," Quentin says, lifting his finger from the band of the shoe.

"There's blood."

Scowling, I round on him. "All the more reason to look for them."

Quentin takes a long breath, lets it out. "Can we talk about this for a minute?"

"No. I can't believe sitting and talking is even an option for you." I throw my bag down at his feet. "Sit here, then. I'm going to look for the others."

As I stalk away and the rocks close behind me, my light-stick is my only solace, strong and purple in the black. I feel desperate and confused and frustrated, like when Dad handed me a new puzzle to unravel. I'd spend days in a haze of lost thoughts until I came to the abrupt solution. I wish I could come to the solution now.

And just like that I do. I trip over it, landing with an *oomph* that scrapes the palms of my hands and leaves my knees smarting. Blinking stars out of my eyes, I kick my feet free of what feels like an abandoned bit of cloth. I reach out and find the cloth sticking out from around the corner of a stone column is the synthetic fabric of an Aristocrat's gown. Squinting, I lift my light-stick and a pair of legs appears in the glow. One foot is bloody and missing a shoe. Heart in my throat, I inch around the column.

It's an Aristocrat, for certain. Only Aristocrats are so Custom pale—all the better for Mods and Alts to stand out. As I draw closer, I see the pale blue of her ball gown, the brown-red stain of blood in her white hair.

"Veronica," I whisper.

Shaking, I bend down, hoping against hope that she's just injured and still alive, but as I close my hand on her cold white skin, I know better. Still, I turn her over. Her stiff body makes an awful crackling noise. She folds over, her hair falls away from her face, and I'm confronted with the streams of blood down her pale, Custom face, her glassy blank eyes, her wide-open mouth. Her eyes are accusing. Her mouth is screaming at me.

Something inside of me breaks. I see images I don't want to see again. Hear words I don't want to hear again.

Meems's twitching body and halting words as she died in my hands.

Screaming Aristocrats falling from windows.

Androids ripping at President Cyr's stomach.

The sounds of a gunshot, and the blood and brain of my uncle's head spattering against the perfect white of Lady Cyr's dress.

Opus's crisped and blackened body, the sizzling noise and the scent of it.

Nadine's open eyes turning on me in Nexis, her lifeless foot hitting a door, and her voice echoing in my mind. "You led us here to die."

Over and over and over again.

Clutching myself, I tumble back on my butt. Everything inside of me freezes solid. Cold, cold, more cold. I can't breathe. There's weight on my chest that I can't see. Something inside my mind tells me to back away, turn away from what my eyes are seeing, as if doing so could erase the image before me, could stop what's flashing through my brain.

But hasty backpedaling, turning on my hands and knees and crawling away…it doesn't make what I saw disappear. It haunts me, follows after me like it's burned into my mind, like it's grabbing at my heels. So I stumble to my feet and try to escape from it.

It comes at me, closing in around me, drowning me. Some dark foreboding thing that, if it catches me, will swallow me whole. I hasten my steps until I'm running as if the speed could cause it to lose pace.

Still, it pursues.

So I run faster, tripping over my feet, feeling my way along the corridor. I slam into Quent, who must have come in search of me.

"Whoa," he breathes, grabbing at me. He's trying to make me go still, but that will only make the image catch up to me faster. So I fight him. I shove at him and squirm out of his grasp and duck under his arms.

"Elle!" he hisses after me.

I don't respond. *Don't look back, don't stop.*

He calls again, closer this time. Is he chasing me? I go faster, my lungs burn. I begin hurtling downed bodies and scattered packs, refusing to see their dead and accusing eyes as well. There is no logic, there is no reason. Only flight.

A hole appears, abrupt and maw-like. I pivot hard, take a turn. Left or right, I don't know. I run down a broken path, half falling, half skittering, still running. My legs are shaking and feel dangerously close to losing their ability to keep pace with my racing mind. And just as I'm thinking it, just as reason is starting to return, just as I realize the only thing chasing me are the ghosts in my head and I need to stop before I hurt myself, my injured leg buckles and I stumble. As I topple, I lose my balance. I throw out my hands and my light-stick slips from my grasp. It flies out…into nothing. My momentum carries me after it. I endeavor to stop, skidding against loose shards and scree, but I'm already going over. And then I'm falling.

I whirl forward, put my arms out and scream.

The darkness eats me down and then I hit. Hard. A wall of shock, cold suffocation pressing in on all sides. It takes me a long moment to realize I've fallen into water and another moment after that to realize I'm choking on it.

I struggle to find which way is up, to get to the air. But

the shock and the cold seem like they've taken something from me, stolen my senses. The last thing I notice is warmth, hands. Someone touching me. And then nothing.

Someone is kissing me…oddly… And then I'm coughing, spitting up water from lungs that are on fire. Someone sits me up, doubles me over so I can gulp huge mouthfuls of air and choke up the rest of what's in my lungs. They pat my back, urging the awful stuff up. Eventually I subside to shakes and gasps and then I start crying because I almost died and everything hurts.

They pull me close. *He* pulls me close, because even though it's pitch dark, I sense the maleness of his rocking body and the low baritone of his "shhhh, shhhh" in my hair. And when he says, "It's okay, I've got you. You're okay," It's a male I know well.

I shove at him, rejecting him, and stumble back to my feet. "No. No, it's not."

I hear him half sigh, half growl in frustration and a light-stick snaps on, bathing Quentin's soaking-wet features in white. He looks up at me, examines me hard. "A simple thank you would suffice."

I touch my lips, hating the phantom warmth of him because I know his lips should be Gus's. "You kissed me. Again!"

Quentin smirks at me. "Oh, come on. I kiss better than that."

I frown at him. "What were you doing then?"

He lifts a hand and shoves a lock of sopping hair away from his forehead. "It's called mouth-to-mouth resuscitation. You do it when someone stops breathing."

Stops breathing? Me? "I was—"

He rocks to his feet and I try not to look at how his wet uniform clings to his muscles. "You wanna tell me why you decided to take a dive off a cliff when you quite obviously didn't intend on a swim?"

I blink at him, muddle-brained. "Swim?"

"Yeah," he says, his brows quirked. "It's that thing you do to prevent yourself from drowning. I know you're capable of it. You should try it sometime. Might add a year or two to the end of my life." He lets out a breath and shakes his head. "Sparks, I thought that was the end of you."

I look away, my face suddenly hot, and attempt to loop my hair behind my ear, but the curls have turned to soggy cords. "I'm sorry."

He shoots me a sidelong glance, examines me for a long time. "You all right?"

I shake my head.

He straightens a little, his expression concerned. "What happened?"

"I—" The image comes back, reminding me that near death doesn't excuse you from the haunts of visions past. I close my eyes, ashamed of how illogical and stupid and fragile I can sometimes be. "I can't."

I turn and try to walk. I have to move, have to do something.

Quentin keeps pace. "Stop."

I shake my head, try limping away faster because I don't want to deal with him. All I want right now is to bury my face in Gus's chest and cry my heart out. But he's not here. He's with Delia…I hope. Circuits, what if something has happened to either of them? I couldn't live. I quicken my pace, fleeing from the awful thought. Quentin grasps for me, I try to pull away, but he's stronger. He has my wrist, pulls me to a stop and swings me around, pinning me against the rock wall. I continue to struggle because I'm afraid of stopping, of looking at what has to be examined inside me and outside in this cave.

"Stop. Stop it," he growls, shaking me.

I still, his tone and strength making me go limp in his grasp. I brace myself against his chest, the tears falling hot and stinging. And suddenly I need to say it, I need someone to know, to validate what I just saw, tell me it's not some nightmare I conjured. So, I give up the ghost that's chasing me. "It's my fault. All of this is my fault."

Quentin doesn't respond, but I know he suddenly understands by the sudden loss of agitated bite to his grip. I was manipulated. I was an instrument. I did this all unknowingly. But it doesn't change that I am the one who did it. It does not and will not make the guilt ever go away. It only increases my need to right the wrongs. But I've let these people down even more and that just makes me fear my responsibility to help the remaining survivors all the worse. He must be feeling all these same things.

A moment later, his fingers are sliding over my cheeks, stealing away the tears. "Don't cry," he whispers.

I jerk away, making him retreat to placing his arms to either side of me. "Maybe you can prevent yourself, but I can't. Just let me cry."

He doesn't respond, just stands close, his arms and body like a shield against the world, his head bent low as if to commiserate, and he lets me sob myself dry.

When it feels like I've drained my soul and there's nothing but burning eyes and sniffles, I try to stand taller, but my legs are shaking with spent adrenaline and Quentin has to grab my elbows to keep me from falling.

"Easy," he says. "Let's try and find Faulk and Aaron. I'm sure they're looking for us. I'll take a look at your leg again when we get back."

"I don't want to go back," I snap. I shake my head. That's not really what I want. "I don't want to go back to that expectation. Not yet." I'm cold, wet, utterly miserable, and so sick of fighting. So sick of people dying and leaving me to see it. Part of me wishes he would have just let me die in that water, but the other part tells it to shut up and deal with the problem because at least I'm alive. "They were attacked, weren't they?"

"Yes, it looks that way. I haven't stopped to take it in yet."

"I-I saw her body." I slide down the rock, plop on the floor. He follows me down, sits across from me. "Veronica."

He grimaces. "I was afraid of that. She must have gone off alone. She did that a lot."

I shake my head. "What if… What if they're all dead?" I whimper. "Bastian? Violet? Delia? What if Gus is dead?"

"He's not dead," he says, voice quiet and eyes on the ground. "Of him, at least, I'm certain."

I blink at him. "How can you be so sure?"

He stares at me. There's something he's trying to decide whether he should tell me. He gets that look.

"Quentin," I say, dropping my voice in warning that he better be open with me.

He's obviously thinking, trying to figure out where to start, what to tell me, what to exclude, probably the best way to sum it all up. "When we were younger and he got his first Modification, he didn't take it so well. My mom sent him home. She thought it would be good for him to spend some time with family."

"He told me about it. He went home, and Max beat him, so he went back to the Cyr estate."

Quentin taps his knee for a moment. "That's what he believes. That's what we told him happened." He breathes in a rush. Then, as if relieved, he adds, "But he didn't walk home that night."

I crunch my brow, confused. "Then how'd he get back?"

Quentin's jaw muscles flex and he takes a deep breath. "They sent him home. In a shipping container."

"What?" I gasp. "A shipping container?"

He nods. "He arrived two days after they packed him in it." He makes a bitter noise in his throat and shakes his head. "It was so small. Too small. I remember thinking that." He lifts his hand, places it against his upper lip, and talks against his fingers. "Before they pulled him out and I really saw. Then I couldn't think at all. I just stared. I couldn't help it. The way the blood had settled, the unnatural angles of his joints and neck, the glazed look in his eyes. They'd beaten him. Tortured him. To make an example, I suppose."

I suddenly can't breathe. My chest feels so tight that I'm not sure if my heart is even beating anymore. "He was…" I swallow, unable to finish.

"Dead." He lowers his head as if nodding. "Or at least so close to it that for all intents and purposes he might as well have been." His voice is clipped and rises and falls a few octaves as he speaks. It's obvious that recalling whatever horrific scene he remembers is traumatizing. "His brain was still alive, but badly damaged. He was comatose and completely paralyzed. Vegetative. Eventually, everything just gave out and the only thing keeping him alive were the machines." He lifts a shaking hand and runs trembling fingers through his ghostly hair. "I kept thinking, 'It's all my fault. I did this to him. If I were better, if I didn't need to be perfect, this wouldn't have happened.' I hated everyone. Me, my father and mother, his mother and brother. I even hated him for doing this to himself, for being a Doll."

"So," I say, trying to understand. "What happened? Some

kind of medical advancement? How did you bring him back to life?"

He shakes his head. "Not medical. No matter how advanced certain medicines are, they'll never be able to do certain things. The human brain, you can regrow it, but you can't recreate a person just as they were or transfer sections of memory into a new brain. We're not that advanced yet. But technology... That's different." His eyes lift. "It was my mother's idea. She'd always loved Guster like a son, and she blamed herself as much as I blamed myself for what happened. She said he'd died too young, that he'd lived too harsh a life for that to be all he had. She wanted him to live. So, she brought your father and uncle in."

I blink, stunned. "Dad and Uncle Simon? What did they have to do with anything?"

"Along with Nexis, your father had another pet project. Something he began working on after your mother died. He was developing better android operating systems, creating androids with more autonomous personalities and a wider range of emotional capabilities. I believe your house android was the original prototype."

I unconsciously touch the personality chip at my breast. "Meems."

"Yes. He always said that he'd hoped he could bring your mother back one day."

I grimace. "You can't bring back the dead."

Quentin doesn't take his eyes off of the ground. "You couldn't be more wrong. It took a few months, but eventually they developed a near-perfect operating system. They re-created his body out of a fusion of prosthetic technology and regrown biological material. Mom wanted him stronger, a better Doll, capable of acting as my bodyguard and also able to withstand whatever his Disfavored family might throw at him, so she Customized him. His body is capable of things most Customized humans are not—things only my family has access to. Then, they uploaded what was left of his mind."

"Wait, what?" I breathe, confused. "What are you saying? Gus is a-an android?"

Quentin glances at me, his expression uneasy, as if he's afraid of how I'm taking the news. "Cyborg, really."

My jaw drops. Gus is a cyborg? I shake my head. "I don't believe you."

"Believe what you like. It's the truth."

I clench my teeth, mentally denying it all. I can't help but look up, some morbid need to see something, anything, to prove Quentin wrong, and I study him. In just a few days he's changed so much. His Alts fading, the grief and fatigue taking bits of his youth and beauty with gusto. I stare at them and think of the last time I saw Gus—his straight back and shoulders, his fret-free face and bright eyes, his strong body. His Alts that didn't fade like everyone else's. I never actually saw him eat. Never saw him sleep. And he never seemed winded when we were running around during the attacks.

"Why didn't he say something about it? Why would he talk about sleeping if he was a cyborg?"

Quentin stares at his hands. "Because he doesn't know he's a cyborg. He thinks he's a real person."

All I can do is gawk at Quentin as if he's slapped me. It feels like he has.

"The ruse to keep him thinking he was a real person was all orchestrated. Real-time downloads for organic experiences like eating, sleeping, defecating, pain, and pleasure. He'd be transferred into a new unit twice annually to exhibit growth and puberty."

At my stunned silence, he rubs his hand across his cheek. He's so drawn and tired looking. He'd always been an obelisk, an ivory tower, but now he's just real. So very real that I don't want to look hard, because I might see myself reflected in his eyes. "We thought it would be best."

"Best," I scoff. "He's living a lie! You brought him back from the dead so that he could be your Doll! Do you know how sick that is?"

Quentin pins me with an acidic glare. "I don't regret what they did! I loved him more than anything and losing him was like dying myself. You've lost friends and family, Elle, don't you dare tell me that you wouldn't bring them back if you could."

"But you've lied to him. He can't have a normal life. He's a freak of nature."

Quentin sits back and takes a long inhale, his expression stony. "Is he? Is that what you thought of your android? Was she less to you because she wasn't a real person? If your father had eventually uploaded your mother into a similar unit to Gus's, would you have shunned her as anything less than your mother?"

"My mother is dead," I hiss. "There is no bringing her back, even if she was an android or a cyborg or whatever. Her mind and personality would be gone."

Quentin breathes a dark chuckle, his eyes rolling. "You know so very little, don't you."

I scowl at him, confused. "Don't I?"

He gives me a knowing expression. "Your mother and father were two of the most brilliant Programmers Evanescence ever had. Do you honestly think Evanescence wouldn't upload and periodically back them up while they were still considered useful to the cause? My father may have done away with their physical forms, but he never erased their data. They're very much alive, not in the flesh, but somewhere on the Main Frame. Just. Like. You." He reaches out and touches my forehead, right where my scar is.

My teeth make a clacking noise as I slam my mouth shut. Is that even possible? I suppose it is. I mean, the Aristocrats change out body parts all the time, have them grown anew. But making copies of the brain? If they could transfer sections of Gus's brain into a nearly android body, why couldn't they put entire brains into all android bodies? "Why haven't I heard of this?"

Quentin hoods his eyes. "There's a lot you and everyone else in Evanescence don't know," he mutters darkly. "And it would have stayed that way, even if my mother or I became President. It's best that way."

I find my fingers tracing the chips. Two of the three chips are identities. My father. Meems. Why did I take them? What would I do if I could bring them back? I couldn't possibly. They're dead. Dead is dead, I can't play God. I shake my head. "I couldn't do it. I couldn't bring Mom or Dad back. It's wrong. They're human beings, not playthings."

Quentin's chest collapses as he lets out a long exhale. "What about your android?"

Meems. Meems, who was nothing but a computer program. Before Evanescence fell, android personalities got transferred into new chasises all the time. Dad had even wanted to transfer her once.

What would Meems think of a new body if I gave her one? She'd never wanted new skin. Her skin was her own, she made that clear. She'd hate it if I gave her a new body. But I'd do it anyway; I'd do it just to have her back and hope she forgave me. "I-It's different."

"How?"

"I'd tell her, for one."

"What if you could give her a body exactly like hers? What if you could save her the pain of knowing her own death?

What if she could live exactly how she was?"

I shake my head. "Still, it's not right. He should know."

"He would have demanded we kill him."

I look away, knowing Quentin is right. His whole body being a machine? Gus wouldn't be able to live like that in his false skin. He'd question everything he was, everything he'd ever done. Right down to his feelings for Delia and me.

"Wait, if he's a cyborg, then..." The word dies on a squeak, and I clear my throat. "How'd he play the game?"

Quentin lifts his chin and stares into my eyes for what seems like an eternity then looks away, his Adam's Apple bobbing and his eyes glistening in the yellow light between us. "Gus first found out about the game from listening to Warren discuss it with my mother. He was obsessed with the idea of being able to create a new life, to make different choices. It was only a matter of time before he began playing it, so we prepared accordingly."

"We?"

"Me, my mother, Simon, your father, the other Dolls." His eyes lift and search over the far side of the tunnel, as if he's uncomfortable. "We knew he wouldn't be able to play. Synthetic life forms can't play virtual reality games, or VR systems aren't yet compatible with the biological and neural layout of synthetic life forms. Simon wanted to just download virtual experiences like we'd been doing for his other life functions. But your father didn't think that would be fair to Gus."

"Fair?" I whisper. My voice sounds hollow and strained to me.

Quentin bobs his head. "Gus had never expressed a desire to carry out life functions. We just gave him those to maintain the guise of reality. But he'd expressed a desire to play, and Warren wanted to honor that. He wanted to give Gus the most authentic experience possible. We discussed everything from creating a virtual avatar programmed with his personality profile to creating experiences from scratch and playing them out like movies in his mind. But the issue was creating a truly organic experience for him. Something reactive and true to being in an entirely new world. Something that elicited true joy and wonder, which are hard to manufacture in AI. Eventually, we decided that someone would go into the game for Gus, play his avatar as he would want it. He'd act exactly as Gus might act and as he played, the experiences he had in the game would be downloaded into Gus's memory. He'd wake thinking he'd played the game."

My chest feels tight. "Who played him?"

Quentin won't look at me. "You already know the answer to that question."

"Still," I breathe, "I need to hear it. To know it's true."

Quentin licks his lips. "I did." It's a tight, almost inaudible response. He puts his hand on his knee and stares at it. "My mother didn't want me to do it. She said that if he ever found out, he'd never forgive me. But…" He pauses, his gaze tracing his broad palm and strong fingers. "I'm the only one close enough to him. He's my best friend, my brother. We know each other better than we know ourselves, I think. And I'm certainly the only one he ever told certain things to—things like what he felt about you…" His fingers tense on his knees, biting into the skin. "I'm the only one who could have believably played him."

"So all that? That was you?"

Why is this all so shocking? I already knew. Deep down, I knew. My confusion between the two of them—times when I thought it was Gus and it was actually Quent; the way Quentin acts around me; Gus's confusion at somehow being in love with two different girls.

His brow creases, and I can tell he's choosing his words carefully. "It was me playing someone else. The guy in that game, he wasn't Gus or me. He's not real, not 100 percent Gus and not 100 percent me. Even I made mistakes playing Gus, things Simon had to go back in and alter."

I blink. "So, he doesn't even remember it the way it actually played out?"

Quentin doesn't answer.

I gasp for breath, fighting a suddenly pounding heart. "It was all a lie, then…all some…some game?" Tears sting at my eyes. I struggle not to let them fall, but they burn at the back of my throat. "Everything we did?"

Quentin closes his eyes. "That's not true."

"How-how could you?" I demand. More tears come then and words start to string together as I rail at him. "How could you do that? Lie to me like that?" I want to get up and run. I want to smack him. I want to scream. But for some reason I just keep sitting there and staring at him through a renewed flood of tears, as if I expect there to be something he says to make it all right. Is that too much to expect? He knew what to say in the game, didn't he? Or was that just him pretending to be someone else, too? Who is this guy? And in whose heart does the majority of the guy I fell in love with exist? Or does he not exist at all?

He won't look at me. If there is any shred of humanity within him, then I'm sure it's because he's so ashamed of what he's done. Maybe ashamed of the tears he's causing. Eventually, Quentin reaches out and touches the chips in my pocket, his fingers brushing my clavicle. "This is your domestic android, isn't it?"

I lean back, pulling the chips from him and cradling them against my chest. "Her name was Meems."

His eyes stay on the pocket, despite my shielding hands.

"Meems," he muses, a slight, sad smirk pulling at his lips as if he's won a bet. His gaze lifts then, flashing amber. "Do you think Meems ever wanted something?"

Sniffling, I press my trembling lips together. I don't have to wonder, I know exactly what Meems wanted. "She wanted to be a human."

Quentin holds my gaze. "If it were possible, if you had the power, would you have given her that wish?"

I hold my breath and stare at him. He's trapped me. Built reason around my emotion, made me see his motives. He used those words of his, said the thing that needed to be said to save himself.

He holds my gaze, intense and powerful as fire, and when I don't respond he says, "Well?"

"Yes," I reply.

He nods his head once, another personal bet won. "Then you understand why I did what I did."

I finally manage to look away, hiding the darkness and pain that I feel. I try to wipe away the tears, to look strong. "It doesn't change the fact that you both used me."

Quentin is quiet for a long moment. "I'm sorry. I never wanted to hurt you. It hadn't been my intent when I started the game. I never even dreamed I'd come across you. The probability of that happening is so—"

"I know what the probability is," I snap.

He closes his mouth as I glare at him, daring him to utter another word. What neither of us says is what we fear—that the game put us together on purpose, that Game Guster was just as much of a tool as Game Ella was. Instead I say, "You could have just left me alone, walked right by me, never approached me in Garibal."

"I'm glad I didn't," he says, his expression some strange mix of amusement and seriousness. It looks too much like an expression Game Guster would make. I look away, denying all of it. Part of me agrees with him. That part would never exchange my experience in Nexis for anything. But another part feels betrayed, tricked, and uncertain.

Quentin must sense my confusion because he says, "I'm sure you wonder why. What was my motive?" He takes a deep breath, his attention sliding off to the side, avoiding me. "The right thing to say to you, the thing that would satisfy my own selfish desire for you, would be to say that I approached you because it is what *I* wanted. But"—he lifts his chin and his brow creases with dismay—"that would be a lie, and I don't want to lie to you. Not anymore."

I clench my fist around the chips, making the silicone edges bite into my skin through the fabric of my uniform. I don't know why his words hurt. I don't know what I expected him to say. I don't know why I even expected those mystery words. It's not as though I like Quentin. It's not as if his opinion of me matters.

Quentin's hand lifts and his fingers slide over mine, cupping my hand in his. And I feel it beyond skin-to-skin contact. I feel that touch down to the very center of my being. The truth is that Quentin touches me in some special way that lets me know he's the boy who touched me in Nexis. There's just something about it—the pressure in the pads of his fingers, the heat of his skin, the gentle deliberateness of his movement, the forward possessiveness of his actions. Something about it is what drew me to Game Guster in the first place. That, and the way he kisses me. They give me a feeling like nothing else.

And it's that feeling that tells me how much of a liar I am. All this hatred, all this denial. I've been lying to myself. The truth is that I do like Quentin Cyr, and I do care about his opinion. I want him to like me. I always have. Except now, the reason for my want has changed.

The want of Pre-Nexis Ella was a flippant, girly obsession with the beauty of the unattainable. The want of Post-Nexis Ella is something born of camaraderie, from knowing someone front to back, inside and out. It's the want of love. Only, that love is for a boy who is a myth, one who is an amalgam of two boys. And I don't know which boy I love more.

As if to hammer home my thoughts, Quentin says, "The truth is that I approached you that day because I knew Gus had feelings for you."

I shake my head, denying it. "He never let on."

"He couldn't," Quentin whispers. "He never thought you'd respond favorably."

Inexplicable pain prickles my chest. I want to say, "of course I would have," but that wouldn't be true. Gus once frightened and disgusted me, which now makes me feel superficial and horrible. I push my self-hatred away. "Then, why in the game if not in real life?"

Quentin shrugs. "Perhaps not in the game, either. If I hadn't been playing him, maybe never. It's another way I deviated from the true path that would have been Gus in the game. But the fact is, *I* played him for better or for worse. I thought I could give this to him. And now?" A bitter scoff escapes him as his arm tenses, pulling me close to him so that our noses nearly touch. "I'm not doing a very good job of it, am I?"

I stare into his eyes, breathe in his air, unable to move even though I have an insatiable desire to lean forward and kiss him. I'm so conflicted. Who is it? Which boy is the one I fell in love with? Perhaps neither? Perhaps the boy in the game is nothing like either of them. "I'm…I'm confused."

Quentin seems to realize himself and draws away a bit, loosening his hand so that it slides teasingly away from me. "You shouldn't be."

I don't know what to say.

He stares back into his lap. "There's only one right answer here."

My voice rasps as I say, "Is there? Because it seems like there are two and I don't know which one to pick."

"There's only one person you love, and that's the Guster that you met and fell in love with in Nexis."

"When you kissed me in the aerovator," I say haltingly, "were you being you or Game Gus?"

He narrows his eyes at the ground. "I was being stupid."

I blink, incredulous. "Stupid?"

"I shouldn't have done it. It was wrong."

Really? Because, confused as I was, it felt right. I cross my arms and look away. I want to demand what's so wrong with kissing me. Doesn't he care? Could he really have done all of that with me in the game and really feel nothing? I cast him a sidelong glance. He looks so hard and unforgiving in the darkness. Maybe he doesn't care. He's an actor, after all. The son of the President. The ultimate manipulator. Maybe his touch is a lie. Maybe his kiss, too. And perhaps my feelings are a lie.

I think of Game Guster and his ability to get exactly what he wanted out of the people around him. I wonder if Quentin only seduced me in the game to satisfy his desire to please Gus. I gulp, hating how much that possibility hurts. I feel sick.

He speaks then, his words low. "I should have told you the moment you pranced up to me at my party wearing Nadine's face. I should have called you out and confessed who I was. But"—he takes a deep breath—"I felt guilty. I was trying to be a good friend. Trying to let Gus have you. That's what I thought you'd want, because I made you believe it's what you wanted, like I'd planned. So, I lied to you. To Gus." He looks up then, meets my eyes. "I created a problem for all of us and I'm sorry."

For what feels like an eternity, I just stare at him, agape. My mind is whirling, swirling. I grasp onto the first concrete thought that comes to me. "What am I going to do about Gus?"

His fingers tighten. "Nothing."

"What?" I huff. "I can't do nothing. What are you saying?"

His grip shifts, pulling me up as if to put me back on my feet, but drawing me away from the wall as well and settling into something softer. I look up at him, confused, only to find myself trapped in his intense gaze.

He stares down at me, and somehow I feel like we must be getting closer even though I don't think I'm moving. Finally, he says, "I'm saying that I'm done." His fingers loosen a little more, slide up my arm in a way that makes my skin tingle. "I'm saying that I'm tired of being a good friend. I'm done pretending it doesn't make me insane seeing you in love with another man. I'm finished with him making you cry because he's in love with the right girl for him. I'm sick of how I feel when you're so close and I can't touch you or kiss you. I can't deal with waking up without you in my arms. It doesn't feel right. I don't like it and I'm fixing it." His fingers slide some more, traveling over my shoulders, up my neck, cupping my face. "I'm saying that I love you, Ellani Drexel."

He pauses a moment, as if he knows I need that to sink in, but then he plows on. "I may have approached you in Nexis for Gus, but *I* fell in love with you. I'm the one who kissed you, who made you smile, who encouraged you. I'm the one you spent all those hours and all those days with. I'm the one you gave yourself to, who you laid down with at night. I'm the one who died in your arms with your tears on my face, loving you more than anything. And it was *me* who went to Simon and tried to see you, even after you told me you didn't want to see me in Real World. I'm the one who found you those Shakespeare sonnets. When Gus remembers a love for you, it's my love he feels, not his. He loves Delia and I love you." His words die. He swallows, his expression anxious.

I stare at him. Everything is such a jumble and it's happening so fast, I don't know what I feel.

But…that doesn't change what Quentin feels, does it?

I was always myself in Nexis, so if he says he loves me, then he's talking about true me. But is it the truth? He's a manipulator, someone who can get whatever he wants from anyone. He's the guy who always knows what to say and delivers it at just the right moment. But what would he gain from lying to me? He has no reason to hurt Gus or me. He has everything. There's nothing beneficial in winning my love.

Unless…

Unless… All he wants is my love in return.

"Say something," he says.

I don't know what to say. All the words in the world don't seem adequate enough. I lick my lips and taste salty tears and murky water. "Say it again."

A quirk graces his lips and his fingers shift on my jaw. "I love you." And then he bends down and kisses me.

And because I can never say no to his kisses, I kiss him back.

There's no confusion after that. With his lips on mine, his body so close, there is no mistaking the familiarity of this dance, of this magnetic pull between us. He may look different, he may smell different, and taste different, but he doesn't feel different. Neither does the way he makes me feel. I am whole with Quentin's arms around me, with his body close to mine, with his lips on mine. It's an addicting sensation—that certainty of rightness after everything has gone wrong for so long. It gives me hope, makes me strong. So I let it carry me away, and for a few blessed moments it's just Quentin and me and the beautiful thing between us.

And then I think about reality and the bodies lying around us and I pull away.

Quentin attempts to chase my retreating lips, but I turn my head. He goes still against me, his whole body alert. We're interlocked together, his body pinning mine against the rock wall. I blink, I hadn't even noticed him lifting me, hadn't mentally acknowledged drawing my arms and legs around him. I try not to think about how intimate a position we're in as I timidly glance at him.

There's smolder in his eyes, the cool melting stuff that's trying to urge me back to the edge. His heavy breathing falls soft on my face, his body is hot and ready. He's so *alive*.

Shifting my weight, I let down one arm and press my fingers to his neck, count his thudding heartbeats excited at the prospect of me.

He glances at my hand. "What?" he whispers, his voice thick.

I close my eyes and swallow. Heartbeat. This boy has a heartbeat. I have a heartbeat. I feel mine echoed beside his, thudding with just as much urgency. "There are dead people all around us," I whisper. "Why?"

He leans in, places his forehead against mine. "I don't know," he admits. "I found a body, too—when I went looking for you. But it's not one of ours." He hesitates, then says. "His teeth were filed. Pointed."

Stomach sinking, I close my eyes. "Cannibals."

"If that's the case, then I'm sure mostly everyone is alive. Most likely the only deaths were to those who struggled or spotted something they shouldn't have."

"Gus would have struggled," I reason. "He's a fighter and he'd want to protect Delia at all costs."

"Yes, but like I said, he wouldn't have died easily. Not with a body that's more machine than man."

I think about that. "If he fought, they would have tried to injure or silence him. He would have been wounded, but he most likely would have gotten away."

Quent's head bobs to agree then pauses, realizing what I've just realized.

If Gus was injured, his chasis—be it biological or synthetic or some combination of the two—would have been damaged and he'd most likely come to the fast realization that he's not a real human. But then, so would the cannibals. And if they couldn't eat him, they probably wouldn't have made the effort to chase him. But because he was a machine, they'd also not try to pursue him if he chose to save a person or two. "You think he's got Delia with him?" Quentin asks.

"It's a fair bet." I smile, because there is some ray of hope for at least some of our group. "Hopefully, there are some others with them and we'll locate them. But…if he realizes what he is…What are we going to tell him?"

Quentin steps into me, letting me slide back to the floor. He hooks a finger under my chin and angles my gaze up to meet his. "Let me talk to him. This is my fight, not yours."

I frown at him. "But your fights are my fights."

Quentin scowls. "Not this one. You getting involved would only confuse him."

"As if you have any right to corner the market on clarity," I mutter sarcastically.

"He's my best friend, Elle. I can talk to him, get him to see. He knows I'd never hurt him because he knows I love him."

"Well, I love him, too," I reason. And realize too late that it's not the right thing to have said.

Quentin's face shuts down and he takes a step away from me. "I see."

I put a hand to my head, as if that could keep all the thoughts that are swirling around from spilling out. "No, that's not what I meant. It's just…"

He closes his eyes, as if shielding himself from the truth. "You think you might love us both."

Sighing, I lower my hand. "No, that's not it." I struggle to find the right words, to explain that it's hard to disconnect from Gus—I have an ingrained love for him and his wellbeing I don't know if I'll ever be able to shake. But I don't want to admit that to this boy who just dumped his heart out to me. Not when I love him, too—more and differently. With *that* kind of love. I cross my arms, shielding the weird place where the cold of the situation and the warmth he brings me collide. "Sparks, you make me want to run away screaming sometimes."

He turns back to me and gives me a long look. "I'll chase you until I catch you or I'll die trying. There is no other option for me, Elle. One day you'll figure that out."

I remember what Violet told me. About the right one following me. And it makes my heart flutter. Trying to hide the smile his words bring, I turn away and shrug it off. "You already died once in Nexis and I didn't like it. Try to stay alive this time. Okay?"

Amusement enters his voice. "Yes, ma'am." His fingers slide over mine, closing around my fist. "If we find him, I'll tell him about the game, explain his misplaced feelings for you. I can't hide the truth anymore."

I swallow. "Doesn't that mean that the love he has for me doesn't actually exist at all? He just remembers loving me?"

He shrugs. "I don't know. He had a strong admiration for you once. And"—he cups my cheek—"there's so much about you to love. Thanks to those memories of my game with you, he sees and interprets everything about you the same way I do. Even without that, I can't imagine any man not loving you."

I smirk at that.

His fingers tense. “I’m serious. You may have your flaws, but those only make you more beautiful to me. No one is perfect, but you can be perfect for someone. And for me, you are. He does love you. Because I love you. He has to, those feelings have been implanted in him. But the reality is he also loves her.”

I lift my chin, meet his eyes. “This is an absolute mess, Quentin Cyr. Perhaps the best option for both of us would be to walk away and start fresh elsewhere.”

He bites his lip, looks away, and a second later he disappears from my side, his fingers leaving a teasing caress in their wake as if saying “Go ahead and try.”

I know that touch is right. I can try to walk away from the love I have for the boy who played Gus in Nexis. But it would be a fool’s errand. Just like there is no other girl for him, there is no other boy for me.

Sighing, I turn and follow after Quentin. Because, like he can’t stop chasing me, I can’t stop following him. No matter where it leads.

chapter sixteen

POST-AMERICAN DATE: 7/7/232

LONGITUDINAL TIMESTAMP: 5:57 P.M.

LOCATION: DISFAVORED TUNNEL SYSTEM

Quent comes back to the mouth of the tunnel and hands me a small pack. "Faulk and Aaron have disappeared. I assume they went back to report what happened to Mac."

"Or maybe they're looking for us?"

"Maybe. It looks like the cannibals are gone, at any rate." He gestures to the pack between us. "These are all the useful things I could find."

I reach into the pack. A few light-sticks. A couple of nutra-packs. A water jug. A sticky thermal-blanket. A few lost personal items, including Angelique's scratch-pad. I close the pack up and struggle to put it on. "Any sign of the others?"

"None who are alive, no."

His words force me to halt, a sudden stillness in my chest. "Who?"

He avoids my eyes. "Don't ask me to tell you that."

I cover my mouth to keep my lips from trembling. He means someone I know is dead, someone whose death would matter. Of course, I care that any of them are dead. That our small group of survivors had gotten this far made me want to cheer for all of them and their survival. "I…I need to see."

"Elle…"

"Please, Quent, I need to see them. There's no one else to remember them in death. Just us. We need to do this for them."

I squint at his frowning face. "You'll have more nightmares," he warns.

"What's a few more out of the thousands to choose from?"

Lips tight, he grasps my elbow and helps me limp back into the cavern.

The first body we come across is Beau's. His eyes stare upward at the ceiling, he lies in a near-perfect circle of his own blood. Seeing his face makes my stomach turn, but I fight to keep the contents down as, wincing against the pain in my reinjured leg, I crouch close to him and close his cold eyes. "I'm sorry," I whisper.

"I took too long," Quent says, voice distant. "Too long to get them food and water. If I'd come back, led them away…"

"No," I say, "don't start thinking that way. You'll go mad."

He looks away. "He was my responsibility. My Doll."

"Your Dolls came down here with you willingly. They knew the risks."

He makes a growling noisc in his throat. "Then why do I feel so guilty?"

"For the same reason I feel guilty? Becausc you're a good person, and you feel like the things you've done are the cause of it, even though they aren't. We're one drop of many in a bucket of lies and deceit."

Shoulders slumping, he stops moving and gives me a pained expression.

I force myself to stand and turn away from Beau. Then I take Quent by the hand. He's shaking. "It's not our fault he's dead, that any of these people are dead. The cannibals killed them. Not us," I say, trying to believe it myself. I lift his hand, kiss his knuckles. "We were trying to save them, to make them safe. We need to remember that."

"I know." His voice sounds raw. "It's just— I'm so sick of losing people. What am I going to tell Cam?"

My heart sinks. Cam. Poor Cam. He'll feel the same way I did when Quentin died in Nexis to save me. Falling apart, no reason to live. "If we find him, tell him the truth. That Beau died valiantly, and Cam should be proud of him. Cam might even already know, so don't stress too much over a course of action that may never take place."

Face twisted, he looks away, and I think he might start crying. Reaching up, I touch his face, and he grasps my hand to his cheek as though it might give him strength. I tug at his other hand. "Come on."

We pass the body of a cannibal. Quent gives him a dark glare as we pass him.

"He's dead. Be nice."

He turns his glare on me then looks back down at the cannibal. "He kidnapped people and ate them for a living." I feel his hand slide along my back, pull me closer to him in a possessive gesture. "If he wasn't already dead, I'd have made him suffer first and I wouldn't have felt bad about it."

In my mind, I hear the gunshot going off, my uncle's brains spattering, and a chill shimmies up my back, despite Quentin's hot touch. "It scares me, how you can turn cold sometimes. How death seems so easy, so cut and dry for you."

His hand disappears and he takes a few steps away from me. Back turned, he says, "When you're filled with so much hate and anger, it's easy to keep a fire inside. It's easy to let it swallow you up, let it burn you. It's cleansing sometimes. You come out a different person. Harder, like steel." He glances over his shoulder. "I have to be hard, Elle. For me"—he turns away again—"for them. Sometimes I don't have the luxury of a soft heart or ethics and morals. I'm a trained Leader. The Manager. Judge. Jury. Executioner. I can't afford remorse." He's quiet for a long moment. "At least, that's what I tell myself. But it's not easy. And their eyes…"

"Haunt you." I finish his thought, remembering Veronica and Nadine and Meems. "You've done the right things up until this point. Even killing Uncle Simon. Don't let what I say make you question that. I'm just jealous. I wish I could handle what I've done as well as you do."

He doesn't answer me. Just begins walking. I hobble after.

Next comes Veronica again, face nearly destroyed. I assume someone struck her, most likely ruptured one of her facial Modifications. Quent avoids looking at her.

Then a boy named Twine I'd gone to school with and a man I don't know.

Four more cannibals.

Karl was shot point-blank in his bedroll and Jayn beaten beyond recognition. "Oh," I breathe, and turn away from them, hiding my face against Quent's chest.

He holds me close, and I feel him fighting not to shake. In rage? Or grief?

After a few moments, I continue on. The last body is farthest from the others and hardest of all. Violet. Not surprisingly, she looks the most prepared for the death that came to her. Perhaps she was ready. Still…

I collapse beside her and stare at her face. Shot in the head. Her eyes are closed and her arms have been laid across her chest. Someone arranged her body. Out of respect? Grief comes hard and fast, making it difficult to breathe. I might have been able to handle the Dolls and the other Aristocrats, but Violet?

Quent stands beside me, face completely closed down, and I just sit there, shaking with rage and hyperventilation. I should be crying, but I think I'm all dried up. Too numb, maybe? Although I feel everything keenly, right down to my bones.

He bends down. Touches my shoulder. "We need to get moving."

I ignore him. "Why?" I gasp the word. "Why would they kill an innocent old woman? She couldn't fight. She could barely breathe."

"Maybe that's just it," Quent says, voice quiet and clipped. "Perhaps she couldn't have kept pace with them, would have dragged them down. They move quickly, I'm told. In and out."

That doesn't help, only makes me close my eyes and shake against the rage inside of me. "She was such a special person."

"I know."

Silence stretches for a long, long time. I stare at Violet's serene features, lovely even with a hole in her head. After what seems like forever, Quent grasps my elbow. "Come on, we can't stay here. They might come back."

"Back?" I say, blindly standing at his tugging grasp. "For what?"

He slides his arm around me, guides me toward a different tunnel. "Considering what they're known for? I can't imagine they'd leave bodies behind for long. I don't want to be here if they do come back after they've secured their prisoners."

The cannibals got that title from something. I glance over my shoulder and watch Violet as we walk away. I want to bury her or burn her. I want to do something to save her from that fate. But what? What could we do? I can't ask Quent to carry all these people back to Kairos and we can't bury them in a rock-hard tunnel.

"Wait," I breathe.

Quent goes still.

"Can't we do something? I can't stand to leave them here like this. Can you?"

His shoulders droop. "No."

An idea occurs to me, from something that I read. "Vikings."

"What?"

"They used to do water burials. We could do that—send them off." I point at the dark body of water at the end of the cave.

Squinting at me, Quent looks less than convinced, but he nods.

Quent drags the bodies toward the pond. Even the cannibals. I try to help, but he reminds me of my leg and, annoyed, I have to sit down and watch him do all the work, which I hate. He keeps lifting his head and inspecting the surrounding cave mouths, as if expecting someone to come at us at any moment, and it makes me twitchy and worried because if they come, I can no longer run.

By the time all the bodies have been brought to the edge of the water, he's sweating and panting and I'm a paranoid mess and angry at myself for being so careless with my leg. Though, when he turns to me and I see the pain in his eyes, I remember my own internal agony and I find forgiveness for myself. People do foolish things in their grief, and sometimes it's not smart and it's not safe. I just have to fix it as soon as possible.

We send the cannibals first, not knowing what to say or do for any of them, but giving each a silent moment of respect, even though neither of us really feels it right now. It's the right thing to do. The Aristocrats come next. The man I don't know. Veronica. Twine. Quent drags them into the deep water, then stands waist deep and says something about each. Things I didn't know that makes each a little more human and a lot less like generic Aristocrats who I've come to judge too harshly.

Body after body gets sent off into the water. I try not to think of ends. Instead, I try to think of those who might still be alive. Bastian and Sadie and their unborn child. The other Dolls. There's Carsai and the other Aristocrats. Delia and Gus…if they weren't caught… I hope that nothing more comes to harm any of them.

Jayn. Then Karl. Quent speaks long and quietly to each of them—saying what, I don't know. I don't try to listen. While I counted each as a friend and ally, they were more to Quent and it's his time to grieve. He pulls them both into the deep water, watches them sink.

Then, he wades back in and grasps Beau by the shoulders of his uniform. He drags him out. Stands there, wrists curled under Beau's limp arms. He starts to speak, but at this point, Quent's ragged voice starts to falter and it's obvious that he's not holding it together well at all, so I carefully wade out and put a hand on his chest. "Quent?"

"I-I can't…"

"Shhh," I whisper, smoothing the hair at the nape of his neck. "It's okay, you don't have to say anything. He knows how much you loved him. Just let him go."

Shaking under my fingers, Quent nods. Collects himself. Continues to drag Beau out. He stands shoulder deep, watching the body sink for what feels like eternity. Finally, he turns and together we slosh back to shore.

I glance down at Violet, who is still lying on the ground waiting her turn to be sent off. "Oh Violet," I whisper, a lump in my throat and tears in my eyes again. "If only you got to live long enough to get what you always hoped for."

Quent rummages in the pack. He pulls out a light-stick, snaps it on, and throws it with all his might into the darkness.

It arcs high, making a whistling noise as it goes, illuminating the pointed stone above us before tumbling down to hit the water with a *thunk*. I watch as it bobs back to the surface, creating a tiny orb of wavering light as it floats.

More follow.

Two light-sticks, half a dozen. Four more.

"Quent?" I ask, concerned that he's throwing away our only source of light. "What are you doing?"

He tosses the last one. Waits for it to splash before turning toward me. The last light-stick glows warm and ruddy between us. "Okay, it's ready."

I turn back to the water, squint. The light-sticks glow dully across the water, creating a wavering banner of winking rainbow light. And then I realize what it reminds me of. "Quent," I breathe.

His smile is slow and subdued. He's exhausted, his eyes dull and his movement weary as he turns to Violet. I bend to help him, taking up some of the weight of Violet so he doesn't have to.

"Your leg," he says.

"It's fine," I grunt against the pain. "I need to do this."

He frowns at me, but nods. And together we draw Violet into the pool. I hold her there for an instant. Then I nod to Quentin, who takes her the rest of the way and drops her into the water.

He comes back and stands beside me.

I think about everything that's sinking into the deep with Violet. Lifetimes of experience and knowledge. "She was a very old woman."

"Four hundred and thirty-two."

I glance at him. "You're so sure?"

He nods. "She was one of the original inhabitants of Evanescence. The last remaining Elder. Everything she knew is dead with her. She deserved better than this. A better death. A better funeral. One where everyone in Evanescence is in attendance and they do a special for her on The Broadcast." His face twists, bitter. "And we give her this."

I take his hand, squeeze it hard. "You gave her the stars, Quentin Cyr. That's the only thing she ever wanted. And for that, I love you all the more."

He turns to me, meets my adoring gaze. And in that time, despite the circumstance and place and all the death, destruction, and pain around us, I feel a well of pure and positive emotion. I love this boy. The real one, not the avatar.

I turn away, stare back at the twinkling water. "That song, the one Violet was humming in the tunnel the other day. What was it called?"

"It's called 'My Way.' It was her favorite, I think."

"My Way," I whisper and then, sad, I smile. I start to hum the song. The sad, slow thing. And as I hum, tears fall for my fallen comrades. For many years lost and for memories forgotten, ambitions foiled, and futures untold.

A moment later, Quent joins me. His low baritone lending to my high soprano. And together we send the dead off to the stars.

chapter seventeen

POST-AMERICAN DATE: 7/7/232

LONGITUDINAL TIMESTAMP: 11:23 P.M.

LOCATION: DISFAVORED TUNNEL SYSTEM

We're quiet as we walk away from the cave of the dead and it remains so until Quentin touches my shoulder. "We should be back at the rebel encampment by now."

"Yes, but it's entirely possible we didn't pick the right tunnel out."

We go a bit farther and the tunnel widens into another cavern that looks very similar to the other, water and all, just smaller.

"Your limping is getting worse."

I look down at my leg, hating that I've been foolish again. My legs are too new to me and I've yet to come to terms with the fact that my mobility is a strange in-between of what I had in Nexis and what I had in Real World. I need to learn a balance and learn it fast, just like I have to learn to use a mask. "Yeah."

"Here," he says, turning and offering me his back. "I'll carry you."

"No." While the idea is tempting, I'm not stupid. "You're just as tired as I am. Let's just rest for a bit."

Quentin looks torn by the idea. It's clear he's about to collapse from exhaustion, but, like me, is apprehensive about remaining in the tunnels as long as we know cannibals are on the loose.

"Just for a little while," I say. "We'll turn the light-stick off. It will be safer that way."

He gives the cave a quick once-over then nods. "All right. Just for a bit."

Voices and bright light wake me. I sit bolt upright and scramble to find my gun, my mind trying to pinpoint the last spot I saw Quentin as I struggle for my feet.

As soon as I'm out of my sleeping bag, something hits me hard in the side. A kick. I fly back, knock my head against the rock. For a moment, I wobble on hands and knees, blinking to see through the blood-red sparks and night-black fireworks in my vision. I lift my head, only to be soundly punched in the cheek. As I collapse to the ground, I taste blood. And then I feel adrenaline rage course through my veins, screaming to fight. I struggle to push myself up.

Whoever it is grabs my hair, yanks me to unsteady feet. I lash out with my fists, but he twists his hand in my hair and tosses me back to the ground. He kicks me again, right in the stomach. This time it hurts so bad that my lungs collapse and I can't think. He uses that time to roll me onto my face and bind my hands and legs behind me with something that bites into my skin.

As soon as I'm bound, he abandons me. Fighting the pain

in my stomach and face, I struggle against my bonds and roll around to see that he's turning to engage a new assailant who is coming at him, screaming. I don't know who it is, I can hardly see beyond my tears of pain and the near darkness on my side of the cave.

Someone touches my arm and I gasp, but their hand finds my mouth, silencing me from a scream. "Don't make a sound." The voice is Quentin's.

I feel him begin to untie me, but someone flies at him from the side, tackling him to the ground. They tussle, rolling around. I hear them splash into the water. As they fight, I desperately tug at my bonds, attempting to free my hands so that I can get to the gun sticking out of the front pocket of my pack.

My heart is pounding. I can barely breathe. I try to watch the conflict in the darkness, keep glancing at where I know my pack is. Blood trickles into my palms, yet I can't feel the pain my restraints must be causing me.

A gunshot going off nearby stills me. I hear a muffled yelp, a body hitting the ground.

For a long moment, I lay paralyzed with fear at who might have fallen.

The shot came from the direction of where my assailant and his attacker were struggling.

Quentin and his attacker renew their efforts, fighting hard and dirty, sending up sprays of water that splash onto me. It seems like he might have the upper hand, but then someone comes running from where the body just went down and jumps into the fray. Two against one, and I don't know if the odds are for or against Quentin.

"No!" I scream. "Stop! Stop it!"

A few more minutes of fighting, with me rolling about and ripping ravines into my skin to free myself as the three in the water thrash. I can hear the sound of fist meeting flesh, of muffled grunts of pain. The newcomer holds Quentin while the other pounds him.

"Stop it!" I howl. "You're gonna kill him." I begin a frenzy of tugging to free myself, rolling and thumping on the ground, sending rocks into the water. I knock my pack and my light-stick tumbles to the ground and flickers last bits of energy as it rolls toward the water then dies.

But it's enough. It's enough to see the bloody face of Quentin restrained. Enough to see his legs give out and his body sink to the water. All fight gone.

Yet they continue to kick and punch him.

Unable to breathe or find my voice, I turn away. Shaking comes. Desperate gasps that bring no air to lungs crushed in dread. I need to go to him, but I have no more strength.

Not again. I can't do this again. I already lost him in Nexis. I can't lose him in Real World, too.

Please don't be dead.

Real World is for keeps.

Please don't be dead.

I'll fall apart.

I'll break into a thousand pieces and never come back together.

I squeeze my eyes tight, trying to block out the sounds of his assailants beating him, even though he's not fighting back anymore.

Blood. So much blood on his face.

Images of his blood on my hands and in my mouth play over and over again. Memories of his death in Nexis. Me turning. Me running from him. Leaving him to die when I should have stayed there with him. Died beside him as I should.

Hysterical, I find my voice again and start to yell for him. "No!" The one word cuts through the cave and echoes around like a siren. "Get up. Fight!"

No answer. I lift my head, trying to find him, dead or alive. There's more light and the sound of more people behind me. Someone must have lit a light-stick behind me. His assailants are moving away. There's a dark lump in the water. Unmoving. I squint at him. "Quent," I squeak. "Quent, get up." Nothing. I stare harder, willing him to do something. Anything.

I wriggle to get to him, to get closer, calling his name. "Quent. Quentin. Quentin Balthazar Cyr." No answer. I get to the edge of the water, my face half submerged, see him facedown.

I stare at him expectantly, telling myself he's just playing possum, that he'll lift his head any moment. But then I realize that too much time has passed, that no one can hold their breath for so long, that people can't breathe with their faces submerged in water. If they hadn't beaten him to death, they've certainly drowned him.

"No," I whimper.

The dismay suffocates me, makes me gag. I'll drown like him. I have to. I can't live without him.

The reality of it hits like a ton of foundation steel. Collapsing my ribs, making my spine curl inward and my bones brittle to snapping. Everything falls apart, my body and mind. The world.

I stare on, tears falling and gasps making bubbles as I struggle to free my hands and feet. I have to get to him, have to turn him over, make him breathe. Even though I know he's dead. My body still battles to save him. Like reflex, a primal thing.

My screams slowly die to moans and sobs of despair.

Someone walks toward me. I hear the footsteps, see the growing circle of light from the light-stick he carries. He wades out, turns the body over. I can't see what he sees, he's standing between us. He stares for a long moment, whispering something. Prayer? Then pushes Quentin's body away so that it drifts into the blackness. Rejecting him. The reality of what I already know seeps all the way in, and I close my eyes and collapse, all the fight now gone out of me.

Stillness. Emptiness. Darkness.

It's all over. No point in living anymore.

When I'm shaken, I open my eyes. It's the man with the light-stick. He bares sharpened teeth at me.

Cannibal.

I understand what he is instantly, but it doesn't seem to bother me.

He's going to eat me.

That's okay. I'd give him some spices and salt, make my bitter flesh more palatable. I want him to do it fast, make the pain stop. Death would be better than being alive… Without him.

When I don't shy away or flinch, when I don't even blink, the cannibal's lips close over his teeth and he frowns at me as if he's disappointed I'm not playing into his scare tactic. Why should I? Quent's dead, again. This time in real life. There's no point in anything at all.

The cannibal drags me to my feet, cuts the bonds around my legs. I don't try to escape. There's no longer anyone to chase me. I fall back to the floor, no will left in my shaking limbs. I can't stand.

The cannibal narrows his eyes at me as if confused. I can't stop looking at where Quent's body is slowly drifting off into the hollow darkness.

Don't leave me. Not again.

The cannibal hauls me back to my feet and shoves me. "Get moving."

Blinking, I turn away from the empty black of where his

body disappeared and I look at the cannibal. Then, I look around, lethargic and half nightmare-dreaming. I take a step, drag my damaged leg after me. As I limp, I see the body of a Disfavored rebel on the ground. I can tell by his uniform and his face—I'd seen it in the complex but never met him. He must have been the one who tried to save me. I turn away, saddened though I didn't know him.

I realize Aaron or Faulk or maybe both must have gone back to the complex, brought reinforcements and possibly a search team. But they must all be dead or caught now because this cannibal is collecting me and the fight is over. There's a grouping of light-sticks up ahead. Most likely there are more cannibals there. Maybe they're going to flay me and eat me right now.

A stronger need to survive, despite feeling like half of my mind and body floated away with Quent, kick-starts my brain and makes me start looking for options to escape.

My captor suddenly tugs on my bonds and lets out a strangled *ooph*, then there's a sickening crack and his hand slides away. I stand there, eyes closed for a long moment, but nothing else happens. I open my eyes, blink. It's so quiet.

Someone touches my bloody wrist.

I can't help the sudden joy that overwhelms me, but it's salted with dread.

"You're a ghost," I whimper.

"Shhh," he whispers. I feel the cold metal of a knife slip between my wrists and the plastic cords that are now buried in my skin.

"I saw you die." My whisper voice is frantic and airy. I'm just imagining this.

The cord snaps and my hands fall to either side of me.

"It takes more than that to kill someone like me, Elle. You'll figure that out one day." He grabs my arm and tugs me backward. "Come on, they'll notice us any moment."

Avoiding looking, because I don't want this charade to end when I realize he's not real, I turn to follow. I stumble over the body of the dead cannibal. As Quent catches and rights me, I try not to focus on the body, to know that Quent killed him. I stare at the ground as I hobble after Quent.

Even though I can't see anything, Quent apparently can. He executes a flawless retreat, circumventing the water and leading me into one of the smaller tunnels off of this cave. I can tell it's a tunnel by the way my breath and scraping footsteps seem to echo back at me on all sides. Time passes and we move farther and farther away.

Away from the hands of the cannibals. I can't help wondering if that last cannibal was leading me toward where the Aristocrats were being held captive, if we're walking away from them now. Trying to find strength, I touch Quent's back. His fingers gently squeeze on my arm, though I feel him starting to shake.

Is he scared? I rub away goose bumps at the thought. "I'm glad you're alive." I don't ask how. Not yet, anyway. Not sure if I want to know. I don't think I care. Even if he's a hallucination brought on by severe trauma, I don't want to pry. I'm just happy he's here. "Where are we going?"

"Out," Quent mutters.

After taking a deep breath, I let it out. "Do you think the others were back there?"

He's quiet for a long moment. "I don't know. Maybe."

"We have to save them."

"Yes."

"Will Mac and the others help?"

More silence. "It would be risky for them. They'd need a really good reason to stick their necks out that far. Just about as good of a reason as the Disfavored would have needed to feed the Aristocrats. We'll think of something. But first, we have to regroup, figure out a plan."

I think of the filed teeth of the man he just killed. "Those were cannibals, Quent. The longer we take to get everyone back, the more likely there will be fewer of them when we return for them."

His fingers flinch on my skin. "Why do I get the feeling you don't trust my judgment?"

"I want to." I think of Nexis, and how Nadine and the others pointed out that I always backed him, even when his plans were self-centered or led to chaos. "But sometimes trusting you—supporting you—has led to regretful things. I've learned to question you."

"That's probably wise. I can't blame you."

We don't talk after that. We just keep walking as the distance between us and the others grows and I can't help but worry. "Where do you think they're being taken?"

"I'm not certain. I don't know any more about the cannibals than you do. Zane tried learning more when he was doing his documentary, but the Disfavored don't know much, either. Just that they come at night in strange automobiles, steal people from their beds, and disappear into The Waste."

"No one has ever fought them?"

"The Disfavored keep a night guard and do try to fight them. They had a wall, but they had to break it down to use for new homes as the city expanded. They used these tunnels to hide, but I guess the cannibals know about them now. Anyway, it's not as though they just roll over and let it happen, the Disfavored do their best."

"And no one has ever tried to follow the cannibals? Get the people they kidnap back?"

"The Waste is not a forgiving place. There are very few vehicles in Kairos, most owned by Mac and none equipped for fighting against the likes of what the cannibals drive. And from what I understand, there are a lot of cannibals out there. Any rescue mission would be outnumbered, outgunned, and outmaneuvered."

"What about something covert?"

"That would require intel on the cannibals, and no one has ever returned from their encampment."

As we walk my adrenaline fades and exhaustion and pain seep into my bones. My head pounds, radiating out through the side of my face where I was struck. My ribs and stomach ache, making it hard to breathe and sending a shooting knife of pain up my side every time I take a step. My hands are throbbing and I feel like someone has taken a saw to both my wrists.

If I hurt this bad, how must Quent feel? He'd been beaten unconscious, left face down in the water for at least ten minutes. "How are you still alive and walking?"

He's quiet before he says, "I'm glad I got to see how you reacted to learning that Gus is a cyborg. It gives me a lot more confidence now that I have to talk about what I am. But knowing how you feel about some things, I'm still terrified to tell you."

I stop short. "What does that mean?"

I hear him turn toward me, feel the heat of him as he steps close and takes both my hands in his. "I know you've come to hate the Aristocracy and everything it represents. You frown on Mods and Alts and Customization."

I swallow, uncertain where he's going.

A breath escapes him, washes over me. He still smells like mint. How does his breath still smell like mint when he's this far from the dome? When the nanites should be dead because his G-chip doesn't work. "I'm a monster. Just like Gus, but in different ways. Do you understand what I mean?"

I shake my head.

He lowers our joined hands between us and he starts to light up. Starting at the tips of his fingers, all his fiber-optic inlays begin to illuminate as if we were still standing under a fully operating dome. I gasp as the rainbow of luminescence travels up his arms, glowing under the fabric of his clothing and then his face. It breaks here and there, spreading around dark patches—places where he was struck, where there is bruising. Until it's like his whole body shows an intricate pattern of fiery veins. And then his Argence follows, making the skin glisten something different around the veins. His hair relights and begins to wave despite the still air, eyes explode to life, like two mirrorballs catching a thousand nonexistent LED bulbs.

His face is swelling in places, bleeding in others. I can see spots where the lines of his inlays have snapped, creating darkness and imperfection on an otherwise perfectly symmetrical work of art. His skin is torn and still bloodied from where he's been beaten, but even now it's healing, leaving fresh pink patches, the last remnants of a Modification insert underneath his quickly knitting flesh. Plastic and metal grafted onto the skull underneath.

I feel my jaw drop. I can't help staring at him.

I can see him as if he were standing in a spotlight, except he *is* the spotlight, throwing glitter and rainbows all around us. It's beautiful. And horrible. "How," I say, but my voice cracks and I have to clear my throat and try again. "How is this possible?"

He directs his gaze down at our hands, dimming the light around us. "I'm not normal."

I scoff. "No shit."

A chuckle escapes him, obviously pleased that I've learned one of his phrases. He shakes his head. "You're not backing away screaming. That's a good sign."

Taking a step closer, I duck and meet his downturned eyes. "Why would I?"

He shrugs.

"I'm not like that."

Gnawing at his lip, he looks off into a corner. "I suppose because I hate it about myself, I don't expect anyone else to think any different."

Tentative, I reach up and gently touch his cheek. The lines are split here and it's swelling. He's so warm. I wonder if it's a fever or if it's from the strike or maybe it's all those nanos working furiously to fix him. "I saw them beating you."

"My Mods," he explains, touching his chest, "aren't just to make me look perfect. They're meant to make me better, too. Protect me, make me strong. My bones, my muscles, even my skin…it's not like normal. And the nanites that live in my body, they're not normal, either."

I run my hand down the side of his face, his neck, tracing the lines to the collar of his uniform. And then, because I have to see, I grasp the pull on his zipper and draw it down past his navel. Quentin doesn't stop me, he just watches me study him as his skin is revealed. I tug the Disfavored uniform away from his shoulders, let it slide over his arms. It pools at his wrists, around his waist.

Despite already having seen Quentin without a shirt, it's different close up and with all his Mods and Alts lit up.

"I used to tell Delia you looked like an angel," I whisper.

He blinks at me. "What?"

Smirking, I lift my hand and press it against his chest. "I used to have a crush on you, couldn't you tell?"

His Argence flushes pink across his cheeks and he looks away from me. "I couldn't."

"I presented myself before you. To dance. The night I died. You turned me away and Gus broke my holo-mask."

Avoiding my eyes, he tucks his chin. "I couldn't dance with you."

"Why?"

Lifting his chin, he meets my eyes again. The diamond Alterations in his eyes dim until they're the amber I've come to associate with him. "Because you weren't for me, and I wasn't for you. You were going to marry Zane, and I had to marry Carsai."

Taking a deep breath, I trace my fingers along the cut planes of his stomach. "Not now, though. Now you could dance with me if you wanted to." Not even hours ago, someone had pummeled this stomach until I was certain every rib was broken. I wonder what's under this skin. What did his father put in him to make it so that he could withstand a beating?

His hand comes up, closes over mine, stilling it against his chest. "I don't want to dance with you."

Confused, I look up at him.

As he meets my gaze, his other hand brushes my face, knuckles smoothing against my jawbone. He leans closer, whispers, "I want to kiss you."

I curl my hand under his, grasping his fingers, step closer. "So kiss me."

Quent leans in, takes my mouth with his. Firm and supple, demanding yet gentle. The hand on my jaw slides backward into my hair, cupping my neck. The other tugs my hand down, pulling it back toward his spine, drawing me tighter to him still. I grasp his shoulder with my free hand, tracing his inlays with my fingers. Memorizing the pattern and heat they emit.

My fingers find the medical tape of the bandage he's wearing and I pull away. How is it that he had the stuffing beaten out of him yet he's been battling an infection for days? I start picking at the edges of the tape.

He turns his head into my hair, watching me, and his voice is amused and deep so close to my ear. "What are you doing?"

"I want to see." I pull up the tape, draw away the bandage. Underneath, there is no longer a wound. The skin is smooth and flawless, not even scarred. I touch it because I can't seem to believe it. "I don't understand how you work."

"That makes two of us."

"What?"

He cocks his head, touches his stomach. "I didn't know I could do that. Withstand being beaten like that. Didn't know I could breathe under water, either."

"You can breathe under water?" I repeat, aghast.

His brows knit. "I think so. I mean, I came to and I was face down in the water. That means I didn't drown, right?" He draws away and leans against the wall. He lifts the hand he broke punching an aerovator door—now perfectly healed like nothing happened—and stares at it, expression haunted. "It's scary, learning about this stuff."

"You didn't know?"

He shakes his head. "My mother wasn't allowed involvement in Customizing my genes. It was entirely my father's doing. And once I was old enough for Mods and Alts, I'd go to bed one night and wake up...changed."

"That's why you have trouble sleeping, isn't it?"

His mouth turns down and I know that's an affirmative.

Hateful acid burns at the back of my throat for Quent's father. And yet... "I want to despise him for what he did to you, but at the same time, what he did to you saved your life."

He closed his eyes. "I know. I hate what I am, what he made me. But it has its benefits, I suppose."

"You're superhuman."

He wrinkles his nose. "Don't call me that. I'm no different than anyone else."

I step close to him again. "But you are. Not saying it doesn't make it any less true."

Pouting at the ground, he mutters, "I don't want to be. I just want to be normal. I want to be deserving of someone like you."

A bitter laugh escapes me. "Me?" I think of his breath that smells like mint, tastes like mint. And mine, which is probably awful since I haven't brushed my teeth in hours. "Quent, you're perfect, what are you talking about?"

He shakes his head. "Depends what your definition of perfect is. To me, this"—he gestures down at himself—"is disgusting."

"You're not disgusting," I growl, defensive. It bothers me that he sees himself like this. That he's got such awful self-esteem.

He bares his teeth. "I don't hate myself or anything. I just hate what has been done to me."

Stepping close to him, I slip my fingers around his waist, run them along his spine. "You're perfect. No matter what they do to you, you'll always be perfect. For me."

His dimples appear. "Sweet talker."

I shrug. "Someone has to do it. Now, can we focus on the important stuff, please?"

Closing his eyes, he rests his head back against the wall. "We're not storming the cannibal camp. That's suicide."

"I-I didn't say anything about that."

His smile widens and he looks down into my eyes. "You didn't have to." His hands slide over my back, returning my embrace. "I know it's hard, but we have to get back to Mac and the others. We can get whatever help there is to be had then. This is bigger than the both of us."

I open my mouth to argue, but he catches my jaw with a finger. "Until then, we're going to rest. You're practically dead on your feet, and I want to take a look at your injuries."

I purse my lips. "I'm fine."

"You're not," he argues, his fingers sneaking up my arms and catching my wrists. "You're going to let me dress these and you're not going to fight me on it, are you?" He lifts a questioning brow.

Grumbling to myself, I roll my eyes. "No."

"Good," he says, tugging me closer. "Maybe if you behave yourself I'll give you a lollipop when we're all done."

I chuckle. And then I wince in pain. "Ow…"

"Glad we agree," he says darkly. "Come on, let's get somewhere safe."

chapter eighteen

POST-AMERICAN DATE: 7/8/232

LONGITUDINAL TIMESTAMP: 11:06 A.M.

LOCATION: DISFAVORED TUNNEL SYSTEM

It takes three trips up random tunnels to find an actual exit and by then, Quent is carrying me. This exit leads up a pair of rough stone steps and into a cellar that smells of dirt and rotten potatoes, even though potatoes are a thing of the far past. I lean heavily on him as he sets me down outside in the biting light of the sun hanging high above Kairos.

"Masks," I remind, pulling my own up over my nose. There are smudges of dirt and blood on it and it hurts my face where it lays across the bruise I got from being struck.

Quent's breath hisses audibly as he inhales and examines the sky. "I wonder where we are."

"Closer to the wall," I venture, taking in the height of the stacked buildings above us. I point opposite the shadow of the wall. "This way should lead back to the rebels."

Fingers flying to his gun, Quent glances around the various buildings. "I'd like to take care of your injuries first."

I nod, knowing that neither my leg nor my resilience

against the pain I feel because of it will last much longer.

Quentin lets out a breath of a laugh, then turns to me, grinning. "We're in luck!" I try to ask what or where, but he scoops me into his arms and trots up the narrow street and into one of the buildings. I can just make out the sand-battered sign hanging over our heads as he carries me over the threshold like a bride. Gaming House.

A gaming house? Eager, I turn to the room, interested to see what one looks like. It's set up almost like a barber shop. There are a dozen chairs set at intervals in two rows down the side walls. They're nothing fancy, rudimentary and hooked into boxes with large locking mechanisms so none of the VR equipment can be stolen. In the middle there is a counter for a clerk of some type, I'm betting. We're in a small cell with iron bars, a kiosk on either side of us. This must be some sort of security measure.

Quentin sets me down on one of the kiosk counters and punches a code into the security pad on the iron door. It beeps and opens. He carries me in and sets me on one of the chairs. I hear him punching codes on one of the boxes.

"You want to play? Now?"

Chuckling, he glances up from the innards of the box. "No, I'm just borrowing some equipment."

"Oh. How do you know the codes?"

"I'm a Cyr, remember?"

"Right." Rolling my eyes, I go back to examining the room. Black tile floor, brown synthetic chairs with pneumatic adjustments. As expected, there are no windows. Hung around the walls are propaganda posters and I frown at them as I read them.

I recognize the people in the pictures. There's one of my father and in big letters it says, "In Drexel We Trust."

Another is of me and says, "Ellani the Savior."

There's one of President Cyr—"Down with the Elite Regime!"

There's one of a Disfavored man standing in the square at Citizen's Way, arm upraised, "We built this city!"

A gaming chair sitting inside an oversize set of VR headphones, "Redux is the way to play."

Another just says, "Are you ready to start again?"

"All these posters," I say. "What is this?"

Quentin glances around. "Images from the game, I think. This version."

"Redux?"

"It's called Redux out here. Not Nexis."

I frown. "Why would they change the name of the game?"

He continues pulling wires and mechanisms out of the console as he speaks. "The game for Aristocrats was to bring everyone together. A Nexis. But out here, it meant something else."

"Did my father know?"

He looks at me. "It was his idea." He starts picking through his pack. "Of course, it was probably your mother's first. But he's the one who named this version Redux. He's the one who programmed the beta version of this game as well." He pulls out the small tool box and sets it on the console.

I look away, stare at the In Drexel We Trust poster once more. "What were you thinking?" I muse, staring at my father's Custom face. Nexis, a game of flippant wants and needs for the Aristocrats. Redux, a game of discontent and revolution for the Disfavored. If he was involved in instigating the uprising, then Dad knew about the plan to plant the Anansi Virus, my role in planting it, and the rebel infiltration of the city.

The first protocol, the one that caused the power outage, was meant to allow the rebels to infiltrate the city. And the second protocol, the one that short circuited the G-Chips, was Uncle Simon's doing. But could the third protocol, the one that shut down the city, have been Dad's doing? But why would Dad have schemed to kill the city and then let a horde of murderous Disfavored in? "This doesn't add up. Where's the redeeming factor?"

"What?" Quent asks, coming to my side with an armful of parts he's stripped from the console.

I turn to him. "What exactly were the Tricksters trying to do?"

"I can only theorize. It's something to ask Mom." He pats the chair. "Lay back."

Adjusting myself, I lay back in the chair. Quent hits a pedal with his foot and the chair reclines, bringing him into focus. He reaches up and turns on a light. "There's electricity here?"

"Batteries," he says dismissively as he sets the parts up on the side of the chair.

Unfastening my pants, I continue talking. "Who were the original Tricksters? My mom. The spider."

"My mom, the fox."

I slide my pants down to my ankles. "But you're the fox, too?" When he doesn't respond, I say, "Quent?"

"Sorry." His eyes flash up and he gives me the devilish Game Gus grin. "I got distracted." He goes back to working on the parts. "I'm being groomed to replace her, just like your father took on spider and then you after him."

"Who else?"

"Zane's father. He was coyote. Now that he's dead, Zane is coyote."

That explains Zane's tattoo. "So, who are rabbit and crow?"

He leans forward and starts examining my leg. "Your guess is as good as mine."

"If Zane's father was coyote, then these Trickster personas

came with the refugees from Adagio." I watch him frown at my leg as he starts gently poking and prodding. "Do you think they're the ones who destroyed Adagio?"

He glances up at me and we stare at each other for a very long time. Finally, he looks away and his white hair falls across his forehead. "Are you implying that they brought the horrors of the Undertunnel upon themselves on purpose? That my mother fed my brother his own father just to keep him alive on purpose?"

I grip the arms of the chair, knowing I'm stepping on hallowed ground when it comes to Quentin's mother. Whatever Kit Cyr is, she's not the sort of person who would inspire such faith from the man I love without good reason. And, to be honest, I can't imagine that my own parents would have planned the mass genocide of so many people, either. I don't know my mother, but my father wasn't like that. He loved humanity and all its potential.

"No," I finally say. "What I'm trying to say is that maybe something went horribly wrong with what they tried in Adagio and perhaps, just maybe, they tried a revised version of it here."

"And it failed again?"

"I'm not sure. It's hard to tell without knowing what their goal actually is."

"So, it's back to getting answers from Mom." He leans to the side and retrieves a slap-patch from the first aid kit by his foot and smacks it on himself.

"What are you doing?"

He flicks his wrist a couple of times, testing for numbness.

"Quent?"

"Don't worry about it." He reaches for a scalpel.

I reach out and grab his wrist. When his eyes flash up I glower at him. "What are you doing?"

He relaxes his arm and I let him go. "I need a couple of

pieces of fiber-optic cable."

The gears click together then. "So you're just going to cut them out of your own hide?" I demand.

"It's not like I need them anymore."

"I refuse to let you rip yourself apart on my account."

"It's my body, Elle. I'll do what I want with it."

"I'll never speak to you again," I threaten, stubborn.

Pursing his lips, he puts the scalpel down and lets out a long, exasperated breath. "My entire life, I have not been able to control anything that happened to my own body. Everything that has been done to me, put inside of me, was done for a stupid reason that helped no one with anything. And now? You're telling me I can't make my first decision with my own body to help the woman I love and the people I want to save, because you're going to be guilty about me being in ten seconds of pain over fiber-optic inlays I don't care about, are useless, and won't be missed? Is that about right?"

I look away, ashamed of myself. "When you put it that way."

"Good. Now help me do this or don't watch."

Knowing he can't do the safest, cleanest job on himself with only one hand, I offer my hand and accept the tweezers he puts in it. "You should have picked a different section."

He rolls up his sleeve and pokes at the inlays on his bicep. "There's only one more slap-patch and that's for you, so it's the arm or nothing." He picks up the knife and positions it.

"Not that one." He pauses and, blushing, I explain myself. "I-I really like that one."

"You can hardly see it."

"Still…there's enough pattern left."

Rolling his eyes, he positions over another one and, glancing to make sure I approve of his choice, he cuts a small T shape into his flesh, right where the cable splits from the main unit mounted on his shoulder, effectively severing it from the other cables. He slips the blade under the cable. I look away as blood starts to seep down his pale arm. "Are you gonna grab it or throw up?"

Licking my lips, I lean forward and grab the end of the cable with the tweezers. "I can't believe I'm doing this."

"Can you blot that? I can't see where it goes."

Wiping his blood away with my sleeve, I grimace at how much this reminds me of his death in Nexis. He follows the cable and cuts right where it ends in a lovely whirling pattern.

"Okay, go ahead and pull."

I firm my grasp on the tweezers and tug a little. His skin moves as the cable comes out an inch. It makes my skin crawl and I really do feel bile rising to my throat this time. I swallow hard, take a deep breath, and yank.

He yelps, but I feel the cable come free and tap wetly against my bare leg. I drop the tweezers and shake my hands around. If I wasn't injured, I'd get up and do a complete gross-out dance.

Shaking his head, Quent chuckles at me as he goes right on to another cable. "You're cute."

Regaining myself, I pick the bloody cable up between two fingers and place it off to the side. "Glad this entertains you."

"Go for it."

I pick up the tweezers and grip the piece he's just freed.

An hour later, I sit quiet and patient as Quent works on repairing my leg. "I'm bored."

"Where's your bracelet? Read some of those sonnets I gave you."

Sighing, I say, “I left it with Delia so she could read something I had stored on it.”

“Do you know how hard it was to find those sonnets?” he demands.

“Relax, I took them out.” I pat my pocket for emphasis. “Keep them right here, close to my heart.”

“Bet you haven’t even read them yet,” he mutters.

I reach out and touch his arm. “I don’t need to.”

The corner of his mouth twitches and I smile with him, warmed by the reality of finding him against all odds. I met him in a game, for heaven’s sake! And we still managed to come together in Real World, despite the strangest circumstances.

“You ever miss it?” I wonder. “Nexis, I mean.”

“Every day. Was the most freedom I ever had. It was like dropping a five-ton ball and chain every time I went in.”

“I got that impression from you.” I giggle. I glance around the room. “You think it was like that for the Disfavored, too? I used to see them lined up outside the gaming houses.”

“I’m sure it was. The objective of the game was different, but it still had to play on the side of their desires. It wouldn’t have been addicting in the way the Tricksters needed it to be.”

I nod. “I think… I think I’d like to see.”

He lifts his chin. “Hm?”

“After he died, I went into Nexis to feel closer to Dad. But he had this whole other side to him I never knew about until after the game. I’d like to play Redux.”

It takes him a moment to realize what I’m asking. “What? Now?”

I shrug. “Why not? How much longer do you have on my leg?”

“A couple of hours at least. This is intricate work.”

“Do you need me conscious for it?”

He shakes his head.

"Then will you hook me up?"

Brow lowered, he scrutinizes me for a few heartbeats. "The Main Frame of Evanescence is down, Elle, it may not even work."

"It's worth a try at least. Come on, please?"

He shakes his head but says, "Okay." He lifts his finger in warning. "But don't go falling in love with anyone in there."

Giggling, I push his hand away. "Of course not."

part five:

ELLA TUGS THE THREADS

chapter nineteen

POST-AMERICAN DATE: 7/8/232

LONGITUDINAL TIMESTAMP: 3:32 P.M.

LOCATION: REDUX

I'm lying under a dome sky. Not the blue sky with clouds I've come to recognize from Nexis. I'm not in the white room I started out in when I first entered Nexis. Perhaps when you start a new game after playing once you don't get taken to the Oracle and her acolytes. Perhaps that's only in Nexis. Perhaps that was an episode only Tricksters of Pre-Anansi Virus experienced.

I sit up. I'm on a green lawn, in a huge garden. Lush rose bushes gush in full bloom all around me. White, red, yellow, and every color in between. Fat bumble bees, vibrant butterflies, and sparkling dragonflies flit from plant to plant. I hear water burbling nearby. I get to my feet wondering if this is a type of Utopia Zone.

I'm not in my warrior costume like before. Now I'm in a midnight-blue gown, one that looks like it belongs in Evanescence and from the looks of it? One I designed myself back in my second year at Paramount. I remember really liking this dress because I think it's the first dress that actually drew some attention from the Elite attendees of my school.

Slowly, I walk between bushes. I lean down and examine a flower. It smells as delicate and feels as velvety soft as the bouquets of roses Gus used to sometimes buy for me in Nexis. The VR in this version is just as detailed and perfect, the sensory projections just the same.

I find the source of the sound of water. A lovely fountain set into a clearing in what I'm seeing is a geometric pattern to the rose garden. The stone of the fountain is as white as the marble in the Oracle's temple. The statue from whose urn the water is flowing into the large stone basin is of a woman. My mother. At the base of the fountain, sitting with a book in his hand and a small teacup of something steaming, is my father.

He's dressed in an old sort of outfit, something I remember seeing in Canal Town back in Nexis, although the color set for this is a somber black and white.

"Dad?" I ask.

He looks up, smiles. "Well hello, Ella."

I swallow a fat lump in my throat. It's so good to see the handsome Custom features of my father, to see those warm eyes and that sparkling grin. I take a step, ready to run to him, throw my arms around him. But I remember how I'd thought the Oracle was my mother and she wasn't. She just knew me. And perhaps this Dad look-alike is the same. "Are you really him?"

He glances down at both his arms. "Last time I checked. But then, we're never the equivalent of the bodies we're given, are we? You've learned that this past year, haven't you?"

Either this game is very clever, able to read my memories, or this man is actually my father. But how?

As if reading my thoughts, he says, "G-Corp has been able to download people onto the Main Frame since PA 135, but it was kept secret from the general public. They just… Copied and uploaded at will at various intervals throughout one's life."

I come closer to him. Sit beside him. It's everything I can do not to lunge at him. "So, you're really you."

In answer, he reaches out to me and pulls me against him. A sob escapes me and I fling my arms around him, wrapping him tight, so tight that no one could pull me away if they tried.

"Oof, you've gotten strong."

I ease up and, giggling, pull away. "Yeah, sorry. I've been working out." I flex my arms to show my muscles.

He lifts a brow, impressed. "You? Working out?"

"I know, right? It wasn't my decision, either. Meems practically forced me."

His face grows grave. "Android boot camp. I can only imagine."

I laugh again. I'm smiling so hard it hurts my face, but I can't stop. "It's so good to see you."

He reaches out, tweaks my chin. "You, too."

"Back up, Warren, I want to see her, too."

Startled, I glance up at the voice that came from behind us. There's no one there but the statue.

"You'd get a better view if you came down off that pedestal of yours and actually talked to your daughter like a grown-up, Cleopatra Drexel."

To my utter dismay, the statue moves. She slumps, rolls her eyes, and lets out a sigh like the most dramatic teenage Aristocrat I've ever seen. Then, she abruptly drops her urn into the fountain. It splashes, making water slosh out the side of the basin so Dad and I both get soaked. Then she lifts her skirts, steps down off her pedestal, and walks through the water.

Wide-eyed, I gawp at her when she transforms stone-to-flesh as she steps over the lip of the basin. She shakes her legs like a discerning cat, drops her skirts, and smoothes them. "There. You happy?"

"Minus a wet behind?" Dad asks, leaning in and kissing her temple. "Very."

Mom turns her gray eyes on me and draws away. "Let's have a look at you."

I feel myself straighten and stiffen with anxious tension as she steps around me, scrutinizing and examining with the eyes of a painter. I follow her with my gaze. Medium build with ample curvature and what I learned is called "meat on one's bones" when I was living in Discoland, my mother cuts a voluptuous form. Like me, her skin is a medium-brown color, her springy curls about thirty hexadecimals darker. Although my skin is a few shades lighter and my hair a little darker and my body a little more lithe and leaner—from my Custom father, no doubt.

Our eyes are the same, our brows. I have Dad's nose, her cheek bones. His mouth.

Finally, Mom straightens and looks to Dad. "She's shorter than I hypothesized. There's an obvious difference between her avatar and her Real World form. Do you think that's going to matter to them?"

Dad shrugs.

"Matter to who?" I ask.

Mom blinks at me. "To the Disfavored, dear. They've come to know you one way, we don't want them suspicious of you." She crosses her arms, examines me again. "I am pleased with how well I did, though. They're almost exactly the same." She elbows Dad in the side. "See, I told you she'd lose those chubby cheeks of hers." She leans in conspiratorially and whispers, "He wanted me to make you chubby."

Dad rolls his eyes. "Oh for heaven's sake, Cleo, don't tell her that. She'll be demanding Mods in seconds flat."

"Of course she won't. She's changed, our Ella, haven't you dear?"

"Um, I'm not sure I follow."

"Of course you don't," Dad says. "No one has explained anything to you. Well then, come along. You'll get a chance to be yourself in Redux for a while, see what your other self has been up to. Not something you get to do every day."

"Other self?"

"He's talking about your avatar."

Dreading the implication of what he's implying, I loop my hand around Dad's offered arm and follow him through the garden and out under an arch that leads into Evanescence. As I glance back, I realize we're in the location where the Imperial Garden is, but instead of the holographic garden there's now a real one.

"You," I begin. "You're talking like a day hasn't passed since you died."

Dad stops short, blinks at me. "I'm dead?"

At my horrified jaw drop, he starts guffawing.

"Joking! Joking!" he howls, cackling.

"Oh, you're awful," Mom mutters. She looks to me. "We're both dead, we know."

"But… You're talking like you know what's been going on," I reason.

"That's because we do," Dad says. "Or relatively. Whatever we can get from the Internetwork. We live in the system now."

I open my mouth, feeling like I should somehow respond to that, but the reality of it is just too much to even question. Quent did say this was possible. He wasn't kidding when he challenged me by asking if I'd bring my parents back if I could give them bodies. I really could do it. The thought is overwhelming.

The city is structured much like I remember it, except on

the holo-screens which were flashing Persevere last time I was in the city, there is now my face, Dad's face. It's the posters from the Gaming House.

In Drexel We Trust.

Ella the Savior.

A group of children run past us on Citizen's Way and they make some sort of hand signal to us as they pass. They run into the square, where a large statue of me has been erected, my foot planted on what looks suspiciously like President Cyr's head.

"What is this?" I whisper.

"This is Redux," Mom says. "Sort of a Nexis 2.0."

"2.0?"

"A better version."

"Better is relative," Dad says. "It's a…well, I don't want to say brainwash version. It's just highly persuasive."

I glance back and forth between the two of them. "And just what were you trying to convince these people?"

Mom blinks. "Were?"

"Yeah, were, because no one's playing this game anymore, Mom. All the Disfavored have moved into the city."

Her face explodes with joy and she claps her hands together. "Wonderful!"

"Wonderful?" I repeat. "Do you have any idea what the hell has just happened in Real World?"

The joyful faces of my parents fall a bit as they see my rage.

"Everyone is dead!" I scream. "Everyone in Evanescence is dead. The androids killed them all. The city has shut down, the nano-net has fallen, the Disfavored are doomed. It is not wonderful."

My mother's clasped hands slowly lower and fall to her side. "I-I don't understand. That wasn't in the plan."

"Your plan? Whatever it was? It backfired."

Mom plops down on the street. Dad crouches down beside her, pats her back. "What went wrong?" she wonders, her expression vexed.

"That doesn't matter," I snap, trying to hold on to my rage despite my overwhelming relief that my parents are, in fact, not evil genocidal maniacs. "What matters is how am I gonna fix the mess you two and Uncle Simon started?"

Dad's head snaps up. "Simon? What did he do?"

"Oh nothing much," I say sarcastically. "Only modified your virus to cause all the G-Chips to fail horribly and—"

"Simon," Mom growls, interrupting me. "That rat bastard, he ruined the whole plan!"

"Plan? What plan?"

Dad looks up. "Ella, do you understand what the Anansi Virus was supposed to do?"

I squint at him. "Uncle Simon said it was to create a power outage."

He nods. "Yes. The power outage would allow a small group of rebel infiltrators to gain access to the city."

"Quentin said as much. He said they were supposed to assassinate the President."

"They had two objectives. The first was to assassinate President Cyr. It was a risky task and I wasn't fully onboard with it, but it was the only way we could get Kit to cooperate with us. The second was for the rebels to plant the Redux Program in the Main Frame while the power was down."

I lean forward, despite myself. This is the first I'm hearing about the Redux Program being planted in the Main Frame. "What's that?"

"It's a hybridized version of this game," Mom explains. "The Redux Program was polished and honed while it was being beta tested on the Disfavored. By the time the Anansi

Virus was planted, the Program would be ready and it could be planted in the Main Frame so that the second protocol could take effect."

"What was the second protocol?"

"A mass brainwash," Dad explains. "A real one, via the G-Chips."

I blink at him. "What?"

Mom says, "We were trying to overthrow the Aristocratic rejection of the Disfavored. We thought if we could get them to somehow psychologically accept the Disfavored, they might let them into the city. Or, at the least, give them a little more aid. Something. Have you seen the way those people live? Been to a Doll House?"

I swallow hard. This makes sense. Far more sense than any explanation up to this point. "The secondary protocol didn't work because of Uncle Simon. He did something to the Anansi Virus, caused the chips to fry. I don't know what he did or why. Maybe we never will. Either way, your Redux Program didn't get a chance to happen at all."

"That does explain some things," Dad muses.

Mom nods. "Though, there had always been a risk of something like that happening."

"Why didn't you try to plant the Redux Program through Nexis instead?" I ask. "I mean, you could have just written the Anansi Virus so that it introduced the Redux Program as a piggyback program, right?"

Dad looks almost surprised I'd ask that. "Because it's just as your mother says, there was risk involved. We didn't want that weight on your shoulders."

A scowl fights its way to the surface. "So it's okay for me to pave the way for destruction, open the door for it, but not invite it in?" I demand. "It's that fine of a line for the two of you?"

Mom and Dad glance at each other.

"Well," I go on, "it didn't happen the way you theorized and now things are incredibly messed up. So, thanks a whole bunch." I turn and walk away from them. They let me go, perhaps because there is little they could say to hold me, and they both know it.

I head down Citizen's Way. To either side of me, Disfavored and Aristocrat alike are living in harmony alongside each other. They all wave at me, like they know exactly who I am. A little girl even runs up to me and clasps her arms around my legs before her mother comes and apologetically pulls her away.

I grow more and more confused the farther I walk. This doesn't seem like a game that would teach Disfavored to hate Aristocrats even more than they do. I turn it over and over in my head, but I can't find a solution. Finally, I give up and catch the arm of a passing Disfavored man. "Excuse me."

"Oh, Miss Ella," he says, grabbing his cap from off of his head and grasping it between his two meaty hands. "What can I do for you?" He looks mildly anxious, like he's afraid of me.

Circuits, what has my avatar been doing in this game?

I smile, trying to look reassuring. "Can you tell me, did you hate Aristocrats before you came to live in this city?"

He smiles at me. "Of course I did. As much as the next person in Kairos, I'm sure. Wanted every one of them dead."

"So, why are you living in harmony with them, then?"

"That's 'cause of you, of course."

"'Cause of me?"

He nods, his brows indicating his perplexity at my apparent confusion. "Wouldn't be the glue that holds us together otherwise, would you?"

I frown at him, more annoyed than anything at the lack of answers I'm getting. "Thank you."

He nods and hustles away, glancing back at me once.

I turn around and return to the Imperial Garden. Dad's sitting on a wrought iron bench that's painted white, his head back and eyes closed as if he's basking in the artificial sun.

"Dad?"

He cracks his eyes open, smiles. "More questions?"

Nodding, I cross my arms. "I've been trying to figure out the brainwashing thing. You said you honed the Program while the Disfavored were playing it, using them as a test population, right?"

He nods.

"So, you taught them to like the Aristocrats?"

"No. Not at first. We made them hate the Aristocrats even more."

"But why would you need to do that? They already hated the Aristocrats," I reflect, thinking about Gus being beaten to death for just becoming a Doll.

"Brainwashing via a program planted on the G-Chip isn't the same as brainwashing a normal brain. The only way to fine tune the Program was to explore the full gamut of the human to hate and love. We used the Disfavored as the first batch of guinea pigs."

"Guinea what?"

He waves his hand. "Test subjects."

"So, you taught them to hate the Aristocrats and then live with them in harmony?"

"In so many words. When a Disfavored plays this game for the first time, they begin on the Exo-Dome level. They are taught to completely despise the Aristocracy, to live as part of a rebel movement to bring down the President and all the Domites. The game gives them incentives to destroy the Aristocrats, because they gain things that belong to the Aristocrats. Food, valuables, wealth, etc. However, there is a point in the game where everything turns quite badly for the Disfavored. He's given an opportunity to join the Aristocrats inside of the dome. This will save the lives of him and those he loves. But he must learn to love and appreciate the Aristocrats, because they are the ones who keep him alive. He learns that to show cruelty and hate toward the Aristocrats will get him ejected from the dome and he will die."

"That's not learning to love. That's control with fear."

"At first, yes. But he learns over time that the strongest hate can be replaced with the strongest love—as the brainwashing is meant to do. The game greatly rewards players who excel at this turnaround."

I'm quiet for a long moment, trying to wrap my head around what he's implying. "But it's wrong to manipulate them like that."

"If you look back at human history, it's no different than a thousand other similar situations. People chose to fold, to give up hate because it was somehow beneficial to them to try and do so. A generation or two later and everyone lives relatively happily."

"You can't be certain that's really what it was like. Weren't you the one who taught me that history was written by the victors?"

He narrows an eye at me. "If I didn't know any better, I'd say you didn't agree with our goals."

"I don't!" I growl. "I think it's wrong to control people's minds. It makes you no better than G-Corp controlling the citizens of Evanescence through the G-Chips."

He takes a deep breath. "The G-Chip may have been the bane of your youthful existence, but eventually you would have come to accept that it was the only way to control the populace—to maintain peace. Humans are inherently destructive; they need to be controlled to some degree."

I feel acid at the back of my throat. I'm so disgusted with what he's saying, and yet, at the back of my logical brain, I know he's right. My head and my heart don't agree and I'm confused.

"Sometimes, people don't know what is best for them. Most times, they want to be told. They don't want to worry, they don't want choice."

"That doesn't give you the right to step up and assume control for them. The Disfavored played your game in order to be free, not to have their brains tinkered with so you could fulfill your awful idea of a utopia. You're not God, Dad."

Dad slowly folds his arms. "I'd never be so bold. All this game does, or did, is subconsciously show the Disfavored what one choice will provide for them. It's meant to greatly encourage them to make the choice we want them to make, but in Real World they are still entirely themselves, and it is up to them to make the final choice to accept the hand of friendship when the Aristocrats extend it. Or…at least, it was. Seems it is all for naught."

"That doesn't change the fact that you intended to brainwash all the Aristocrats."

He shrugs. "Are you going to tell me making the Aristocrats a little more compassionate toward their fellow man is a bad thing?"

I want to agree, but I know better. "Part of being human is to have free will, even if it's to make the choice to hurt someone else."

"Well," Dad says, voice quiet, "in that we disagree. Because to me, to show one's humanity is to be compassionate toward others. So, if you ask what I meant to do with the Redux Program, it was to make humans out of monsters, civilize a lot of heathens."

Taking a breath, I hold my tongue. There is no point in

arguing with a man who can't see the crimes against humanity he planned to commit. To him, the Aristocrats were nothing but test subjects, lab animals, monsters. Maybe Uncle Simon saw things like I do. Maybe he didn't agree with what the Tricksters were doing. Maybe that's why he fried the G-Chips before the Redux Program could be uploaded.

I plop down beside him. "I can't believe you did this. It's like I don't even know you." I lift my hands. "And to drag me into it?"

"You were necessary."

A scoff escapes me. "You sound so clinical."

He glances down at me. "Don't get me wrong, Ella. You're the light of my life. I love you more than anything and I only want the best for you. It's because of that that I—we—did this for you. To give you a better world to live in."

"I didn't ask for that."

"You didn't need to. It's what every parent wants—to give a safe, beautiful world to their child. We'd do anything to that end."

I can't help my bitter smirk. "I doubt many parents have gone this far."

"We set everything up so that you'd come out in a favorable position. I wanted that most of all for you. Seeing you struggle to fit in, one foot in each world, it nearly killed me. I wanted a world where your unique identity was something special, not just to me but everyone."

"I talked to a Disfavored man a little while ago. He said I was the glue that held everyone together. What did he mean by that? Does it have to do with why they call me the Savior?"

He grins. "That's my favorite part of the whole game. Your mother came up with it. The best ideas are always hers."

I stay silent. I don't know if I agree with him.

Seeing that he's not going to get a gush from me, he

continues, "I don't want to give too much away, but in this game, there is an avatar of you who allows for the integration of the Disfavored into the city. Your avatar is the one who convinces the Aristocrats to allow the Disfavored in and the one who convinces the Disfavored to play nice or reap the consequences."

"What on earth possessed her to make an avatar of *me* do something like that?"

"Because isn't that exactly what you were doing in Real World? The avatar here is meant to echo the mission you were given in Nexis. A virtual you to work hand in hand with the real you."

I shake my head. "I didn't sign up for all of this."

"But you planted the virus. Didn't you know what you were doing?"

"No, I wish I did," I say, disgusted by my own naïveté. "Uncle Simon explained that there would be some kind of power outage, that it would just emphasize to the Aristocrats that they rely too heavily on technology. He never told me anything about the rebel infiltration, President Cyr's assassination, the planting of the Redux Program, or the G-Chips getting fried. I never would have planted the virus otherwise."

"I see," he reflects, voice grave. "Things didn't quite go as we had predicted."

"Clearly."

He bangs a fist on his knee. "If only Simon had stuck to the plan. This all would have gone so perfectly. The Redux Program would have gotten the Aristocrats to open their hearts to aiding the Disfavored, and the Redux Game would have primed the Disfavored for just such an occasion."

"No. The Disfavored are still just as bloodthirsty, still in their hate mode. They'd kill an Aristocrat if they saw one."

"That's because Ella the Savior hasn't come to them in

Real World yet. She's the trigger, the switch over in Real World that will make the Disfavored choose to cooperate."

"How could one person do that?"

"The game subconsciously taught them to trust you. If you tell them the Aristocrats will aid and accept them, then they will trust you because the game taught them to."

Everything he's saying sounds crazy to me. "Why me? Why would you put so much responsibility on me?"

"Isn't this what you want? A world where Naturals and Customs can live side by side? Where you're no longer an outcast?"

"By shoving me into the spotlight?"

"Isn't that also what you wanted? To stand out and be loved by your peers? Wasn't that what you struggled for?"

He's right, of course. I wanted to be popular, to be loved despite being a Natural among Customs. "I didn't want it this way." I touch my forehead—my head feels like it's going to explode. "This is so much."

His face falls. "I'm sorry to have burdened you with this, then. We assumed you'd be a willing participant. It was agreed among we Tricksters that, should something happen to Cleo or myself, you'd be brought into the fold when the time came and you'd be apprised of the plan. It's one of the reasons we secured your marriage to Zane."

"That didn't happen. Uncle Simon falsified my death and kept me captive for the past year. He most certainly never explained anything to me, especially this."

"His actions were regrettable. He should have taken more care."

That's an understatement. "You didn't know what was going on with me at all? Even though you seem to know some things?"

He wrinkles his nose. "As I've said, we had some access

via the Internetwork, but it's limited and spotty here."

"I-I don't even know if I believe what you're telling me. People living beyond the grave in virtual realms, brainwashing… It's all theoretical."

"That's only what G-Corp wanted the citizens to believe, Ella. G-Corp has had incredible scientific capability from the very beginning. From its inception, it brought on the best and brightest minds in the world, put them all together in this isolated dome, creating a fast and strong eugenics program, and the results were stunning. Add to it the ability to upload those brilliant minds on the Main Frame, allow access to them for certain qualified personnel, and we can do many, many wonderful and horrible things."

"Is that what happened? They killed you, but you kept helping the other Tricksters to fine tune this Program?"

"Yes, I've had a hand in this Program from the very beginning. But remotely, of course. The Main Frame knows when certain people are being accessed, so your uncle thought it was safest to export me into Redux itself. Same with your mother. We live here, on this virtual plane in the utopia we imagined with you." He smiles.

I can't help my heated words. "But the avatar in this game isn't me," I argue. "I was out there, alone and without either of you. And you were connecting with people from Real World, pulling the strings on my life like I was a little puppet and you never once thought to reach out to me?"

He closes his eyes, takes a deep breath. "It was too dangerous."

My lip is trembling and I feel hot tears threatening to fall. "I needed you."

His smile is gentle as he reaches out and touches my hand. "No. You didn't. Clearly you've done everything wonderfully, Ella. I'm very proud of you."

"Wonderfully? Nearly everyone in Evanescence is dead because I made a horrible mistake. And now the Disfavored may all die, too." Angry, I pull away from him. "I don't deserve anyone being proud of me and you don't deserve to be proud of me. Go be proud of Other Ella, your little Savior."

The skin around his eyes tighten. "Jealousy does not and never has suited you. You're better than this. How can you be jealous of yourself?"

"The person in this game, whoever she is, is not me."

He scoffs. "Oh, my Ellani, she is exactly you. Your body in this world is a bit taller, as your mother miscalculated your final growth results. But the brain that inhabits your avatar on this level? It is your brain. The same brain that regularly copied, uploaded, and exported to Redux every time you entered Nexis."

I shake my head, rejecting what he's saying. "Then she's not me. I'm a completely different person than I was just last week. Where is she? I'll prove it."

"She doesn't exist."

"What?

"Not while you're here, anyway. Can't have two of you existing at the same time."

I roll my eyes. "All of this is insane, Dad. Every last convoluted bit of it."

"Insane and convoluted as it is, it's the truth. It's the virtual reality behind the reality. Two timelines, two Ellas working in conjunction with each other."

And now they've collided. And Real World Ella is left picking up the pieces. Sighing, I drop my shoulders. "So, the plan is all screwed up. What am I supposed to do?"

He rubs his chin in thought. "That is a bit of a conundrum. We didn't hypothesize for the plan running this off course. But you're a smart girl, you'll think of something."

"Gee, thanks."

"Your mother and I gave you every possible resource you could need in Nexis and in Redux. You did a momentous thing in both games. I have every faith you can do exactly the same in Real World."

I grip my hair in both my hands. "Ugh, I don't have the same resources in Real World. I don't have the threads like my avatar did in Nexis, and I don't even know who half the Real World Tricksters are—let alone trust them."

"It doesn't matter who the Tricksters are or how many."

"What's that supposed to mean?"

"The Tricksters in Nexis were just symbolic. Bodies that held something important to your success."

"They were people," I hiss. "They were my friends."

Dad lifts his chin. "And what is a friend but someone who helps you succeed in life? Who is a lover? A mother? A father? In the end, when you take all the humanitarian fluff out of people's minds, other people are nothing but tools. Things that make you laugh, cry, cope, things that comfort you, things that push you or drag you down. They are the most important tools in our kit, because without other people, we are nothing. And each one of us, every human alive, is a special kind of tool, unique in what they can offer or take away from the people around them. That's what makes each of us important. That's the big thing that humanity lost sight of when it chose who got to live and who got to die, when it closed off the domes and left the Disfavored outside to die in the aftermath of what we'd all created. And that's the wrong your mother and I and the other people on our teams were trying to correct. The Aristocrats are valuable, but so are the Disfavored. There is something both sides have to offer, and we need to find balance." He holds up his hand, presenting the city around us in demonstration.

chapter twenty

POST-AMERICAN DATE: 7/8/232

LONGITUDINAL TIMESTAMP: 8:02 P.M.

LOCATION: KAIROS

The silence of the gaming room is nearly overpowering after being submerged in the virtual version of Evanescence for so long. I pull off the cap and blinders, blink in the bright battery light.

Quent glances up at me from my leg. "All done?"

"Yeah."

"Did you have fun?"

I knit my brows, rub my temples. "I'm not sure fun is the right word."

He pauses in his ministrations, looks up again, giving me all of his attention. "What was it like? I've always wondered about Redux, but everyone was always so hush, hush about it."

"That night at the ball," I venture. "Zane put something in your pocket and then Gus took it from you. What was it?"

"Zane told me it was some kind of reboot program. I was supposed to upload it onto the Main Frame right before the Anansi Virus kicked in, but Dad wanted me to do that stupid birthday toast. So I stayed behind with you and Gus did it instead. It's what rebooted the power."

I shake my head. "It wasn't."

He squints at me, waiting.

I shake my head. "It doesn't matter. What matters is what's currently happening. What's ahead of us."

"Okay," he says slowly. I can tell he wants to ask questions, but he refrains. "As soon as I'm done, I suppose we'll go back to the rebel base, let them know what happened to the Aristocrats, appeal to them to help rescue them."

"Except you've already mentioned that's not going to be so easy."

"No. It won't be. The rebels have just about as much reason to save a bunch of Aristocrats from the cannibals as the Disfavored inside of Evanescence have for helping to save them. We'd need a miracle reason."

I lean back, press the butts of my palms against my tired eyes. "Is nothing easy? Just a little bit of luck, that's all I'm asking for."

"I think we're lucky I spotted this place," he's saying. "I've fixed this to almost new now."

I smile at the ceiling. "And I'm so lucky you're an Engineer."

"Yeah," he says, "an Engineer and a Programmer, fate sure worked in our favor. There's practically nothing you and I couldn't fix."

A snort escapes me. "If only life were as easy to fix as machines and electronics." And then something occurs to me, and I sit up suddenly.

Quent jumps and pulls both his hands away. "What? Did you feel that?"

"All the Aristocrats!"

He blinks at me and lowers both his hands, which are

holding tools I don't even know the names of. His expression tells me he's not following my line of thought. "Tools, Quent." I point at the instruments he's holding. "We're all finely honed, specialty tools."

He looks at his hands, looks at me.

I'm grinning like a madwoman now. "And *they've* got a broken city."

And then he gets it. And he grins just as big. That beautiful, mischievous grin that made me love him in the first place. "Elle, you're a genius." Then he leans forward and kisses me.

I lean into the kiss, wanting more of him. I want so much to just make him part of me, to rise with him on a different level. I want to make us code and stitch us together. I want to be water so I can mix with him. I want to be air so we can be the same thing. The kiss becomes more and more fervent. I hear tools fall to the floor as he gets to his feet and kneels over me on the chair. I feel his hands in my hair, along my neck, my shoulders, my skin.

Everything is alive, tingling and twisting. His fingers slip over my hip, brushing against the edges of my underwear. He breaks the kiss, pants against my lips. "I want you," he whispers.

I kiss him, hungry, letting my fingers grasp at the zipper of his uniform and tug it down. I slip my hands in, touch the heat of his bare stomach as I slide the uniform over his shoulders. "So take me."

He growls into my lips, lets his body slip between my legs. He kisses my neck, my chest. His fingers slide under my shirt, slide it over my head. There's no strange awe at him seeing me for the first time. It's an odd comfort knowing he's seen my Natural body a hundred times already in Nexis and loves and accepts it for all its flaws. He reveres them. Just like I find that I revere him, even though his body is new to me. We're not strangers. He knows just the right ways to touch and titillate me. I know him just as well. So when we finally do come together, it's like puzzle pieces rejoining. Perfect and whole, and it takes a lot of time and convincing ourselves to come apart again.

chapter twenty-one

POST-AMERICAN DATE: 7/8/232

LONGITUDINAL TIMESTAMP: 11:04 P.M.

LOCATION: KAIROS

It takes us a while to find the right building. Quent and I shuffle down the stairs and Delaney looks up from a game of cards he's playing with another Disfavored man. Quent says, "Some guard you are. You don't even have your gun within reaching distance."

Startled, Delaney shoots to his feet, upsetting both the crate and the cards. "Where have you two been? They've been combing the tunnels looking for you for hours."

"We had to go topside," Quent explains. "Ella was injured."

Delaney straightens, takes in my bruised cheek, the bandages around my wrists. "You okay?"

I shrug. "As good as I can be after a sound beating."

Delaney's eyes stray to Quent, who is without a scratch. "Where the hell were you?"

Quent catches the implied inability to look out for me. "There's a reason we're here and the man that touched her is dead. Now, where are Zane and Clairen? I need to speak with them."

"They're getting ready to out a rat."

"A rat?"

"Yeah," Delaney says. "Come on." He leads us into one of the larger main rooms of the complex. People are pouring in from a number of shoot-off tunnels and before long there must be at least fifty standing among the few old vehicles, crates, and pieces of equipment stored here.

After a few moments, Clairen climbs a few steps onto a short dais on the other side of the room. She makes a hand signal and the room goes silent. Her teal eyes scan the group of people and her features, made sharper looking by her high, tight ponytail, look murderous.

"Five dead," she says, very suddenly. "Five. Dead. Twelve missing. In *our* tunnels. Our *safe* place."

There's a murmur now, a wave of outrage.

"Even more, with the dead and missing Aristocrats from the dome," she adds.

"No one cares!"

"Yeah, they're just Aristocrats!"

"I care!" she screams, and she's like a demon, her expression is so fierce. This shuts everyone up again. "Do you know why?" Clairen continues, scowling. "Because someone has sold us out. Someone has given away an entry point. And that's not okay." Her eyes search again, as if that will ferret out the traitor. She glances down to where her closer administrators are gathered. "Bring her up."

Aaron and Mac slowly climb the steps of the dais. Between them, they hold a young woman about my size and shape. She wriggles and I can hear her screaming behind the gag tied around her mouth. As they move more squarely to present her to the crowd, I notice something about her thrashing body that makes me grab Quent's wrist. She's missing a leg. They drop her unceremoniously to the floor. With her arms tied behind her back, she tries her best to struggle to balance on her one leg and her stub.

Clairen steps to the side of the girl and grabs a fistful of the girl's hair, wrenching her upright so that everyone can see her face. Broad cheek bones, black hair, black eyes, surprisingly well dressed for a Disfavored. She's got strange tattoos on her neck. "This girl is one of the cannibals," Clairen announces.

There's more murmuring.

"Considering how hard those with her fought my unit? I'm gonna say she's important to the bastards." Clairen tosses the girl's head away so that the momentum of it knocks her back onto the ground. A moment later, Clairen's gun is drawn and sighted on the girl. "Come forward, or I'll kill her."

Everyone remains still and quiet. I feel Quentin's arms come around me, realize I'm shaking. He presses his face into my hair.

Searching more, Clairen snarls. "You don't believe me?"

Bam.

I scream and flinch. The girl screams and flinches. Someone screams, "No!"

And the next thing I know, Faulk is struggling forward, arms outstretched. "Don't! Don't kill her!"

The group parts and he's climbing onto the stage, grabbing the girl into his arms. I realize that Clairen hasn't shot her, that she only shot the floor, a bluff to draw him out. Mac and Aaron and a few others are on the stage now, drawing the two apart.

"No! Stormy!" Faulk is shouting, trying to struggle out of Mac and another man's grasp. "Don't hurt her. Promise you won't hurt her."

The girl named Stormy is dragged off the stage; so is Faulk. And then it's very quiet and still. I'm gasping. Quentin's arms are tight around me, and my heart pounds against him. He gives me a kiss on the temple. "Come on, we have work to do."

Numb, I draw away and walk toward where Clairen and the others are talking in a tight circle. "Where's Zane and my mother?" Quent asks.

"They're out searching for you," Clairen says, eyes showing her surprise. "We'd almost given up hope and thought you'd been snatched like the rest."

"We got delayed," I explain.

Clairen examines my face. "Not without incident, it seems."

"You're aware that the others have been captured then?" Quent asks.

She nods. "Aaron came back and reported after he got separated from Faulk." She says "Faulk" like it's a swear word, and I suppose it is now. "Ugh, I can't believe I trusted him."

"We all did," Mac reasons. "It's best to just let it go. Can't be helped now."

"Oh," she huffs, "it can be plenty helped." She shakes a fist like she intends to use it.

Mac rolls his eyes. "I doubt violence will be necessary. We have something he's keen on keeping safe."

"There's nothing he could know that I care to keep him alive for." She turns away.

"Don't be hasty, Claire," Mac warns.

She flashes him the one-fingered hand signal. "Mind your own business, old man. He's my subordinate, I'll deal with him any way I like."

"Actually," I say, stepping up to follow her as she walks away, "would you mind if I talk to him before you kill him?"

I hear a number of people following us, and I assume Quent is among them.

Her face contorts. "What could you possibly want to ask that rat-faced motherfucker?"

"A lot, actually. No one has ever returned from the

cannibals' camp, right?" I glance back and Quent nods to double verify. "That's why you don't know anything about them? Why you can't ever save the people they snatch?"

She remains quiet, waiting for me to continue as we walk down the canvas corridor.

"He has. And you're in a position to get answers."

She stops, turns on me. "I don't need answers. The answer is that once people go to the cannibals they die with the cannibals. That's all I need to know. That's the only truth."

I stare up at her for a long moment, glance to the side to see how far back Quent, Delaney, and Aaron are, then lower my voice accordingly. "They took someone from you, didn't they." It's not a question, it's a statement.

Her brow twitches and she looks away.

"Well," I say quietly. "They've taken someone from me, too. And I have to try and get that someone back. You may not want answers, but I do. Those answers are knowledge I can use. And knowledge in my hands is power." I make a fist in emphasis and lift my chin. "I need all the power I can get, Clairen, and I'm asking for you to help me."

For the expanse of a number of breaths, Clairen examines me. Then she smiles a little. "You might be short, but you're exactly like how you are in the game. It's kind of creepy."

I lower my fist and let out a nervous breath. "Yeah, you're telling me."

"All right," she finally says. "I'll let you talk to him."

"Thank you."

She turns and I follow again. "Don't thank me, there's no point. You can find out everything you want from him, it's not gonna make a difference. The cannibals are powerful."

"I know."

Her eyes slide sideways. "I sense a scheme. What are you planning, Ellani Drexel?"

I shrug and play innocent. I'm not pulling the lynch pin until I'm certain all of this is going to work how I theorize. "Nothing."

"Don't go putting yourself in unnecessary danger. We need you."

As I smile at her, I sense a bit of mischief in my expression. "Oh, I know. I'm counting on it."

Her expression grows uneasy and she glances back at Quentin. "Is she always like this?"

Quent says, "I think she learned it from me," and there's no apology in his voice.

Delaney and Aaron chuckle at that.

"You're as bad as your brother," she mutters.

We walk for a few more minutes in what I'm feeling is satisfied silence, when suddenly we pass a room, and I recognize the people in it. I stop, backpedal. "Gus? Delia?"

Delia looks up from unbuckling a taser from her hip and gives me a wide-eyed stare through twin black eyes and a swollen nose. It's Gus who comes forward, grabs me into a big, asphyxiating hug. "Elle." I hug him back, feeling awkward and fully aware of Delia's expression becoming a scowl.

"It's good to see you made it out. I knew you would." I hear Quent say behind me. Gus's body grows tense and he pulls away. As he draws away, I see the full extent of the damage the cannibal attack wrought on his body. His face is split open in a couple of places, revealing his robotic interior, and his dominant hand has been stripped at the knuckles. Obviously he beat someone quite well, and his expression says he's ready to start in on Quent.

I step forward and hold up my hands, but he's too fast.

Before I know what's happening, Gus hits Quent. Hard. So hard he stumbles back and hits the wall.

Delaney, Aaron, and Clairen move to intervene, but Quent

holds up the hand that's not cradling his face. "No. It's fine."

Gus remains still as Quent straightens, rolls a shoulder, and pulls his hand away. His skin is stripped clean of his cheek mod, hanging ragged. "I suppose I deserved that," he says, examining the blood on his hand.

His only response is a stony glare from Gus.

"I suppose I owe you an explanation."

Gus's eyes narrow. "Too late for that. Cam and Sid did it for you."

Quent lowers his hand. "They made it out, too, then?"

A chin lowering from Gus.

"They're with Zane and Kit," Clairen provides, voice uneasy, as if she's still not sure whether Gus is gonna attack Quent or not.

"Sorry," Delaney adds, "I guess I forgot to tell you that Aaron found some survivors."

Gus's head twitches. "They're not dead. I've told you that. The cannibals took them alive." His voice is agitated and it's clear he's argued this point a number of times, that he's just as annoyed by the Disfavored knack for writing people off as dead as soon as the cannibals take them.

"Some of them," I correct. Gus glances at me, like he's only remembering I'm there right now. He stares at me for a long moment and it's clear that there's a confused war of emotion within him.

I stare back, wondering how much he must have figured out. How much Cam and Sid told him.

His gaze finally breaks away, swings around the room, then back to Quent. "I need to talk to you."

Quent nods. "I'm sure you do."

"Alone."

"Of course." Quent glances at Clairen, and, making a face like this is all rather stupid and taking up her time, she lets out a big sigh, slumps, and leads them into another room. A moment later, Clairen comes out alone and zips up the door.

She rejoins us and we stand awkwardly as muffled baritone voices begin talking in the room beyond.

I glance at the others who seem unsure if they should stay or continue on. "We'll catch up," I say, dismissing them. "This might take a while."

Clairen nods to the others and they hurry away. "We'll be waiting."

Delia is watching the room, inching toward it. I do the same. We both stop a fair distance from the opening, a few paces from each other. She, like me, probably wants to give them some privacy but still wants to be within reach. This is a big moment, emotional, and I doubt either is going to come out with a smile on his face.

We eye each other uneasily as the discussion in the room beyond escalates from Gus's elevated voice to elevated growls of rage. In a similar tone, Quentin's voice joins his, just as agitated. I can't hear what either is saying. They're deep enough in that the words are garbled, but the emotion and heat are evidence enough the conversation isn't going well.

Long minutes tick by, their voices eventually lower.

I feel myself taking a few steps closer, wanting to hear how Quentin is explaining himself to Gus, but Delia's words pull me back. "Did you know?"

For once, her voice isn't laced with venom, and her face holds no hate. She's just tired and vulnerable. It occurs to me how very much she must love him and how this discovery is affecting her as well.

Slumping my shoulders, I focus on her. "Of course not."

She looks away, her bald brows knit so that they pucker over the bulbous implant in her face. I hate that thing, hate how it makes her even more of a stranger to me. I have no idea how to talk to her anymore. "I should have guessed it." Her voice is wavering and I sense she's going to cry.

"Oh, Dee. You couldn't have known that."

"But I always sensed something about him was off. I think he did, too." Her eyes search the ground. "At least now we know."

"I hope this doesn't change things between you two. He's still the same Gus." If it was me in her place, I'd love him even if he wasn't real. I learned from a young age to love and appreciate Meems; Gus isn't that different. But Delia's closer to the Aristocratic way of thinking than ever, so maybe she won't.

Head whipping up, she scowls at me. "I'm not like that, and I'm disgusted you'd ever think that about me."

I avoid her glare as I admit, "I don't know what to think of you anymore."

She examines her feet and gnaws her lip. "I read your letters," she finally whispers.

I cock my head, but she's still staring at her feet. "How'd you do that?"

"Gus did it for me. He rewired it into a light-stick."

"Huh, that's smart."

"Yeah. He's really smart."

I want to say, "I know," but I don't. Not really. "Quent, too," I say instead.

"It's weird, how this all ended up. With us. With the game and what your uncle did. I don't know if I understand it all. But I at least think I get where you were coming from."

"I'm so sorry, Dee. You have to believe that."

She closes her eyes and a tear escapes down her cheek. "It's just hard. There's a lot of pain."

The emotion in her voice makes my heart ache. I touch my chips, drawing strength from them. "Not that it's any use, but if you want to talk…I-I've lost my parents, too. But I've never lost a sister. I mean, I lost you when Simon locked me up. But you were alive at least."

She takes a deep breath, lets it out. "It's not the first time I've had to deal with losing my sister. You knew I was alive, but to me…to me, you were dead, and I had to deal with that all over again with Nina. I think I was mad because you were actually alive, and all that pain and suffering I went through had been senseless and cruel punishment."

"I never wanted you to go through that."

"Didn't make it hurt or feel like betrayal any less. Especially when Gus suddenly came at me with these notions of being in love with you."

"But you realize now that he's not, right?"

"I read your letters. It's not as though his feelings wouldn't be returned if he told you about them."

"I—" I rub my forehead. "I do have feelings for the boy who played Gus in the game, but that was Quent. I love Quent, not Gus. And Gus loves you, not me. And yes," I continue, seeing she's going to argue, "Gus has residual feelings for me, but they're not his feelings, they're Quent's. I'm aware that doesn't change it. I wish I could somehow fix all of this for you."

"You can't. I have to convince him to forget memories that aren't even real. Anyway," she eventually breathes. "I lost one sister, and I got another one back. For that, at least, I'm grateful. Especially since it seems like I get to keep Gus, too." She finally shoots me a sidelong glance and smirks. "And hey, you finally got Quentin."

I smile back at her then look away. Despite that small triumph, it's a hollow victory. One that came at too high a cost. "I planted that virus so that I could see him again."

"Yeah." Her voice is strained. "Though, I'm not sure I'd

do anything different if it came to me and Gus."

"Is this worth it? Love?"

She's quiet for a heartbeat. "I suppose that depends what you do with it. If a million people died so that you could reunite with the boy you loved, then you two had better save two million in return. Nina was worth that much, don't you think?"

"No," I whisper, creating a fist around the chips in my pocket. "Nina was worth a hundred million." I take a breath. "Dee?"

"Hm?"

"We have to save the others."

"Yes."

"I have a plan."

Delia's eyes light up, but we're interrupted by the sound of the door unzipping. We've been so busy talking I didn't realize the room behind me had gone silent and now Gus is opening the door in sharp, clipped motions. I take a step toward him, wanting to comfort him in some way. "Gus?"

But he doesn't even look at me. He brushes right past me, goes to Delia. Right into her opening arms and kisses her hard. I close my mouth, lower my chin, and close my eyes in internal satisfaction. This is how it should be and it feels right.

Gus grasps her hand and tugs her in a particular direction. "Come on, we're leaving."

Delia glances back at me, eyes wide, but speaks to him. "Where?"

"Anywhere but here. If I don't get out of here now, I'm going to kill him. Come with me."

Delia turns her attention back to him. "Okay." They begin walking away.

"Gus," I call out.

He pauses, looks a little confused for a second. It's clear

it's hard for him to shake his memories. "What," he growls, not turning toward me.

"Don't go far. I need you." Then, realizing what this sounds like, I add, "I need you both. So does Quent. Don't leave us again. Either of you. Please."

He doesn't respond, just keeps walking. And Delia goes with him, but she looks back and nods at me, and I know I'll be able to find them later. Because we have work to do.

When they're both gone, I enter the room Gus came from. Quent is sitting on a crate, arms braced on both his knees and head hung between his shoulders. I get to my knees before him and press my forehead to his hair. His hands lift, gently cup my jaw, his thumb brushes my cheek.

"He's really pissed at me."

I grasp his ankle. "Do you blame him?"

"No." Then he says, "I'm still not sorry."

I smile, though I know he can't see it, and think of the passionate way Gus loves my best friend. "Deep down? I don't think he is, either."

chapter twenty-two

POST-AMERICAN DATE: 7/8/232

LONGITUDINAL TIMESTAMP: 2:03 A.M.

LOCATION: REBEL BASE, KAIROS

When Clairen lets me into the room Faulk is being detained in, he's lying on a cot staring at the ceiling. His hands aren't bound, but there's an iron shackle on his ankle and he's connected to a massive stone in the middle of the room.

I glance at Quentin and Clairen, who are both standing at the plastic observation window by the door. I'd asked to be alone to talk to him.

"Faulk?"

He opens his eyes, glances at me. I see his mouth is bloody and as I approach, I see a pair of bloody false teeth sitting on the floor. I assume they weren't willingly removed. "So, that's how you hid what you are."

Despondent, he turns over on the cot, faces the wall.

I pull the small chair close to the cot, sit down beside him. "I'm going to assume you've been planted as a spy here for quite a while. Clairen doesn't trust easy. How long have you been running with the Disfavored?"

He doesn't respond.

"Look, I know you have no reason to talk to me. But if you don't cooperate it's going to come out of that girl's hide."

He stiffens and I know I've gotten to him.

"What's her name, Stormy?"

Haltingly, he nods.

"She your girl?"

He lifts a shoulder.

"She's important, either way."

He speaks so low I can barely hear him. "She's Taurus's daughter."

"Taurus," I repeat. "Who's he?"

"Leader."

"Ah."

"Soon as he realizes she's gone, he's gonna come looking for her. He'll kill all of you. She's his treasure."

"Well," I say, and I'm glad he can't see my face because his words rattle me. "Perhaps an agreement can be reached. He has some people we'd like back."

"Taurus don't do negotiations. Doesn't need to. He could pound you to bone dust in an instant. 'Sides, even if he negotiated, he'd trade and just turn round and come after you. You don't cross Taurus."

"He seems very powerful."

"He's fuckin' Satan incarnate."

I glance at Quent and he narrows an eye. I know they can hear what we're saying—there's an arcane microphone wired into the ceiling of the cell. "Why hasn't he crushed us in the past?"

"'Cause that would be bad for business."

"What?"

The chuckle that comes from Faulk is so evil sounding

that I can't help but think the Satan analogy is pretty fitting, considering this Taurus person has demons working for him. "It's amazing how gullible and stupid you people are. File your teeth, spread some rumors, and act a little wild and crazy, and suddenly everyone thinks you're a fucking man-eater."

I knit my brow. "You're not?"

"No," he says, like the idea disgusts him. "None of us are."

"Then what do you do with the Disfavored you kidnap?"

"We sell them. As slaves."

Creasing my brow, I say, "So the whole cannibal thing is a lie?"

He raises a hand and rings an imaginary bell as he says, "Ding, ding, ding, give the girl a prize!" He lowers his arm again. "We capture the Disfavored and Taurus sells them."

"Where?"

"Annex."

"That's the Disfavored settlement just outside of Cadence, right?"

He nods. "He'll sell them at market in Annex. Most likely, they'll be spread all over Annex as slaves. Most of the men will go to the coliseum and the women will go to whore houses."

"Coliseum? What's that?"

"You ever read about the Romans?"

"Yeah."

"They'll train them up, turn them into gladiators. They'll fight against each other. To the death."

I gasp. "But, why?"

"To entertain the wealthier Domites. If you win, you can get into Cadence. At least, that's what I've heard. People make journeys to Annex to try their hand at the games, but I wouldn't want to try. It's suicide."

"And that's what's going to happen to the Aristocrats you sold out to the cannibals?"

He shrugs. "No."

I stare at his back for a long time. If they aren't going to be sold, then what's the point in capturing them? "Why did you give them away? Why couldn't you have just let them be?"

He finally glances over his shoulder. "Same reason you want them back so bad."

My stomach drops. No…he couldn't possibly.

Faulk sees my expression and grins at me, bloody, sharp teeth hideous and awful in their mockery. "Now she gets it."

chapter twenty-three

POST-AMERICAN DATE: 7/8/232

LONGITUDINAL TIMESTAMP: 2:22 A.M.

LOCATION: REBEL BASE, KAIROS

I don't bother zipping the cell up behind me as I rush out and round on Clairen. "I need to talk to that other prisoner. That girl, Stormy."

"What?" Clairen squawks. "What's going on?"

"I don't have time, Clairen. Now."

A growling noise escapes her but she turns and leads me down another tunnel.

Quentin catches my hand. "What's going on?" He asks it low, low enough that Clairen can't hear and I match his tone because I don't want her to panic or upset the plan.

"Taurus is going to try and take Evanescence."

"What?" he hisses.

"Shhh," I glance at Clairen. "I'm almost positive that's why he went after the Aristocrats."

"So, what are we going to do?"

"Rescue them and get them to do what he stole them for before he does. The good part is that they'll definitely still be at his main camp, wherever that is. He'll want to keep them close."

"Yeah, but how are we gonna find the camp, let alone rescue them?"

We come to a stop at the door Clairen is currently unzipping. "That's what I'm about to negotiate."

Inside, Stormy's cell looks much like Faulk's did. Except she's sitting in her chair, facing the door. When I come in, she looks up, grabs both sides of the bottom of the chair as if to brace herself.

This girl...she could be me.

"Hello, Stormy," I say. "My name is Ella."

She lifts her chin, stares at me with defiant black eyes.

"You don't want to talk. That's fine. You don't need to. I can talk for us both." I cross my arms, turn on my toe, and slowly pace the floor. "You're the daughter of Taurus. Taurus is the leader of the group we've come to know as cannibals. But you're not cannibals. You're slavers. And Faulk gave away a location of a tunnel entrance so that you could kidnap the Aristocrats in the hopes to take over Evanescence." I turn to her. "Did I leave anything out?"

She looks away. "Faulk spilled, then."

"He did it to save you."

She scoffs. "He did it because he's afraid my father will string him up if he lets anything happen to me. Any one of my father's men would do it." She leans forward. "My father would do anything to save me."

Unmoved, I lift a brow. "Is that supposed to scare me?"

This unsettles her; I can see it in the sudden unease in her face. I take my dominance and run with it. Grabbing the other chair, I swing it around and plop myself down in front of her so that I'm straddling the chair back. I rest my arms on the back of the chair, cool and confident even though I'm terrified. If I botch this, we're screwed. Everything is riding on my ability to sway Stormy.

"Do you know who *I* am, Stormy?"

She shakes her head.

"My name is Ellani Drexel. I'm the daughter of Warren Drexel. The people of Kairos call me The Savior. Want to guess why they call me that?"

Her tongue darts out, moistening her lips and, swallowing, she offers me a less vigorous shake.

I lean forward a little bit. "They call me that because I'm the one who killed all the Aristocrats in the city you're trying to steal. Any idea what I do to people who steal from me?"

She's frightened now.

"Why don't I show you then, huh?" I say, standing.

Yelping, she holds up her hands like she expects I'm going to attack her. I give her a look like she's pathetic and stupid. Deep down, I'm so sorry for her and I feel awful for manipulating her like this. She's terrified and alone and absolutely useless in her disability. I know what that feels like. But I can't let that show. So I mock her with my eyes and my smirk as I lift a hand and call, "Clairen, bring me a knife."

"No," Stormy blubbers as the zipper opens behind me. "What are you gonna do?"

I feel the leather handle of the long knife Clairen wears at her belt enter my hand. I grip it, brandish it. I take one last moment to relish the terrified look in Stormy's eyes before I look away and begin hacking at my pant leg.

I can hear Stormy's heavy breathing as I slide the knife under the fabric and work it at an angle. I relish the tearing noise it makes, the suspense of the moment, and Stormy's sudden gasp as I allow the pant leg to fall, revealing that I am just like her.

I chose the same leg as hers for a reason. A good one. And I'm glad that it's my undamaged prosthetic, because it makes the impact on Stormy even stronger. I can see the surprise of our shared state, that warring with empathy and kinship. But it's soon replaced with an expression that warms me to the core, because it's just what I want her to show me. A sudden realization that her state isn't something she has to live with. That there is a possibility to stand on two legs once again. And then I see the want. The jealousy. The envy.

Before I lose her too far down the hole, I toss the knife to the ground at my feet. It hits point first between my toes. I knew those nights of practicing knife throwing with Opus back in Nexis would come in handy one day. Stormy's eyes snap up.

"They took my legs. They took my freedom and my father," I say, drawing close to her, leaning into her face. "So you know what I did?"

Her eyes are wide as I lift my hand, make a gun shape with my fingers and hold it to her head. She flinches as I pull an imaginary trigger and make a shooting noise. I smile at her, letting a little bit of madness show. It's not hard. There is so much riding on this that I feel a little like I'm going mad.

"Now," I say, squatting down in front of her and gripping her good knee. "Do you love your father, Stormy?"

Mouth tight, she nods her head.

"He'd do anything for his little girl. Spoils her rotten, doesn't he? Even lets her go out on raids when she's nothing but a burden to his men. Isn't that right?"

She doesn't answer. She doesn't have to. Even if she had a crutch, which I assume she did at one point, she'd still be slower than everyone. And because of who she is, everyone would be worrying about her. But Taurus must humor her, despite the risk. He must rely on his men's ability to protect her. On their fear of him and his wrath. Every man has a chink in his chain.

"How pathetic," I spit, standing and turning away. "You rely on Daddy for everything. You're nothing but a burden. You wouldn't even make a decent slave," I rail as I swoop down and pull the blade out of the floor. I turn and point it in her face. "I'd be doing him a favor if I put you out of his misery right here."

"Th-that's not true," she whimpers, tears brimming on her lids. "He-he loves me. He'll do anything to save me. You'll see, you'll regret saying these things to me."

I lift my chin, scoff a breath at her as I pull the knife away and tuck it into my belt. "And then what? You'd still be just as useless, wouldn't you? You'd still be legless Stormy having to be rescued by Daddy, putting everyone else at risk because you can't help yourself. When's it gonna stop? When are you going to prove you're actually worth the blood and bones you inhabit?"

I leave the question hanging between us, examining her expectantly.

Her face grows pink and she looks away.

"Look," I say, trying to make myself sound softer, but still authoritative. "I've been where you are. I've felt those feelings, hated having to be taken care of. I thought of killing myself a lot. I bet you have, too."

Her shoulders fold as she sinks into herself.

"What if I gave you a chance to do something all on your own?" I ask. Her chin jerks and I take it as a good sign. "What if I gave you the power to save yourself? What if I gave you a choice that could save the lives of your people and your father?"

Her gaze shoots sideways. "You don't have that kind of power."

"Don't I?" I bluff. "I destroyed a city no one else could get into. I took it over. The Disfavored love me. They'd jump the first second I told them to. It wouldn't be hard, they hate your father and your people. I could bring a hundred thousand of them down on your heads. A whole army. I can do all that." I hold out my hands. "And I'm only a Natural."

Casually, I walk back to the chair. I take a moment to grin and wink at Quent, who's staring at me with wide eyes, before turning around and taking a relaxed seat on the chair once more. "I have all the power, Stormy. I could show you how to have some of it. I could give a little to you. The chance to stand. How would you like that?"

Her eyes go to my leg again.

"You don't have things like this back home, do you?" It's clear that they don't. Taurus must make a decent bit of coin on his slaving, and he'd have gotten her the best prosthetic if his money could buy it. "Maybe something more rudimentary? Daddy probably had someone make you a pretty bit of clockwork. It's gone now, though."

She looks close to tears again.

"Do you want what I have?" I demand.

Stormy closes her eyes and two tears slip free. "Yes," she breathes. I want to go to her, wrap her in my arms, but I grip my leg instead.

"Do you want power? Do you want to be called Stormy the Savior, like me?"

She nods.

"Then I'll make you a deal. Your father has royally pissed me off, Stormy. I'm not feeling terribly forgiving toward him, but I might be persuaded not to kill him or completely squash your people if you make this a little less taxing. I'll give you a leg that's just as good as the real thing, and you give me information." I stand then, turn away. "You've got two hours to make the decision."

I remain straight backed and quiet as I walk out the door.

Quentin flanks me as I walk down the corridor. When we're far enough away, he finally speaks. "That was crazy."

"Yes."

"It was also brilliant."

"I thought so."

"Should I assume the worst case scenario for this deal your hashing with her?"

"You got it, Prince Charming."

"I don't like this."

"I wasn't too keen on ripping fiber-optics out of your skin, but I did it for you because I love you."

"We did that for *you*," he reasons.

"I'm doing this for you." I turn on him. "And all these people. So you better not hesitate to disconnect it or hook her up to it when she comes back in an hour and five minutes saying she wants my damn leg."

Quent looks like he's about to argue. But I say, "My body. My choice. Greater good and all that. Don't try and talk me out of it, because I'm liable to turn yellow," I say, borrowing a line from Morden, one of our teammates from Nexis. I reach out and grasp his hand. "Just do this for me. Please."

His gaze begs me not to expect this of him, but he doesn't argue. Clairen appears the next moment, following us. I turn to her, hand her back the knife. "I'm sure you get my plan by now."

"That you're a lying sack of shit?" She sheaths the knife. "Yeah."

I laugh. "I'm not lying, Clairen. You're all going to help me get the Aristocrats back."

Her nostrils flare at that. "Oh yeah? Why's that?"

I glance over my shoulder. "Because I can't restart Evanescence without them."

chapter twenty-four

POST-AMERICAN DATE: 7/8/232

LONGITUDINAL TIMESTAMP: 2:40

LOCATION: REBEL BASE, KAIROS

The little girl, Ani, comes in with a tray and sets it down on the table between Quent and me.

"Thank you," I say.

She only ducks her head and runs away.

"You have a way with kids," he teases.

Half starved, I pick up my bowl, tuck into my gruel. "Shut up." I shovel in a few bites before I realize that Quent isn't eating with me. Looking up, I see he's watching me with an expression that I assume he'd make if I were peeling off sections of my flesh. I swallow what's in my mouth. "What?"

"How are you eating that?"

Looking into the bowl so he can't see my annoyance, I say, "Because it's what was put in front of me and I'm hungry. I suggest you eat, too. You need your strength."

"I can't eat this."

I let my hands slip off the table, ball my fists on my knees. "Quentin, you're being a spoiled brat. This is all they have because it's all you fed them, so just eat it."

He's quiet for a long moment. Then he slowly says, "Okay. Okay. I'm gonna ignore the implication that I'm the one who personally packs and ships the aid containers that come down the tracks for these people. I'm being spoiled, I'm sure I am. I'm only being that way because I honestly don't know how to cope with eating salty cement, but"—he takes a deep breath—"I'll try my best."

"Good." I go back to eating.

Out of the corner of my eye, I see him lift his spoon and take a bite. It takes him a long time to chew. I can hear him swallow and he takes a large gulp of water afterward. "Can I just ask you something?" he says, voice light. "How are you managing? I mean, you've always loved food. I could never fathom why or how you managed to eat so much in Nexis. It's always seemed like you could eat anything. Maybe you can hand me a few pointers."

"Practice," I hedge, mouth full.

"Practice? Who would wanna do that? I mean, you don't eat stuff like this unless you have to." He lifts a spoonful of it and lets it fall back into the bowl with a *splat*. Then he turns and grins at me in that playful, mysterious way that lets me know he's joking.

But something inside breaks and I look away, unable to keep eye contact. I don't want to admit I developed a tolerance for gruel out of necessity. I don't want Quent to learn what happened to me while I was being held captive, or how I suffered. I don't want him to know the depths of my shame and desperation, that I resorted to theft and trickery—things he taught me in Nexis—to survive in Real World. But Quent can tell when something is up with me, and it's clear in his tone as he says, "Ella?"

My cheeks heat. "I've had some practice."

"Why would you want to practice something like that? The only reason to eat this is if you were forced t—" He takes a breath in sudden comprehension.

I can feel the strands of data coming together in his head, the code executing and being read, and it makes my heart break. I curl my arms around myself, sheltering the ache in my heart and the remembered hollowness in my stomach.

A moment later, he's on his feet, his chair collapsing behind him, and he's pulling me to my feet, making me drop my spoon and upset my bowl, and folding me into his embrace.

And just like that, I feel burning tears escape. I brush at them, frustrated with all the tears I've cried in the past few days. I try to be strong, try to explain myself. "It's hard. I can't keep myself from feeling it all again." I suck a desperate gulp of air. "That kind of hunger… It's insane making."

"Elle," he utters. But no other words come. There's just this shaking reinforcement of his embrace on me. Rage shaking. "Never again. Not while there is breath in my body." He draws me back, his hands wander up my arms, slide up my neck, and he kisses me. I kiss him back. And then he draws away slightly and speaks against my lips. "Why didn't you tell me? I could have gotten you out. I could have saved you that pain, this memory."

A desperate choke escapes me and I look away. "I wanted to, but"—I make a guttural noise and pull away—"it's so complicated, I can't explain it."

Quent steps into my line of sight. "Try."

I grind my teeth, searching for words.

"We're not in the game anymore, Elle. We can't hide this stuff from each other. This is real. Repercussions are real."

"I know," I snap. "Trust me, I'm well aware of repercussions. Even when it's a game, there are repercussions. Or hadn't you noticed?"

He doesn't respond.

I drop my shoulders. "I'm sorry, I shouldn't take this out on you. It's not your fault."

"Maybe it is," he says quietly. "I knew something was wrong. I knew you were hiding it. I could have looked into it, could have poked my nose in places you didn't want me to, but I didn't. You suffered because I didn't do anything about it, even though I sensed I should have."

I look over my shoulder at him. "Don't you dare blame yourself for what happened to me in Evanescence. You were only respecting my wishes."

He meets my glare. "Maybe I shouldn't have even done that."

Holding his gaze, I say, "You did the right thing. I trusted you to respect my wishes, just as you trusted me to tell you something important, not keep secrets. I'm the one who betrayed that trust, not you. I should have told you what was going on." I rub my arms, suddenly feeling cold. "I didn't know what I'd be asking you to get yourself into. At the time, I didn't know what was going on or who was holding me captive. I had no idea why they'd faked my death or why they were starving me or why I wasn't able to communicate with anyone from the outside except through the game. I didn't know if they were dangerous. I didn't want you to get hurt."

He scoffs. "You do realize I am—or, was—one of the most powerful people in Evanescence, right? No one would have dared touch me."

"I didn't. Not then. How would I have known you were Quentin Cyr?"

Brows lifting, he concedes my point. Then he reaches out and his hand slides over my hip, pulling me near again.

I shut my eyes and rest my head against his shoulder. It feels so good to be close to him. I'm strong, I know that. But he makes me feel stronger. "I'm sorry I hid what was going on from you."

His hand snakes up, cradles my head as he leans over me, protective and strong. "And I'm sorry I hid who I was from you. It was wrong of me to have done what I did with you and Gus. But I don't regret it. I never would have gotten to know you…to fall in love with you if I hadn't."

"Love? Well," a sharp female voice sounds from the doorway. Quent tenses. "That's a far cry from pretending in a game, isn't it? And when were you going to tell me about this little secret?"

Quent draws back, revealing Lady Cyr standing in the doorway. Tall, lean, and carved to perfection, Lady Cyr is like a Grecian statue. It's hard to believe that, like Zane, there is a Natural under all that. Like her sons, her Alts have burned out, leaving a fine tracery of scar-like lines all over her still-pearly skin. Though, I have to wonder if, like Quent, she can light up at will.

"Mom," he breathes. And he sounds like he's been caught with his hand in the cookie jar.

She smiles at him and holds her arms out, and he gladly goes into her embrace.

"It's good to see you're alive and well," she says, holding him. And then she grabs his ear and twists, making him double over with a wince. "And it's not so good to see you acting like an idiot. What did I say about leaving Ella alone?"

"Ow, Mom, come on," Quent grunts.

She growls at him, but I can see in her bright blue eyes and quirked mouth that she's not really meaning to hurt him or that she's really mad. She releases him and gives him a light slap on the shoulder. "Womanizer, you're as bad as your brother. Let me see her."

Quent rolls his eyes and steps out of her way.

I hold my breath as Lady Cyr breezes toward me. Impulse kicks in and before I know what I'm doing, I'm moving to curtsy to her.

"Ah!" she says, holding her finger up in admonishment. "Don't you dare, Ellani Drexel, or I'll box your ears as bad as I do that foolish son of mine. You stand straight and tall when you talk to me. We're equals now, thank the network." She puts her fists on her hips and gives me a critical eye. "You look just like Cleo."

"Thank you."

"It's not a compliment. To be honest, it's a little off-putting."

"Mom," Quent hisses in embarrassment.

She waves her hand in dismissal. "Oh please, there's no need to worry about feelings here. Your girl, she's got a steel frame. Haven't you?"

I clasp my hands behind my back so she can't see how bad I'm still shaking from my memories about being starved.

"You're aware I was your mother's friend?"

I nod. "I know a little about you and her. And what she was all about. Not much, though."

She nods, making strands of her now gray hair fall from behind her ear to brush her high forehead. "You'll figure it out. We're a complicated lot, we Tricksters." She offers her hand. "I'm Kit Boyd."

I scrunch my brow, confused. "Not Kit Cyr anymore?"

A shadow tangles her expression, narrowing her lips and flaring her eyes. "Not anymore, no."

I feel Quent step up close behind me and touch my back in reassurance. He must understand how unnerving standing before his mother is. Her presence practically ignites the room. I guess I never noticed it when she stood beside President Cyr, but alone, she's an obvious force to be reckoned with, and I wonder if this is what drew Quent's father to her in the first place. "Boyd is mom's first married name. She prefers it."

I nod. I can understand her wanting to shed Cyr's name. Especially if he was as awful as they've painted him to be.

Kit crosses her arms and stares at us for a long moment. "Just look at you two. The fox and the spider. Together again. Cleo would be crying, it's so beautiful. We always did talk about our children carrying on the tradition," she notes, expression wistful. "Although, the arrangement had been with Zane and Ella, not you, Quent. You were supposed to end up with Carsai Sheldon, secure the strength of the Presidency with a political marriage. Sheldon's support would have provided us a seamless coup."

Quent rolls his eyes. "It's a good thing the dome fell, then, isn't it?"

She frowns. "That set us back."

"Oh come off it," he shoots back at her. "Zane went off track with Clairen, and if you wanna split hairs, you can blame Simon for killing Ella off in the first place. How was Zane gonna marry a dead girl? Besides, you *knew* I was playing with her."

"That's why I told you to stop your silly pursuit of finding her Real World player."

"So, you were aware Ella was actually alive, weren't you?" His tone is a dangerous accusation.

A flash in Kit's eyes and then her face settles to a deadly calm neutral. "Yes."

I step forward. "Then you knew about the virus. Uncle Simon had said 'We've been watching.' He meant you and him, didn't he?"

She grins at me. "Who else would he mean? Only Simon, your caretakers, and I knew you were alive. It was best to keep you hidden from the President and his suspicious inclinations. I couldn't have him going after you like he did Cleo and

Warren. It was important you get in the game, important you complete your intended role."

Quent stiffens against me. "Then you knew what Simon was doing to her?"

As I watch Kit visibly think through her next words, I hold my breath. Though, there's nothing she could say that would get him to forgive her. I know Quent well enough for that. And she must, too, because she doesn't answer, just clears her throat and turns away from us. "As I've always taught you, Quentin. Sacrifices needed to be made for the greater good. Now, I've come to talk to Ella about her plan to—"

"That's it?" Quent demands. "All you have to say? You stand complicit in the imprisonment and torture of your best friend's child—the woman I love—and your only defense is that sacrifices must be made?"

She goes still, lifts her chin. "What else would you have me do?"

He straightens. "Apologize, at the very least."

Kit lifts a brow, examines him, examines me. "I would, but I'm not sorry."

"What?" he breathes.

"I'm sorry it had to be Ella, I really am. Sorry it was the girl who my friend birthed. Sorry it was the woman you fell in love with. But she's the lynchpin. The tool. She was destined to be for more generations back than I can count. The Tricksters have been working toward this pivot point for hundreds of years. Perhaps one day you'll understand that. But she had to go in, had to plant that virus. And it had to be perfect. We did what we had to. Me, Cleo, Warren, Simon." She meets my eyes.

I swallow hard. "And that included torturing me to the point of near insanity?"

She grasps the doorway. "You needed to be pushed to the point where you realized what needed to be done. To make you evolve, grow stronger, ascend this place of purgatory. Your father assumed that simply explaining it to you, giving you the choice, would be the thing that swayed you. But come on, let's look at the girl you were. Simon didn't believe you'd volunteer to plant the virus unless you were given a very good reason. I agreed with him. None of us wanted to hurt you, Ella, you need to understand that. But you need to comprehend just how important you are. You're going to save us all."

"Yeah," I say. "I sort of got that message."

"Good. I'm glad you're finally getting onboard. It makes everything so much easier. Of course, way off course." She grasps her chin and turns in thought. "I'll have to completely recalculate everything."

I step forward. "No."

Her eyes are sharp as she looks over her shoulder. "Excuse me?"

"I said, no."

She spins fully now, obviously ready to fight me.

"I'm done being your puppet. I'm done letting you decide what I'm doing and where I'm going. I'm done with you playing God."

She scoffs and the danger in her eyes makes Quent's hand flinch on my back. "You don't have a choice. We made sure of that."

"I'm well aware." I have to step into this savior role. "I have to do some things, only because there's no other choice. But," I say in emphasis, "your role is over. There's only one fox I trust and it's him." I toss my chin to indicate Quent. "We new Tricksters inherited this mess you fools made with your little games and we're going to fix it. And we're doing it our way. You don't like it? Well, I've got a bullet with your name on it." I stand, drawn tight as a bow with my face red and my fists balled, and I stare at her, huffing; I'm so angry I could punch her.

Quent is so still and tense beside me that I'm pretty sure I could flick him and he'd shatter.

And Lady Cyr? She just stares at me, long and hard. Finally, she smirks. "You're a lot like your mother. She'd be very proud of you."

I don't want to be like my mother.

Her gaze shifts to her son. "You picked a good one. You've got my blessing and my support. Fix this hideous mistake. Oh," she says, hand poised on the doorjamb, "I came to get you. Mac wanted a round table, get you to tell us what your plan of attack is."

"So you were willing to give Ella the lead all along?" Quent asks.

"*He* was. I told him he was an idiot and we'd let you take command over my dead body. But I've changed my mind. I think we're in fine hands."

I stare after her, even after she disappears.

Quent says, "I can't believe you threatened to shoot my mother."

A scoff breaks free and he suddenly laughs with me and when we've giggled so hard that we're tearing and neither of us can breathe, he drapes his arm around me. "Come on, let's take over this joint."

"Don't tease me." I wheeze, still trying to catch my breath.

"Me? Tease you?" He grasps my hand, swings me around in a twirl like we're on the dance floor, then dips me. "Never."

Still in the dip, I smile at him. "I'm glad you're my fox."

He pulls me up, sets me back on my feet. "And I'm glad you're my spider." We start walking and he sets a hand on my shoulder. "Even more glad that you only have two feet."

"I don't have any feet, actually."

He shrugs. "That doesn't change anything. You're still you."

Biting my lip, I look away from him. "I know. That's why

I'm giving one of my legs up. I know my disability doesn't make me who I am. I'm just scared."

"Don't be. I'll make it quick and painless."

I shake my head. "I'm not afraid of the pain. I'm afraid of the physical limitations."

Quent lowers his chin, traps me with his amber eyes. "Elle, real legs, no legs, VR legs, fake legs, one leg—you have no limitations. You get through locked doors that no one else can get through."

"This time I need help doing it."

"Have you considered how you're going to make all of this happen?"

"I'll explain it when I've gotten everyone in one place."

chapter twenty-five

POST-AMERICAN DATE: 7/8/232

LONGITUDINAL TIMESTAMP: 3:12 A.M.

LOCATION: REBEL BASE, KAIROS

"—and that's about the long and short of it," I say, finishing my explanation of how I intend to make magic happen. And it will be magic. With a healthy dose of technology for good measure.

Everyone just stares at me, mouths agape. Finally, Mac says, "I don't think I understand half of what was just said to me."

Zane sits back, scratches his chin. "The logistics of it…"

Cam and Sid glance at each other, then Sid says, "It *is* theoretically sound."

Mac shakes his head. "You're asking us to put a lot of faith in you."

I turn to him. "You put a lot of weight on my shoulders to begin with." I look around the table, meet everyone's eyes. "All of you. You let this happen. You brought it about with your revolutionary fervor and now I have to pick up the pieces and try and save everyone's asses."

"Follow you or die, is that the option?" Clairen asks.

"No. None of you are gonna die if I don't restart Evanescence. If this Taurus guy doesn't strike first and completely obliterate you, if he doesn't use the Aristocrats to his own ends in an effort to enslave you all, you could go on doing your day to day. You'll be living in masks, figuring out how to survive without the dome's meager support of the very basics like food, water, and medicine. I'm sure there are other cities doing it somewhere, you could send out envoys, maybe learn from them. Maybe you'd survive. But I have to wonder, what was the point of all of this if you're not going to carry it through to the bitter end? Even if it means putting a little faith in a figurehead you created on a whim. Even if it means sticking your neck out for other people you may not like very much."

Eyes avoid mine, look at the table, off to the side, at the ceiling, examine nails. I feel Quent's hand find my knee and he squeezes it. "If anyone could do it," he says, "it's you, Elle."

"It's not just me," I correct. "It's all of us. Everyone in this complex will be just as important as the Aristocrats we're trying to save. Everyone is instrumental here."

"But," Delia says, "if something goes wrong?"

"That's what this whole plan is built on, assurance against something going wrong. Right?" Gus asks, glancing up at me with bright eyes.

I nod. "If we spread our assets, we have a higher chance of at least some of us getting through. Some is better than none."

Clairen worries the end of her ponytail. "We don't have much time to pull this all together."

"No," I agree. "That's why I need everyone's help." I swallow hard, look to the faces around the circular table and offer my hand at the center. "Who's in?"

Without hesitation Quent puts his hand over mine. "You

have me. And my Dolls."

Delia puts hers on next. "Where Gus goes, I go." She smiles sheepishly. "But I would have helped anyway."

I grin at her in thanks.

Zane and Kit put theirs on. Zane looks to Clairen and she looks to Mac.

Mac doesn't unfold his arms. "I don't like making agreements when I don't know the terms of what I'm getting myself into."

I bite my lip, start wracking my brain for a different way to explain myself. A way that a Disfavored man who knows nothing about virtual reality games or technology can understand.

"But you've got my support. If only because I don't have any other options."

Held breath is released around me and I can feel it on my skin. "Then by proxy," Clairen comes forward, enthusiastically slaps her hand down on Zane's, "you've got mine, the Unmentionables, and the rebels."

"Good," I say, pulling my hand away. "Now we just need the Aristocrats and Disfavored to cooperate like we expect."

Quent says, "What do you need us to do?"

"Delia and I will handle the programming end. I'll dip back into Redux if I have to, ask my mother and father for some help, but I'm pretty confident that I'll be able to come up with the patch program for The Broadcast and the Main Frame. Delia, since it's your specialty, you're in charge of individualized touch points for the Aristocrats."

"I'd need their personal information for that," she says.

"I can help you there," Kit says. She slides off her slap-bracelet and pushes it across the table. "Personal files for every resident in Evanescence. You'll just need a way to read it."

Delia hands it to Gus. "Done."

Smirking, I glance to my other side. "Quent, you, Gus, Sid, and Cam have an Engineering think-tank between the four of you. I assume you'll guess what we'll need."

Quent touches my knee. "Even before you."

"Ugh, gag me," I hear Delaney mutter.

"Delaney, I need you and Aaron to make sure we have quick and easy access to equipment and transportation. I need something for Delia and me to work with and anything Quent and his Dolls need to get the gaming houses up and running and to remodel the access chips."

"Clairen and Mac, I need all of your people debriefed and prepared with their own drop points and equipment. You think you can coordinate that and get total compliance?"

"Easy peasy," Clairen barks.

"Zane, have you got your part?"

He nods. "I just need to know where to go and I need Angelique to be there, too. I can't pull the whole show off on my own."

I glance at Clairen, who nods. "We'll make it happen."

I sit back, trying to think if I've missed something, and when I can't think of anything, I look up. "Anything else?"

There doesn't seem to be, though I'm sure everyone is just highly overwhelmed.

One of Clairen's Unmentionables pops her head in. "She folded."

Quent checks the arcane clock on the wall. "An hour and four minutes. Not bad."

"Don't congratulate me yet."

"This is a big sacrifice, Ella," Kit says. "Are you sure you want to do this?"

Avoiding everyone's eyes, I nod.

"Has anyone considered that this is going to deeply alter how the Disfavored see Ella?" Zane wonders. "We're hinging on them folding to the Ella the Savior protocol right? What if this new body shape does something to alter that?"

"I've thought of that already," I say. "Let me handle it."

"I don't like not knowing what you're planning," Mac says.

"You've already admitted you don't understand half of what I'm doing but you've already dedicated yourself to it. Don't get cold feet now, it's bad for morale. If you'll all excuse me, I have to go hack my leg off for the sake of your skins."

chapter twenty-six

POST-AMERICAN DATE: 7/9/232

LONGITUDINAL TIMESTAMP: 8:08 P.M.

LOCATION: REBEL BASE, KAIROS

Clairen's teal eyes slice over the rebels, meeting the gaze of each man in turn. "Remember, this is a quick in and out. The top priority is stealth. We get in, release the prisoners, and get out. Aristocrats are our primary objective. I can't stress enough how important this mission is. Without them, the city is dead. We're all dead. You got that?"

There are perhaps five dozen of them, dark and scarred, ready for anything. These are not the broken and bedraggled creatures I used to watch from my web in my father's workroom.

"Each of you has been designated a specific drop point and an access chip. You're to break into small groups. Each group is responsible for releasing and protecting one Aristocrat. You are to get that Aristocrat to your drop point at all costs. If, for some reason, your comrades fall and you find yourself needing to take on more than one Aristocrat, you are to do so. So long as the Aristocrats arrive alive at a drop zone, have an access chip in their hand, and insert that access chip, the mission is a success."

Quent shifts on the crate beside me, his knuckles brushing mine. We're sitting at the back with Delia, Delaney, Sid, Aaron, and Gus near one of the vehicles. Zane and Kit are with Mac somewhere in the honeycomb network of canvas tunnels the rebels call a base. Around us, the rebels mill around, preparing to go out to rescue the captured Aristocrats.

As Clairen moves toward us, Delia steps in front of her. "What happens if what this Stormy girl told us is a lie?"

The pale skin under Clairen's eye twitches, as if annoyed that someone would invite such bad luck with speculation. "Then we're screwed and I shoot her in the head."

"And," Quent says, "if she's telling the truth about the layout and the numbers, it's still gonna be a tough rescue."

Clairen doesn't answer. Instead she points at Aaron. "You, head up Razor team. Guard from the east." She looks around to Quent. "Where's your other Doll?"

"Cam's not coming," Quent says. "I excused him from duty for a few days. To grieve."

I lower my chin, hiding my expression as an image of Beau lying in a pool of blood flashes into my mind.

Annoyed, Clairen growls under her breath. "God, you'd think we weren't all in the midst of a constant funeral dirge." She spins on her heel.

Sid says, "I'll help."

She gives him a sidelong glance. "You any good with a gun?"

"I'm a Doll," he says, as if that should answer all the questions.

She tilts her head, considering this.

"Plus, I'm an Electrical Engineer with some medical background."

"Then no." Clairen waves her hand in dismissal. "Gus, you

think you can take Talon to the west, while Delaney takes Fang to the north, and I'll go to the south with Spur?"

"Sure," Gus says, but Clairen is already walking away, not caring whether he thinks he can or not, apparently.

I grasp Quent's sleeve as I struggle to stand on my one good leg and hobble after her on my crutches. Realizing I won't catch up to her fast pace, I call to her, "What team do you want us on?"

Clairen turns, looks at me, and lets out a half laugh. "You're *not* coming."

Stunned I blink at her. "What?"

She turns to me fully. "You're too valuable to take into Taurus's stronghold, Ellani." Her eyes glance toward Delia. "As is your friend." Then back toward Sid. "And that one."

"Wait, what?" Delia squawks. "That's not fair!"

Clairen gets in Delia's face, stares her down. "It's perfectly fair. You couldn't fight if your life depended on it. And we need you *alive*. If, for some reason, we can't get your friends back, we'll be relying on the few of you we have to reboot the city. We need you safe."

Scowling, Delia turns to me. "Say something!"

I don't know what she wants me to say. If the whole point is to satisfy my argument they need as many Aristocrats as they can get to reboot the city, I can't argue with Clairen. Instead, I say, "Then maybe you shouldn't take Gus or Quent, either."

"Elle," Quent hisses, nudging me. "I have to go."

"What?" I turn to him, eyes pleading. "I don't want you to go. Not if I can't protect you."

"Protect him?" Clairen spits. "You? You're missing a leg!"

I scowl at her. "Yes, me. I've always got his back and he's got mine." I meet his eyes. "I don't trust anyone else."

Quent touches my shoulder. "I'll have my brother with

me and Gus has our back. It'll be okay."

I don't like it. Not one bit. It feels all wrong, being separated from him again. "We should stay together. This doesn't feel right."

"I know." Then he leans forward and plants a kiss on my forehead. "I'll be back. If you stay, then I'll have a reason to come back."

Sid gravitates closer to us. "I agree with Ella, Quent. It's not right. I'm supposed to protect you. It's my job."

"You've got new orders," Quent says. "Your new orders are to protect Ella with your life. She's the new me—the most valuable person to Evanescence—so you'd better get used to it."

As much as I know Sid likes me, he still frowns and I don't blame him.

Behind me, I can hear Delia saying, "I swear on the Main Frame, if you don't bring him back in one piece, I'll never help you reboot Evanescence. I'll kill myself first." She's talking to Clairen, who looks bored by all of it. Delia grabs her lapel. "You hear?"

Clairen grabs Delia's wrist, wrenches herself away. "Yeah, I hear, Domite. Back off."

Gus intercepts them, grasping Delia's shoulders and easing her back toward one of the trucks. They share a heated few words before Delia storms off and Gus goes chasing after her.

Quent's fingers slide over my elbow and I look back at him. "Please be safe."

He leans in and kisses me again, this time on the mouth. After a long, hot kiss, he pulls away and rests his forehead against mine. "Wish me luck. All the luck because we're going to need it to get everyone back."

"Don't say things like that. I'm likely to tie you up and

refuse to let you go at all." I hold my breath against my thundering heart and the panic it wants to cause. Reaching up, I just hold him close. And I hope, more than anything, this isn't for the last time.

"We're out in two hours," Clairen announces. "Better prep yourselves." She turns and disappears down a corridor.

Silent and stiff, I sit with Quent as he begins checking his weapons. Wanting something—anything—to do to occupy myself, I pick up a semi-automatic pistol and begin cleaning it as I try to wrap my mind around everything that is going on.

I stare at the gun in my hand. Determined. I wish I could be there to help them. "It should be me doing this. Not you."

"It should be both of us," he says. "But you're helping in your own way."

I look up. "How?"

"You're the one who pointed out how much the Disfavored need the remaining Aristocrats." He smiles and studies the pistol he's holding. "All that brain wracking I've been doing trying to figure out a way, and all you had to do was breathe a few obvious syllables to get them to understand how important those refugees are. And you've managed to orchestrate this whole plan, all on your own. We've reversed roles. This time you know what's right to say, and I'm the one going in, guns blazing."

I slam down the weapon and stare at it. "Don't you dare go in guns blazing."

He's quiet for a long time. So long that I lift my gaze and meet his troubled expression. I drop my shoulders. "Will you please stop looking at me like I'm going to break?"

He lifts a brow. "I'm just worried. You've been through a lot lately."

"We both have. You have just as much reason for a meltdown as me." I point at his gun. "And have you even thought about the fact that if you draw that gun out here, you'll be killing for real?"

He looks away and mutters, "I've already killed for real, remember?"

I close my mouth. Right. He shot my uncle. And he snapped that cannibal's neck like a twig. "Is it bothering you?"

His face twists. "You know how I feel. But I'm trying not to think about it. This isn't the time, so I'm just outrunning it for now."

"I understand. One day, we're both going to wake up from a decent night's sleep and not think about what's gone on the past few days."

He closes his eyes. "One day. Maybe when this is all over, when you're designing dresses and I'm engineering some foolish vehicle, and we have a dog."

I lean against the steel frame behind me and smile at the resuscitated dream we once shared of a future together in Nexis. "Dogs don't exist out here."

"I know."

"Still, I like the idea."

He takes a deep breath. "We've had this discussion once already, this whole 'we might die thing.' I don't like the idea of even doing this. It's dangerous."

A small light glimmers before me. "Then don't go."

"I have to go. I'm the President of Evanescence. The reality is, if we manage to save those people, I'm going to be in charge of them. And, therefore, I need to be the one who goes in there and orchestrates their release. I have to do this. Just like you have to stand up and become the leader of the Disfavored."

I nod. I can't let my fear of losing him damn more lives. And I can't let my fear make him even more afraid. The only time I've ever seen him looking this unsure is the moment when the aerovator doors closed between him and Zane. "Hey," I say, trying to be lighthearted for him. "Where is that daredevil I fell in love with?"

He gives me a dark grin. "I believe I left him back in Nexis—bleeding on the floor in the Central Dominion—and he's going to stay there because out here, shit's real. Out here, I die for real. I lose you for real. Game over. For real."

I look away. "You just had to say it out loud."

"Had to make sure you realized that. Just in case you got any stupid ideas about coming after us."

I frown at my shoe. "The thought had crossed my mind."

His amused voice says, "I'm aware."

I huff, hating that he understands me so well. I couldn't sneak up on him if I wanted to. "I need to fantasize about being there with you, otherwise I'm liable to completely melt down and force you to stay behind. Because I'm really scared, Quent. But we both have a responsibility, promises to keep. And we can't be selfish."

He rubs his eyes. "Yeah."

I touch his knee. "I love you. You know that, right?"

He smirks. "I had a suspicion." Then his expression sobers. "I wouldn't endanger us unless I had to."

part six:

ELLA THE SAVIOR

chapter twenty-seven

POST-AMERICAN DATE: 7/10/232

LONGITUDINAL TIMESTAMP: 1:00 A.M.

LOCATION: REBEL BASE, KAIROS

"Time," I breathe. "Such a strange thing when you think about it."

Delia stirs next to me; she's not sleeping. She's no closer to sleep than I am. How could she be? Gus is out there. With Quent. I'm just as worried about Gus as I am Quent, but I don't tell her that. It's not my place.

"I don't believe in time," Delia finally says. "Not anymore. It's just a dumb way to measure how empty our lives are."

I turn on my side, stare at her profile in the darkness. "Why emptiness? Why not fullness? Why not measure in good things, Dee?"

She takes a long breath, lets it out. "I suppose you could. I just remember the bad things so much more clearly."

I sit up and when I do the faint light coming from the mostly extinguished light-stick catches the tears on her cheeks. Trying not to notice, I wrap my arms around my leg. "Why can we only seem to remember bad things so clearly?"

She turns her head away from me. "Gus says that it's the bad things that shape you into who you are. That's why you remember them so well."

Where do the bad things start? "If that's true, then I start much further back than I think. I mean, my mother and father came together under bad circumstances, her being brought in from living a nightmare in the Undertunnel." I shiver, thinking about the prospect of resorting to cannibalism to survive. Mom lived, so did Kit and Zane. That means they *must* have eaten what was available to them. The idea that I'm born of a body who ingested another human's flesh makes my skin crawl. I change the subject before I venture too far down my mother's dark rabbit hole. "And my father betrayed the woman he loved to be with my mother."

"I don't think my parents ever did anything bad," Delia says.

I force a smile. "That means you were born innocent. You're a good person, Dee, not like me."

"No," she grunts. "I'm not good at all. I've done a lot of bad things."

"You?" I breathe with a laugh. "Not the Delia I knew."

She hitches her blanket up over her shoulder, as if she's cold. "The Delia you knew is dead. I killed her and I liked it."

Bastian told me about this. About the person Delia is now. For a long moment, I just stare at her. Her abrasive voice, her brisk tone, the words… I don't know what to make of them. How could the girl I knew be this person? And then it seems clear. "When I died… That was the first bad thing, wasn't it?"

"Death is powerful. Transformative. The person who dies goes through the last transformation—puts a period at the end of their story. But the people left behind?" She shakes her head. "That's a new paragraph, a new chapter. For some it's the climax. Everything falls after that. Maybe they become the villain."

"I'm sorry you had to go through that."

"I'm not," she says. "I like who I am now. That girl was weak and small. She was incapable of being alone or standing for what she believed in. She would have crumpled into a ball during the attack. This one grabbed her best friend and saved them both. This one is handling the death of her family far better than those around her. This one is a rock."

"Are you?" I ask. "A rock, I mean. Rocks are hard, immovable, unfeeling. You're not like that. You feel a lot. Just like I do."

"You don't know what I feel."

I smile at her. "You love Gus. And you're scared for Carsai. You miss your parents, though you try hard not to show it. And losing Nina was another bad moment that transformed you into something else."

She turns, looks at me in the darkness, and her eyes are a mixture of dark hate and bewilderment, but it doesn't faze me. She wants to pretend she's a rock and doesn't like that I can see the soft interior. I can't fault her for that.

"You're a good person, Delia. No amount of convincing yourself that you have no heart or that you're made of stone will change that fact. You care for your own deeply, which is what makes you wonderful. You shouldn't deny that about yourself because it's your biggest strength."

She looks away again. "I hate you."

I grin bigger. "No you don't."

"I want to hate you," she argues. "Gus is right, it's impossible not to love you. And I hate you because you make it so easy for him to see those things in you that he doesn't see in me."

"What are you talking about? Gus sees a lot of good things in you. He wouldn't have started dating you otherwise. He has feelings for me because they were downloaded into him. But he chose *you*. That means he favors you, Dee. Don't you see?"

She's quiet for a long time. "You think we could be happy? Gus and me?"

I shrug. "As happy as anybody. I don't know what they're gonna do with us when we get to Evanescence, but I hope we can just live out our days in peace. Don't you?"

A siren begins to blare.

We both sit up. "What's that?" she yells over the noise.

"I don't know."

We sit, paralyzed with uncertainty, then Sid practically rips the door as he tears at the zipper. "Get up. Both of you. We need to leave."

Dee is on her feet and shoving them into boots in less than a second. I move to do the same, struggling to stand on one leg and grab at my crutches. Sid slips in and lifts me. "Sorry, but it'll be faster this way."

Cam appears behind him. "Got 'em?"

He glances behind himself, checks us up and down, and steps forward. The corridor beyond is dark, but there are flashing lights in the main chamber at the end of the hall. I can hear boots pounding on the stone and yelling. In the distance, shooting begins.

"What's going on?" Delia asks as she trails us to the main chamber.

"I think we're being raided," Sid answers. A few of the remaining rebels run past us, guns lifted. Knowing Sid can't defend with me in his arms, I reach for my gun, only to find I don't have one. He grabbed me before I could grab it.

I reach down and take his out of its holster. "What do you mean?"

"I don't know, but we have to go. Now."

I turn to Cam. "Go get Stormy."

"What?"

"You heard me."

"But—"

"Damnit, I made a promise to her, I'm gonna keep it. Either you go get her or I'm getting down and going to get her myself."

Frowning, Cam turns and hustles off.

I tap Sid on the shoulder. "Okay, let's go, we're sitting ducks out here."

I keep one arm around Sid's neck as he runs and the other outstretched with my gun. Once we reach the central chamber, we slam into a wall of bedlam. Screaming, running, things being hastily loaded and thrown onto the backs of trucks that are already rumbling and belching black smoke. Sid steps toward one. I hold my breath as he sets me on the floor, and I help Delia climb in. Inside, there are already half a dozen Disfavored rebels, their faces covered in masks. Sid glances around.

I cover him with the gun. "You scc Cam?"

"Not yet."

"Hurry up, Cam," I whisper. Then, "What about the others? Are they back?"

Sid doesn't look at me as he begins to wrestle things out of a box under the bench seat. "Don't know."

Grabbing the bar, I slide to the end of the truck. "I'm not leaving without Quent." I move to climb out, but Cam appcars, carrying Stormy. He chucks her practically on top of mc and it takes me precious moments to untangle myself from her. Whcn I finally get my balance and grab for my crutches, I'm once again knocked to the floor with a clang as someone suddenly hits the gas and the truck lurches backward, nearly running over Cam, who only manages to save himself from being backed over by grabbing the sidebar and hauling himself up.

Delia grasps my arm, helps me back onto my butt as the

vehicle turns in a wide arc that makes us all tip to one side. A few thuds smack at the bottom and sides of the truck as it drives over what I hope are just boxes and not bodies.

A sudden burst of gunfire opens up. Metallic pinging hails the side of the truck, and then bullets are coming through the canvas. Delia screams.

"Get down!" someone yells.

The truck swerves again. Bodies fall around me. Most alive, a couple dead.

Sid crawls toward us. "Here, put this on." He shoves something onto my face. I fight him because whatever it is, it's uncomfortable. But then I realize it's a mask. I struggle into it, hoping it's on properly. The goggles fog instantly, blinding me to everything except the blood that's slowly circulating around the bed of the truck as our driver wrenches the wheel back and forth. I gasp and gulp at strange, stale air. It's hard to breathe with a mask on in normal circumstances, so it's three times harder now that I'm certain that I'm hyperventilating. My fingers twitch. I need the gun that flew from my hand when Cam tossed Stormy at me. I need the spider threads I used in Nexis. I don't have either.

As Cam laces the canvas backing closed behind us, I check my surroundings. Delia is on the floor next to me, Sid is helping her into a mask. Two dead. Eight others alive. I reach for the rifle trapped under one of the bodies and above all the noise, I hear a bullet slide into a chamber at my temple.

"Don't."

It's Stormy. I recognize her raised voice.

"Are you threatening me with my own gun?"

There's a pause. "Yes. Yes I am."

"I give you a perfectly good leg and this is how you repay me." Rolling my eyes, I kick out with my good leg. My foot hits her square in the chest, sends her flying. It takes her too long to recover and by the time she does, I have both the rifle and my gun aimed at her. "Just because you can stand now doesn't make you invincible. Now take cover and shut up."

She remains crouched where she is. "They're here for me."

"Well they're not gonna get you."

Another volley of bullets. *Rat-tat-tat-tatta. Ping. Tink. Tink.*

Stormy screams and hits the floor. Instinct kicks in and I'm throwing myself over her, defensive.

She's not hurt, just scared. "They're shooting at me!"

Delia reaches out, grabs Stormy's hand. "It's gonna be okay!" she hollers over the thundering rumble of the truck as it accelerates up an incline. From what I remember of the base's layout, there are ramps that lead up and out at the city limits. I feel the truck gain momentum underneath me, opening up and speeding across The Waste.

In the half-light of the LED floodlights mounted on the truck following us, dust wafts through the shredded holes in the canvas. Outside for real now.

Something thumps hard on the top of the cabin in front of us. The truck swerves hard to the left. Stormy shrieks again. So do I, because it feels like we're going to tip. But then we're righted and we rock back and forth a few times. I'm about to breathe a sigh of relief, when I hear more ripping. This time from behind me.

I look back in time to see a body, stark in the light outside, climbing through the half-closed canvas. Gun raised, sharp teeth bright.

Cannibal.

Stormy struggles underneath me. "I told you!"

If the cannibals are here, what does that mean?

I curl around Stormy, half crush her, but I don't care. This way she's protected by my body, and the cannibal can't see her.

I raise both guns and it's like I was born with them in my hands. Screaming to match the howl of the creature among us, I shoot. He shoots, too. But my draw is quicker and his aim is thrown off by the bullet sliding home in his left shoulder. He falls backward, his momentum pushing him out of the canvas opening. I hear him hit the ground and roll behind us.

But there's another one just behind him.

This time it's Sid who takes him out. "Get behind me!"

"Like hell," I yell back. I scramble over Stormy, half sitting on her as I take up a crouched position beside him. "Cam, get your ass back here."

He doesn't have to be told twice.

There's silence. As silent as it can be, considering my thundering heart, Stormy's frantic breathing, Delia's cooing shushing, and the moan of one of the Disfavored who was injured in the second volley of shots.

Seconds turn to minutes, but that's eternity. The engine continues to hum under us and we drive straight, gravel and the sorry remains of long-dead vegetation kicking up under the truck as it eats the wasteland beneath it.

"Is it over?" Delia asks, voice shaking.

"No," Cam whispers. "Stay quiet. We're being followed."

"Followed?" she asks, sitting up. "But I don't—"

Something jars the side of the truck, clipping the back of it so that an awful metallic noise rattles me to my teeth, and I can suddenly see a vast section of desert passing behind us.

Anchored in a massive hole in the tailgate is a large metal hook, like the kind Quent once used to fish with in Nexis.

"Brace!" someone behind us yells.

I do as I'm told, grabbing hold of a bench seat leg just as another awful jarring slams my bones together. A body rolls past me.

"Stormy!"

I let go, slide along beside her. Screaming, her hands go up. Mine go out. I grab one just in time. Just as her body slides out of the back of the truck. I realize too late that I'm going with her, and we're both going down.

My ankle snags in something and it's like my body is on a medieval torture device I once read about in Dad's files. *Snap. Pop.* Pain. So much pain that black shoots around the edges and vomit explodes from my throat. But I don't let go. Can't let go.

Stormy's wild eyes, big and black as night. Her mouth, bloody and open wide in horror. The ground rushing just past her. Her hand in mine.

Don't let go.

Don't let go.

Don't.

Don't.

It's a mantra I repeat over and over again against the pain and the black.

More pain, hands grip me. Sid climbs over me, pulls Stormy up by her wrists. Her shaking body passes over me.

In the ghostly light of oncoming desert dawn, I see not one, but two vehicles following us. Each spilling over with cannibals.

"Gun!" I scream. But I'm already raising it. I didn't let go of that, either. Clever me.

I lift it. I take aim. I fire.

I pull the hammer back, load the next round in the chamber. Around me I hear more guns firing, filling the space between my rounds.

Again. *Boom.*

And again. *Boom.*

And again. *Boom.*

I keep going. I keep firing. Bodies fall into the desert

behind us. Roll, go black and still.

One of the trucks draws closer, overtaking us. Metal spikes eat at the world around me, shredding so that I can see more outside than in.

Someone shoots the driver pursuing us. A couple of cannibals jump at us in a last-ditch effort. They're shot before their hands can cling.

Bodies fall around me. I refuse to look at who they are. Instead, I fire another round, this time aiming for the driver. The next time aiming for the grinning grill at the front of the truck.

Boom.

Reload.

Boom.

As long as one of us is still firing, as long as the truck is still going, there's still hope.

Keep going.

Keep going.

Until there's nothing left.

Until all the bullets are gone and darkness and pain finally take me.

chapter twenty-eight

POST-AMERICAN DATE: 7/10/232

LONGITUDINAL TIMESTAMP: 6:02 A.M.

LOCATION: THE WASTE

"Ella? Ella!" Someone is shaking me. Groggy, I open my eyes but I wish I were back asleep almost as quickly, because the pain in my leg is so intense it makes me want to scream.

Delia blinks at me. "Are you all right?"

Trying to see through the pain spots, I squint at her and focus in sudden bright light. I still have my mask on. Around us, the yellow-brown miasma that is the sky passes over us like an unhealthy soup. Moving. We're still moving. Still in the truck.

I sit up, biting my lip against the pain.

"Careful," Sid says, grabbing my shoulders and supporting me from behind.

I glance around. Sid, hands bloody, but upright and okay. Cam next to Delia. His uniform has been torn to shreds and used to bandage a large bloody wound in his chest. He smiles, weary.

I search the floor. "Stormy?" Then I sit bolt upright. "Stormy!"

"I'm here." A small voice reports from behind me. In the darkness remaining in the cabin, Stormy sits grasping her knees in a pool of sticky blood. There are no bodies, only two remaining people who look just as wounded as Cam does.

I let out a breath of relief. "You're all right?" She seems shaky, sitting alone and scared. Eyes wide in the darkness. "Stormy?" I ask, confused why her terrified eyes are fixed on me.

"Ella," Delia breathes, placing a hand on my arm. She tosses her head downward and I follow the gesture. Only to find nothing there are all. A few feet away, my remaining prosthetic is caught between two of the legs of the bench-seat. The end is ragged and bloody, the neural links laying limp like white worms.

I look down at my leg. Or, my stump. Not even a stump anymore, just a gaping thing where a stump used to be. It's all crusted over with blood, but I can see the smooth bits where the scar remains and the rough patches where the prosthetic limb was once attached. Circulation to the sections has been tied off with part of what, I assume, is the rest of Cam's uniform and radiating around and up and all over is an intense pain that beats with my fragile heart.

My mouth tastes bitter. No wonder Stormy is looking at me like that.

"Oh, Ella," Delia whispers. She folds her arms around me, embracing me. "It's okay. We'll get new ones for you. We're almost home!"

"Home?" I glance around, confused.

"Here," Sid says, bending to lift me into his arms. "Looks like we've circled halfway around the city. We're coming up on the main gate." He sits me on a bench seat so I can lean out one of the rips in the canvas.

Dry wind beats at my matted hair, flakes of dust and debris bite my skin. To our left is nothing but brown, cracked earth. I can see where there used to be vegetation—trees and grass. The occasional foundation, picked clean of everything but the concrete. It smells metallic and musty. To our right is the outskirts of Kairos and beyond her, a massive blue moon fallen to earth.

Around the moon is a black belt and around the belt, a skirt of geometric shapes.

Evanescence. With her blue nano-glass dome. Her black wall to keep out the Disfavored. And the Outer Block, Kairos, spilling out all around her. Nothing ever looked so beautiful.

The truck takes a turn up a road that seems fairly wide for the ones I've seen in Kairos so far. I stare as she gets bigger and bigger until the only thing that I can see is the black wall and she's blocking the light like an angry parent come to frown on the creatures below.

But there's nothing to frown at. Only the toys left behind. The forts, the cars, the building blocks, and the spilled things.

Kairos abandoned.

Tin-sheet doors left ajar, ragged clothes still hanging on lines, pots of muddy water left by the wells, broken dishes in the streets, dirt collecting against the sides of buildings as wind blows it in and no feet shuffle it back out.

The stench remains. A deep, lingering scent. Defecation, decay. A few bodies lay rotting in the gutters, bloated and heaving in the sewage. I lift my uniform up over my mask, preferring the scent of my own vomit and the blood of strangers to this filth.

After traversing what seems like an endless approach of desperation and decay, we turn a corner and suddenly it's there. The gates of Evanescence thrown wide, with no care as to who enters.

Unquestioned, the truck advances, rolling over the bodies of Disfavored and droid alike—ground zero for the rebel infiltration that took place the night the Anansi Virus activated. The droids on the other side of the gate have gotten their just desserts at the hands of the Disfavored they kept out of the city. Torn to the very basest of components—easy targets once they were struck immobile by the city shutting down.

And the devastation continues. Block upon block destroyed, broken, decimated, violated, and vandalized. It seems as if nothing is untouched. Even the broken bodies of the poor Aristocrats who were either still alive or—circuits, I hope—dead before the Disfavored entered the city have been given the same treatment. Torn, decapitated, clothes ripped from their bodies, obscene things done to them.

Someone's trembling fingers find mine. I hear Delia whisper beside me, "Monsters."

And I believe what she says. This is the vilest display I have ever witnessed here or in the game. And I'm here to save these people? What's to stop them from doing the same thing to me? It's hard to tell if the initial experimentation through Redux created these monsters or if they would have acted like this on their own. Part of me hopes it's the brainwashing. It gives them some kind of excuse for this behavior. And it gives me hope. Because if this is the brainwashing, then there is hope that the secondary stage will work— that they will listen to their Savior.

I swallow hard, suddenly terrified. What if I'm not a savior at all? If I'm walking into a trap? If they want to do to me what they've done to these bodies piled along the street like trash? Rape me, beat me, cut off my remaining limbs, rip out my innards and string them along the street like festival garland, put my head on a pike. It smells in here like it smells out there and that doesn't compute. Evanescence always smelled fresh and clean, like machine oil and plastic. Not offal.

"I'm going to be sick." Delia pulls away and begins heaving over the side of the truck, leaving a trail of her own foulness to add to the abomination.

The truck continues on, holo- and nano-glass cracking and snapping under its tires. As we draw farther in, we start to pass Disfavored. Shuffling and lost in the streets like they don't quite know what to do with themselves. Many of them wear the opulent Designer clothes and jewelry of the Aristocrats they displaced. Some still wear their bloodstained clothing. None of them seem to know what to do with themselves, so while some continue on with destruction and devastation, some scream and twirl about as if drunk and at a party, others sit on benches, walk in and out of shops, and stare at displays as if they're trying to act like an Aristocrat. All the windows are broken. None of the doors are open. Pods stand immobile in the streets and on the hover-ways.

We head toward the Central Block, where the towering white buildings of Bella Adona, Central Staffing, and the People's Tower stand. Now there are only two towers. The People's Tower is nothing but a mess of rubble. The hover station has come down, collided with the tower, it seems.

We stop at the base of Bella Adona and as the truck backs into the sheltering alcove of a service bay, I stare up at her opposing frame. Just days ago I was here, staring at her with a mind full of possibility, and now there is only dread. Where once I was enamored at the idea of reuniting with my lover and my best friend, now I'm terrified of what might have become of Quent while Delia quietly shakes and sobs beside me. The rock girl has cracked and her true feelings are spilling out like magma.

The truck bumps against the back of the bay and the engine cuts off.

"Best unload, I suppose," Sid quietly says. He unlaces the torn canvas backing, as if we couldn't all just climb through the giant hole in it, and steps out onto the bay.

Ready to stand, I grasp the end of the seat, but then realize, once again, I can't. My crutches are gone, most likely had slid out of the truck during the attack. "I, uh, I'm gonna need some help."

"Right." Sid comes to my rescue, lifting me to the edge of the truck bed then sliding me into his arms once he's dismounted. We wait on the sparkling street for the others to get out. Delia, Cam, Stormy, the two rebels who were with us. Everyone is still clutching their weapons, so I do the same, holding it at ready, even though I'm out of ammo. Perhaps we can deter someone from messing with us.

I hear a door open and close and then feet on the sidewalk. I crane, looking to see who it is. And then my stomach drops. "Clairen?" I breathe.

She lifts her hand to run it through her hair, but then stops and pulls it away with a wince when she finds the source of all the blood that has matted her hair and run down her face and neck. She looks like she showered in it.

"I-I thought you were with the others? With Gus?" Delia says, stepping forward.

Clairen looks down, licks her lips. "I was. Until I wasn't."

"What happened?" I demand. "Where's Quent?"

"I-I don't know," she admits. "My objective was to head back to base and get you all to safety once we realized what was happening." She lets out a long breath and rubs her palms on her thighs.

"But… But… You just abandoned them?"

Clairen's brows knit. "I— "

"Coward!" Delia yells, running at her. One of the other rebels steps between them, grabs her wrists to detain her. "Let me go. I'm gonna kill her!"

"Delia, don't," Cam says, voice tired. "She was only following orders. Just like Sid and me. Our goal was to get you two to safety. That's what we did."

Sid says, "If Clairen hadn't come back to warn us, we'd probably all be dead. It's clear Taurus was planning to attack us while the bulk of our defense was away. Perhaps they even walked into a trap."

I close my eyes, rest my head against his neck. I suddenly feel very tired. Weak. My head is pounding. "So, no one got out? None of the other Aristocrats were freed?"

"I don't know," Clairen says, voice tired. She drops her gun on the ground, sits down on the steps, and stares down Citizen's Way. "When it was clear we were driving into the midst of an attack heading your way, we all got separated. I brought who I could of my unit back, we held them off as long as we could to get you four secured. Somehow, Taurus knew about our base. I'm sure Faulk told him about that, too," she mutters darkly. "He came to look for his daughter, as promised."

"Well." I lift a hand and indicate the quiet girl standing on the loading dock. "Obviously they're not going to find her."

"He'll regroup," Stormy says, voice quiet. "Come looking." Her eyes examine her feet and she sounds almost upset about it. "You should have let him have me."

"Maybe we should have," Delia mutters. "At least Ella wouldn't have lost her other leg."

Stormy's eyes come up and her mouth opens, but she looks at me and whatever syllable she's about to utter dies on her lips and she avoids my eyes. She suddenly looks like she's in pain.

"I'm sorry to keep you from your father, Stormy," I say. "We made a deal and you held true to your end of the bargain.

You gave us good information. I just need to keep you a little longer. You're the only bargaining chip we have. If something happens, if our efforts to rescue the Aristocrats are thwarted and more people taken captive? We'll have to use you in negotiations and damn the consequences once your father has you back."

She nods. "I understand. I would have done the same thing in your shoes."

I smile. "You are in my shoes. Well, one at least."

And just like that, she starts crying and as she cries, she yells at me. "I can't believe you! I-I didn't know you were going to give me *your* leg. Just that you were going to give me *a* leg. And now-and now you don't have any legs! And you saved me back there. Risked your life. Why would you do that?"

Smiling, I try to talk gently to her. "You would have died otherwise."

"So?"

"So, I don't want you to die. You've got a lot of living to do. Especially now. You've got that new leg, you can stand up. Some practice, and you'll be running around and it will be like you were never missing one at all. That kind of gift is valuable. I expect you to make good use of it, not throw your life away."

Her tears are huge and her face contorted with so much emotion that everything's twitching. "I-I don't know what to say to that."

"Ugh, just stop sniveling. Say sorry and thank you," Delia answers. "And let's get back to more important matters. Like, what we're going to do when Taurus does decide to look for Stormy again."

"We'll do as Ella suggested, use Stormy as a bargaining chip," Clairen reasons.

"Keeping Stormy will be pointless unless we can prevent him from getting into Evanescence," Sid says.

I nod. "Once he's in the city, it will be almost impossible to eject him and because he has the Aristocrats, he'll take over and there will be no point in keeping her."

"This is all supposing the Aristocrats are still under his control," Delia says, crossing her arms. "I'm preferring the option that Gus and the others actually managed to free them."

"If they did, then we'll know it shortly," I say, hoping beyond hope that when it comes time to log on, I see all the avatars we've prepared for. "So long as everyone sticks to the plan."

"That doesn't answer the problem of my father," Stormy says, stepping forward.

"If everyone is logged in, and I can convince them to help me, then we should be able to shut the gates and keep him out. I'll send you out after everything is all squared."

Stormy stakes her head. "He won't give up. He knows now that most of the Aristocrats are dead, that this city is ripe for the taking and nearly defenseless. All your droids are smashed. What are you going to use to defend yourselves?"

"Then we'll just keep you here as assurance he won't hurt us," one of the Disfavored says.

She shakes her head. "That won't stop him. He's gotten it into his head that he's going to own this dome. Once he gets an idea, he doesn't stop until he's achieved it. Even if it involves me coming to harm." Her hand absently grabs at her thigh and it tugs my heart. I know that phantom gesture all too well. "He gets what he wants. Always. And he wants this city."

A small seed of an idea takes root in my mind, but I don't humor it. I have too much to do. "He can't have it. Sid, get us into Bella Adona."

"With what? Open sesame?"

His comment almost makes me giggle, because I remember a very similar line in a similar situation in Nexis. "Can't you short circuit the door like you did in the aerovator?"

"That requires electricity, remember?"

Right. I'd forgotten about that. "We need another way."

Everyone thinks for a moment. "When all else fails," Cam says quietly. "Physical force."

"We don't want to use explosives. It could damage the dome," Clairen reminds.

"Not what I was thinking." Cam holds up his hand. "Toss me the keys."

She looks put off by the idea, but she does as she's asked. Cam gets into the truck, starts it, pulls out, and disappears around the side of the building. We're all in the process of gravitating after him when we hear tires squeal and then a sudden crashing.

Sid picks up his pace, comes around the corner, and stops short. Cam has driven headlong into the main doors of Bella Adona. And now they're sitting wide open.

I hear Clairen say, "My truck!"

Sid mutters, "He's off his gourd. Beau's death pushed him off the edge."

I beam. "I think this is therapeutic for him."

He begins carrying me toward the doors. "If he's even still alive to benefit from the therapy."

Cam appears the next moment, grinning like an idiot. "That was deceivingly fun."

"I'm going to kill you!" Clairen screams at him as she bends, picks up an abandoned Clara Silvertree handbag, and throws it at his head.

He ducks behind a column just in time.

"Uh, guys?" Delia says.

Cam appears again, blows raspberries at her.

"Guys!" Delia growls again.

I glance at her, so does everyone else.

She gestures toward the bodies appearing in the shadows of the buildings around us. "You're attracting attention," she mutters. "And if you haven't forgotten, some of us aren't so safe here."

I gulp. Standing among the Disfavored who are with us, she sticks out like a florescent-pink elephant in a herd of zebra. I'm sure Sid and Cam do as well. "Get inside, all of you."

No one has to be told a second time. Once we're in, the Disfavored close the doors behind us. "We can't lock it."

Clairen gives Cam an accusing glare. "'Cause someone broke the lock."

"I got this," Stormy says, lunging forward and plucking the keys out of his hand. Everyone is a little too stunned by her sudden leap to action to run after her, until she's already in the truck and starting it. "You gonna get out of the way or what?" she demands through the busted out driver's side window.

Nervously, Sid and the others shuffle out of the way. Stormy expertly backs the truck right up against the closed doors. She shuts off the truck, gingerly gets out, and tosses the keys back to Clairen. "There. That ought to hold 'em."

"But," Clairen breathes. "You just helped us."

Stormy shrugs and walks by her. "Needed to be done." She stops when she realizes no one is following. "Uh, what now?"

I grin at her. Perhaps it's a mad grin, perhaps I've gone completely off my rocker at the thought of losing Quent and Gus and Bastian and Sadie and failing all the other people who are counting on me. Or, perhaps I'm only just starting to fight for them. "We're going to get the Main Frame back online."

chapter twenty-nine

POST-AMERICAN DATE: 7/10/232

LONGITUDINAL TIMESTAMP: 10:06 A.M.

LOCATION: DOME 5: EVANESCENCE

The halls of Bella Adona are silent and still. The air feels stale and I can smell the death high above us, even from this distance. I glance around in the darkness.

"I can't see anything," Delia whispers.

"Here," Cam says. A light-stick flashes on, bathing us in eerie green light.

Delia gasps, grabbing my arm. I turn my head and find half a dozen bodies littering the floor.

"Are they…?" she whispers.

"Droids," I say, keeping my voice low, even though there's nothing these dead machines can do to me now. They look like wilted flowers, or perhaps like the people in Sleeping Beauty's kingdom after her fairies put everyone under a spell. Guns in their hands, mechanical faces blank. Security droids don't look like normal androids, they don't have anthropomorphic chasises to make them seem like humans. They look like Meems did after she gave up her skin to give me new legs.

"It's so sad," I reflect. At my companions' disgruntled faces, I add, "That this happened at all. That they rebelled against us. Killed us."

Sid says, "It's possible their rebellion was part of the virus, right? I mean, I can't imagine the entire population of robots trying to kill us. There must have been one happy android."

I think of Meems and how she'd reacted when I finally found her dying on the floor of my father's workroom. The normal Meems would never have wanted to hurt me. But if a virus had made her go rogue… Had she wanted to kill me? I couldn't tell, she was so badly broken. Would she have, if she'd been able? "I don't think so," I say, but not wanting to deal with the repercussions of such a debate, I change the subject. "Cam, which way to the Main Frame?"

He gestures down the hall. "This way."

Their footsteps echo as we step around downed machines and pass under a magnificent golden arch held high by ornate white pillars. Their boots squeak on the tile floors, the noise grating against my spine.

"Do you honestly think we can do this?" Delia asks.

I shrug. "We have to try, right?"

She looks away, focusing on the dark hall in front of us. "Do we? We don't owe these people anything."

"You're wrong," I say. "As a human being, you owe it to every other human—and the world—to be the best you can be. We have the potential to be great." I take a moment, try to collect my thoughts. "What if we'd taken all this technology, all this intelligence, and actually put it toward something good? Rebuilding the world, feeding the hungry, curing true ills, educating others so they could continue on with the cause?"

She gives me a sidelong glance then lowers her voice so the Disfavored, who have fallen behind us in their fascination with the downed droids, can't hear. "You realize that's an absolute farce of an ideal to work toward, don't you? Humans are evil, destructive creatures. We'll always only care about ourselves and what's best for us."

"We don't all have to be. Some of us can fight that programming, can't we?"

She doesn't respond, and we continue on in silence.

When we get to the first closed door, Sid looks to Cam and asks, "You think the truck will fit down this hall?"

Cam chuckles. "I have a better idea." He kneels down, digs in his pack, and comes up with a light-stick. He snaps it on, pulls the power plate off the wall, and starts tinkering with wires.

Sid adjusts me as he watches. Feeling bad about him having to carry me, I say, "You can put me down and rest if you want to."

"Nah, I'm fine. You don't weigh much."

"Right. You're only like half a person at this point," Cam says, as he twists some wires together.

"Gee thanks," I mutter.

"She's more of a man than you'll ever be, that's for sure," Stormy says, coming up behind him. "What are you doing anyway?"

"You'll see, pipsqueak."

"Hey, I'm not a—" The door suddenly slides open with a pneumatic hiss.

I drop my jaw. "How did you…?"

He holds up the light-stick, which he's plugged the wires into. "I saw Gus do this with your flex-bracelet so Delia could read it. I'd forgotten about batteries. Useful little buggers."

Stormy slaps him on the back. "Nice job, Sell-Skin."

He gives her a withering glare. "Are you trying to get me to gag you? Because I'm sorely tempted."

"Play nice," Clairen warns. "We need the brat alive."

"I'm right here, you know."

"Oh, how could we not," Delia mutters.

I whisper to Sid, "What's a Sell-Skin?"

"It's what the Disfavored call Dolls."

"Oh…"

Cam hot-wires door after door after door. Doors we'd never have been able to pass through if the G-Chips in our frontal lobes were still connected to the Main Frame and the city was still online. Even if we'd somehow gotten through the doors, the city's security programming would have zapped our minds, would have sent droids after us, would have alerted someone to our intent. Now, we move unchallenged. All of us are on edge, waiting for something to spring out and challenge us.

And then we're there.

A vast cylindrical room that goes up and up and up. A narrow walkway stretches out into the center, over more length of cylinder that goes down and down and leads to a single workstation.

It's like the final room I came to in the Central Dominion. The final level of my game in Nexis, the place where I cracked Dad's final code and planted the Anansi Virus.

At the workstation, there is one holo-screen lit, black with a single line across the center. I can't see what it says from here.

"Let's get closer," I say. Sid obliges, putting me down in the chair at the end of the walkway and then stepping back and sighing like he's glad to be rid of the weight of me. I turn and smile at him. "Thanks for helping me in here."

He flashes a tired smile that doesn't reach his eyes and then lowers himself to the floor.

Delia is slowly making her way along the walkway that circles the room, examining the dark and quiet facade of server units lining the room for stories in either direction. I know from my memory of the same room in Central Dominion that if the light-stick were out and the Main Frame up and working, the walls would be twinkling with lights—like the synapses of a brain. But the brain of Evanescence is dead.

"Are you ready, Dee?" I ask.

Delia comes over and takes a seat at one of the chairs beside me. "As I'll ever be."

I redirect my attention to the workstation. Before me are ten unshattered holo-screens. I have no way to interact with any of them without my G-Chip. The one just before me, a black screen with a white line of writing:

Anansi Initiative complete. Activate Redux Program?

Six small rectangular boxes flash after the question mark. Indicating input of a password is necessary.

"Dad was right," I sigh.

Delia's chin turns toward me, though she doesn't look away from the screens. "What do you mean?"

"It's like what I said when I explained the whole plan to everyone back at the base. There was a secondary program that was supposed to run in conjunction with the Anansi Virus. This Redux Program that's supposed to bring on some kind of renaissance for Evanescence."

"And that's why we created those chips?"

"Yeah. We're going to need a couple of VR consoles," I say, turning, but half the group is gone.

"Cam already left to get them," Clairen responds. "And Sid is looking for some alternate power sources."

Stormy comes toward us. "What are you guys doing?"

"Attempting to reboot the city," Delia says.

"Well yeah, I got that. But how? This computer is dead, isn't it? How are you even going to restart it?"

"It's not dead, just asleep," I say, pointing toward the lit screen. "I surmise it's on a sleep mode. I have to get this password in."

"Do you even know the password?"

I frown. "No, but I'll figure it out. I'm good at this sort of thing."

Stormy's eyes explore the workstation. "There's no keyboard, no holo-board, and aren't your G-Chips dead? Isn't that how you Domites in Evanescence control your technology?"

"I'm impressed you know so much about us."

"Dad says you have to know your enemies."

"He's a smart man. I'd liked to have met him under better circumstances." I point at the screen. "The reason the city shut down in the first place is because I planted a virus in the system. I was able to do that because my parents created a virtual reality game called Nexis that was designed to overlay the system. Through the game, I was able to bypass all the security programs and get into the Main Frame. I'm hoping to be able to get back into the game and, from there, reboot the city."

"You see," Delia adds, "we could try and hack our way into the Main Frame from out here. It's not like Ella hasn't created the bypass codes before, but that would take time we don't have. In the game, Ella has already gotten past all of that and we should, theoretically, be able to get straight to work."

Stormy nods. "I think I get it. But what about the other Aristocrats? Didn't you say you needed them?"

I grin at her. "Oh, I definitely do."

"But they're not here."

"No," I agree. "And they won't be coming into the city until I make sure the Disfavored aren't going to kill them on sight. I've arranged for their safe entrance into the game alongside me." I point at one of the screens. "If I'm calculating right, you should be allowed to watch what's happening in the game. You all should."

"If the Aristocrats were safely rescued," Clairen adds.

The sobers me. "Yes. If."

A few minutes later, Cam and one of Clairen's Disfavored return carrying two consoles. They begin unpacking them and hooking Delia and I up. Sid and the other Disfavored return with a small generator. "I found this in the archives. I hope it still works."

"Shouldn't you be able to hook everything to light-sticks like the doors?" Stormy asks.

"No, we need too much power," Sid says, distracted as he and Cam puzzle out wires and exchange bundles of cords.

While they attempt to hook everything up, I turn to Delia. "You have your access chip?" She reaches into her pocket and pulls it out. "These have everyone's access codes preloaded, so as long as they're inserted at entry-time, they should all get redirected to Central Dominion."

"I'll take that," Cam says, taking the chip from Delia. "You girls ready?"

I sit back in the chair, give one last glance to Delia, and pull my blinders over my eyes.

chapter thirty

POST-AMERICAN DATE: 7/10/232

LONGITUDINAL TIMESTAMP: 1:05 P.M.

LOCATION: FREE ZONE, CENTRAL DOMINION; NEXIS

The Central Dominion is just like how I left it. Literally. I wake up, and I'm suspended from a massive tangle of light-shot spider webbing. I'm not just caught in it, I'm part of it, each line shot through my body like it has been threaded through me with a needle, though it doesn't hurt. There's a sudden bit of screeching beneath me. Panicked, I glance around, trying to pinpoint the echoing hysteria. "Delia?"

"I'm here." I hear her call from far below me.

I tilt my head back, see her standing on the narrow walkway in front of the bank of computers I'd used to input the last of the coding required to insert the virus. Around her are a number of the Aristocratic girls she's become friends with since I was forced to abandon her. Including Carsai. Not everyone is here yet, but there is time. I let out a breath of relief. "You made it!"

Delia grins at me. "Was there any doubt?"

"Yeah, but how?" Farouza asks.

"Where are we?" Carsai demands. "And what are you doing up there, Ellani?"

"This is such a long story." I shake my head. "Dee, what do you see?"

Lowering her gaze, she squints at the computer. "It's the same screen as the one out there. Wait, there's something appearing under it… S-P-I-D-E-R." She looks up. "Must be the passcode to activate the Program."

As she speaks, the lights around us start flickering, and the computer whirs and clicks and beeps. Shots of light come down the wires strung through my body, travel out.

"What's happening?" she calls. "Are you okay?"

"I'm all right." It doesn't hurt. This all sort of makes sense. If I'm the lynchpin and Nexis is just another layer of reality over the Real World, then a physical manifestation of my role in the process makes sense.

"Holy sparks." I hear from below. This time the voice is older and male.

"There are more people coming in," Delia calls up.

I nod, annoyed I couldn't have at least been strung up in a direction that allowed me to see what was going on around me. Knowing there is nothing I can do until they've all arrived, I hang and I wait while the noise below grows and grows as more people connect out in Real World and are dropped onto this level. Every so often, I twist and glance down. Even though they have all been pulled from whatever game they were playing in Nexis when the city first went down, Delia's access chip has not only transported them from their games, but it has also stripped them of their avatar's clothing and design. They all look like how they do in Real World, Mods and Alts glistening on Custom skin clothed in Elite, Neo-Baroque opulence. I can't stare for too long because it's almost too painful to look at. All that color and cheer, all that innocent Aristocratic frivolity. It reminds me too much of a time when I was naïve to the woes of the world, before all of us were touched by darkness and pain.

Eventually, Delia calls up to me. "I think this is the best we're going to get." There's a tinge to her voice, which tells me some faces are missing, but I expect that. Some are dead. We've orchestrated this plan so some of our group are doing other things. Cam and Sid are still outside, making sure nothing goes wrong with our bodies or the connection with the game. Zane and Angelique should be in Central Staffing, working hard on patching this scene out through The Broadcast so the Disfavored inside the dome can see their Savior convincing the Aristocrats to save them.

But her voice tells me Gus isn't here. And if Gus isn't here, Quent isn't, either. My heart sinks, but I try to stay focused, try to tell myself there are a hundred reasons why they aren't here, and they are perfectly logical. I can't wait forever for them to appear here in Nexis. Time is of the essence.

Pushing my dread away, I swallow. "Okay, it's show time." As I've learned from playing Nexis, I manipulate the threads. Slowly, they slide out of me, lower me. I come down in the center of the Aristocrats and as my feet touch the ground, more threads bloom up out of the floor, wrap around me, knitting me into a dress made of silken silver threads that glisten and move like mercury around me.

Bastian comes forward, grabs me into a massive hug, and Sadie follows. "I'm so glad to see you."

"And I you, but it's not the time for a reunion." Nodding, Bastian steps away, drawing Sadie with him.

I stand tall, meet the piercing eyes of the Aristocrats around me with a sense of pride. Delia has written my avatar to look the very best I can while still being my Natural self. My hair is Primped, I've got both my legs, and I'm dressed in a gown of my very finest design. I need to appeal to both sides of this long-standing war.

"Thank you all for coming."

"I didn't have a choice," one Aristocrat man says. "I was held at gunpoint."

I smile at him. "I apologize for the rough treatment. I know this is all a little abrupt, and you've had a very traumatizing few days."

"That's an understatement," Carsai mutters.

"I'd like to show you something." I move toward the control panel and type in a command. "Zane, are you there?"

A screen flashes and his face appears. As Delia programmed him to look, he's in top Anchor form. He sits back, and Angelique and Kit are beside him at the table. A sudden murmur goes up in the crowd around me. Like me, most of the Aristocrats in the group assumed Zane and Kit were dead. We were all there when the aerovator door closed between us and them.

"Angelique!" Carsai squeals. "Circuits, I was so worried when those Disfavored men took you!"

Angelique smiles at her. "I'm fine. They were very good to me, very gentle. And look!" She holds up her scratch-pad. "They even saved this for me. They're not like what we thought."

"That's a matter of opinion," Carsai mutters. "And Lady Cyr!" She turns her attention to Kit and curtsies, her voice dripping with reverence. "I'm so very glad to see you. I have an urgent matter to speak with you about."

"In time, Miss Sheldon," Kit says, folding her white-gloved hands before her. "Right now, we've got serious matters to attend to. It's time to save our home."

Another murmur goes up then. I examine the surroundings behind Kit, Zane, and Angelique. I've only been in Central

Staffing a few times, and I've only seen The Broadcast studio once, but the Nexis version of it looks similar to what I remember from my one class trip. "Are you all hooked up?"

"Yes," Zane responds. "I'm live and rolling. The drones we use when filming in Kairos are in operation and circulating the city, and the main holo-screens have been powered up. Though, I don't know how long this auxiliary power cell is going to hold up."

The Central Staffing building is equipped with an auxiliary power cell that allows for emergency Broadcasts to be made, and we've tapped into that. "Give me a feed from one of the external cameras."

"All right, one moment please." He clears his throat and, in his best Anchor voice, he says, "Ladies and Gentlemen, reporting to you live from Nexis's Central Dominion, this is Zane Boyd here with Lady Kistune Cyr and Junior Anchor Angelique Foreman. We're about to show you a lively and disturbing image which is not for the faint of heart."

I roll my eyes. "Today please, Zane."

"Okay, okay. No appreciation for proper news coverage." He flips a switch and the screen splits. On one side, the newsroom remains the same. The new image is a live feed from Evanescence. The camera pans out and circles a large group of Disfavored people half dressed in our clothing, half dressed in their own, staring wide eyed and dumbfounded at one of the large holo-screens set up at the corner of two of the main streets. The wall behind them is painted with large letters. "In Drexel We Trust." On a wall farther down the street, I can see even larger, "Ella the Savior." The camera finishes panning, stopping so we're staring at the backs of the Disfavored, seeing what they are seeing. And what they are seeing is us, staring at them.

Zane just can't help himself. "A hush falls over both

crowds as the Disfavored and the Aristocrats behold each other for the first time. How strange a thing, to see clearly for the first time the people from beyond the wall."

"Zane shut up or I'll put you on mute."

He drops his shoulders, but says nothing else.

"As you can see," I say, voice hushed, "this is what our city now looks like."

"Are those Disfavored?" Sadie asks.

Someone else says, "In our city?"

"Who let them in?" another asks.

"The city did," Delia says quickly, cutting off hysteria before it can gain momentum. "After we left, the doors flew wide open and the Disfavored moved in. We don't know how or why, but we're trying to cope with it."

"How are we going to get them out?" Carsai demands.

"We're not going to," I say.

"What? But this is our home, not theirs!"

"And what have you done to earn it?" I demand, irritated. "What has any one of you done to even earn the right to still be alive?"

That shuts them up. For a moment.

"These people have scratched by and struggled just to survive. They've done nothing wrong. Their only fate is to have been born on the wrong side of a wall. And the only reason you grew up the way you did, why you're fat and happy with comfortable clothing, educations, and stupid Mods and Alts is because you were born on the right side. These people didn't have to save you from those cannibals, but they did. Every one of the people out there"—I point at the screen—"has every reason to want to kill you."

"They would if they had the chance," an older Aristocrat woman says, voice frantic. "Just look at the bodies in the street. Those are people we know. Clearly, they'd do the same to us if they could."

"But they won't. The Disfavored are ready to learn to live in harmony with the Aristocrats. Like you're soon going to find, they've learned that only with cooperation between our two sides can we manage to make it through this crisis. You needed them and they saved you. Now, they need you and you're going to save them. We're going to fix the city." I finally turn so my face appears to the Disfavored who are watching us.

The reaction is instantaneous. They react to me like the Aristocrats react to the Presidential family when they appear on The Broadcast. There's this sudden stillness, and then people start cheering. One voice, then many chant, "Drexel! Drexel! Drexel!"

They go on and on and on. The sound grows and grows and grows until it echoes around the chamber and makes the room feel like there's a living heartbeat in it. It unnerves me.

Reaching out, I allow a number of threads to flow from my body and connect to the control panel. The screen flickers off. Silence falls like a guillotine, and I turn to the Aristocrats.

They are still and bristling, like so many statues. I might shatter them, like glass. "As you can see, the Disfavored are willing to cooperate."

"That answers nothing," Carsai spits, taking a step forward. "What *is* that?"

"That," I say, trying to make my voice knifelike, "is what happens when people play games with other people's lives. It's what happens when brilliant minds, like yours, and yours, and yours, and yours"—I point at different people—"are allowed to have what they want. It's exactly why we're all standing here and why we have to fix this."

Carsai crosses her arms. "I'm not fixing anything."

"Carsai," I say, losing my patience.

Delia reaches out, touches my arm. She takes a step forward. "Look, you don't have to listen to Ella, Carsai. If you listen to anyone, listen to me, to Kit, to Zane, and Angelique." She holds her hand out toward the screen. "The Disfavored have moved into the city. And we're what? Twenty-five strong? How are we going to get them out? Even if we did, what the heck are we going to do with a whole city all to ourselves? These people have always lived on the Outer Block. Because we left them out there to die. They've been waiting for a moment like this, to be allowed in where it's safe. They even tried to force their way in a couple of times and I don't blame them. We've all been out there, we've all seen what they've been forced to live in because of us. And now, the city is dead, the only thing that ever protected any of us is dead, and without it we're all dead. Carsai, you're mean and selfish sometimes, but you're not a bad person. Can you honestly look me in the eye and tell me these people deserve to die? They've done *nothing* to you."

"They've done plenty," Carsai growls. "I was there. It wasn't just droids going nuts and killing people. There were Disfavored, too."

"A small group of them, yes," Kit says. "But they were there at my bidding. The city fell because I allowed for the virus to be planted, even encouraged it. What happened to our fellow citizens and our city was a terrible mistake. A mistake caused by my trust of someone who betrayed me. I wanted us all to live together in peace, Disfavored and Aristocrat alike, but I didn't want it to happen in this awful manner. I'm..." She pauses, her voice wavering. "I'm so very sorry. If you want to get angry, get angry at me. I humbly accept whatever punishment awaits me at your hands."

Everyone seems stunned. They've always loved, trusted, and blindly followed the Presidential family. And now their internal programming to follow like sheep is at war with the logical minds they've been bred to possess.

"Ellani and the others are trying their best to fix the mistakes that I and a few others have made. Please help them do this. If you don't agree, then we will all die. I couldn't live with myself if anything happened to the precious few of you who still exist."

The Aristocrats glance around at each other, each as uncertain as the next on what to do.

I step forward and I bank everything on my hope that my father's Redux Program works on the Disfavored. "I personally stake my life against the guarantee that the Disfavored in this city will make every effort to live in peace and protect those of you who are still living."

"Why on Earth would they do that?" someone demands.

Smiling, I turn back toward the screen. "Okay, Zane, open up the audio line."

"Let me introduce you?"

"This isn't the time for theatrics."

"Oh come on, Ella, this might be my last day in the limelight."

"Ugh, fine, make it fast."

Grinning ear to ear, he says, "Citizens of Kairos, may I present to you your Savior, Miss Ellani Drexel."

More cheering and chanting as the camera angle narrows in on me until I'm the only one on the screen the Disfavored can see. I hold my hand up for silence, and it takes quite a few minutes to get it but when I do, it's eerie. I feel sweat pouring down my back, and my gown itches. I can't believe I'm about to speak with all of these people, that I'm about to step up and take the reins on a runaway stagecoach my parents basically left me on a whim. No, I've been on this stagecoach all along. They may have dropped the crumbs, but I picked them up and followed the path. There's always an option, and this is what my choices have led me to.

I take a deep breath, level my eyes at the Disfavored before me. "People of Kairos. Or should I say, People of Neo-Evanescence." There's a cheer at that. I hold my hand up again. "I welcome you to what, I hope, is a new future. One where we can cancel out and overwrite the sins of our forefathers. Humanity as a race has done a terrible thing. It destroyed the world we once had, it broke us apart, it left some of us for dead. But we didn't die."

More cheering. I wait. They settle.

"Now, we are at a turning point. A point where a new challenge is on our doorstep. This beautiful utopia, this sparkling domed city that is your new home, your salvation, this city is dead."

I'm met with confused silence and I grab the thread, the half-lie half-truth, and I weave the story for them.

"Yes, I've given you a dead city." I make it sound entirely on purpose. "And now you all have a choice." I spin the thread of Real World with the thread of the virtual world. "You've learned to hate the Aristocracy. You've learned that the only way to survive, to get by and succeed in this world, is to take from them. You've taken, and they've paid dearly. And now, I present you with a choice." I see some nodding. They expect this, they've been programmed—brainwashed—in Redux to react to this moment.

"Your old home is dead. Your new home is dead. You will not survive on your current path of hate and destruction." I step backward and hold my hand out, indicating the Aristocrats standing behind me. The camera backs up, showing a panorama of sparking alien creatures who promise a strange future. "I have with me here, the keys to the future. You know them well. You're thinking you hate them, you want them dead. How did some get through? The simple answer is that I saved them. Because without them, you would destroy everything." I pause, let that sink in.

"This city, Evanescence, is beautiful and offers so much to its occupants. You wanted it, lusted for it. Yet you failed to realize that, like any machine, it operates on individual parts. Cogs, pistons, springs, wheels, belts, fuel, wire, chips, grease, protocols... Without these things, machines are useless, aren't they? Without tools to fix the parts in a machine, it's just as useless."

I turn to the groups of Aristocrats, continue speaking as I walk among them. "Each of these people is a part, a tool. They are the most valuable thing this city possesses, the only thing that can get it up and running." I touch shoulders as I realize who is capable of what. "Engineers, Programmers, Designers, Medics, Geneticists, Machinists, Horticulturalists, Biologists, Nutritionists," I list, and those are just the few occupations that I know from the people I went to school with. "These are the people who can get the city back online. Who can maintain it. Who can teach your children and your children's children how to keep it going and make it even better as the years march by. But—" I turn back to the screen, meet the dark eyes of the hundreds of Disfavored amassed in the square before me. This image is repeated in a hundred different places throughout the city, they are all seeing and hearing this because The Broadcast penetrates everything. "I need you to help me keep them safe, to let them into this city, and let them stay. I need you to forgive and forget the past, to take my hand and move forward with me and with them. Will you do this for me?"

I reach out my hand, offer it as if waiting for them to take it. I don't know why I choose this gesture, as there are virtual worlds dividing us and I cannot touch them, but it feels right.

One by one and then dozens by dozens by hundreds, hands outstretch toward mine.

It's not everyone. I don't need it to be. There will always be dissenters, and perhaps they will become the next generation of Tricksters. But for now? For now there are enough. An overwhelming number I know are going to try.

I hear an intake of breath behind me.

"Thank you," I say. And then, Zane cuts the feed.

"I think that's a good place to end it," he says. "Dramatic pause."

I force a nervous smile. While I've got one group onboard, I still need the other. The important one. Stiff, I turn back toward my fellow citizens. "You've got your guarantee." There is nothing else I can really say. "Will you help or not?"

One of my classmates, a boy named Hunter, says, "What makes you think we can restart the city? None of us even know how the city works. I was taught she operates entirely without human assistance. Everything is autonomic, so why are we necessary?"

"I thought that, too," I say, "but then I had to wonder why she shut down at all." There were a few things that just didn't make sense—the robots trying to kill us and then the city shutting down entirely. In none of the plans were either of these factors a beneficial goal. It's clear that neither the robots nor the city were in the Tricksters' original plans. I don't even believe they were Uncle Simon's doing. Clearly, he was attempting something. Perhaps once everything is settled, I can do some exploring on the Main Frame and try to decode his virus to see, but I don't believe success rides on him.

What I do believe is that everything I've learned from Meems, from virtual worlds that allow you to touch reality, from my parents still living beyond the grave, is that artificial intelligence is far more advanced and capable than we believe.

But the most well executed programs are still fallible… Even cities that can run on their own.

“I think,” I say haltingly, “that Evanescence is like a body. The supercomputer that is Main Frame is her brain. Like any living thing she needs cells…tools, parts, things that make her operate and carry out her normative functions. Evanescence had a balance of both: human and machine. When whatever Uncle Simon did blew our G-Chips, the human parts of the body were disconnected from the artificial intelligence that runs the city. The city no longer recognized us as part of her—we were viruses, bacteria, foreign bodies that had to be expelled. So, one part of the body started attacking another like—white blood cells no longer recognizing red blood cells as good and killing them. That’s why the robots turned on us. The city, being connected to all of them like a hive mind, told them we were the enemy. As soon as the last living being fell in the city, she realized there were no longer any red blood cells to protect, so she shut the white blood cells down. But without any blood cells, the body dies entirely. So, she shut down.”

“So,” Delia says, haltingly, “you think the city accidentally tried to kill us?”

“Something like that. It’s obviously a bit more complicated, but the only thing that marked us as citizens was our G-Chips. Disconnect them from the network and we’re considered no different than Disfavored.”

“What about the androids?” Zane chimes in. “My assistant droid, Ruby… I can’t imagine she’d ever try to harm me.” There’s an underlying tenderness in his voice that lets me know that he feels as strongly for his assistant as I do Meems.

I lift my hand to touch the chips, but I realize they aren’t here in Nexis with me. “The city controlled the droids. They were our security—meant to kill trespassers. It would have been nothing for the city to direct them that we needed to be eliminated. As for the androids, I don't necessarily believe that they had full control of their own free will. We may have felt they were autonomous beings, but deep down they were still machines connected to the Main Frame, like a hive mind."

The idea of it terrifies me, but it's no different than a virtual reality game reprogramming entire populations.

"And you want us to wake this city up again?" Sadie asks. "So it can try to kill us again?"

I shake my head. "What I want to do is tell this city there are still red blood cells to accept and keep safe. We have to give her a transfusion and her body can't reject it."

"And how, exactly, are you going to do that?" Carsai demands.

I hold out my hands and let a number of glowing threads fall down to the floor. "From what I understand, my avatar is a bridge. In Nexis, I connect Central Dominion and Main Frame. In Redux, I connect between Kairos and Evanescence. I'm capable of converting other avatars into code and as long as they're with me, I can bridge them back and forth. That's why you're all here in Nexis even though you're playing Redux because I need you all here, so I can upload you into Main Frame."

"Wait, what?" Carsai squawks. "You want to upload our consciousnesses into a computer?"

I shrug. "In so many words, yes. We don't have the chips to connect with her anymore, so this is the only way to tell her we're here and she needs to keep us alive."

"But," someone else says, "isn't that risky? Couldn't we maybe die if we try moving our consciousnesses?"

Sparks, I was hoping no one would notice that part. "It's possible, but I don't think you will."

"Can you guarantee that?"

"No," I admit. Faces turn sour and I can tell I'm losing

them. "But," I hedge, "if I get you onto the Main Frame, it's very likely you'll find your loved ones again."

"What do you mean?"

I glance at the screen where Kit and Zane are watching everything silently unfold. "All your friends and family, everyone who died? They're there… On Main Frame."

"She's telling the truth," Kit says. "The city created regular backups of each of the citizens via the G-Chip."

"So," one woman says, stepping forward, "you're offering us heaven?"

"I don't know what it's going to be like. I don't know if you'll even find them in there."

"But"—her eyes, faceted like garnets, flick up and meet mine—"it's possible?"

I nod. "It's possible."

She chews her lip. "What if we find them and don't want to come back?"

"I'd encourage it. At least for a little while. If I get you in, if I connect you and you manage to find who you're looking for? There's no reason why you can't connect with them as often as you'd like. But after I wake up the city, after I convince her to accept her new inhabitants, I'm going to make an effort to get you back into your bodies and get you all safely into the city. I need you all alive so you can help these people learn to live with Evanescence. After that, I'll help you carry out whatever wish you may have."

She lifts her hand, her fingers stroking one of the threads. There are tears in her eyes. "If it means I can see Nadine and my grandson again, I'll help you."

Nadine. There's nothing that says that this woman's Nadine is my Nadine. There could have been a hundred Nadines with little boys in Evanescence, but somehow I just know she means the same one. I lift the thread, let it slide along her arm, wrapping around her wrist and up her body like a coiling snake. I turn my hand, touch her outstretched fingers. "Tell her I say 'hi.'"

The thread glows silver and the woman bursts into nothing but golden code. The code spirals along the thread and together they move up and up and up, like a strand of semiprecious DNA. And then it shoots out, connects with a section of the darkened column around us. The thread injects the golden code with the speed of a bullet and it sticks there, the first strand in my web.

Half a dozen lights flicker on along the column, the first synapses firing after a brain long asleep starts to wake up.

Delia steps forward next. "Send me right to Nina."

"I'll try my best."

Like the woman before her, Delia turns to code. Hers is a glowing bright blue as she disappears into the column. My heart aches because there's a chance I won't ever see her again.

Bastian comes then. "I uh, I need some answers."

"Ask some for me, too." I send him to Uncle Simon.

Sadie. "If he's going, I'm going." And off to Katrina.

Quent's few remaining Dolls come next.

More Aristocrats join them, drawn by the prospect of reuniting with loved ones or possibly because they want to help. I inject them into the Main Frame, giving our city more and more reason to live. Each is a different color, each disappearing into the column, lighting more lights. Waking her up after a long nap.

Until finally, it's just Carsai and me.

I stand there with twenty some-odd silver strands shooting out from my body, connecting me to the inside of the column. "What's it going to be, Carsai?"

She scowls at me. "You stole him from me."

"Yeah. But he wasn't yours to begin with."

"He was," she argues. "It was prearranged. It was our destiny. We were born into it."

"There's no such thing as destiny. Anything you're born into, you can get yourself out of. Anything life throws at you, you can fight. Quent was never yours. He was his own, and he made his own choices."

Tears prickle her eyes. "He's not here, Ellani. Why isn't he here?"

I swallow hard. I've been asking that question since I lowered myself to the floor and didn't see him or Gus standing here. He was supposed to be here. He was supposed to help me convince the Aristocrats to help.

"Is he dead?" she demands.

My voice cracks as I answer, "I don't know. I hope not." I hope he's just late, detained, couldn't get to a gaming house on time. Anything. There's still hope. Not being here in the game means nothing. He could be fine in Real World. I have to hold on to that hope.

"Was he periodically backed up, too?"

"Yes," Kit answers because I can't seem to find words. I'm barely holding it together. It was easy not to examine the idea too hard, to push it off because things needed doing, but it's hard with Carsai making me think about it.

"Then I want to see that version of him. I want to be with the virtual him. Like how we were in the game."

I force myself to talk. "I-I don't know if I can do that."

Carsai steps forward, holds out her hand. "Try. Give me this one thing, Ellani, and maybe I'll come back. Maybe I'll help you."

Nodding, I let the thread reach out to her, convert her. Carsai's color is red gold, like fire. Like the dress I wore the night of the virus. I watch her rise, I watch her disappear. I watch another set of lights turn on.

chapter thirty-one

POST-AMERICAN DATE: 7/10/232

LONGITUDINAL TIMESTAMP: 3:58 P.M.

LOCATION: FREE ZONE, CENTRAL DOMINION; NEXIS

"Ella," Kit says, voice quiet and gentle.

I sniff, trying to get my head back in the game. "Yeah?"

"We're ready over here."

"Yeah. I just need a minute."

I take a few breaths, trying to calm my racing heart, the heat in my chest. Why is it that every time I'm in this chamber, I'm dealing with the sudden loss of the man I love? *No, he's not gone in Real World, you have no proof.*

"Quent's strong," Zane says, voice quiet, though I can see the worry in his eyes. "And he loves you. He'll do everything he can to get back to you."

"I know." The tears are falling now. I can't help it. It hurts so much, not having him here with me for what could be my last few minutes. Despite it all, despite wanting to curl into a ball and sob, despite the shaking and the feeling like parts of my insides are peeling away and falling into a black hole,

I send three strands out into the control panel. I let them travel down virtual highways, let them find the place in Nexis where Zane, Kit, and Angelique are sitting at a desk in Central Dominion's version of The Broadcast studio.

I let them rise up through the floor, coil up legs, wrap around bodies, curl out to fingers. "Thank you for having faith in me," I say. And then I break them apart, into components that the massive supercomputer around me recognizes and understands them as. I turn them into their chips—things without bodies, just strands of data to be read. Virtual bits of DNA, bits of genetic code that I add to a giant puzzle, hoping the Main Frame of Evanescence will take these small glimpses and remember the big picture.

And then I break myself down. I let my body dissolve, flow down the different strands, up and in. The line between Nexis and Real World blurs, everything inverts, and suddenly I know I'm inside of Main Frame. From everywhere and nowhere at once, my mother's song—the one that started to play after the virus hit—is still playing on repeat. Main Frame is stuck on her final moments, stuck in a computer's version of a dream.

I see the image of my mother singing me the song, demonstrating the hand game. I see images of her staring furiously at a holo-screen as she works on Nexis. The image of my father finding her slumped over her workstation, a steaming laser-hole in her head. I see his resolute face as he sits down at the station and takes up her mantle. I see my face, over and over again as I walk into his workroom and see him tirelessly toiling away. I get older and older and my face never changes.

I reach beyond myself to the Aristocrats. The ones I'm connected to, the ones stored in Main Frame's memory.

I see more. Thousands of images from thousands of households. Strangers eating, laughing, bathing, arguing, working, sleeping. The excitement of waking up to a new Mod. The frustration of a Medical protocol not being successful. The angst of trying to satisfy demanding parents. The yearning for another you can't have. The disappointment of not being accepted by the other Elite. All ages from all over the city and all different time periods. It's a hodgepodge, in no particular order.

I reach farther still, beyond the formless and through the city, trailing the streets and the different floors of all the buildings. I reach up and into the bodies of the Disfavored standing around staring at the screens—at the web being built in the heart of the city.

I see images from outside.

Droids on the wall looking down with featureless faces.

Cameras flying down, staring with glass eyes.

The city of Kairos rising up, falling, rising up again.

A gang beating a man to death for a sack of gruel meal.

A woman brutally raped in an alley.

That same woman selling herself into servitude to feed that child born of violation and degradation.

The child taking up a gun and killing his mother's enslavers.

I feel the empty bellies. The dry tongues. The needling of acid rain, the asphyxiation of scratch-lung, the tight burn of radiation exposure.

It goes on and on. I see a hundred thousand sunsets and sunrises on a world that blazes and dissolves in Post-Apocalyptic heat. One sparkling world of white towers, cool mornings, and glistening streets. One world of blackened shanties, sweaty mornings, and bloody streets.

Evanescence sees everything I see through the eyes of the habitat systems, the eyes of her citizens, the eyes of her robots, the G-Chips, the games she houses. She sees us and she sees them, Aristocrat and Disfavored alike. She sees both worlds rise and fall. She sees both persevere.

In the back of my mind, I'm jumping thread to thread to thread. There are countless numbers of them now, each representing a life. I'm connecting one life to another through similarities. We're all the same in a million little ways. Love. Hate. Happiness. Sadness. Desire. Common language of the tongue and heart make it easy to do so. And in the end, we're not so different. And when I'm done, Evanescence can't see the difference, either.

In the end, she can't see what makes Aristocrats different from Disfavored. She can't discern physical body from virtual body. We're all humans and we are inside of her.

I sense her programming coming to a few rapid conclusions, her artificial intelligence taking a few more vital steps toward true consciousness. And like a great behemoth of a creature long asleep, feel her get slowly to her feet and shake her great mane. I feel her wake up.

chapter thirty-two

POST-AMERICAN DATE: 7/10/232

LONGITUDINAL TIMESTAMP: 7:07 P.M.

LOCATION: DOME 5: EVANESCENCE

I watch from the roof of Bella Adona as the Aristocrats are escorted into the city. Each has at least one armed Disfavored with them, but the security is unnecessary. The Disfavored within Evanescence are lined up along Citizen's Way, cheering and throwing what they deem as valuables into the street like flower petals.

Leaning forward in the hover chair Sid found for me, I prop my elbows on the rooftop and sigh. Beside me, a small holo-glass screen has materialized, showing me a rolling flicker of the spectacle from different angles. The Broadcast cameras are back in action and Zane has them covering everything. Along with the flickering of images, Evanescence is displaying her progress with her reboot. Habitat systems are 32 percent online, dome cleanup initiative is 10 percent complete, nano-net retrieval is in full effect.

I don't need to know most of these things. The gray smog of miasma rises up from Kairos—the nanite swarms waking up and heading back into the air. The machines under the city hum back to life, churning out new robotic units to clean and repair.

Beside me, Delia frowns at the screen. "I don't see them."

"Don't," I whisper. I can't have her point it out. I can't get that close.

"Ella," she whimpers, not listening to me.

I close my eyes. I've already scanned all the faces that came through the gate. The gate that, even as the procession moves forward and the Disfavored close in around the last stragglers from the outside, is closing. It has to close. The cameras have picked up the impending threat—the massive dust cloud of oncoming vehicles. Without the droids, something I didn't allow for when I woke her up, the city is defenseless. Eventually, the citizens will learn to use the weapons the droids have dropped, but until then, the best defense is offense.

Evanescence knows my fear of leaving anyone behind, and she has calculated the distance and has allowed for the largest margin of error. The gates will shut fully just in time, only allowing for anyone who needs to get into the city before Taurus gets here.

One camera stays trained on the closing gate.

The bodies of Disfavored, Aristocrat, and droid alike have been moved out of the way and there's a clear view all the way out to the small army of oncoming cannibals.

"Is it going to close in time?" Stormy demands, nervous.

"You act as though you don't want your father to come rescue you," Cam says.

She turns away. "Of course I do."

Cam grins at her back. "If you wanted to stay here, you could."

"No," I say quietly. "Stormy has to go back out. I need her

to deliver a message."

"You do?" she asks.

I request my chair spin around and when it doesn't, I'm momentarily confused. Oh right, no G-Chip. I grasp the side of the wall and turn myself toward her. "I have a deal I'd like to offer your father. Something I hope he'll accept, but we can talk about that later. Right now, why don't you go join the festivities?"

She gives me a skeptical brow crimp but turns and gets into the aerovator. "Clairen, make sure she doesn't get into trouble, would you? I'm sure you'd like to go see the others anyway." Nodding, she trots after Stormy. "And Clairen?" She turns on her heel, gives me a questioning look. "Can you send Bastian to see me when you find him? I'd like to know what he found out from Uncle Simon."

Of all the things we still haven't learned, it's why he tampered with the virus in the first place—his true intent. I need to know, because if he really intended to cause ill to these people, then I'm going to have to hunt down his cyber-self on the Main Frame and contain him somehow. Because free? He's still a threat. Clairen's mouth turns grave as she continues her pursuit of Stormy. Her Disfavored follow, leaving the Dolls, Delia, and me on the roof.

"You should go with them, see your friends," I say to Sid and Cam.

Sid frowns at me. "We're here for the same reason as you."

Biting my lip, I nod and look away.

The gate is more than half closed now. Delia grasps my hand, shudders. I hold my breath, heart hammering. It feels like it did when the boys closed the door to the Undertunnel. An end, a beginning. And I don't want this door to close because I want hope to still be there. I feel myself shaking, and Delia squeezing my fingers does nothing to stop it.

The door closes and closes. The trucks get closer and closer.

I'm not scared of them getting in. I'm scared of someone getting locked out.

"Come on," I whisper. And then I yell it. "Come on, Quentin, move your ass!"

But I'm cheering for no one. Because there's no one there to cheer.

And the door shuts. *Boom.* And I feel myself shatter, my muscles turn to liquid. I'd collapse if I wasn't sitting. Delia's grasp fades out of mine. She pools to the roof beside me, starts sobbing into her hands.

I don't register much after that. I just stare and stare and stare. A holo-screen flits in front of me at one point, trying to show me footage of the cannibals throwing a fit outside the gate. Evanescence apparently thinks this is funny. But I don't care. I swat at the screen and it ducks away.

Evanescence tries to cheer me up, she plays Mom's "Itsy Bitsy Spider" recording for me.

"Stop," I growl at her. "Just leave me alone."

The holo-screen drifts away and I'm left in relative silence. The larger screens flicker on and it catches my attention. There's a line flashing across. *The Savior has returned.* I roll my eyes at it. Yes, I've done what needed doing. I've saved the survivors, I've saved the Disfavored. I've rebooted the city and even managed to somehow fulfill an underlying desire to bring peace between the Aristocrats and the Disfavored.

But, the victory feels hollow.

There's movement in the streets, congealing around Bella Adona like a clot. Clogging the streets and the hover-ways as far as I can see are thousands of people. The dark clothing and faces mark them as Disfavored. Little ants milling around pods and bodies. An army of them. People start yelling, and the yelling moves like wildfire. They begin cheering in a unified mass that sends a chill to my bones.

The longer I listen, the longer their cheers start to make sense to me, forming into a single word they're chanting over and over and over again.

Drexel.

Drexel.

Drexel.

And it just seems like they're screaming. *Empty. Empty. Empty.* Because despite all these people, despite a bright future, despite everything I've managed to do, it all feels pointless. Bitter tears come as I stare down at the people. I hate that they're so happy and have so much potential when I have sacrificed everything to give them this. It feels like I should get something, too, but I don't.

Part of me just wants to throw myself off the side of Bella Adona. But I still have to be something to these people. Eventually, I'll have to go back inside and be a Leader to them. But right now I'm alone and I can break down and be weak, so I let myself sob.

"You know," a voice says from behind me, making me tense. "I never did like it when you cried."

I gasp, despite myself, and more tears come. "Then maybe you should stop dying on me."

"Oh come on, Elle, I was going for the dramatic entrance thing."

I look over my shoulder, take in Quent's beaten, bloody body, and I know he just went through hell to keep his promise to me. "How?" I whisper.

He beams. "We came back through the Undertunnel."

"We?"

"Gus, too."

I try not to grin too hard, because I'm also furious with

him. It's a strange feeling being both happy and angry. "You scared me half to death."

He saunters closer, examines me. "Hmm, half a person, maybe, but not half dead." I open my mouth to yell at him, but he dips down and kisses me, stealing all the anger and grief, all the gray and broken. I kiss him back, because things are finally upright.

Somewhere, there's another pair of prosthetic legs that fit me. Even now, Clairen's men are searching for them. When they find them, we'll reattach them. And then I'll go out and I'll walk among the new citizens of Neo-Evanescence. And together, we'll start our renaissance.

Quent draws back. "What do you want to do about Taurus?"

"I'll take care of it." If he doesn't accept my offer, things could get ugly. Especially if he manages to get another dome interested in what we have to offer here. A Disfavored wouldn't take interest in Evanescence unless he thought there was something uniquely special about it. The people who came from Adagio were smart, yes, but they didn't seem to have some of the technology we have here. It's possible that the other domed cities aren't like this one. It's possible that other cities may want what we have and will come and try to take it now that they sense we're weak.

But they're out there. And we're in here. We are many and, with a little effort, we'll soon be one. And when people act as one, they can do almost anything. I have faith in that. Because I am Ella the Savior.

acknowledgments

I'm going to be ridiculously candid right now.

Being a creative person is nearly as terrible as it is wonderful. I'm convinced of that.

To me, creativity is a way to interpret and understand what's inside and what's outside. This is what I call the muse. She's not a person, music, or a place like she is for many other people. She's an interpretive force. And through her, a creative person is able to express things via whatever medium they're best suited for.

For me that medium is words.

Sometimes your muse is kind, she gives you a million ways to express yourself and it's nearly overwhelming how creative you are. Other times she gives you dry spells and taunts you with a complete inability to understand or articulate the tempest within.

And because you can't figure out or express things, you get really lost.

The creation of this book was a lesson in the fickle behavior of the muse.

Writing *Redux* was not like writing *Nexis*.

While *Nexis* was a voluntary stream that flowed, constant

and strong—lending me a near perfect manuscript in just a few months; *Redux* was something I really had to dig deep for and coax out under what felt like a reign of bullets.

I wrote *Redux* 1.0 in the summer of 2015. It was very difficult and when I completed it, I knew something was wrong. I could not—for the life of me—figure out what.

I gave it to my beta-readers who gave me fabulous feedback and helped to improve it, but we still couldn't quite get it where it needed to be.

So, I handed it in with a plea for assistance from my editor, Liz Pelletier. We were in the midst of the release of *Nexis*, so it got shelved and my focus was drawn to touring for quite a few months. By the time that was over, my patience with the writing world was shot. I was frustrated with my inability to create new content, with how hard it was just to organize and keep in touch with all the balls that were up in the air, with how difficult it had been to write *Redux* 1.0 and my dissatisfaction with it, and I was jaded by *Nexis* not becoming the next NYT bestseller that I dreamed it would be—despite the amount of work I put into it.

On top of that, I was in the middle of a personal crisis. Every avenue of my life seemed like a dead end that would not make me happy. I wanted to drop everything, move to some place new, and start over as a completely new person. I was deeply considering walking away from my path as a writer. I couldn't eat, I hardly slept, I started having chest pains. I dropped nearly 20 pounds in less than three weeks.

Clearly, I wasn't in a good spot.

It was at this time that my agent, Louise Fury, organized a phone call between me and Liz. We talked about *Redux*. We talked about a few of my other projects. Liz wanted more of my work and I started to feel a little bit of hope...

It was also at this time that Liz introduced me to Robin

Haseltine—my new editor. I was a little nervous to work with a new editor. I love working with Liz—we make a good team—and I wasn't all that keen on the change. However, Robin and I hit it off from the start. I'm beyond thankful for Robin who, out of everyone, was able to empathize with my feeling that something was off and able to really work with me to isolate what plagued me.

The biggest problem? Ella wasn't herself. She wasn't shining like she had in *Nexis*. Sound familiar?

So, Ella and I were in the same boat. I'm not saying Ella is, in any way, a Mary-Sue character (we don't have much in common and I wrote her to be like that, and of my existing characters, I think Jeanette from *For Your Heart* is the most like me); however, the trials I put her through are universal and we just happened to be going through the same ones.

Knowing this, I decided that the best thing to do was gut and do a full rewrite of *Redux*. Perhaps I was living vicariously—gutting and revamping her story like I wished I could my own. A character's story is much easier to rewrite than one's own. I had just a few months to do this, wasn't wholly sure what I needed to do, and I was clearly overwhelmed.

I met with my best friend, Christen, for dinner and I explained to her what I needed to do, but that I didn't know what, exactly, to change the story to. She helped me reconnect with some long lost thoughts I'd once shared with her and that pushed me in the right direction.

I came up with a solution, sent it to Robin, and got approval.

Then, I disappeared into the writing cave—hunkering down in my small corner at my local Panera Bread every evening, every weekend. I toiled and toiled.

My friends and family, though they missed me, were blessedly patient with me despite having to cancel a number of cons, girl's weekends, dinner outings, and dates. Letting down my friends—the one area that hadn't been suffering—wasn't helping ease my anxiety.

Despite now knowing what to do, it wasn't easy to write *Redux* 2.0. Every other aspect of my life was still a shambles—directionless and clambering for my attention. I kept getting distracted and the days slid by.

The impending due-date of *Redux* 2.0 forced me into myopic hyper-focus, but the more I pushed the more the muse resisted.

A close friend of the family, Irena, took one look at me and told me I should go for hypnosis. She gave me a reference. I like to think I straddle the logical and whimsical in equal parts, so I kept my mind open about it and I went—half skeptical but sort of desperate for help at the same time.

...It actually helped. It may sound woo-woo to you, and it could have just been a placebo, but it lead me toward an opening in my soul that allowed me to channel my muse in a way I haven't been able to do since I initially wrote *Nexis* a few years ago.

With less than three weeks until the second re-write was due, the dam suddenly broke and *Redux* 2.0 flowed forth with the same ease and intensity as *Nexis*.

The need to redirect and strengthen Ella's character allowed me a form of control. Ella was constantly being knocked down and put in bad situations, but I had to make her persevere. I had to keep her from getting drawn down by the darkness. She couldn't just get up and walk away. She had to do the same things I did. A dozen problems were clamoring for her attention, but she prioritized, took control, divided, and conquered.

Through Ella, I was able to control and change in a way that I could not in my real life. She became my avatar—much like her own character did for her in *Nexis*. Ella did for me as a writer what many books allow for readers—a chance for escape, a chance to be someone else, a chance to find hope through a similar situation that has been removed just far enough to give you insight.

As I continued to toil away in my corner at Panera, my friends and family supported me on all sides. I took strength from that as I didn't want to make the sacrifice of time spent away from them go to waste.

In their avid desire for more, my fans gave me hope and kept me focused. I didn't want to disappoint them any more than I wanted to disappoint myself. *Nexis* may not have been a best seller, but there are some readers out there who esteem it as their favorite book and they, with their guaranteed sales, are the ones I have to please most—not the potentials.

My own near-comical love-life gave me fuel as well. This year has been a thing of intense highs and lows and tragic swings for me. People claim that love triangles don't happen in real life. Well, they do folks. I've been on all sides and angles of that. So I am writing what I know in that respect. XD

I cried when I finished *Redux* 2.0. It was the first thing that felt right in a very long time.

Robin made me cry again when I read her email about how much she loved it. It wasn't perfect, obviously—nothing ever is, but it was where it needed to be and I had hope.

They say writing is a lonely affair. But, no writer is an island. We have baristas who keep our teacups filled. We collect friends and family who love and accept us despite our lapses into artistic introversion. We're cursed with loves that consume, desolate, and fertilize like fire. We encounter sagely women who introduce us to spiritual guides. We're blessed with editors who understand us and with their kind, uplifting words, unknowingly talk us down from career suicide.

We accumulate fans who poke and encourage us even when all we want to do is curl up and forget the world exists. And, of course, even when we're knee deep in other worlds, our muses provide us with characters who act as mirrors, allowing us to see into the very depths of what it is to be human and provide us with paths to follow out of the darkness.

I'm so very happy you're all my neighbors on this continent called creativity. I cherish and thank you all.

Grab the Entangled Teen releases readers are talking about!

Remember Yesterday
by Pintip Dunn

Sixteen-year-old Jessa Stone is the most valuable citizen in Eden City. Her psychic abilities could lead to significant scientific discoveries, if only she'd let TechRA study her. But ten years ago, the scientists kidnapped and experimented on her, leading to severe ramifications for her sister, Callie. She'd much rather break in to their labs and sabotage their research—starting with Tanner Callahan, budding scientist and the boy she loathes most at school.

The past isn't what she assumed, though—and neither is Tanner. He's not the arrogant jerk she thought he was. And his research opens the door to the possibility that Jessa can rectify a fatal mistake made ten years earlier. She'll do anything to change the past and save her sister—even if it means teaming up with the enemy she swore to defeat.

Infinity
by Jus Accardo

There are three things Kori knows for sure about her life:

One: Her army general dad is insanely overprotective.
Two: The guy he sent to watch her, Cade, is way too good-looking.
Three: Everything she knew was a lie.

Now there are three things Kori never knew about her life:

One: There's a device that allows her to jump dimensions.
Two: Cade's got a lethal secret.
Three: Someone wants her dead.

Island of Exiles
by Erica Cameron

On the isolated desert island of Shiara, every breath is a battle.

The clan comes before self, and protecting her home means Khya is a warrior above all else. But when obeying the clan leaders could cost her brother his life, Khya's home becomes a deadly trap. The council she hoped to join has betrayed her, and their secrets, hundreds of years deep, reach around a world she's never seen.

To save her brother's life and her island home, her only choice is to turn against her clan and go on the run—a betrayal and a death sentence.

SHADOWS

BY JENNIFER L. ARMENTROUT

The last thing Dawson Black expected was Bethany Williams. As a Luxen, an alien life-form on Earth, human girls are...well, fun. But since the Luxen have to keep their true identities a secret, falling for one would be insane. Dangerous. Tempting. Undeniable.

Bethany can't deny the immediate connection between her and Dawson. And even though boys aren't a complication she wants, she can't stay away from him. Still, whenever they lock eyes, she's drawn in. Captivated. Lured. Loved.

Dawson is keeping a secret that will change her existence...and put her life in jeopardy. But even he can't stop risking everything for one human girl. Or from a fate that is as unavoidable as love itself.

PROOF OF LIES
BY DIANA RODRIGUEZ WALLACH

Some secrets are best kept hidden…

Anastasia Phoenix has always been the odd girl out, whether moving from city to international city with her scientist parents or being the black belt who speaks four languages.

And most definitely as the orphan whose sister is missing, presumed dead.

She's the only one who believes Keira is still alive, and when new evidence surfaces, Anastasia sets out to follow the trail—and lands in the middle of a massive conspiracy. Now she isn't sure who she can trust. At her side is Marcus, the bad boy with a sexy accent who's as secretive as she is. He may have followed her to Rome to help, but something about him seems too good to be true.

Nothing is as it appears, and when everything she's ever known is revealed to be a lie, Anastasia has to believe in one impossibility.

She *will* find her sister.